You a

A journey into a wondrous land whose boundaries are only that of the imagination.

You are entering The Twilight Zone.

New Line Television unleashes the seminal classic series into a modern incarnation featuring all new tales from The Twilight Zone. This awesome book features two stories with a sting in the tale that will draw fans into a world of fantasy and suspense like no other!

Upgrade

A harassed mother escapes the mayhem of her home life by fantasizing about the ideal family, but then she wakes up to find her old family has been replaced!

Sensuous Cindy

Ben starts to enjoy the delights of a hot new virtual reality program called Sensuous Cindy. But it isn't really cheating when it's with a computer, is it?

THE TWILIGHT ZONE

UPGRADE • SENSUOUS CINDY

Novelization by Pat Cadigan

BLACK FLAME

This one is for Jay Slater with mass quantities of appreciation.

A Black Flame Publication
www.blackflame.com

First published in 2004 by BL Publishing, Games Workshop Ltd., Willow Road, Nottingham NG7 2WS, UK.

Distributed in the US by Simon & Schuster, 1230 Avenue of the Americas, New York, NY 10020, USA.

10 9 8 7 6 5 4 3 2 1

ISBN 1-84416-131-5

A CIP record for this book is available from the British Library.

Printed in the UK by Bookmarque, Surrey, UK.

UPGRADE

Based on the Teleplay by
Robert Hewitt Wolfe

Virtually everybody is familiar with that old bit of folk wisdom about getting what you want. You know the one:

The only thing in the world worse than not getting what you want is getting it.

But exactly what makes getting what you want such a terrible experience? Well, this is one of those things that varies from person to person. After all, no two people are exactly alike. Everybody wants something different. In fact, even those who appear to want the same things don't want them in exactly the same ways. And yet each outcome would seem to be remarkably similar for just about everyone.

Why is that, do you suppose? Could it be because all these different people want all these different things for what amounts to the same reason?

And what reason could that be?

Why do you want the things that you want? Are they really just things?

A mother, for example, may want to live in a better home in a better neighborhood because of what those things can give her family; the comfort of better surroundings, a sense of security, the reassurance of knowing that there will always be a place where life is good because they are loved and cared about.

A mother knows that these are among the elements that make for a good home life, healthy and happy children, and a healthy and happy marriage. Ask any mother and she will tell you that she only wants the best for her family, she wants to make everything perfect for them.

Of course, we all have our own idea of what is perfect and what isn't even close to perfect. As well, what might be perfect for one person—or one family, or even shall we say, one person in the same family—can be unacceptable, intolerable, or even inconceivable for another. This is where things start to get either interesting or complicated, depending on your point of view.

Something else to consider, though: What happens if your idea of what would be perfect is wrong? Not completely wrong that is, not wrong in every way, but just off-kilter enough to require certain alterations before all can be right with your world. Not to mention the people in your world.

But what kind of alterations? How many of them, and to what degree? Is there some point beyond which everything has changed so much that it really isn't your world any more?

In the world we know as ours, the idea is plain and simple; all of us only want what is best for our loved ones.

It's when we get it that everything starts to get interesting, or complicated, or perhaps something even more than that. At that point, we find that we have traveled well past the border of what is familiar to us and crossed over into The Twilight Zone.

ONE

ONE

Once, it had been the perfect house squarely in the middle of the perfect neighborhood. Now it was so much more than that.

Now, it was officially the address that Annie Macintosh could call *Home Sweet Home* and today was the big day when she moved into it with her family. Who were most certainly not, by any stretch of the imagination, perfect.

That was all right with her though. Annie had always tried to maintain the awareness that there was a great deal of difference between doing whatever she could to bring out the best in her loved ones and the irrational demand for the patently impossible. If there was one thing that she had never asked her family to give her, it was perfection or anything even remotely like it.

Well, not really. While she certainly would not have described herself as low maintenance or completely undemanding, perfection was the one thing she had never asked of her husband, nor had she ever expected it. And yet, paradoxically,

Philip managed to be perfect anyway, at least for her.

As for their children, she had always done her best to let them know that she loved them unreservedly. In turn, they reacted to even the slightest, most reasonable request with so much grief that anyone would have thought she demanded the impossible of them on a regular basis.

Of course, she did feel that it was absolutely necessary for her to take into account the fact that Sean and Tess were teenagers. After all, teenagers always considered their parents to be impossible. Impossible to put up with, impossible to please, impossible in just about any way a person would care to name, even under the most favorable of circumstances. So perhaps, on Planet Puberty, she was actually the embodiment of impossible demands just by virtue of the fact that she was their mother. While for her, the reverse was true; their world was pretty much impossible to live in.

And wasn't that an odd thing to be thinking about on a happy day like today, Annie reflected. When they were finally moving into their new home. Which was perfect, the perfect house in the perfect neighborhood.

She brushed back a strand of dark blonde hair that had escaped from her untidy ponytail as she stood in the hallway at the foot of the stairs and gazed around with a mixture of excited anticipation and contentment at those perfect surroundings. This house had everything she had ever dreamed of. It seemed that she simply could not stop admiring any of it. The hardwood floors, the crown molding, the separate dining room, the immaculate ceilings so completely devoid of cracks and stains, and last but most certainly not least, the gorgeous fireplace in the living room.

She thought she must have looked like some kind of vapid, grinning idiot to the burly men who were ferrying in all of the Macintosh family's worldly possessions from the moving van outside. They probably thought she was the biggest hick they had ever seen.

Probably? No, try definitely. But so what? Was it really any kind of big deal? She was in her own home now; she could be a hick or a vapid grinning idiot if she wanted. Or just look that way.

Besides, these were moving men, for crying out loud. They weren't asking anything of her, except that she cough up their fee when the job was done. By the time these guys called it a day and drove away in their truck, they would have forgotten what she looked like, along with anything else about her. If they hadn't already that was.

What was running through her mind right now, all that was nothing but silly stuff, Annie told herself. It was ridiculous for her to stand there worrying about what some moving men—total strangers!—thought of her as they carried the furniture and boxes into the house.

After all, this was what these men did for a living. They got paid to move people into new homes, or out of old ones all the time. For them, this was just one more job in a series, no different than any of the other jobs they'd ever done. All of the furniture and the various boxes marked "kitchen" or "bedroom" or "living room", all of those things that made up the family's personal possessions was all just cargo to be loaded into the truck at one location and then unloaded somewhere else.

They weren't even really looking at any of it except in the process of finding a spot in the house to set it all down. Then, as if on cue, she heard one of them call out, "Take that to the downstairs bath!" and she felt her grin become even bigger.

Take that to the downstairs bath. She, Annie Mac-intosh, now lived in a house that had a downstairs bath. This was most definitely a step up in the world for her; for the whole family.

The moving men could not have cared less one way or another. It would hardly occur to them to study the old broken-down sofa or the worn-out chairs or the scratched and scuffed dining set with a critical eye and whisper to each other about what a shame it was to put such shabby, dilapidated stuff in a place like this, the perfect house in the perfect neighborhood.

Her gaze fell on one of the men as he hefted a large, somewhat unwieldy box labeled "Lamps, Bookends, Bric-A-Brac, etc." and realized a bit belatedly that he was waiting for her to tell him whether it was all right for him to put it down somewhere in here or whether she wanted him to take it upstairs instead.

She felt a moderate rush of heat to her face as she pointed to an area next to the hearth, her smile becoming slightly embarrassed. No, the moving men most certainly were not looking at all the goods and chattels belonging to the Macintosh family and evaluating them as to whether they were of a quality that was good enough for the current new digs.

After a strenuous day of heavy lifting, all they were thinking about was getting everything on the truck unloaded as quickly as possible so they could knock off, get the hell out of there and go have a beer or something.

There was only one person in a hundred mile radius who was making any judgments of that nature and she knew it couldn't possibly have been the movers. No, it was just good old Annie Macintosh herself, busily projecting her own insecurities again. As if she were some self-conscious ten year-old with growing pains, instead of an adult woman with the real and much more pressing concerns of a family to look after.

Lately, she seemed to be making a habit of this kind of thinking and that certainly wasn't good. If she didn't make a serious effort to break herself out of it, she was going to wake up some morning and find out she had turned into one of those people who was never satisfied with anything. Then she would never be happy, no matter how perfect the house or anything else in her life was, because she wouldn't know how.

Besides, when she gave it some serious consideration, what did that word perfect really mean anyway?

"Congratulations, Annie!" said a cheerful voice to her right.

She turned to find Yasmine beaming at her. The enthusiasm of her best friend's lovely, flawless features was a reflection of how she was feeling herself. Yasmine took a step back and, with a ceremonious flourish, presented her with the "Sold" placard that she had just removed from the signpost in the front yard.

"Here you go, girlfriend" she announced. "It's all yours. Signed, sealed, and dee-lightful."

Annie laughed. "Thanks" she said happily and held the sign out at arms length to admire it before she set it down on one of the many large cartons nearby. Then she took a deep, happy breath and indulged herself in another look around, drinking in all the beautiful features of her new home for what might easily have been the zillionth time.

"Hard to believe" she said, speaking as much to herself as she was to the woman standing next to her.

Two of the moving men began to stack some more cartons around them and she thought it might be a good idea to surrender the space to them before she and Yasmine got blocked-in completely.

Motioning for Yasmine to come with her, Annie drifted away from the staircase and down the three small steps that led to the living room. Did the steps make it a sunken living room? She kept forgetting to ask Yasmine about that. Even if it could not officially be described as sunken according to the realtor's book of rules (or whatever they used) it was classy. So elegant and tasteful. She loved it. But the one thing she loved most of all, more than anything else by a long, long way, was the fire-place.

It was not the old-fashioned, ornate kind of fire-place, so large that it unrelentingly took over the entire room. But a sophisticated, elegant hearth in pure, snowy white. The only decorations were the moldings which Annie had been delighted to see were also painted white rather than the antique gold flake stuff that so many interior designers seem to favor. The mantle was just wide enough to accommodate the usual knick-knacks and framed snapshots, with plenty of space left over for stocking-hangers at Christmas.

Annie had a sudden mental image of how the fireplace would look decorated for the holidays, with five stockings—the dog had to have one, too—dangling side by side, waiting for Santa, and felt a sharp, bittersweet pang in her heart. If only she had been able to do that for the kids back when they had still been little enough to believe in Santa.

She had never lived in a building with fireplace. Back in her years as an apartment dweller, she had never been able to afford anything but minimal lay-outs with the most minimal of features. There were times when she had counted herself lucky to end up with air conditioning.

When she and Philip had gotten married, their happiness had not been dimmed in even the slight-est way by the realities of life on the austerity plan. Then the kids had come, one right after another, and the always-tight household budget turned into a serious exercise in how to produce something out of nothing on a daily basis. Those had been lean years for sure.

But they certainly had not been unhappy ones, not by a long shot. For little kids, the concept of things like rich and poor simply had no real meaning of any sort and Sean and Tess had enjoyed their childhood. They had been a couple of happy little kids with absolutely no awareness that Mommy and Daddy constantly had to make do and even, from time to time, go without.

Not that the two of them hadn't begged vigorously for practically every new toy they saw on TV or in their friends' homes. What had saved their parental sanity in that area, Philip liked to joke, was the fact that Nature gave children such blessedly short attention spans. Joke or not, Annie had a feeling that there was probably a great deal of truth to that.

Fortunately, one of the things that she and Phil never had to joke about was how they had always managed to provide their children with everything they needed. If not everything, or even most of, what they had wanted.

All told, the only things the Macintosh family had ever really lacked came under the heading of "frills" and "extras". As hard as that had been sometimes, it had paid off. Now here they were, living proof that the failure to obtain all (or even just a few) of the latest CDs, clothes, and electronic gadgets was not, in fact, fatal. Or even slightly debilitating, for that matter.

This was definitely the sort of thing she ought to remind herself of once in a while, Annie thought. Especially now that the leanest of all those lean times had been left well behind them. It had taken them years of hard work and belt-tightening but they had managed to do it. They had succeeded in achieving a higher standard of living, a better quality of life. After all the time she had spent making two eggs go three ways and serving pasta for dinner five nights in a row, they were finally, finally better off; the way she and Philip had always promised each other they would be.

The thing she had to do now was not to let herself get fixated on material objects as a barometer of personal worth. Her life, always good for the most part, had just become better. What she really ought to concentrate on, she told herself firmly, was simply to enjoy it.

There was only one way to do that, she had to focus on living in each moment as it came, and not spend her precious time and energy dwelling on superficial matters like things or appearances. She didn't have to center her life on things or appearances just to appreciate the upgrade.

She couldn't help chuckling a little at the word her mind had chosen; upgrade. It just went to show you, she thought, amused with herself, that even though she had made a conscious effort to keep all that cyber-computer-techie stuff at arms length—and a very generous arms length, at that—somehow, she had become infected with the jargon after all.

Still, upgrade was kind of a good word for it. She felt it was a very appropriate word, really; it fit the situation pretty well. *Le mot juste*, as the French put it. Upgrade. What the hell, she thought, if the word was good enough for multi-billionaire computer software moguls, then it was good enough for Annie Macintosh.

And besides, she remembered, upgrade wasn't just limited to the computer industry. Airlines had been giving upgrades to passengers for years. Yeah, that was more like it. She could think of this house as being like an upgrade from economy to first class. It certainly felt like one.

Yasmine slipped an arm around her shoulders and gave her a brief, affectionate squeeze. Annie smiled and squeezed her friend's hand in return. If it had not been for the very canny and observant Yasmine Haleem, she would not have been standing there in front of her very own fireplace, watching moving men bring their belongings into the perfect house, in the perfect neighborhood. Having a best friend with a real estate license was definitely "A Good Thing".

For years, Yasmine had been listening to her, with a seemingly endless supply of patience, while she went on and on and on about what she imagined her dream house would be like.

"First of all, it will have a backyard, big enough so that the dog can romp around in it to his heart's content," Annie had said. "But not so big that we have to spend every waking moment of our free time coaxing the grass to grow and ripping up dandelions and all that lawn and yard maintenance stuff people do. I don't want us to have to devote our lives to tilling the soil."

In fact, Annie had not been telling Yasmine the whole truth about her feelings around yards, or "gardens" as her Great-aunt Lauren, who had spent most of her life in England, had called them.

Great-aunt Lauren's garden was the real problem. It had been so perfect, so full of everything that a garden should have, like a real-life English country house garden.

Its perfection was the problem, compared with the messy reality of Annie's own yard, especially after they got Czonka and he tore it up and after they got the kids, and the kids went out there with Phil to play ball and tore it up some more. But she hadn't been about to go into all that with Yasmine, so she just continued in a more positive way.

"Still, even though I've never been into gardening in a very serious way, I would still really like to plant some tulips. I just love the way they look when they come up in the spring. Oh, and I'd like one of those red-bud trees," she had added, "just a little one. I love the way they look too, before the leaves finally turn green for the summer."

"How about the inside?" Yasmine had asked her. "I mean, you are planning to live indoors rather than outside in the back yard with the dog?"

"What are you talking about? Do you seriously believe that anyone would stand for the dog to live outside?" Annie had replied promptly. "Oh, please. I want hardwood floors. If there's any one thing I'm sick and tired of, it's wall-to-wall carpeting. After a while, it all looks like the same old worn-out, stained stuff you can see on every floor in every sad little rental house in the entire world.

My dream house has hardwood floors and area rugs. Oriental, of course. Like magic carpets that will carry me away from boring, everyday things like dishes that need to be washed, laundry that needs to be done and groceries that need to be shopped for—"

"Girlfriend," Yasmine had interrupted, "that is not carpeting you're describing now. That's what we in the trade refer to as widescreen TV with a satellite hook-up."

"And full internet access," Annie had added, laughing with her, "all the magic carpets have them these days, didn't you know?"

"Okay, you're probably right about that." Yasmine had said, laughing again. "So, what else does this dream house of yours have?"

"Stairs."

"Stairs?!" Yasmine had gaped at her in surprise. "Now I know you've completely lost your mind. If the Good Lord had meant us to climb stairs, He wouldn't have given us all those nifty step machines and cross-trainers to use in air-conditioned health clubs."

"You heard me," Annie had chuckled. "I want stairs. Because my dream house is not one of those cookie-cutter ranch things, and it's not a split-level ranch thing with the bedrooms over a two-car garage, either. It's a real, house-shaped house, with two, no, make that three storeys. And all the staircases have a landing to split them up and make climbing them easier."

"Are you sure you don't want an elevator with that?" Yasmine had teased. "How about fries?"

Annie had stuck her tongue out at her. "The top floor is a sort of combination attic and loft style place," she had gone on, "except it's all done up nicely. No dust, no cobwebs, no rafters, and no teenagers. It's a private club where the admission is strictly limited to people over thirty who want a place to go where they know they'll be able to hear themselves think."

Yasmine had been highly amused. "So there won't be a widescreen TV with a satellite hook-up, then?"

"Oh, sure, there'll be a TV. The biggest one that will fit in the room." Annie had grinned. "It just won't be able to receive any sports channels."

"I hear you!" Yasmine had said feelingly, as they both laughed again. "Is there any way that I can get an invite to this place?"

"You don't have to worry, you're already number one on the VIP list." Annie had assured her. "There are lots of special benefits with that, you know. For one thing, you get unlimited complimentary frozen strawberry margaritas made fresh in the deluxe, ultra-modern kitchen on the first floor."

"Deluxe, eh?" Yasmine had said. "And just what makes this kitchen of yours worthy of the term 'deluxe'? Tell me more."

"It's deluxe because it has one of those island counters in the center of the room, to be used only for preparing gourmet treats and fancy cocktails. It even has its own little white enamel sink for washing fruit and vegetables."

"Now, you know that Phil and the kids will probably just use it as a breakfast bar, then dump their dirty dishes in your little white enamel sink don't you?" Yasmine had said.

Annie shook her head firmly. "No, they most certainly will not. I'm talking about a kitchen that's big enough to accommodate both a counter and a table. They'll be eating their breakfast at the table and washing their own dirty dishes in the regular stainless steel sink, or I'll know the reason why."

There had been even more laughter at this. The idea of a stern Annie, ordering her husband and children around with an iron hand, had been funny to both of them for a number of different reasons; Yasmine, always tactful, had showed restraint by not laughing too hard, something which Annie appreciated.

"So you'll have lots and lots of counter space," Yasmine had said. "I hear you there, too. Counter space is tied with closet space as the number one request I get from people looking to buy a house."

"Believe me, I can relate," Annie had replied. "I don't think there could ever be such a thing as too much counter space. And while I'm asking for miracles, I would like my counters to be marble, if you don't mind, a nice rosy pink color. A dusty rose on a white or pale-ish background, I mean, not the stuff they make headstones out of for graves."

"Check." Yasmine had mimed marking something off on an invisible clipboard. "Anything else, madame?"

"Well, since you asked—" Annie had hesitated then, wondering if continuing to talk about this wasn't just going to leave her feeling dissatisfied, frustrated, and mildly depressed, as it sometimes did. "I want a separate dining room with an old-fashioned, frosted glass light fixture. I want the living room to be large enough that you can still walk around freely even after we move the furniture in. I wouldn't say no to some better furniture either, but I don't guess there are any houses that will morph a broken-down sofa into something that isn't an eyesore."

"I don't think so." Yasmine had said, her large dark eyes twinkling. "But I will double-check on that for you, just to be sure. After all, they probably laughed at the idea of central vac back in the old days, too. Any other requests?"

"Well, now that you mention it, I think I'll take central vac, too." Annie had said with a laugh. "Thanks for reminding me! Let's see, what else? White walls in every room in the house. Ceilings without cracks or water stains. Woodwork that has no scratches or scars from decades of suffering the slings and arrows of outrageous misfortune. A roof that doesn't leak. Pipes that don't burst and a hot water heater large enough so I can take a shower that lasts longer than thirty seconds, and make that quite a lot longer, thank you.

"Oh, and while I'm at it, more than one bathroom. Please, more than one bathroom. More than two would be even better. More than three..." now she made a pained face. "No. Thank you. Just the idea that I could have more than three toilets to clean could give me nightmares for the rest of my life."

"But four toilets would mean one for each of you," Yasmine had said, looking slightly surprised,

"which would mean no waiting. Wouldn't something like that outweigh any other disadvantages?"

"You would think so." Annie had said with a
short laugh. "But only if you have never had the
experience of cleaning a certain variety of porcelain fixture in the Macintosh household, and I
know for a fact that you haven't. Given a choice
between having one more of those to clean and
having to wait, I really do not mind waiting. Just
take my word for it."

"I guess I'll have to," Yasmine had said, "what
else does madame require?"

"Madame requires a laundry room in the base-
ment, not just the hook-ups for a washer and dryer,
but a room specifically for doing laundry in. Of
course, if the room should happen to come with a
washer and dryer, I certainly wouldn't refuse to
keep them. That would be ungracious." Annie had
given a long sigh of yearning. "Oh, and in that
nice, spacious living room? I want a fireplace."

"What kind?" Yasmine had asked her.

"Surprise me." Annie had sighed again. "Believe
me, that won't be hard. In fact, surprising me will
probably be the easiest thing that anyone ever
did."

Annie Macintosh's "Idea Of The Perfect Place To
Live" had been her favorite subject and one she
had never tired of; running through chapter and
verse over lunch, over drinks on their occasional
Girls' Night Out, and over the phone when they
indulged in one of their yak-fests like a couple of
teenagers.

Or rather, like teenagers from their own past. The teenaged yak-fests of today occurred without the benefit of the human voice, conducted as they were in online chat rooms with only the *click-click-click* from your own computer keyboard as an indication that you were saying something, and maybe an electronic *boop* or *beep* when someone else replied.

Annie was quite frankly mystified as to how anyone could possibly get any satisfaction out of a conversation conducted by typing instead of talking. How could you possibly feel as if you were having a conversation if you were typing? Where was the satisfaction in that? She would have found the absence of another human's voice too disconcerting. Too weird.

Naturally, Sean and Tess thought she was out of her mind. Of course, there were a lot of reasons why her teenaged kids thought she was out of her mind; this was just one more. Fortunately, Yasmine was a kindred spirit where the traditional telephone yak-fest was concerned, although the call she had made to tell Annie about a house that had only just come on the market, this house, had barely lasted thirty seconds.

"I am most certainly not going to talk to you about it on the phone," Yasmine had informed her. "You are going to see it first. Then we can talk all you want. Well, up to a point. Now, grab a pen, I'm going to give you the address and you're going to get in the car and drive over there right now. I want to see you there in fifteen minutes. No arguments."

Annie had obeyed, telling herself that she was just humoring her friend. But the moment she had pulled up in front of the house, she had known there was no going back, this was where she and her family were going to live. She was going to do whatever she had to do in order to make that a reality.

Yasmine had met her at the door with a big, knowing smile and then taken her through the place room by room. "This is what is known in the trade as a model home," she had explained, while Annie explored every part of it with wholehearted enthusiasm. "The company that built it has been using it to show off their work to anyone who might be in the market to have a house built for them."

Annie had shaken her head in bewilderment. "But why would anyone want to go to all that trouble," she said, running a finger over a section of crown molding (crown molding! God, how classy was that? She hadn't even thought of crown molding when she had been fabricating her dream house), "when this place is already finished? Who could possibly bear to wait to have something else after seeing this house?"

"People who want this house at a different address." Yasmine told her, laughing a little. "It's those three little words no working realtor ever forgets: Location, location, location."

"Oh!" Annie had made a show of gently hitting her forehead with the heel of her hand. "Of course. You would think that since my best friend just happens to be a realtor herself, even *I* would know something like that. I guess I have just demonstrated that without a doubt I have absolutely no future in the real estate business."

"That may be true," Yasmine had said, laughing again, "but you do have a future in this house. There's only one thing left to decide: do you want to take one more tour through the place, or shall we go back to my office and get started on the paperwork?"

And the rest, as the saying went, was history. Or to be more precise, it was history currently in the making.

"You know, I have never seen myself simply as a person who sells big boxes for people to live in," Yasmine had said to her. "I have always preferred to think of myself as a sort of matchmaker for real estate."

In Annie's case, truer words had never been spoken. She was definitely in love all right, and this was a match made in heaven with a dream come true. And so what if that was a major cliché, even the very mother of all clichés? It just so happened to be the perfect way to describe how she felt.

But now, as she admired the mantel on her fireplace and her exquisite hardwood floor, she felt something inside herself start to falter a little bit.

Having a dream come true was wonderful, but it was not a completely carefree experience. There were still certain facts of life that had to be dealt with and Annie found that just thinking about them was enough to let realism spill in, like cold water on her happiness.

"I don't know how we're ever going to afford it," she sighed, turning around slowly in the middle of the living room to admire it again, "but it certainly is perfect."

Yasmine grabbed her arm and gave it an admonishing shake, looking at her as if to say, "Don't start with that one now, girlfriend. You'll get by like you always have and you know it." Annie could see it as plain as anything on her friend's face, practically hear her thinking it.

It was so nice to have a friend that close, Annie thought, and smiled back in silent answer: "You're right, sorry, I won't let it happen again. Today at least."

Then she turned and caught sight of two of the moving men coming in. One was carrying yet another of what seemed to be an endless series of large boxes full of the family's belongings and the other holding a large flat rectangle wrapped in brown paper.

Annie brightened and went quickly to intercept the latter. "It's only missing one thing." she announced, taking the package from him and unwrapping it to reveal her most prized possession. The Macintosh family portrait.

The elegantly framed photo: herself, Philip, Tess, Sean, and even Czonka, the family dog with a highly ambiguous ancestry they couldn't even begin to guess at, was one of the few luxuries that Annie had insisted she couldn't live without.

She knew that her use of the word luxury, in terms of a professionally-shot family portrait, was probably more than a little on the grandiose side.

Annie didn't care. For her, this immaculate photo of her family could be nothing less than a luxury item.

Getting all of them together in one place for the requisite amount of time had taken some heavy-duty people-wrangling on her part. Even Philip's schedule had been tough to work with, in spite of the fact that he had insisted he wanted to have a family portrait taken just as much as she did. But in the end, it had been worth it. The result had turned out even better than she had hoped. The expression on each of those faces that she loved so much was open, relaxed and unguarded, their smiles pleasant and sincere.

In fact, Tess and Sean had come out looking so much at ease that she could almost forget what a battle she'd had with them about their clothes. No T-shirts, ripped jeans, baseball caps, leather, studs, or sunglasses. And by some miracle, she had managed to get her way.

Anyone who might have seen only the portrait would never have known that her daughter was not, in fact, always impeccably groomed and tastefully dressed, but went around in shapeless, mismatched skirts and blouses with her flyaway hair uncombed and her face set in what seemed like a permanent expression of pained distaste.

Nor would anyone have ever guessed that her brother Sean wasn't given to neatly tailored shirts and sweater vests, but to those awful baggy jeans that seemed to be de rigueur for the skateboard set, along with torn sweatshirts and hoodies, and a baseball cap. Worn backwards, of course.

Looking back on it now, she thought it must have been some kind of miracle that she had managed to persuade him to let go of that skateboard long enough to have his picture taken. It hadn't been easy and at one point, she had begun to think they might have had to have the thing surgically removed.

Even Czonka, the family dog, was well-groomed for a change. His normally unruly white fur had been scrubbed clean, neatly brushed and trimmed, courtesy of a fancy dog beauty salon. That kind of service hadn't been cheap, either, in fact, it had cost as much as the portrait itself, but it had definitely been worth it. The dog looked so good that if Annie hadn't known better herself, she might have thought he was some sort of obscure breed, rather than simply the product of generations of random encounters between undiscriminating canines.

It had all been worth it: the bill from the dog salon, the battle with Tess and Sean's clothes, the highly exasperating and nearly impossible struggle to get the entire family's schedules aligned and synchronized. In the end, it had been worth every bit of effort. Every time she looked at this photo, she felt as if the photographer had somehow managed to capture the exact image of them that she carried in her heart. Her family may not have been perfect, but in this one, ever-so-brief, photographically-preserved moment, they looked perfect.

"I remember that photo," Yasmine said, admiring it with her. "Even Czonka is smiling. You sent it out as your Christmas card last year."

Annie could detect just the slightest hint of envy in her friend's voice and, as always, she couldn't help feeling a certain amount of bafflement mixed with a kind of reluctant pity for the woman. This was something they had talked about from time to time. Of course, she and Yasmine talked about virtually everything together, in detail and at great length. The subjects they covered included their respective personal lives, which were very different in just about every possible way.

Annie would seem to have epitomized the very essence of middle America. At thirty-five, she was, by her own description, your basic WASP, married to another basic WASP with two basic WASP children and a basic WASP house-pet. All in all, the kind of nuclear family most likely to be found living on a tree-lined street in the suburbs.

As a genuine card-carrying member of the PTA, Annie not only had to synchronize her schedule with the calendar for the school year, she also had to volunteer for the car-pool, bake for the school fund-raisers, and keep track of what extra-curricular activity was on what day, or try to. If there was any time left over, she could get her hair done (or try to).

Yasmine, on the other hand, was two years younger and single by choice, exotically Middle Eastern. She was the classic, high-powered business woman who owned and ran her own realty office. She lived in a luxury condo in a high-rise, and occasionally nipped off to the Caribbean during a lull in the housing market or even on a whim, either alone or in the company of one of several

boyfriends whom Yasmine referred to somewhat
wryly as her suitors. And she didn't need to find
time to get her hair done, since it was naturally
thick, dark, and wavy.

Annie would have thought that Yasmine would
find someone like her far too domesticated and
mundane, even for polite conversation about the
weather, let alone a longstanding friendship of virtually intimate closeness. But ever since they had
met in an exercise class at the local health club,
they had been, in Philip's words, peanut butter and
jelly, completely different elements that came
together to make an unbeatable combination. Yasmine had concurred, congratulating Philip on
possessing such a high degree of insight, especially
for a man, Annie had added, making them all
laugh, Philip included.

She and Yasmine had been doing their peanut
butter and jelly thing for ten years now, a duration
that Annie sometimes found rather amazing. Only
Philip had been such an important part of her life
for longer. Well, the children too, to be technical.
But of course her relationship with them as their
mother could not really be even remotely the same
sort of thing.

In any case, she very much enjoyed her friendship with Yasmine. She enjoyed listening to her
talk about the real estate business, her various
clients, her island vacations and the men in her
life, whether they were arriving, departing, or still
under consideration.

To Annie's secret delight, however, she had long
ago discovered that, as fascinating as she found

Yasmine's life, it actually held no attraction for her. She really had no envy for her friend's comparative freedom to come and go as she pleased. She didn't even really covet her friend's obviously more substantial bank account.

It was immensely reassuring, as well as gratifying, to discover that she really was satisfied with the choices she had made for herself. Getting married, having children, putting all of her energies into family-related things. Maybe her life wasn't the sort of thing that would have made her a poster-child for NOW, but it was her life, the one that she had chosen, not something that had been chosen for her or simply conferred on her.

That was what Yasmine envied, she knew. Not what she had, but that she was so secure in the knowledge of what she wanted, as well as what she had to do to go about getting it. Annie had still found this just as surprising, perhaps even more so, as she had never thought that there was anything tentative or uncertain in Yasmine's approach to living, but as Yasmine had tried to explain to her, that wasn't quite it, either. It was the way Annie just seemed to have so much faith in herself and in her capacity for making the right decisions.

Annie, in turn, had tried to explain to Yasmine that these were the same qualities that she saw in Yasmine herself; that perhaps her friend couldn't help perceiving her as being stronger or better in that area simply because Annie's entire lifestyle was unfamiliar territory to her. But Yasmine had insisted there was more to it than just the differences in the way they lived.

"Of all the people I've ever known," Yasmine had told her over some after-dinner drinks one night, "you are the only one that I would ever describe as someone who really has her shit together."

Her friend's choice of words had jerked a surprised laugh out of Annie. Yasmine virtually never used profanity of any kind, not because she was especially prudish, but because some people were and her work could have been adversely affected by it. More than one real estate agent, she had told Annie, had seen a client disappear simply because someone had let the wrong word slip out.

"See?" Yasmine had said, laughing with her. "That's how strong my feelings are—strong feelings, strong language. But all kidding aside now, we both know I'm right about this. Don't try to deny it, girlfriend, you have really got your shit together and *you* know it."

Annie's sense of modesty, either innate or instilled in her as part of her upbringing (even she wasn't sure which), would not quite let her accept Yasmine's praise as being completely true. On the other hand, there was no question that the family's circumstances would have been very different if Annie had not been so focused and capable enough for all of them to rely on.

Her family really did rely on her, and for so very much, the big things and the little things and every single other thing in between, she thought as she smiled fondly at each face in the photo. She would not have had it any other way.

It was this certainty which she held in herself that made this more than simply a family portrait for her. When she looked at it, she saw a portrait of her happiness and that was something very few people could say they had in their possession.

She turned and, standing on tiptoe, hung it on the picture hook already in place over the mantel-piece. "Belongs right there, doesn't it?" she said to Yasmine, who made a murmur of assent.

And, without a doubt, it did. It was as if the picture hook had been placed there to wait expressly for that photo in that frame and nothing else. If any moment of her life could accurately be described as perfect, Annie thought, suffused with happiness, it was right now, while she was standing in the perfect house, in the perfect neighborhood, gazing at this perfect picture.

And then, her family came in and that was the end of that illusion.

TWO

Actually, they didn't really come in so much as they burst in, starting with Tess.

"Mom!" her daughter whined shrilly at top volume, making Annie wince. "Sean says I have dragon breath!"

"You don't believe me?" said her brother Sean, his baggies flapping as he came in behind her, hefting his ever-present skateboard. "Go ahead and sniff her!"

Even as a toddler, Sean had shown a fondness for teasing his sister. At first it had been playful and she had teased him right back with gusto. But as the two of them had gotten older, Sean's voice had acquired more of an edge, whereas Tess's had become strident, even shrill, and the exchanges between them had become openly and unremittingly mean.

These days, it bore absolutely no resemblance at all to anything that Annie would ever have called teasing. Now it was a couple of bickering teenagers, who just kept on sniping and jabbing and poking at each other with remorseless anger and bitterness until one of them—Tess, of course, it was always Tess—went over the edge and blew up.

Of late, the fighting between them had become a war with virtually no let-up. Annie couldn't stand to listen to them. Two seconds and she was ready to tear her hair out.

The sound of them at each other's throats was not improved by the way their voices echoed around the still unfurnished house. Before Annie could tell them to give it a rest, however, Tess spotted the family portrait hanging over the fireplace.

"I hate that photo!" she announced, teenage distress putting an even sharper edge into her whine. "That dress makes me look chunky!"

"What dress doesn't?" said Sean, as prompt as ever.

"MOM!"

Annie felt as if Tess's wail had gone right through her and she cringed, thinking it was a miracle that none of the windows had broken. Sean only laughed at her nastily and began to step up the torment even more by thrusting his fingers at her face in odd, cryptic little gestures.

"It's called 'throwing gang signs.'" Phil had explained to Annie helpfully when she had asked. "All the kids do it. They all want to be like that rapper. You know the one. What's-his-name. Like the candy. Eminems. Don't ask me whether he's plain or peanut, though."

And then right on cue, her very helpful husband half-stumbled, half-skidded into the living room in

the wake of the hyperactive bundle of fur that was
Czonka, part sheepdog (had to be), part terrier
(could be), part everything else (probably).

"Whoa! Easy, Czonka, easy!" Phil said good-
naturedly. He was fighting the dog for control of
the leash he had wrapped around one hand while
attempting to juggle a precarious pile of large,
unwieldy boxes with the other.

Czonka paid no attention.. He was even more out
of control than usual, panting and slobbering in
pure canine ecstasy, as he lunged first in one direction and then another, trying to make up his doggy
mind which of the many wonderful new smells he
wanted to investigate first. Complicating this doggy
dilemma for him was the slippery polished floor;
Annie could hear his claws clicking and scraping
on the wood as he scrambled for balance.

Well, that was just great, she thought miserably;
by this time tomorrow, she could expect to find
that every hardwood floor in her gorgeous new
house had been decorated with wall-to-wall
scratches.

Her shoulders slumped. "So much," she sighed,
"for my perfect moment."

As if to underscore her feelings by scoring the
floor, Sean dropped his skateboard onto the hardwood surface in the hallway and zoomed off into
the kitchen, probably on a mission to find out if
they had finished moving the refrigerator.

"I told you, no skateboarding indoors!" Annie
shouted after him, wishing with every fiber of her
being that she didn't have to sound as helpless as
she felt.

She turned to her husband, who was trying to put the boxes down without dropping them whilst not letting go of the dog's leash.

"How about backing me up here?" she demanded unhappily.

Phil gave her one of his pained smiles. "Aw, c'mon honey," he said, managing to drop only half the boxes as he set down the rest of them. "It's moving day. Czonka! Czonka, you bad boy!" he added, not meaning a word of it.

Instinct told Czonka that this was the moment he had been waiting for and he made the most of it. With an energetic lunge, he pulled the leash out of Phil's hand, then began the serious canine task of giving this strange new living room the thorough sniffing he felt it required.

Feeling more helpless than ever, Annie turned to look at Yasmine. "Help?" she asked, only half-kiddingly. "Someone? Anyone?"

But at this point, her deep and virtually intimate friendship with Yasmine Haleem suddenly, well, not ended, exactly; bottomed out was a better term, perhaps.

Yasmine was more than happy to listen to her talk about any aspect of her life, including motherhood, the joys of raising children, the frustrations, the problems, the worries, and everything else. She had been especially good about sitting patiently through Annie's cute-baby anecdotes, much more so than any other non-parent that Annie was acquainted with.

But when it came to some kind of substantial interaction. Well, it wasn't so much that it was a no-go area between them as it was simply a total blank. It was as if this kind of participation in Annie's life was an idea as incomprehensible for Yasmine as fifth-dimensional quantum physics. Or as Yasmine herself would have put it, they just don't have that stuff back where I come from and I never saw anything like it around here, either.

Whatever it was, Annie found it more disheartening than if Yasmine had just given her a flat-out "No way, girlfriend, they're your family, you have to handle them." There had been times in the past when for one reason or another Yasmine had been unable to help her out with other sorts of things and she had not felt nearly so alone or let down then as she did right now.

Especially right now, since she could tell just by the expression on Yasmine's face that she was about to make an exit.

Yasmine's suddenly finding a reason why she had to be elsewhere seemed to have become all but a conditioned reflex now, Annie thought. She looked directly into the other woman's eyes in a last-ditch attempt to make Yasmine see she needed her to stay just a little bit longer, just for the moral support Annie would get from the mere fact of her presence.

In any other situation, Yasmine would have understood that look and she would already be urging Annie to tell her what was buzzing around in her mind, talk it over so they could lay it out together, analyze it and see how it really broke down. Her smile wouldn't have become faintly mask-like and her large dark eyes wouldn't have looked so, well, not empty but actually flat. As if they were only pictures of eyes.

Spooked by the sudden bizarre turn her thoughts had taken, Annie found she could not help drawing back a little as Yasmine put an affectionate arm around her. As far as she could tell, however, the other woman didn't seem to notice.

"You're doing fine, Annie," she said, giving her a kiss on the cheek, "call me if you need anything."

Annie looked after her sadly as she headed for the front door with quick, busy little steps, appointment book already open in one hand as she checked her always-demanding schedule.

This is Annie calling Yasmine, come in Yasmine, she thought at her closest friend who was suddenly so far away. You know how you said call if I need anything? Well, I am and I do. I am calling because I do. Need something, that is. Anything from you, anything at all.

A little voice, in some distant part of her mind suggested that this might actually work better if she said the words aloud, rather than just thinking them. As comically obvious as that might have been, however, Annie remained silent anyway. Partly, she told herself, because actually saying it out loud would sound so melodramatic that she would embarrass everyone, even the moving men.

But it was also partly because she was afraid to find out that it wouldn't work, that Yasmine's only response would be an even blanker look of utter incomprehension and any further attempts on her part to break through it might result in that awful blankness spreading to all the other areas of their friendship.

Then she would really be alone. She would be forced to walk the high wire of her life completely without the net of her best friend's support. No, that would have been intolerable. Her friendship with Yasmine meant entirely too much to her to risk.

It would be better all the way around if she didn't push this, she decided. Although, at the same time she could not help feeling somewhat uncertain as to what her thoughts actually meant. Assuming that they made any real sense in the first place.

She ran an anxious hand through her hair, tucking a few loose strands behind her ears. The strangest things seemed to be running through her mind today.

"Have to say, Annie, it already looks like home."

The sound of her husband's voice broke in on her thoughts then and brought her back to the immediate situation, dispersing the odd melancholy that had settled over her. In spite of everything, Annie felt a broad sunny smile spreading over her face. She turned to find that he was already reaching for her, pulling her into his arms to give her one of his warm, comforting hugs. Automatically, she started to put her arms around him in return and then froze in horror.

Czonka, the Wonder Mutt, had discovered the fireplace and apparently was just as thrilled about this new feature as Annie was, if not even more so. He was so enamored of it, in fact, that he was demonstrating his approval in the only way he knew how: by giving it the Five-Star Mark of Approval in traditional canine fashion. The salute with one leg lifted.

"Czonka, no!" Annie wailed in horror and ran over to chase him away from the hearth.

The dog turned his head, almost casually, to see what all the fuss was about and then bolted immediately at the sight of her flying at him all wild-eyed, hollering and waving her arms. He came to an unsteady, skidding stop several feet away between two large moving cartons and gave her a baleful, offended doggy stare that suggested he found her reaction not only completely unreasonable, but also symptomatic of a deeper problem requiring professional attention.

Furthermore, his reproachful eyes seemed to say, this was all nothing more than a complete waste of energy on her part anyway because, as anyone could plainly see, his work here was finished.

Annie let out a wordless, strangled shout of anger and frustration that actually made the animal flinch. She leaned heavily on the mantelpiece and stared down at the mess Czonka had made. A moment or two passed and then she could hear Phil whispering to the dog, shooing him out of the room. She tried without success to block out the sound of the dog's claws clicking on the wood as he slunk off to wait out the controversy generated by his salute to movin' on up.

Have to say, Annie, it already looks like home.

Oh, please, no, not that, she begged silently. She squeezed her eyes shut and let her forehead drop down on the backs of her hands still clutching the mantel. Please, please. If it really does already look like home, I don't want it to look like that home. Not the home with the dog pee in the fireplace. Please, please not that. Anything but that.

Behind her, Phil started to say something to her and she whirled on him.

"And don't you dare tell me it's moving day!" she snapped. "Don't you dare!"

Without waiting to hear what, if anything, he might possibly tell her instead, Annie fled to the kitchen. She grabbed the first box she saw on the counter next to the sink and began to rummage through it blindly.

The movers had packed up every single thing from the kitchen cabinets at the old house so there were bound to be some paper towels or cloth wipes somewhere that she could use to clean up Czonka's housewarming mess. Maybe, by the time she found them, she would also have managed to pull herself together and calm down.

It never failed, she thought broodingly. It just never failed. And if it ever did fail, if anything ever *did* happen differently, she would probably drop dead from the shock. God, it wasn't like she was asking for the moon. All she wanted was a little bit of space in each day—just a little bit— when she could enjoy some sense of peace and contentment.

Those moments, which had always been too few and far between, were now becoming so cruelly rare and brief that sometimes she could almost have believed that someone, or something, was playing with her. Which was a completely lunatic idea that would make sense only if you were a complete lunatic.

Which she wasn't, of course. But if for some reason she started thinking she really was a complete lunatic after all, she could just phone her best friend. Yasmine had that part covered.

If what she needed was to hear someone tell her how much of a complete lunatic she wasn't, she could count on Yasmine to do that for her at least. It was something that Yasmine understood with no trouble at all, since she had already told Annie that she really had her shit together.

Depsite the fact that Yasmine had not gone on to state in so many words that this was not a quality found in complete lunatics, Annie could almost certainly take that as a given. No matter how crazy her beloved family made her.

Her feelings for her family were never, ever in question, she did love them. But, oh, God, they did make her crazy and they'd been doing it for years.

The moment Tess had become a teenager, she had apparently lost the ability to pitch her voice in anything but a shrill whine. This less-than-attractive feature had been accompanied by a rather substantial and very unfortunate increase in her weight.

All of that combined with the disposition characteristic of adolescents the world over—sullen at best and just plain bad the rest of the time—had made her easily offended, hard to please, and generally inconsolable about the world and her place in it. The teasing she had to endure from her brother didn't help a bit, of course.

These days, Annie seldom saw anything but the briefest flashes of the happy little girl that Tess had been. Sometimes, she found herself thinking that she virtually didn't recognize her daughter, that she could almost believe an unknown entity or force of some kind had somehow managed to perform a bizarre swap, taking the original and substituting a different version.

This was obviously another completely lunatic idea, suitable only for complete lunatics. But in truth, it wasn't something she had come up with on her own. She had heard a number of other parents describe life with teenaged children in the same way.

Or, to be perfectly honest about it, she had overheard them here and there, standing in line at the grocery store, sitting nearby in restaurants, chatting over coffee at PTA meetings. At the time, however, both Tess and Sean had still been quite small and it had sounded awfully harsh to her, even after she had survived the "Terrible Twos" twice.

Well, live and learn. The thing was, she still couldn't help feeling that old description was awfully harsh, and she always felt slightly guilty when the thought crossed her mind. But then there were certain other days when she found herself almost wishing that were the real explanation not only for Tess's behavior but for Sean's as well.

As for Sean. Oh, God, that boy! With his baggies and the skateboard he carried with him everywhere, even into the bathroom. It was impossible to have any sort of conversation with him these days because he was always making those gang signs while blathering a stream of "Yo, yo, yo, down with my homies, hey, dawg, word to yo momma, oh, gee!"

The ever-helpful Phil had explained that he was actually saying OG, which stood for Original Gangster, but it sounded like "oh, gee" to her.

And if he wasn't rapping in tongues or risking permanent disability on his skateboard, it was only because he thought it would be more fun to torment his sister about her weight. To make matters even worse, the boy had the appetite of a water buffalo combined with the metabolism of hummingbird. Well, all right, a hummingbird who was just a bit on the husky side, but, unfortunately, nowhere near as husky as his sister.

As a result, every meal the family ate together would more often that not turn into a turbulent ordeal that always came to an end with Tess storming up to her room in tears before the antacids came out for dessert.

Antacids for Annie's dessert, that was. Her husband's stamina surpassed hers by far. Somehow, Philip always managed to take everything in his stride, no matter what it was.

Even when the kids provoked him to the point where he finally raised his voice in anger and exiled one or both of them to their rooms, he never lost his equilibrium altogether. Mr "Steady-As-A-Rock"; Annie had once joked that he could have been a walking advertisement for Prozac, except he didn't take any.

She heard him come into the kitchen behind her and realized that she had been standing there like a woman in a trance, taking things out of the box and putting them back in over and over. Wasn't that constructive?

Still pulling myself together until I can find something more constructively therapeutic. Like, say, a basket weaving class, she thought darkly.

She finally found the paper towels and started unrolling several sheets so she could clean up Czonka's salute to the upgrade in their standard of living.

"Honey?" Phil slipped his arms around her waist and kissed her shoulder. "Relax."

Relax? Easy for him to say—Mr "Steady-As-A-Rock". But she might as well take advantage of that particular feature, she thought and, closing her eyes, she let herself lean back against him. Only lightly at first, but then he pulled her closer, encouraging her to let him take more of her weight.

"We've been here fifteen minutes," she said bleakly. "One quarter of an hour, that's all it's been, and already the hardwood's scraped and the fireplace is stained."

"They're kids, Annie," her husband said softly with his lips close to her ear. "They're just kids. And the dog? Well, Czonka just got all excited."

She pulled away sharply and turned around to face him. "Philip, this is supposed to be a fresh start," she said in an anxious, pleading tone. "It's supposed to be a new beginning for us."

"And it is. But," he added, trying to pull her close for another hug and then yielding to the restraining hand she put on his chest, "just because we have a new house doesn't mean we're going to turn into a new family."

"Maybe it doesn't," she said, "but sometimes I wish we would."

The words were out of her mouth before she could think better of them. What a thing to say, she scolded herself, not resisting now as Phil put both arms around her and pulled her close again. After all those high-minded thoughts about the foolishness of concentrating on material things or looks, and not expecting the impossible from poor fallible creatures that were only human, she had to go and blurt that out.

She pulled away from Phil again and looked up at him, her anxiety deepening. The perfect thing to say, of course, would have been, "I didn't mean that." The problem was, they'd have both known it wasn't the truth.

Besides, she needed to talk this out no matter how silly it was. If she couldn't turn to her husband with it, then she must have married the wrong man, something that she would never have believed in a million years. There just wasn't anyone better than Philip; there couldn't be.

"Does that make me a terrible person?" she asked him, her voice timid with guilt.

Phil smiled down at her, with the gentleness that had made her fall in love with him in the first place.

"Don't worry, sweetheart," he said softly. "It'll be our little secret."

No question about it, Annie thought, she had the best husband in the world. Feeling consoled and on the way to cheering up again, she sighed and leaned into him as he hugged her, grateful for the comfort of his acceptance. That was the key to Mr "Steady-As-A-Rock", she thought, that enormous capacity for acceptance.

All the things that she could never seem to stop worrying about, Phil was simply able to accept. And that included her own lack of perfection, which she had just demonstrated by opening her big mouth. But instead of finding fault with her at length and in extensive detail, he simply accepted that, too.

Very handy to be married to a guy who was so good at making everything feel better, she thought with another, more contented sigh. And by every-thing, she meant everything, the big things and the little things. Even the sound of Czonka's claws on the hardwood floor as he trotted through the din-ing room toward the kitchen didn't sound quite as awful to her now. It was as if Phil had somehow managed to give the mutt's claws an instant pedi-cure, just to make her happy.

Poor Czonka; she felt a surge of guilt. The dog certainly wasn't to blame for anything that might be bothering her. Phil was right. The excitement of their brand-new home had just been too much for him and his basic house-training had been com-pletely over-ruled by the far more powerful canine instinct to mark his territory.

She could only hope that this was a strictly tem-porary lapse and that his house-training would be making a timely return. Especially since it was pretty much the only training Czonka had. One more thing that was in no way his fault, either.

The dog's saving grace was the fact that his naturally sweet temperament made him the quintessential lovable mutt, so that he did not appear to be quite as out of control as he actually was. Well, maybe out of control was kind of an overstatement. That made him sound more like he was wild rather than energetic and that really wasn't quite true, at least not in general.

If Czonka was out of control right now, however, there was a perfectly good reason for it, she realized suddenly. He was hungry. In all the activity and excitement of moving day, the poor guy had yet to be fed.

He had probably been cowering behind a box somewhere ever since Phil had shooed him out of the living room, doing his best to stay out of sight and out of trouble, until he could no longer ignore the hunger pangs and he finally had to give in and risk another hysterical display by approaching her for food.

Poor, poor Czonka, Annie thought as she pulled away from Phil. The mutt was also a bottomless well of unreserved love and acceptance, she reminded herself, and he had never been stingy with his affections. Or his time, for that matter, which was a lot more than the humans in residence could say for themselves.

What Czonka required in return was hardly unreasonable. As Phil had once joked, there were no pockets in his shaggy fur coat so he had no need for either a wallet or any money to put in it. Ever since that trip to the vet, he lacked a weapon of mass distribution so he couldn't infiltrate the neighborhood to produce a new generation of Czonkas or even indulge in a series of self-destructive love affairs. Therefore, expecting regular meals was hardly asking too much of him. She could take a moment to feed him before she worried about cleaning up the mess he had made in the fireplace.

Annie turned to say something soothing to Czonka by way of apology and froze, staring open-mouthed at the dog standing just inside the doorway. He was looking up at her and Phil with an air of expectant adoration that said, "I was put on this earth to give you my utter devotion. You are here to give me food." It was a look that Annie had always thought of as being pure Czonka at least in style.

The white dog standing expectantly in her brand new kitchen was not the lovable mutt with the impossible-to-determine pedigree but an immaculate French poodle, perfectly coiffed and clipped and unmistakably purebred. The only thing this dog and Czonka had in common was the color of their fur.

Annie blinked at the dog and it blinked back at her as if in reply, cocking its frizzy head to one side slightly.

"Did I mention that I was put on this earth to give you my utter devotion and that you are here to give me food?"

She turned to say something about the strange dog to Phil but he was smiling fondly at the poodle.

"Go give Mommy some lurve," he told the dog in a deep, Barry White rumble.

Immediately, the poodle trotted over to Annie and gave her hand a gentle lick, still gazing at her with unreserved love.

Okay—will worship you for food. Is that any clearer?

"Very funny." Annie frowned as she gave the dog a perfunctory pat on its fuzzy puffball head. "Don't tell me Czonka's already made a friend."

Phil raised an eyebrow, looking honestly mystified. "What are you talking about?" he asked her and then, before she could say anything, turned to the dog and added, "Sit, Czonka."

The poodle planted his haunches on the kitchen floor with matter-of-fact obedience. His head swiveled to Phil, as if he were checking for confirmation that this was the correct action.

"Who's my champ?" Phil asked approvingly, scratching the dog behind his frizzy-wool ears. "That's right, you are. Czonka is."

Annie stepped back, trying to stare at both Phil and the dog at once. Her husband had always enjoyed kidding around with her, but practical jokes and deadpan put-ons had never really been his kind of thing. Still scratching the poodle's head affectionately, he turned to say something else to her, then saw the expression on her face.

"What is it, honey? Something wrong?" he asked, his forehead wrinkling with genuine concern.

The poodle, who was enjoying his attentions, seemed to be equally curious. In fact, the longer she looked at them, the more their expressions resembled each other.

Annie had to shake her head sharply to clear it. "Stop screwing around, Philip," she told him. "I am most definitely not in the mood for it right now. I mean it."

His puzzled expression only deepened.

"This isn't funny," she said impatiently. "If you bought another dog—"

Phil hesitated and then looked down at the poodle again. "Do you know what Mommy's talking about?" he asked the dog conversationally.

The dog leaned into him, obviously enjoying the attention in a very calm, quiet, and definitely non-Czonka sort of way.

"No, of course, you don't." Still scratching the dog's head, Phil looked up at her again, his smile fading. "And neither do I."

"Come on, Phil, weren't you even listening to me? How many ways do I have to say it before I can make you understand?" Annie folded her arms. "This is the wrong day for silly games."

But instead of dropping the act, he just kept staring at her, as if he really had no idea what she could possibly be talking about.

Annie drew back from him a little more. Something about the way he was looking at her, maybe the degree of sincerity in his expression was starting to make her feel distinctly uneasy now, rather than simply irritated. If she hadn't known better, if she had been, say, a neighbor who had just dropped in to say hello, she wouldn't have doubted Phil for a moment.

Since when had her husband become such a good actor, she wondered, her uneasiness becoming more intense. Even more puzzling, why would he be doing something like that now? Was it possible that their son's puerile compulsion for unmerciful teasing had finally rubbed off on him in some way? Or could Mr "Steady-As-A-Rock" simply have crumbled all of a sudden?

Well, everybody always said it was the quiet ones you had to watch out for; you'd think they were just fine and then suddenly when you were least expecting it, kablooie! They lost it completely.

What was even worse, everybody also said, was that this sort of thing could happen to anyone. No one was immune. All human beings had their breaking point, but that didn't mean you would always be able to tell when someone was getting close to it.

But still... her husband? Philip?

She had visualized herself going to pieces a million times, but not Philip. Anyone else, maybe even Yasmine; as unlikely as that was under normal conditions. Even the self-possessed and highly competent Yasmine Haleem might have been capable of losing her grip, depending on the combination of circumstances. But not Philip. Never Philip, never in a million years. Never in a billion.

If she had invited not just the people next door, but everyone in the entire neighborhood to come into her kitchen and then demanded that they choose which one of them was compos mentis, she knew what the result would have been.

They would all have taken one look at her and agreed it was Phil without hesitation. There would have been nothing she could have done to convince them otherwise. They wouldn't have believed her even if she showed them some kind of proof. Like a picture.

Like the family portrait—

Abruptly, she straightened up and marched past her bewildered husband, who was still stroking the purebred impostor and into the living room.

All right, she thought, now she was taking the gloves off. If he was really going to insist on kidding around with her like this, she was just going to have to call him into the living room and let him see for himself that one of the first things she had done was to unwrap and hang the family portrait. Then he would have to own up and admit that his little joke had never had a chance. And, maybe, then they could finally get back to the job of moving in.

The movers were unloading the furniture now and to her displeasure, she found herself suddenly doing a sort of little dance with the two men who were carrying the more-than-slightly threadbare sofa. They kept trying to get out of her way while she kept trying to dodge around them, unfortunately always in the same direction, and with a timing that was virtually supernatural. For several seconds, Annie was strongly tempted to believe that they were deliberately playing with her, indulging in a little bizarre moving-day humor.

The expressions on the men's faces, on the other hand, suggested that they were wondering why they'd had to have the bad luck to be carrying the sofa when she had suddenly decided she simply had to dance with it.

Finally, she managed to get the men to shift to the right at the same time that she was moving to the left, and the three of them executed something that reminded Annie a great deal of a square-dancing step: Do-si-do, quick step to the left and swing that sofa, yeehaw.

Lovely, just lovely—and how nice that she could have the opportunity for a close-up look at her sofa, Annie thought sourly; otherwise she might have been in danger of forgetting exactly how shabby the thing was.

Then she simply stood, openmouthed, in front of the fireplace, unable to move, gaping at the portrait.

The four of them, Phil, Sean, Tess, and herself, smiling out at the world with joy in their faces and contentment in their hearts and in their midst, the fifth member of the family: Czonka, obviously coddled, doggily devoted, and unmistakably one hundred per cent American Kennel Club certified French poodle.

THREE

All right; she had to give in, Annie decided as she glanced up briefly from the photo album in her lap to look at her husband. She had no other choice but to believe him.

Which was to say, she believed he wasn't trying to pull something on her. Whatever kind of bizarre joke or stunt this was, Phil was definitely no more a part of it than she was. That was the good news.

The bad news was that this only made it even more difficult for her to imagine what could possibly be going on.

The only thing she understood, as she sat leafing through photo album after photo album, was that somehow every single picture that had included Czonka had been altered, so that the familiar lovable mutt had been replaced by this poodle with the pristine pedigree.

No, that was wrong. She didn't understand it. She couldn't understand it. She could only see it with her own eyes. She could see that every single picture Czonka appeared in, no matter how old or how recent, whether it was in one of the photo albums or still languishing in a one-hour-photo envelope, had changed. She could see all of that as plain as anything, but she did not, and could not, in any way, understand it in the slightest.

"Satisfied?" Phil asked, pausing in the middle of wiring up the stereo to look over his shoulder at her.

Satisfied? Annie shook her head slightly. What the hell kind of a question was that to ask her? What was she supposed to be satisfied by?

She kept flipping through the photo albums. The images passed before her eyes, one after another. Here was one taken on the day Phil had brought the dog home from the animal shelter. Czonka had been a small shaggy ball of fur that wouldn't stop licking all their faces.

"I asked if anyone had any idea what his lineage might be," Phil had said, amused, "but all anyone could tell me was that they just about one hundred per cent certain that he is, in fact, a dog."

Here was a photo she had taken of Tess and Sean on Christmas Day in front of the tree. By some miracle, she had caught them during one of the three separate seconds of the day when they hadn't been bickering. Sean was holding up a videogame and the dog was sitting beside him, regarding the cartridge in the boy's hand with a comical expression of doggy bewilderment.

Here was Phil grinning into the camera on his birthday with Czonka on his lap, both of them wearing identical party hats, the dog far more interested in the plate of birthday cake on the table in front of them.

Here was a shot of Annie herself taken by Phil; she was holding a Frisbee™ out for the dog's inspection and Czonka was sniffing it with what seemed to be a somewhat skeptical air, as if he had never seen anything like it before and wasn't sure it was something he approved of.

But it was not the dog she knew. Not Czonka.

None of the photos included the familiar mutt with the mysterious, mixed lineage, the white four-legged rag-pile that had stolen all their hearts as a pup in the animal shelter. That dog was nowhere to be seen; all evidence of the dog had vanished without a trace.

The only dog in any of the photos was the white poodle with the puffball head that Phil kept insisting was, and always had been Czonka. The one, true Czonka, and the only dog they had ever had.

"I don't understand," Annie said, closing the photo album and reaching for another. "What happened to our dog? What happened to Czonka?"

Phil made a frustrated noise as he fiddled with the stereo wires.

"I really wish you would stop saying that." He glanced down at the poodle stretched out on the floor by his feet. "If you keep it up, you're going to give him a complex. You know how sensitive he is."

Annie looked at the dog with a troubled expression. Without raising his head, the dog stared back at her with an almost-human look of rebuke in his dark eyes, as if silently asking her whether she really thought she could go on liv-

ing with herself if she had something as terrible
as his damaged self-esteem on her conscience.

It wasn't funny. Anne pressed her lips together in
a firm line. "That is not my dog," she said.

Her husband made an even more frustrated noise
and turned away from the stereo to look at her.

"Well, then, I don't know what to tell you," he
said, sounding impatient as he stood up. He went
over to the coffee table and pointed at a mess of
official-looking papers scattered over it along with
a collection of ribbons, almost all of them blue
except for one or two red ones.

"Look at his AKC papers," he said to her, pushing an official-looking form toward her with his
index finger. "And look here, look at his ribbons,
his champion certificate." He grabbed a leather
folder and opened it to display the engraved docu-
ment inside. "See for yourself. Now just how much
proof do you need?"

Annie stared at it, knowing, as surely as she
knew her own name, that she had never seen any
of those papers or ribbons or that folder before this
very moment when her husband had picked them
up and showed it to her. She looked past him to the
poodle, who had raised his head and now looked
as if he were waiting for her to capitulate.

"That is not my dog," she said a bit more insis-
tently. It was like a mantra now: *Om mane padme
hum. The jewel may be in the lotus but that is not
my dog.*

"Annie." Phil put the folder down on the coffee
table and went over to her. "You love this dog.
You've always loved this dog. Hell, there are days I

think you like him better than me. No, scratch that. There are days when I *know* you do." He knelt down in front of her and took one of her hands in both of his. "Why are you pretending you don't recognize him?"

She stared at him, completely at a loss for words. Why was she pretending not to recognize this poodle? Was she pretending?

She looked down at the photo album in her lap again.

Here was a picture of Phil and the poodle on the sofa; Phil holding the open newspaper so that they both seemed to be reading it. Anne could remember when she had taken the original of that particular photo; it hadn't been that long ago.

She remembered how later on she'd had to brush so much white mongrel hair off the upholstery that she could have knitted a sweater for one of Tess's old dolls out of it.

And here was another photo she remembered taking: Czonka and Sean shaking hands, which was one of the few tricks Czonka had been able to learn. Of course, he usually decided when he wanted to shake hands and, friendly as he was, he wasn't usually in the mood. His favorite time to make your acquaintance, however, was right after walking through a muddy puddle and if he couldn't get you to offer your hand right away, he would dab his grimy paw on any part of your body that he could reach until you cooperated.

Here was a photo of Czonka trying to lick Tess's face while she unsuccessfully fended him off. Just looking at the picture made Tess's voice echo in her memory: "Mom, make him stop! He's going to lick off all my make-up!"

Czonka had always been partial to the taste of trendy teen cosmetics. He found anything marked "NO ANIMAL TESTING" particularly delicious. Annie had never been able to decide whether that was really just a coincidence; she also wasn't sure whether anything labeled "NO ANIMAL TESTING" was technically entitled to continue making that claim once Czonka had ingested it.

She raised her head and looked up at her husband again, wishing that she could see more in his face than his obvious and genuine concern about her mental state.

As crazy as what she was saying may have seemed to him, why didn't it disturb him enough to make him question the whole situation rather than just her sanity? Why wasn't he questioning his own? Was it really just because the evidence of the photos was backing him up?

Abruptly, the poodle got up and came over to her. He stood for a moment wagging his pom-pom tail tentatively and then licked her hand.

"Go away, you," she said, drawing back and turning to her husband. "Philip, get him away from me."

Surprised hurt seemed to radiate from the poodle in all but palpable waves. His big liquid eyes seemed to ask: how can you be so cruel, after all we've meant to each other?

Phil started to say something but was drowned out by the shrill complaining whine of their daughter as she came galloping heavily down the stairs with her brother behind her.

"Mom!" The word was always two syllables when Tess said it: Mah-ahm. She stumped toward the living room, her bare feet showing under the shapeless, ankle-length skirt she was wearing, but didn't come down the steps. "Sean is stapling his posters to the wall!"

The family informer strikes again, Annie thought wearily, forgetting all about the poodle for the moment. Tess's eagerness to report any and all infractions of the house law by her brother, no matter how great or small, was as dismaying to her as Sean's eagerness to violate any and all rules laid down for him, no matter how great or small.

"You're a traitor, you know that?" Sean said, giving his Mom a significant look as he poked Tess's shoulder. He was well aware that neither she nor his Dad were terribly pleased about Tess's inclination to tattle. It was probably another reason why the boy never missed a chance to go out of his way to flout every rule, no matter what it was—even if it was more difficult to break a rule than it would have been to obey it.

"And they shoot traitors," he added, giving his sister another hard poke in the arm. "Did you know that?"

"Leave me alone!" Tess wailed, putting up her hands to fend him off. She fled to the kitchen and he followed closely behind, trying to poke her some more.

"Hey, is that a new zit?" he said with mock fascination.

"I hate you!" yelled Tess, sounding desperate now as she ran back past her brother and pounded up the stairs to her room.

Closing her eyes, Annie took a deep weary breath. She felt as if she had heard this exchange repeatedly, over and over again, day in and day out, week in and week out. It was getting so that she could practically recite everything they said before it actually came out of their mouths.

There was almost no variation except in perhaps the most minor details; the same arguments over the same issues, the same angry words and the same reactions.

"Someday, I'd like to find out who the hell is writing their dialog so I can fire them," she had said more than once, to Yasmine as well as to her husband. "That constant fighting and sniping and bickering might be easier to take if it wasn't the same damned thing over and over and over."

It occurred to her, now that she was thinking of it, that the response she got from both Yasmine and Phil was just as predictable. Yasmine would smile, give her an encouraging word and a sympathetic squeeze and then leave; Phil would hug her and tell her to relax.

Always the same thing, without variation, as if they had all been programmed. Herself included. Obviously the kids aren't the only ones who could use some new material, she thought, feeling another, stronger wave of weariness pass over her.

Then she opened her eyes again and her gaze fell immediately on the poodle, still staring at her with expectant, imploring eyes.

What was that you were thinking just now? Something about how you had to get some new material, wasn't it? asked a tiny voice in her mind. Don't you think this is something you could call "new material?"

No. This had nothing to do with new material, she thought, drawing back a little more from the animal. Phil started to speak again but she paid no attention.

"That is not my dog," she said emphatically.

The poodle stayed where he was, looking more expectant than ever now, as if he had been trained not to move a muscle until he heard exactly the right command.

Still crouched in front of her, Phil stared at her unhappily for a moment and she could feel that he was waiting for something from her as well. She had no idea what that could have been, only that she couldn't possibly give it to him. He straightened up with a small sigh of resignation and then hovered over her a bit longer, as if to give her one last chance to do or say whatever it was he was hoping for.

Finally, he let out a frustrated breath and went back to the stereo, snapping his fingers at the poodle, which followed him with the unmistakable easy air of longstanding obedience. Obviously, they were old pals and this was one of those old, familiar routines they'd been doing forever...

Annie got up and left the room, not quite running to the kitchen.

* * *

OFFICIAL MOTHER OF THE YEAR COFFEE MUG
(so keep yer grubby paws OFF)

The sentiment had been printed to order on the sixteen-ounce porcelain cup, complete with a design of grubby prints both human and canine. A Mother's Day gift from Phil and the kids.

And Czonka, of course. That had been several years ago, when the kids had still been solidly in their childhood and Czonka had still been more of a puppy than a full-grown dog.

Annie had always loved the mug not only because it was one-of-a-kind and non-fattening but because Phil had gone to the trouble of supplying the family's actual prints, including Czonka's, for it.

The prints weren't full-size, of course—large as the cup was, it wasn't quite large enough for anything that authentic. But the fact that each of the prints was the real thing just reduced in size had touched Annie in a rare and highly meaningful way. She wasn't sure that any woman who wasn't also a mother would understand.

Now she sat at the marble-topped island counter in the middle of her perfect kitchen, staring at it with her chin on her folded hands. Yasmine sat across from her, looking concerned as she sipped green tea from one of the handmade pottery mugs that Annie had brought back as a souvenir from a family vacation in Amish country several years ago. She could feel how Yasmine was waiting for her to say something. To unburden herself. Share everything that was bothering her, talk it over.

Annie said nothing. She kept her gaze fixed on her old Mother's Day present and wondered if there was any way she could pick it up without touching any of the paw prints. That made no sense at all, of course, but as far as she could tell, making sense was not exactly the order of the day anyway.

Finally, Yasmine leaned forward and put a gentle hand on her forearm. "Annie, listen to me very carefully," she said.

Annie stared down her friend's long, graceful fingers; soft, flawless skin, perfect manicure. What kind of dishwashing liquid does she buy that leaves her hands looking so young and smooth?

Oh, for heaven's sake—where had that absurdity come from, she wondered? Slightly appalled at herself, she put the thought out of her mind altogether as Yasmine went on.

"Believe it or not, I have seen this sort of thing before," the other woman was saying. "Buying your first home can be very difficult. There's so much involved, so much paperwork, so many procedures. You've got escrow, you've got inspections: mechanical, termites, then the surveyor. It's a lot of stress. A lot." She squeezed Annie's arm for emphasis. "No one knows that better than I do."

"Uh-huh. So now let me see if I've got this right," Annie said, finally giving in and lifting her gaze to look directly at Yasmine. "What you're saying to me is, I've owned a poodle for five years but never realized it?"

She turned and looked over at the dog lying on the floor in the far corner of the kitchen. His choice of spot had not been accidental; it happened to be close to the cabinet where Czonka's dog food and treats were stored. This was a typical Czonka thing to do.

The mutt's complete lack of training and discipline had not interfered with his ability either to locate edibles or to position himself so he could be sure to benefit from someone's sudden impulse to reward him just for existing. And since he knew Annie was no less prone to it than anyone else in the family, she could always be sure of having a little company in the kitchen.

Czonka's company. Czonka the mutt. Her Czonka did that. Which made it a reasonable assumption that a lot of other dogs did the same thing, including this one. But that didn't make any of them Czonka. Including this one.

Especially this one.

Yasmine had turned to follow her gaze; now she turned back to Annie and gave her arm a little shake. "Look, girlfriend, I know what the stress can do to people. I've had clients forget their own names, what year it was, even how many children they have," she said. "I knew one guy who, every day for three months, drove back to his old apartment after work."

Annie pulled her arm free of Yasmine's grasp and sat back in her chair.

"But what would any of that have to do with me?" she asked, feeling mildly annoyed. "I've got two teenagers, I eat stress for breakfast. And again for lunch."

"Which is why I'm not worried about you," Yasmine replied, the anxiety in her face deepening.

Annie noticed and gave a short, humorless laugh. "Then you ought to stop looking so worried."

"I just want you to remember that we ran the numbers," Yasmine said, tapping one perfect finger on the marble countertop between them. "You are not in over your head. You got a great deal here, you really did. I told you buying a model home was the way to go."

"So now what are you really trying to say, Yasmine?" she asked her friend, feeling slightly bewildered. Did Yasmine really believe that she was freaking out over a mortgage?

"What I'm saying is, relax." Yasmine reached over and captured her arm again. "It's all going to be okay. This is your home. Every square inch of it." She made a graceful flourish with one hand that took in the whole of the kitchen and ended with her pointing at the poodle. "And that is your dog." She gave a small chuckle. "If you don't believe me, just ask him. He'll tell you. When it comes to knowing who feeds him, he's the final authority."

Annie refused to laugh or even smile just for the sake of politeness. Apparently, her best friend did think the trauma of a mortgage was giving her delusions or hallucinations or something. She had a powerful urge to grab the other woman by the shoulders and shake her till she rattled. She might even have done it, had it not been for the fact that Yasmine had shocked the hell out of her by being there at all.

Not that Annie had called her. That had been all Phil's idea, and he had simply gone ahead and done it without thinking to ask her about it first. If he had, she would have simply told him that he shouldn't bother Yasmine, that Yasmine was really too busy. It would have been a lot easier than attempting to explain that her best friend probably wouldn't have the faintest idea of what Phil was talking about.

But it seemed that she had misread Yasmine completely, Annie thought, because here she was. Maybe she didn't know her best friend as well as she thought she had. Or maybe it was just that Phil was a lot better at explaining what was going on with her, and she actually didn't know herself as well as she thought she did.

None of that made sense, of course. Not in terms of the day's events. And as long as that poodle was in her house instead of the dog she remembered, nothing would, or could, make sense. Which, today, was business as usual.

She turned back to Yasmine, intending to tell her how she felt, and then changed her mind. Something about the expression on the other woman's face, friendly concern mixed with something else she wasn't sure she could identify, a kind of knowing look, told her that in some way, Yasmine still wasn't really hearing her after all. Maybe because this had to do with the part of her life that Yasmine simply didn't understand.

So there was one thing at least that still made sense. Too bad it could not have been something that would do her some good.

* * *

Their first night together in their beautiful new home should have been perfect, Annie thought as she pulled back the covers and got into bed. But then, she had been imagining it as the perfect end to a perfect day.

What she had not imagined was that anything could make the day so much less than perfect. Or less than happy, at least. Well, nothing short of a disaster of global proportions, like an asteroid striking the earth, anyway.

She had not really expected that everything would go smoothly, without even the slightest hitch. She knew better than to expect anything of the sort. Things like the dog peeing in the fireplace, the kids and their constant bickering—as much as those things had upset her, they were at least in the realm of the familiar, not to mention the possible.

But this thing with Czonka being replaced by a poodle and everyone insisting that they had always had a poodle when she knew better...

God, she didn't have the faintest idea of what to call that, other than inexplicable. She had never even heard of anything even vaguely similar happening to anyone and somehow, she thought she would have, if it had been something this bizarre.

The only thing even faintly like it that she could think of was something she and Phil had seen on the Discovery Channel several months ago. It was a program about a famous neurosurgeon whose patients had highly unusual conditions that caused them to believe that one of their arms or legs didn't actually belong to them, or that everyone in their families had been replaced by impostors.

At the time, Annie had found it incomprehensible that none of the people affected could accept even just the possibility that their perceptions might be faulty. And it was not so much that they categorically refused to consider the notion as it was that it never occurred to them, any more than it would have occurred to her to question whether the Czonka she had seen every day for the last five years might not actually be a furry white mutt but a horse or a rabbit. Or a pedigreed poodle.

So what was she supposed to conclude from all of that, she wondered as she picked up the bottle of papaya lotion from the nightstand and squeezed some onto the back of each hand.

Should she have been considering the idea that she was funny in the head? That she had some kind of exotic brain condition even more bizarre than any of the famous neurosurgeon's patients, but it only affected her memories of the family dog?

That is not my dog.

The truth of that statement went all the way through to her core, she thought, and she just wasn't going to be able to get around it by ignoring it or pretending otherwise. Which still left her without even the faintest idea of what she could do, Annie thought glumly as she continued to massage papaya lotion into a few chapped spots on her knuckles.

The lotion was some kind of aromatherapy formula that Yasmine had given her and it was supposed to have some kind of stress-relieving properties. While it certainly was great-smelling stuff and it made her skin feel wonderful, she could feel no reduction whatsoever in her stress or anxiety.

But then she had known deep down that there wouldn't be. She knew better than to put any faith in a smell being able to cure anything because she knew the difference between a marketing ploy and a fact. Just as she knew the difference between her dog and some other animal.

In her mind's eye, she could see her dog—her dog, her *real* dog—standing at the fireplace with one leg in the air. Czonka, the shaggy white mutt, the same one who had been dragging Phil into the living room, straining at the leash, trying to smell everything at once; the dog she had just been looking at in the family portrait over the fireplace only seconds before.

The original family portrait, which existed now only in her memory, it seemed.

Her memory was extremely vivid. Even if, by some fantastic turn of events, she actually had forgotten all those things Yasmine had mentioned—her name, what year it was, how many kids she had—she still remembered plenty of other things.

She remembered, for example, how every few months she had to get Phil to hold Czonka down so she could cut the knots and snarls out of the unruly fur dangling down from his belly.

She remembered how they had all learned never to forget to lock the door when they took a bath or he would jump into the tub with them.

She also remembered the time that she had finally managed to sneak up on him with the camera so she could get some pictures of him lying on the floor with his back legs extended, looking like a dog-skin rug.

A mutt dog, not a poodle dog.

No, she knew her dog when she saw him and that poodle wasn't her dog.

Before she could start another round of worrying about what that meant in terms of the photo albums and the family portrait, the bedroom door opened and Phil came in. She saw that he had a bottle of champagne in one hand and two long-stemmed glasses in the other.

Normally the sight of his loving smile would have been enough to banish all of Annie's troubled thoughts, but normal was still too far away tonight, with no sign of it getting closer again any time soon.

"And what's that you have there?" she asked him, smiling a little in spite of everything. It was just a tiny smile, though, and it didn't last.

"Champagne." He wiggled his eyebrows. "And by that I do not mean zee sparkling wine, I mean zee French champagne. Zee real thing, no substitutes accepted. Zee product of zee one and only champagne grape, ma cherie."

The fake French accent got a small laugh out of her. "Talk about optimistic," she said, wiggling her own eyebrows at him.

Still smiling at her, he put the champagne and the glasses on the nightstand and sat down on the bed facing her as she undid her ponytail and shook her head, letting her hair fall loosely around her shoulders.

"Sorry it's been such a tough day," he said, taking one of her lotion-covered hands in both of his and giving it an affectionate squeeze.

Her own answering smile was tentative. "Sorry if I freaked you out." It was the most neutral thing she could think of to say to him.

But apparently it was the right thing. He moved closer and ran his hand through her hair. He had always told her how much he loved the way she looked with long hair. It was a bit stringy and ragged and needed washing right now but that didn't seem to bother him.

"Does that mean I can open the champagne?" he asked.

More than anything else in the world, Annie wanted to forget every single thing that had happened in the last eight hours. Or, if she really couldn't forget, then she wanted at least to pretend that she had.

She would have been more than glad to pretend that the most disturbing things she'd had to deal with all day were the chronic bickering of a couple of bad-tempered, ill-mannered teenage children and a little dog pee in the fireplace. Then she could look into Phil's eyes and say yes, open the champagne and let's celebrate like a couple of newlyweds who have just moved into a palace. That was the way she had always imagined they would spend their first night in their own beautiful home.

But instead all her happiness was being overshadowed by things she couldn't understand, and she could barely manage to force a smile.

"Down, boy," she said with a nervous laugh.

He ran a gentle finger along the line of her cheek and turned her face so that he could look directly into her eyes.

"Annie, I just want to say… Well, I know I was reluctant to move, but I'm glad you talked me into it." Pulling her closer, he kissed his way down her face from her forehead to the end of her nose. "Now, how about I talk you into something?" he added.

Annie let herself relax into his embrace, trying to give herself over to the reassurance and comfort that he had always been able to provide, no matter how awful a day she might have had. The knowledge that he was always there for her to lean on when she had to was the perfect constant in her life.

Perfect. There was that word again. Perfect house, perfect neighborhood, perfect moment, perfect, perfect, perfect. She used that word so much when in reality it described so little in her life. But then, wouldn't most people say the same thing? And how many people would be able to say that there was anything perfect in their lives at all? Very, very few people were so lucky, but it just so happened that she was one of them. Because Phil was perfect for her.

All at once, Annie became aware of the sound of the dog whining at the closed bedroom door.

Czonka always did that. He never could stand to be left out of anything and he seemed to have an unerring instinct for knowing when Annie and Phil wanted to be alone. Czonka the mutt, that was. The real Czonka, the true Czonka, the one that she

remembered. Not this strange poodle that everyone
kept insisting was her dog. She couldn't help going
stiff in her husband's arms and drawing back a little.

"Pretend he's not there," Phil whispered,
stroking her as he tried to bring her back into the
moment.

The whining outside the door continued. It
didn't sound exactly like Czonka's whine to her
but it was similar enough to give her the creeps.
Annie drew back from him slightly.

"I can't," she said with a small shudder. "I just…
I can't."

Phil looked at her for a long moment, searching
her face for something that she knew should have
been there but wasn't. She wished again more than
anything that she could simply make herself let go
of the day—or make the day let go of her—even
just temporarily. But as much as she wanted to,
she just couldn't and instead, with a heavy sigh of
defeat, Philip let go of her.

He said nothing as he lay down and turned out the
light, which made her feel worse than if he had been
angry or impatient with her. Mr "Steady-As-A-Rock"
didn't anger easily, particularly with her. Talking
things over like rational adults was his style. As a
result, their disagreements seldom grew into heated
arguments about more sensitive underlying issues.

This was something that had always appeared to
work in their favor. As near as Annie could tell,
they seemed to have fewer arguments in general
than most of the other couples they knew, probably as a direct result.

Things had changed. She could feel it. Now they seemed to have one of those lousy sensitive issues in actual development. The poodle whined again.

She raised up a little so she could see his black nose snuffling at the space under the door. This was something else Czonka always did when he was faced with the problem of a barrier to ready access. As if he really believed that he might be able to smell some secret way through it so he could take part in whatever human thing was so fascinating that he had to be kept from it.

Except it wasn't Czonka out there. It was a dog she had never seen before. No matter what anyone told her, no matter what it said on all those official AKC papers, no matter what she saw in the photo albums or in the family portrait, that poodle was not Czonka, had never been Czonka, and would not ever be Czonka.

Almost as if it had heard her thoughts, the poodle outside the bedroom door gave a louder and more insistent whine.

Annie lay down and put her hands over her ears in an attempt to shut him out. It didn't work. She lay in the dark for what seemed like forever, feeling alone and lost, before she finally got to sleep.

FOUR

When she woke up the next morning, she discovered to her dismay that Phil had let her sleep in almost an hour later than usual. Perhaps he had been aware of the long and complicated dream she had been having about her Great-Aunt Lauren and her oh-so-English, oh-so-perfect garden.

The dream had been a confused amalgam of things that had really happened in the garden, and things that, as a child, she had wanted to happen. In her drowsy state, it was hard to distinguish the two, but it was easy to remember the dream in detail because it had been so vivid.

Annie had been about eight, and she had been sitting with her friend Trish in the rose arbor listening to a story told by Auntie Lauren. Whatever had happened to Trish and all her other friends from school and college, wondered Annie? At best, they were a few lines of type in an email or an online chat. Or a Happy Holidays card, sometimes with a family photo in which the old friends seemed to become more and more distant, more and more out of touch with the world that Annie had been making for herself, especially since her marriage.

She wondered how she had arrived at this place in her life when the only real friend she had was Yasmine—who was also, of course, her realtor.

Yasmine, who was so interested in the house and what Annie wanted it to be, and yet so uninterested in anything else. Which included Great-Aunt Lauren, her garden and her stories.

Great-Aunt Lauren had lived a couple of blocks over from Annie's parents' home, when Annie was a child. She had been living in the same house and tending the same garden for some years before Annie's parents had moved into the neighborhood.

In fact, part of their reason for moving to that area had been the closeness of a reliable and retired relative, who could take care of Annie—and was only too happy to do so. Even when Annie had been at her most high-spirited, Great-Aunt Lauren had somehow managed to keep up with her, to engage in her play and her exercise, and in all kinds of ways to help to make her a better person.

That had always been a theme in Annie's family; making the best of yourself. Which also meant making the best of what was around you: your home, your garden, your job, and of course any children. Annie's parents had pushed her quite hard in school to achieve good grades, stressing that she needed to do well, especially when she reached the age to go into high school, so her grades would be strong enough to allow her to go into college.

Annie had not been an especially gifted child academically, but she had excelled in enough areas to live up to her parents' wishes. Of course, it had been hard work.

Hard work meant plenty of time spent reading and doing work at home to supplement what she had been learning at school. But hard work was something Annie didn't mind, even as a child. And the upside of all that work had been that her parents had allowed her lots of free time to play, to exercise, or just to lie in the sun making plans.

Annie had always had a head full of plans. Plans about her life ahead, what kind of house she would like to live in, what kind of man she would like to marry, and what kind of children they might have together. She had supposed that it was all to do with the family, with their insistence on always making the best of everything.

One of the people who had managed to live up to that ideal most strongly had been Great-Aunt Lauren. It was because her great-aunt's life and her home seemed to represent an almost perfect achievement that Annie had enjoyed going over to see Lauren and going out, whenever the weather was good enough, into the garden to sit and to talk.

When they had been out in the garden together, and Lauren was taking a break from weeding and pruning and generally tending to all the flowers, shrubs and other growing things, their favorite place to sit had been in the old rose arbor. It had been there even when Lauren had moved to the house. Of course, it was just a wooden construction, with a raised deck and railings around, the upper part of the sides open. Topping it off was a conical roof, with a weathervane standing proudly in the center of it.

The profusion of roses had been Lauren's addition to the place and that had truly turned it into an arbor. Annie had thought of it as not just an arbor, but also "a harbor". It was somewhere safe and sheltered where she could be at home.

Wherever she had gone, even on trips to summer camp involving a three or four hour bus ride, she had always been able to come home to the rose arbor, to dock the little ship of her body on the cane chairs, and to find a place that was home. There had been few times in her childhood when she had been happier than when she was in the rose arbor with her Great-Aunt Lauren.

On one side of the arbor there had been a swing seat, like the ones many people had on their porches. Great-Aunt Lauren had loved to sit in the swing seat and rock gently backwards and forwards while she chatted to Annie. Sometimes she would tell stories. Her stories had seemed timeless and always with a meaning for today, and yet they seemed to have come from a far-away place.

That faraway land must have been a magical place, because there it actually was possible to have your wishes come true. It was possible to meet your Prince Charming and to marry him, and to live happily ever after. It was possible to live in the perfect house. It had been possible to have wonderful children who grew up straight and strong and brave.

All of Great-Aunt Lauren's stories had been associated in some way with that magical land of perfect husband, perfect homes and perfect children. But that perfection had always been achieved at a price. This was because there really had been magic involved, and it had been necessary to keep on the right side of all the spirits, the magicians, the wise men and women who had controlled that magic. Not to mention, of course, the animals who had a special spirit within them. They may have looked like regular rabbits, with cute floppy ears and sleek fur and bobbly tails, but they were anything but ordinary.

On the occasion all those years ago, when her friend Trish and she had been sitting on the cane chairs, listening to Great-Aunt Lauren telling a story, the magical animal had been a cat. Now, from her reading of the Alice stories, Annie had imagined that all magical cats must look special in some way, like the famous Cheshire Cat. But the cat that Great-Aunt Lauren talked about had been quite an ordinary looking one.

The cat's name had been Callie, and she had been a mackerel tabby, just like thousands of other mackerel tabbies. She was, perhaps, a little on the plump side, because everyone had loved her so much they would always give her treats. And since the cat had been ten years-old—which Annie had known was really, really old in cat years—perhaps she could have been forgiven for putting on a little bit of weight and being comfortable about it.

Whilst Annie as a child had always loved both dogs and cats, her great-aunt was definitely a cat person. That was most likely the reason why the magical creature in the story she had been telling to Lauren and Trish had been a cat—though one that was very different from the elegant pair of Siamese cats which Great-Aunt Lauren kept.

So, there they had all been sitting, calm and quiet in the late afternoon sunshine, a gentle breeze blowing through the rose arbor, wafting the scent of roses all around. Great-Aunt Lauren was rocking on her swing seat, relaxed on a comfortable cushion which had been predictably decorated with a floral pattern, one dominated by roses.

It couldn't have been any other way. Great-Aunt Lauren's life, her garden and her home, had been so much in harmony, every piece making beautiful music with every other piece, that of course the cushion on the swing seat had been a floral pattern, with mostly roses. It was, after all a cushion in a rose arbor.

Great-Aunt Lauren's eyes had been almost closed, just like her cats when they were happy and content. Her spectacles—which she needed both for reading and for doing any close work in the garden—had been resting on her chest at the end of their cord. The cord was itself an intricate thing, twisted threads of gold and red and silver, and Annie had imagined that there had been a story attached to the cord, just as the cord was attached to the spectacles.

The tale was slowly spinning out, as if Great-Aunt Lauren had been some exotic and wonderful spider at the center of a complicated and lovely web. If it had been a real web, thought Annie, it would have been one of those achingly perfect ones that you sometimes saw early in the morning, when the dew was still on everything. Every strand of the web would have been heavy with tiny droplets of water from the dew, as if the slightest touch or the gentlest breeze would cause a cascade of miniature raindrops to fall.

"So, the little girl—let's call her Susie—had decided that the help she needed would only be available from the magical cat, Callie," Lauren had continued. They had just taken a break from story-telling in order for them to go into the kitchen, which was cool and dark at this time of the day, to take out a jug of lemonade from the refrigerator.

The lemonade—home-made, of course, and from lemons grown in the greenhouse—had been chilling all day.

Lauren, Trish and Annie had each filled a tall glass with lemonade and gone back into the rose arbor. As they had sat there, glasses resting on their laps, Annie had been able to feel the moisture from the air condensing on the cold glass, tiny droplets forming, just like those tiny droplets that fell from the perfect, dew-covered spider web.

The lemonade that her great-aunt had made in those days when Annie was only eight, had seemed to her like the most perfect lemonade she had ever tasted. Sometimes she thought that it would always be the most perfect lemonade she would ever taste in her whole life.

Even though her Great-Aunt had shown Annie the exact recipe and the method for making the lemonade, somehow Annie herself could never get that exact, correct and perfect flavor that Lauren achieved. Although, of course, she had tried over and over to manage it, and sometimes felt as if she were getting a little closer, as if she were perfecting her lemonade-making skills.

Annie had taken a sip from her long, cool glass of lemonade as her great-aunt picked up the thread of her story. Lauren seemed to be drifting in and out of being fully awake, as if she were spending so much time thinking about that faraway, perfect and magical land that she had actually been there for part of the time. Maybe she'd had one foot in each world, her feet in their old tennis shoes, which dangled sometimes touching the floor, sometimes in the air, as she rocked back and forth.

"In order for Susie to consult the magical cat about her problem," Lauren had explained, "it was necessary for the girl to go to where the cat was. Callie did not make house calls.

It was the afternoon, perhaps not quite as late in the afternoon as we find ourselves today, but late all the same. At different times of the day, the cat would be in different places. So it was necessary to know where Callie liked to be at any time of the day, on particular days of the week, for she was a cat who loved to have a varied routine from day to day. Susie had consulted her wise old uncle, who had known the cat's schedule to the last detail. So, off Susie went to the hollow log at the edge of the woods, where Callie liked to rest at this time of the day, which happened to be a Friday.

"She was clutching in her hand a small parcel containing a special gift for the magical cat. Everyone who consulted Callie took her a gift, and they all knew the kind of things she would love. In Susie's case, she had taken some of Callie's favorite cat treats. Her old uncle, who used to make up batches of the treats for his own cats, had given them to Susie in a small paper sack, which glowed whiter than white in the afternoon sun.

The paper in those days, in that land, was made from flax, not from the coarse wood pulp that is used today. It made a beautiful, soft, white paper, perfect in every way and ideal for every application. Susie had used her drawing skills to decorate the paper sack with pictures of flowers and trees and hedgerows, all colored in her special drawing inks. Susie knew that this would be like an extra gift for Callie the magical cat and would help to ensure that her problem was solved in one visit.

"When Susie reached the hollow log, and bent down to see Callie inside, she saw that the cat was resting, lying full length on the bottom of the log, with her head resting on her paws. But despite this pose of resting, Callie's eyes were open, bright and alert, taking in every detail of the world in front of her, which was now dominated by this young girl.

"Callie looked at Susie and then the cat briskly enquired: 'So, my little Susie, what is it that you need help with today? For I know that few people will come all the way out to this old hollow log where I love to rest on a Friday afternoon, unless they have some problem which I may be able to help with.'

"Susie smiled. It was impossible to fool the magical cat. She gave over to Callie the bag of treats.

After admiring the drawings and their shining colors, Callie sniffed in approval at the treats. 'From your old uncle,' Callie said. 'I'll warrant he made up a batch specially, and gave you the best of the batch, as he always does, so that you could in turn give them to me.'

"Susie nodded that this was so, and then, having received a nod of approval from Callie, began to set out her problem.

"You must have been wondering," said Great-Aunt Lauren, her eyes opening wider as she tilted her head up to look straight at Annie and her friend Trish, "what kind of problem an eight year-old girl, living a happy life in that wonderful faraway land, could possibly have.

"What would take her across the fields and meadows, past lakes and ponds, to the very edge of the great wood where the magical cat was resting in her hollow log on that long ago and far away Friday afternoon? Well, if truth be told—and of course, there was no dealing with a magical cat that did not involve the telling of the truth—it was actually the problem of Susie's eldest sister, Karen.

"Karen was a beautiful young woman of full nineteen years, and she was betrothed to a handsome young merchant in the nearby town. The young man had promised to build for Karen her dream home, a perfect house in a perfect setting, where they could both live happily for ever and ever. Wanting the home to be Karen's dream home, he had asked Karen to tell him all about it, to tell him her dream.

"There was only one problem: Karen did not dream. By great bad luck, when she had been only eight a wicked wizard had cast a spell on her, so that her dream life was empty. Perhaps she did still dream, but just never remembered when she awoke. Perhaps she did not dream at all.

"Either way, no dreams and no dream home in Karen's head—and thus no dream home to tell her wonderful fiancé about. So Karen had turned to her youngest sister, who had skills in drawing and painting, with inks and chalks and pastels, to help her plan out a dream home, to put it all down on paper for her love to create for her in reality.

"Now, designing someone else's dream home is not the easiest thing in the world. You have to know that person really well and try to get inside their head and see the way they think and feel. In their favor, however, was the fact that Karen and Susie were loving sisters, who despite their age difference were very close.

"Susie, who was a bright and intelligent as well as a loving and caring sister to Karen, was able to determine most of the things that would be part of a dream home just from her knowledge and insight into her sister. But on one important factor—or, at least, it seemed so to Susie—she was at a loss. What would be the perfect pet for Karen, her dream pet in her dream home?

"Well, who better to consult about your sister's dream pet than a magical cat, since cats are so popular as pets with so many people? Surely Callie would know Karen's perfect pet.

"Susie explained her problem to Callie, who watched the girl's young face with a kind of ancient wisdom in her lustrous cat eyes. Those eyes glazed over a little, as if Callie were deep in thought, and then she said: 'Susie, I must think on this and dream on it. Perchance I will fall asleep here in my log and the solution to the question of what would be the perfect pet for your sister will be revealed to me today. Or perchance it will not be until the moon is full in the sky tonight and I am asleep under the stars. Either way, if you return upon the morrow to the place where you know I will be on a Saturday afternoon,' and here Callie gave Susie a knowing wink, 'then we will have the solution. And now, my child, let me rest and think.'

"So Susie went away, leaving the magical cat to think on the problem and wended her way back through the fields, where the shadows were beginning to lengthen as the sun sank in the sky, to her home. When she went to bed, it took her a while to relax and fall into a slumber, for she was so excited about finding out the answer to her question from Callie the next day. But when she did fall into a deep sleep, she dreamed a strange and mysterious dream.

"And now, young ladies," Great-aunt Lauren had said, sitting upright and planting both her tennis-shoe clad feet on the floor, "now it is time to be thinking about some tea. How do toasted English muffins sound to you both?"

FIVE

English muffins, thought Annie drowsily as she fumbled for her slippers and dressing gown. That was the last thing in the dream that she was able to remember. Had there been more of the dream, which she could not remember in half-awake, half-sleeping state? Or would it resume on another night, perhaps tonight? Either way, it would be fascinating to know what the dream pet turned out to be.

Though Annie could almost taste those toasted English muffins and the sweet honey that her Great-Aunt Lauren had put on them for her eight year-old Annie, she could not remember any more about the solution to the dream pet problem. Hardly surprising, though, she thought to herself, that I was dreaming about pets, given the downright weird thing that has happened to Czonka.

With that thorny problem of her own to deal with, Annie Macintosh dragged herself off the bed, started looking around for some clothes that were in a reasonable sate to wear and thought about breakfast. Were there any English muffins in the house, she wondered? She couldn't remember getting any, but maybe Phil had, which would make up for him letting her sleep so late. Which meant she was going to have one of those groggy and next-to-useless mornings.

Damn, she thought. He must have done it in the hope that she would sleep off the stresses and strains of yesterday and awake refreshed and untroubled.

Or, if not completely carefree then burdened only by the usual concerns—bickering teenaged children, dog pee, scratched woodwork—rather than anything out of the ordinary. Like, say, a surreal waking nightmare involving the family dog.

She shoved the thought away, splashed cold water on her face until her skin was stinging, and pulled on an old pair of jeans.

While there was no faulting her husband's intentions, she had never been able to make him understand that she was one of those people for whom sleeping in was actually no help at all.

No matter how tired she seemed, or how much he thought she needed to rest, the extra time in bed would only result in her waking up even groggier and more lethargic than if she had had too little sleep. Just the way she felt now, she thought, yawning, as she started to put her T-shirt on backwards for the third time.

From here she would go dragging through most of the day in a fog which wouldn't lift until sometime late in the evening, so that she found herself wide awake when she should have been winding down and getting ready to go to sleep. Then it would be yet another day before she completely recovered.

Exactly what would have made her husband think, after all these years, that this time would be any different she couldn't imagine.

Some sort of extra-strength optimism on his part, perhaps, that her natural tendencies in that area would undergo a complete change and she would respond the way he wished she would—and probably the way most other people would have—just because he wanted so much to do precisely the right thing to help her.

Could she really call that extra-strength optimism? She stumped down the stairs to the landing, leaning heavily on the banister. Or was it more like extra-strength stubbornness?

I want to make you feel better but only if you'll do it my way.

She paused for an extra-wide yawn before going the rest of the way down the stairs.

No, definitely not, not in a million years; there was absolutely no reason for her to associate that kind of control-freak behavior with her sweet-natured husband. Not Phil, Mr "Steady-As-A-Rock", Macintosh.

If anyone around here had a little touch of control-freakiness to them, it was Annie herself. That would certainly explain her ongoing desire for the perfect house and the perfect furniture and the perfect family.

Oh, she could say she didn't really expect her family to be perfect. But if she were going to be completely honest with herself, she would have to admit that she did have a standard that she measured them against and too often she was dissatisfied with the results.

She stopped at the bottom of the steps and looked around, yawning again.

Only yesterday she had been standing there telling herself that she didn't want to turn into one of those people for whom nothing was ever quite good enough.

She had vowed that she wasn't going to let herself become one of those sad, sour souls who was never satisfied with anything, who always found something to complain about instead of something to enjoy and be happy about.

For the woman who had stood here in this very spot yesterday, this had been the perfect house and she had been excited about moving into it.

Today, she could stand in the same place and look around at the multitude of boxes that needed to be unpacked and the well-worn furniture—which was to say, well-worn at the very best, and the rest of it being just plain old worse-for-wear—and it was still the perfect house, the house she had dreamed of.

Furthermore, even if the dream had been only hers in the beginning, Phil shared it with her now completely. He had said so, just last night...

The memory of the dog whining at the bedroom door came back to her. That bizarre waking nightmare about the strange dog, the poodle that had appeared out of nowhere, that Phil kept insisting was Czonka.

Regardless of the fact that she knew differently, however, there wasn't a shred of evidence to back her up. Every photo in every one of their albums, the family portrait…

The portrait was still hanging over the fireplace, looking no different than it had last night when she had paused on her way up to bed to take it down for closer study, searching for some sign of it having been altered.

After studying the photo itself, she had turned it over and carefully inspected the back for any evidence that the paper seal had been removed. Then she had gone over the frame inch by inch, even though she had never examined those physical details very closely in the first place and therefore didn't have the faintest idea of what she might be looking for.

What was obvious to her, however, was the fact that both the paper seal and the frame itself had been intact since the glue had dried. And she had a very strong feeling that even if she had had both the knowledge and the equipment to dust the thing for fingerprints, she wouldn't have found any but her own.

Annie now took a couple of steps toward it and then abruptly grabbed hold of the banister, forcing herself to stop.

It's the family portrait, she told herself. Or, to be more accurate, the most recent in a series of family portraits. All of which had been taken by an established photography and portraiture business, which had been owned and run by the same family almost since the area was first settled, since the first townships grew up.

Walt Whickers, who was the chief portrait photographer there, had been taking the Macintosh formal family portraits ever since the children had been born. Of course, the portrait albums which Phil and Annie had so carefully maintained, selecting the best shots, were different. They contained photos taken by Phil, by Annie, by the kids when they got old enough to use a camera; in fact, before they got old enough to use it properly. But that was another story.

Some of the pictures in their albums, the very recent ones, had been taken on a small digital camera that Annie had bought Phil as a birthday present a year or so ago. By linking it to his PC, he was able to crop the pictures, make colors brighter or darker; change them in almost any way.

But that was digital photos on a computer, no way could that have been done with the family portrait hanging on the wall. The one that now so strangely showed a completely different Czonka from the one that Annie remembered. Although it was the Czonka, so the rest of her family assured her, that she could see in her own new home, and that had always been the same.

She could picture in her mind the occasion when they had last been to visit Walt Whickers and his studio, to have the current family portrait taken. Of course, Annie had wanted it to be perfect, the loving family and their pet. She had wanted it to be a picture that she could send out to all of her friends, just as they had a habit of sending Annie and Phil their family portraits with the Happy Holidays cards. Of course, just as in everything that Annie had wanted to be perfect, nothing had gone right.

For starters, they had all been late arriving at the photography studio. Annie had picked up the kids after school let out, and Phil had left work early to drive to the studio. Well, first there had been the delays while she had talked Sean's science teacher out of holding him back in school to finish a project which should have been done a week before.

Then there had been Tess spending forever in the bathroom at the photographers when they did finally arrive, trying to make herself look beautiful. Or perhaps the thing for teenagers now to be was "cool" rather than beautiful? Whatever it was, Tess had taken the longest time messing around in there, almost driving her mother to distraction. Of course, she hadn't managed to achieve whatever she was setting out to do, so she had been whining at Annie about it. Sean, of course, made things worse by standing in the background going on and on about how he had tidied his hair and smartened up his clothes all in a couple of minutes.

The photographer, Walt Whickers, had seen it all before, and took it in his stride. He patiently guided them to their seats, making sure the air conditioning was turned up high enough to compensate for the heat of the studio lights.

Which had all been very well, but where had Phil been? He was over twenty-five minutes late arriving. Traffic was backed up on the Overlink Parkway, as a truck lost its load of wood all over the freeway; the usual kind of disruption that just seemed to occur at the worst times.

When Phil finally did get to the studio, to find the rest of his family, even the rebellious Czonka, in place, he was hot and bothered. Walt Whickers did his best to calm Phil, brought him a glass of ice water, gave him time to straighten his tie and his jacket, splashed cold water on his face to cool down, talked soothingly to all of them about "No hurry" and "Plenty of time" and of course, Annie's favorite, "Worse things happen in war."

Eventually they had all been in place. Sean and Tess had stopped teasing and picking at each other, Czonka had been on his best behavior—aided by the ever-resourceful photographer having some doggie treats to hand. Phil had calmed down a bit, but of course the whole thing had made Annie fraught. She tried her hardest to put on her best smile, to hold her face *just so* in order to minimize the signs of wear and tear that the years of raising the kids had put on her. Eventually the photographs had been taken, Walt Whickers had seemed happy, and they were all able to go home.

Of course, even going home had not been easy. The traffic was still bad because of the earlier truck accident, and Tess and Sean had decided to have an argument in the car. In Annie's car, of course, since Phil had remembered he needed to go back to the office to collect some papers he had forgotten.

The argument Tess and Sean had been having had been so stupid and pointless, as far as Annie was concerned. Tess had been complaining about how she would never look her best, and then Sean had started trying to creep her out by telling her that photographers stole your soul when they took your picture. "How else do you explain how healthy old Walt is, after all these years?" said Sean. "I mean, man, he is ancient. And yet he's got the moves of a guy half his age. It must be all the recharging that his batteries get from the soul power he's stealing from his subjects."

Tess obviously didn't know whether to take her brother seriously and get really weirded out, or just to make like a mature person and laugh it off as nonsense. It was exactly the kind of conflict in knowing what to do and say that was enough to send any teenager into a fit.

Annie, tired, hot and frustrated at the wheel of the car in the nose-to-tail traffic jam, had tried to intervene. "Listen, Tess, he's just trying to start an argument. And Sean, cut it out and leave your sister alone."

That was what Annie had wanted to say, and to say it in the authoritative, commanding manner that would show she would brook no argument. She wanted to be the perfect mother, friendly and supportive and understanding of her children when they needed it, but strong, rational and definitive with her advice and, yes, instructions, as was necessary to keep them on the straight and narrow.

What actually happened, as so often, was that before she could say a word, Tess had responded to Sean herself.

"You know nothing!" she spat out at her brother. "That stuff about cameras stealing the soul is just an old superstition, something that the native

Americans thought. Tribes in the Amazon are the same, even now."

"Yeah?" replied Sean. "You think you know so much. You think you're all grown up. You think that you're the ultimate perfect Tess, always right. Well, maybe those old native Americans and the tribes in the Amazon all know something you don't."

Annie knew that each time he said "you" to his sister, he was pointing at her with his index finger, each time getting closer and closer to actually poking her. "That's all I need," she thought. "If he pokes her they'll actually start scrapping in the car. If they do that, I'm just going to lose it."

The traffic was now at a complete standstill, which allowed Annie the opportunity she needed to turn around, face her squabbling children, and try to stop this once and for all.

"Okay!" she shouted at them. "That is enough. Enough, enough, too much and a lot more than anyone can stand. Not a word out of either of you until we get home. Otherwise you're grounded for the next two weeks."

Annie's shouting at her children—which was something she rarely did—must have convinced them for once that she was serious. The rest of the journey home was conducted with only a sullen silence coming from the back seat. But it was a tense and fretful silence.

The upshot of all this was that by the time Annie got Tess, Sean and Czonka home, she felt well and truly frazzled. She had been angry enough that even Sean had agreed to take cloths and disinfectant to clean up the mess that Czonka had made in the back seat. Tess had flounced off to her room, no doubt to stare at herself in her vanity mirror and convince herself that she wasn't beautiful, or cool, or hot, or whatever it was Tess wanted to be.

Czonka had just slunk off and hidden somewhere. The dog must have realized that he had put himself in Annie's bad books.

Annie had slumped on the couch with a glass of iced water, convinced that what should have been a perfect family portrait would never turn out that way. She had been convinced that when they saw the proofs, there would not be one picture in which all of them were looking good.

In the event, however, and when the proofs were delivered, Annie was proven wrong.

There were two or three pictures in which, while everyone might not be looking perfect—how could they, when they were far from perfect in reality?— the whole family, Czonka included, were looking pretty good.

Annie and Phil had made the final decision over their favorite, and that was the picture which had been enlarged and framed and generally made to look impressive, before being hung on the wall. And now, here the self-same portrait was hanging on the wall in Annie's dream home.

She could go over there, take the portrait down again, and study it even more carefully using a magnifying glass or even a microscope. It wouldn't matter, though, because she still wouldn't see her dog. That fuzzy-headed poodle would still be in the middle of the photo, looking for all the world as if he belonged right there with them and nowhere else.

Except he didn't. He never would.

As cute as he was—and she had to admit she did think he was as lovable in his own way as the real Czonka—he was not the shaggy, barely-controllable mutt who had christened the fireplace.

Surely Phil must remember *that* even if he didn't remember the real Czonka? He had to remember how upset she'd been, the way he had made excuses for the dog as well as Tess and Sean—

Just then, she became aware of the kids' voices in the kitchen. She tensed automatically at the sound, waiting for the inevitable explosion of shouting and furious tears. When it came to starting the day, Sean preferred making his sister cry to an eight-course breakfast.

But half a minute or so went past and she heard nothing that was even the bare beginnings of an upset: no shouting, no wailing, no Tess storming out of the kitchen on her way up to her room in hysterics. The voices in the kitchen never rose even slightly above a normal conversational level.

Maybe she was wrong, she thought. Maybe that was actually Phil she was hearing in there having breakfast with Tess rather than Sean.

Then she heard Sean's laugh and knew that she hadn't been mistaken after all. Her son had a very distinctive laugh, quite pleasant when he wasn't indulging his nasty side.

And from what she could hear coming from the kitchen this morning, he was about as far from nasty as he could get without changing into some-one else altogether.

For anyone else, this might have been reassuring but Annie found herself tensing again.

Could Sean and Tess really co-exist peacefully in the same room instead of going for each other's throats? That was far too good to be true and she knew it.

She was actually afraid to go in and see what they were up to, afraid that what sounded like peaceful co-existence would actually turn out to be some new and especially horrible thing they had come up with to make each other miserable.

Another minute went by without all hell break-ing loose and Annie really began to wonder.

Some impulse made her look over at the family portrait again. One perfect moment, captured for-ever, the image of her family that she carried in her heart.

Except there was a poodle where their dog had been, both in the picture and in her life.

But not in her heart. And not in her memory, either, she told herself.

She knew what she knew, and she remembered what she remembered, and nothing Phil or Yas-mine said to her would change that.

All right. She had settled that to her own satisfac-tion, if not to anyone else's. At least she knew what was in her own mind. So, on with the day then.

Annie took a steadying breath, tightened the belt on her dressing gown, and went into the kitchen to see what new horrors Tess and Sean were visiting on each other.

Hidden behind the open refrigerator door, Sean was hurriedly assembling a sack lunch for himself while his sister sat quietly at the table, poking at a dry waffle with a fork.

"Mom, you forgot to buy syrup," Tess said as soon as Annie came in. "I'm stuck eating my waffles plain and they're awful. You know how I hate plain waffles."

Annie blinked at her.

The harsh, complaining edge that rubbed her nerves raw was all but absent from the girl's voice this morning. She found it startling enough that it took her a little time before she actually registered exactly what Tess had said. Even then she wasn't sure if she had heard her right.

She couldn't have, Annie decided. Her daughter would never, ever ask for syrup or anything remotely like it within earshot of her brother. It would never happen. It was one of several ways to guarantee that Sean would let loose with an onslaught of cruel taunts about her weight. Tess knew better than to leave herself open to something like that.

To cover her surprise and confusion, Annie turned to a carton sitting on the kitchen table and pretended to sort through it, handling the items inside with no idea of what they were.

Sean kept rummaging in the open refrigerator, giving no indication that he'd heard Tess say anything at all. Nor did Tess seem to anticipate any sort of response from him.

"Syrup," Annie said finally, feeling a bit dazed. "That's what you said?"

Tess nodded, looking a bit impatient.

"Syr-up," she said, enunciating each syllable on its own.

"Syrup," Annie repeated, feeling even more dazed. "All right. I'll go shopping today."

"Oh, Te-ess," Sean singsonged teasingly with his head still in the refrigerator, "I made you a special surprise lunch."

Here we go. Annie winced.

Of course, it had been too good to be true and she, of all people, should have known better. Sean's I'm-a-good-boy act had simply been part of the build-up to something particularly brutal. The last special surprise lunch he had made for his sister had consisted of crushed houseflies on stale saltines.

"It better be egg salad," Tess singsonged back at him in a tone of voice that was far more good-natured than admonishing.

"That's amazing, young lady!" Sean's hand came up from behind the open refrigerator door dangling a sandwich bag between two fingers. "How in the world did you ever guess?" He chuckled as he put the sandwich back in the fridge. "Wait, don't tell me," he added. "I've got it. You must be a mind-reader!"

The name that Sean had just called his sister was mind-reader?

Annie felt her jaw drop. She was already struggling with the idea that her son would really lift a finger to make a sandwich even just for himself instead of asking her or Phil to do it. That he would actually go so far as to make one for anyone else, especially for his sister—and especially something edible—was about as absurdly improbable as the idea that she could have failed to notice that the dog they had owned for the last five years was an AKC-certified champion poodle.

Then Sean straightened up and closed the refrigerator door and Annie found that she had been transported from the realm of the absurdly improbable to a whole new dimension of the incomprehensible. It seemed that the boy who was standing there smiling at her, who had been poking around in her refrigerator a moment ago and was now looking at her as if she was supposed to know him wasn't her son after all.

He was a total stranger, someone she had never seen before, even though he had sounded exactly like Sean right down to the laugh. As if he had been deliberately trying to fool her.

Or maybe that had been Sean she'd heard laughing earlier, Annie thought suddenly, but he had gone out the back door by the time she had reached the kitchen, leaving Tess to finish having breakfast with this boy and introduce him to her.

But good God, where could he have come from? He had to be some new friend, Annie decided, because she was absolutely certain she had never seen him before. This boy was taller and more muscular, the epitome of the classic high school athlete. His curly hair had been neatly trimmed rather than shaved down to the skull in the traditional skater-punk fashion that Sean favored, and his skin was clear and healthy. The only spots he had were a light sprinkling of freckles across the bridge of his nose.

He dressed a bit like a preppie, but not overly so. Perhaps a more tasteful sort of preppie. Definitely someone who didn't aspire to be a gangsta, or even just dress like one. Whoever he was, she knew for certain that he had never come over after school with either Sean or Tess. Nor was he someone from the old neighborhood; Annie was sure of that, too. She knew just about all the kids from the old neighborhood by sight at the very least. This boy wasn't one of them.

But even if he had been, he wasn't the kind of kid that Sean would ever have hung out with. He obviously didn't have a skateboard, a pair of baggies, or a rapper vocabulary. He probably didn't even know any gang signs. Her son would never have bothered with him.

Neither would Tess, but for an entirely different reason. Tess would have taken one look at him and then locked herself in her room so she could weep copious, bitter tears for hours if not days while she wailed about the unfairness of having to be trapped inside the body of a girl too ugly to talk to any of the good-looking boys.

All right, then, maybe he lived in the house next door and he was one of those outgoing, confident types, a rare example of well-adjusted adolescence that most parents could only wish their kids could be like. Very cleverly, he had come over so early that he had caught both kids off-guard, which had allowed him to charm them out of their usual monstrous behavior, at least temporarily.

He'd even had enough time to find out what Tess's favorite sandwich was so he could make it for her. Then, still having a spare minute or two, this Einstein of social interaction had decided to help himself to anything else that looked good for his own lunch.

The thoughts seemed to zoom around in Annie's head like runaway pinballs while another part of her mind insisted that she was making entirely too much out of this. Kids invited their friends over for breakfast all the time, it was perfectly normal.

She tried to say something to him, anything at all, even just "hello", but her voice refused to work. Her mouth opened and closed without a sound while she went on gaping at him.

He must think I'm an idiot, she thought, helplessly as he came toward her, his smile broadening.

"Morning, Mom," he said cheerfully and kissed her on the cheek. "Love you."

Annie's mind simply stopped functioning altogether. She stared after the boy as he walked out of the kitchen. A few moments later, she heard him trotting up the stairs. God, his steps were so very much like Sean's, so similar that she would have sworn it was her son if she hadn't known better.

At the same time, she could hear Tess behind her getting up from the table so she could take her plate to the sink. The noise gave Annie an odd sensation of being disconnected. It was as though she had suddenly become aware that the world, having been set in motion, would stay in motion with or without her participation. With an effort, she made herself turn around and look at her daughter, who was pushing the remains of her waffle into the garbage disposal.

"Who…" Annie's voice faded immediately. She cleared her throat and tried again. "Who was that?"

Tess paused to look over at her sharply, one hand on the hot water tap, the other holding the plate under the faucet. She had been about to rinse off her own plate without anyone telling her to. The improbability of such an occurrence wasn't completely lost on Annie, though it was fairly tame compared to everything else that was going on. It did serve as a definite indication that nothing was running normally around here.

"Mom," she said with a hint of her old whining tone in her voice. "Cut it out already, Okay?"

Annie felt a surge of anger and impatience. "Tess, I asked you a question," she said hotly. "Who is that boy and what is he doing in our house?"

Her daughter proceeded to rinse the plate and then set it down in the sink before she turned around to face her, one hand on her hip.

"Come on, Mom," she said. "This isn't funny. First it was Czonka and now Sean?"

"Sean?!"

Annie looked over her shoulder at the doorway, as if the strange boy might reappear. "What are you talking about? That wasn't Sean!"

Tess's round face went from exasperated to wary as she took a step back and somehow the girl's expression was so open that Annie could perceive exactly what she was thinking down to the smallest detail.

For the first time that Annie could ever remember, her daughter was actually scared of her. As if she were the real stranger here, and not that boy who had just kissed her on the cheek and then gone upstairs as if he were one of the family—

"Dad!" Tess yelled, backing away another step.

She was holding her fork out in front of her, Annie noticed with a heightened surrealistic feeling. Did she think she might have to use it to protect herself? Did she actually think her own mother was dangerous?

"Dad!" Tess yelled again even more urgently. "Mom's acting weird again!"

Annie's jaw dropped. "Mom's acting weird again?"

A cold knot of dread began to gather just below her breastbone as she realized that there was no reasoning with Tess. The girl—her daughter, her own daughter—was gaping at her as if she had never seen her before, as if they really were strangers to each other.

Impulsively, she started to run a hand over her own face and then caught it with her other hand, lacing her fingers together as if she were about to pray. Then she turned and ran out of the kitchen, through the dining room to the foot of the stairs.

"Sean! I want to see you right now!" she yelled. "I mean it, Sean, you get down here! Get down here right n—"

Her voice cut off. She had not even been aware of turning her head to look at the portrait over the fireplace. There had been no conscious intention in her mind to check her memory against the photo.

And yet, that must have been exactly why she had gone to stand at the foot of the stairs instead of just going directly up to Sean's room so she could get to the bottom of this craziness.

The purebred AKC-registered dog that had so obviously not belonged in the picture was now barely noticeable to her. It was still there, of course, and it was still a poodle instead of the mutt she remembered as Czonka, but it had now been completely overshadowed by the smiling face of a boy she didn't know at all. A very handsome young man she had never laid eyes on until this morning, when she had found him rooting around in the refrigerator in the kitchen with her daughter Tess—

Who was no longer in the photo, either.

The overweight, unhappy young woman who had had to be cajoled into smiling for the fraction of a second it had taken to snap the picture was gone, as if she had never been there at all. She had been replaced by a sunny, athletic-looking blonde with long, straight hair, large, blue eyes and delicate bone structure. This girl would have been very much in her element in a fashion magazine, or playing tennis at some exclusive country club, or even on one of those TV shows about beautiful young teenagers growing up rich and privileged and angst-ridden in Beverly Hills. But she most definitely did not belong in the original, unchanged Macintosh family portrait as remembered by Annie Macintosh.

It's a wise mother who knows her own child.

The words blew through Annie's mind like a scatter of leaves in a windstorm. Who had said that? Some classic poet or philosopher? Or someone far more prosaic, like her own grandmother? Who was not in the photo, either, but hadn't been there to begin with and so couldn't be replaced, thank God.

Annie covered her mouth with her hand. For the first time in a very, very long time, she had no idea what to do next.

"Mom?" asked a familiar voice. "What's wrong?"

She didn't want to turn and look at the girl who had just asked that question. Even if she hadn't already known from the photo that she was going to see that strange, pretty blonde instead of the angry, sullen teen who struggled with her weight and her self-esteem, the girl's voice would have given it away. This girl spoke in a voice that was well-modulated and pleasant, practically musical; it was not a sound that would bludgeon your ears and scrape your nerves raw.

As much as she didn't want to look at this girl, however, Annie was already turning towards her in automatic response to being addressed as "Mom".

She knew that when she did finally see this girl, she was going to freak out all over again. In turn, everyone else would claim they had no idea what she was upset about and she wasn't sure exactly how much more of that she could take before she reached some kind of breaking point, but it was definitely not very much. Not very much at all.

It flashed through her mind suddenly that she didn't have to go through this. She could actually defuse the entire situation and save herself and everyone else enormous amounts of trouble and anxiety by simply accepting what she saw and heard over what she remembered. Because regardless of what she remembered, she knew what was going to happen in the next few seconds: this beautiful girl was going to insist that she was Tess and the good-looking boy upstairs was Sean, and they always had been. Annie only had to look at the family portrait hanging over the fireplace to see the truth of that.

But if she really, truly needed more proof, she could pore over all the old photo albums yet again, examine years and years and years of pictures snapped with a variety of cameras—disposables, cheap, sporty Polaroids, the Pentax with the zoom lens that they used to get good shots at Tess's ballet recitals and Sean's soccer games...

Except none of that was real.

Those weren't real memories of her actual life, those were scenes from the wish-fulfillment fantasy she had indulged in when the kids were still babies. The future had still been wide open back then. The possibilities had been endless, and no aspiration was out of the question. And even though she still thought about that from time to time, she wasn't really wishing that she'd had different children.

At least, she didn't mean to.

Suddenly the girl's face seemed to materialize out of nowhere right in front of her, wide-eyed with concern for her, for Annie, calling her Mom and asking her if she was all right in a soft, caring voice instead of complaining and crying with self-pity.

That was not my dog. That was not my son. This is not my daughter.

Better get a second opinion, said a small voice in her mind. Where's your husband?

"Philip!" Annie yelled and bolted up the stairs in full-blown panic. "Philip!"

The steps seemed to flicker in front of her eyes almost like a strip of film that had jumped its sprockets or an old-fashioned flipbook animation. She blinked against the sensation of slight dizziness, forcing herself to see only her husband's face in her mind in an attempt to steady herself.

She reached the landing and started to round the bend for the next flight only to find herself facing something or someone coming down the steps and all but coming down on top of her. She cried out in shock, unable to focus for a moment because her eyes were still all funny from the strange flickering on the staircase and she couldn't quite see anything.

That didn't matter, she told herself, because she could focus on her husband. She could focus on Phil and only on Phil. Husband, partner, best friend, other half; Mr "Steady-As-A-Rock". As soon as she could lean on him, everything else would fall into place.

Then she saw who it really was—not Philip but that strange boy from the kitchen, the one she was supposed to accept as Sean. He was looking at her with the same expression of bewildered apprehension as the girl downstairs. The two of them, the boy and the girl, they were obviously related to each other if not to her, Annie thought with dazed giddiness. The family resemblance was unmistakable.

There was a flurry of movement: arms, hands, the front of a neatly-buttoned shirt, a faint whiff of expensive aftershave. She felt herself wavering, in danger of toppling over altogether. The strange boy who was not her son reached for her arm.

She knew that he only meant to help her, that she had lost her balance and he was simply trying to keep her from falling down the stairs and getting hurt. She knew that was the only thing in his mind and she should let him grab her and pull her to safety.

She knew it even as instinct made her draw back from him; not just pull away but move back, give ground. Her foot found nothing but air for a long moment. Then she felt it slide over the soft, rounded edge of a carpeted step.

Annie flung both arms wide, groping futilely for the railing but her body had already turned too far away from it. The last thing she saw was the lower part of the staircase rushing towards her face.

SIX

Voices kept drifting in and out of her range of hearing, quite clear and distinct but for the most part seeming to come from some distance away.

She might have been floating around a lake half asleep on a raft and hearing snatches of conversation from people on the shore. Except, Annie realized eventually, she could not actually feel anything that might have been even the calmest movement of water. As well, the voices that kept fading in and out were always the same ones, and they always seemed to be talking about the same thing.

She wasn't quite sure what that was; sometimes she thought it sounded like a subject that she might know something about, sometimes nothing she heard made any sense at all. Either way, she had no active desire to find out so she didn't bother to make any sort of real effort to listen.

After a while, however, she became aware that the voices had stopped fading away. In fact, they had actually been increasing in volume for some time and now they were so loud that they seemed to be prodding and tugging at her in a deliberate attempt to get her to pay attention.

Annie tried to shut them out again. She wanted to keep on drifting like this; she felt too tired to do anything else. Perhaps if she drifted for long enough, she would get to a place where the voices faded out again permanently. Then she could rest.

She had a feeling that that would be the more desirable alternative, that she didn't want to hear the voices, not only because she was tired but also because they had nothing good to say and she would be better off in the quiet. But the voices only became more insistent, until finally she felt herself starting to emerge from a dreamy semi-conscious state into full wakefulness.

No! she thought, trying to summon up the sensation of drifting and let it carry her away from the light and the noise and a vague, unpleasant feeling of pressure that was now resolving itself as a really rotten headache.

Too late, she thought as a wave of unhappiness swept through her. I'm awake.

Reluctantly, she opened her eyes to find herself stretched out on the slightly lumpy, threadbare sofa cushions. Phil was hovering over her, his expression a mixture of concern and cautious relief.

"Annie?" he said, looking into her eyes searchingly.

She blinked up at him in bewildered silence. Something was wrong but she couldn't remember what. Elsewhere in the living room, she could hear other people moving around and something that sounded like a CB radio or a police scanner.

"You gave us quite a scare," said her husband, brushing her hair back from her forehead.

"What happened?" she asked, wincing, and raised herself up a little on one arm.

A tall man in a blue uniform was standing at the foot of the couch holding a rugged-looking red plastic case with the letters EMS stamped on the cover in white. A paramedic, she realized, blinking with astonishment. He gave her a smile that she knew was supposed to be full of reassurance and would give her some encouragement to start feeling better.

Annie stared back at him coldly. If he thought she was going to feel better just because he wanted her to, he could just disabuse himself of that notion. She was a human being, not something he could program as part of his job. To her bemusement, she saw that this didn't make him any less inclined to smile.

Another paramedic, a woman almost as tall as the man, materialized next to Phil and tapped him on the shoulder. Phil stood up and they conferred in whispers for a few moments before she handed him a folded sheet of paper. Then she turned to Annie with a smile identical to the man's.

Annie gave her a pained frown in return to show this paramedic that she still wasn't having any but it seemed to have no more effect on her than it had on her partner. Both of them continued to smile at her with the same confident air of people who were absolutely certain that everything was all right in every way. They were still smiling as they turned to leave.

Glaring at their retreating backs, Annie was suddenly positive that she could have thumbed her nose at them or stuck out her tongue or even stripped naked and stood on her head and those professional smiles would not have changed in the slightest. They might as well have been wearing masks, which was a pretty ridiculous idea, she thought, wincing at the sudden twinge in her temples. No wonder she had a headache.

"What happened?" she asked Phil again as he knelt down beside the couch.

"You took a little tumble," he said, the worry lines in his face deepening. "But you're going to be okay. The paramedics say you might have a slight concussion. Very, very slight, though. Nothing to worry about."

With an effort, Annie pushed herself all the way up to a sitting position and tried to get her mind around that one. How on earth could she have gotten a concussion?

She looked around at all the boxes lying everywhere in the general disorder that surrounded them in the living room. This was the way the inside of her head felt, she thought; everything was all disorganized and out of place, nothing was where it was supposed to be, and she had no idea how she could even begin to get it all straightened out. She ran a cautious hand through her hair feeling for any bumps or sore spots and, to her relief, found nothing out of the ordinary.

Well, at least her head was still in one piece. That had to be a good sign, she thought as she swung her legs off the couch and put both feet on the floor.

The beautiful hardwood floor. A floor like that ought to have some protection, Annie thought, and remembered one of several beautiful Oriental rugs she had spotted in a catalog. That rug would have been perfect here, but she would probably never be able to find the catalog again in all the chaos of moving. Not that it would make a bit of difference if she actually *did* find it again, since there was no way they could have afforded the rug anyway. And even if they could have, it wouldn't exactly go with the saggy, broken-down sofa and the rest of their old, worn-out stuff...

God only knew why she was thinking about something like that right now, Annie thought; maybe because she had hit her head. Maybe that was what happened to people when they fell down the stairs and hit their heads—the shock caused their inner interior decorator to come to the surface.

Abruptly, she remembered the family portrait over the fireplace. She turned to look at it but Phil was standing in front of her, blocking her view. Taking his hand, she opened her mouth to tell him about what had happened in the kitchen, how there had been a strange boy who wasn't Sean but had acted as though he were, how Tess had said she was acting weird, how she had come into the living room and seen the changed family portrait with that boy who wasn't Sean and now a girl who wasn't Tess—

A small movement in the corner of her eye caught her attention and she stopped.

There they were, standing a few feet away from the sofa watching her with wide, apprehensive eyes. Not her children, not Sean and Tess but those two teenagers she didn't know, those two strangers that she had never seen before. She turned back to Phil and clutched his arm more tightly than was strictly necessary. "Sean and Tess," she said urgently. "Where are they?"

Her husband hesitated, giving her an odd look. "Kids," he said, making a beckoning motion to the two strangers while keeping his eyes on hers. "Your mom wants to see you."

"No!" She hung onto his arm, pulling herself closer to him so that they were nose to nose and lowered her voice to a whisper. "Those are not our children."

Phil squeezed his eyes shut for a second as if he had felt a sudden but intense pain. When he opened them again, he avoided her gaze, turning to look at the two strange teenagers.

Now he would tell them the joke was over, they had to stop fooling around and go get Sean and Tess for her, she thought wildly. She gripped his arm even harder, waiting for him to say it, willing him to straighten everyone out. He had to make them stop all this ridiculous screwing around now, it wasn't funny.

Instead, he hesitated again and then cleared his throat. "Time for school, you two," he said. "Come on, now, you're late enough already."

The boy looked startled and opened his mouth as if he were about to argue or protest, but the girl suddenly stepped in front of him.

"Come on, let's go," she said, ushering him quickly toward the kitchen. "Bye, Dad."

The degree of anguish in her pretty face was so startling that Annie felt a sudden strong maternal urge to run to the girl and take her in her arms to try to comfort her.

But then the girl added, "Bye, Mom," and she felt herself recoiling in horror.

As soon as she heard the kitchen door open and close behind them, she let go of Phil and jumped to her feet. Immediately, the headache that had been fading came back with what seemed like twice its original strength. She ignored it, intending to search the house thoroughly in spite of the renewed throbbing in her head. But Phil was trying to pull her back down on the sofa again.

"No," she told him. "Sean and Tess—"

"Annie, sit down." He managed to get her back on the sofa next to him.

She shook her head emphatically, trying to twist out of his grasp. "Philip, our children are missing— don't you care?"

"Listen to me—" He was talking over her, trying to wrap his arms around her as she struggled. "Annie, listen to me."

He put one hand on the side of her face and gently but firmly turned her head around so that he could look directly into her eyes.

"Listen, Annie, please," he begged her. "Our kids are on their way to school."

She drew back from him, pushing both hands against his chest but he was holding her too securely.

"No. If you mean those two, no, you're wrong. I never saw those two before in my life," she protested. "What's wrong with you? Don't you know your own children?"

"Of course I do," he said in a soft, soothing voice that was starting to grate on her nerves as badly as Tess's complaining whine. Then all at once her heart gave a painfully hard, panicky leap as it suddenly occurred to her that she might never hear her daughter whine again. "Of course I know our children and so do you. You're just confused, that's all."

She was confused? Annie's panic turned to anger as she stared at him in disbelief.

"No, I most certainly am not confused—you're the one who's confused!" she said. "What's wrong with you?"

She broke free of him and backed away a couple of steps, looking around wildly. There had to be something in the room, something old and familiar that they'd had for ages that she could stick right under his nose and the moment he saw it, he would snap right out of this—this—this weird problem.

What kind of problem was this, anyway? Something with his eyesight? Or maybe when she had fallen down the stairs, he had fallen with her—or, no, she had landed on him and knocked him down, causing him to hit his head very, very hard on the hardwood floor...

On the hardwood floor which had been marred by the wheels on Sean's skateboard.

The real Sean, the one with the pimples and the gang signs and the baggies slipping halfway down his butt, not that idealized fantasy who made egg salad sandwiches for his sister...

Immediately, Annie hurried up the three little steps to the hallway, searching for the telltale lines of scoring that she knew would stretch from somewhere in the area directly in front of the staircase all the way through the dining room and into the kitchen.

Those lines had been everywhere she looked in their old rented house, staining the already-worn carpeting, actual ruts pressed into the kitchen floor so deeply that she knew where they were just by standing on them—one of the many reasons they wouldn't be getting their security deposit back. But she had been determined yesterday when Sean had dropped the damned skateboard down on the hardwood and zoomed into the kitchen that he would never, ever do it again, that she would not have to see these beautiful, perfect floors ruined...

She walked up and down the hallway, paused in bewilderment, and then just stood, staring helplessly at the unmarred floor. There was nothing, not even a faint scuff. But the marks had been there. They had been. She could remember seeing them as clearly as she had seen the dog lift his leg in front of the fireplace.

These hadn't been just a few minor little scuffs that a little polish could take care of, these had been scars cut right into the wood, no different than if her son had taken a knife and deliberately carved the lines into the floor by hand. Marks like that wouldn't just wipe off with some lemon oil cleaner and they certainly didn't fade away all by themselves.

Only apparently they did. Or at least, those had.

The marks that had played such a large role in reducing her to tears yesterday had vanished so completely that she couldn't find the faintest sign that they had ever actually been there. But that was impossible. She looked up sharply at the family portrait. It was as impossible as, say, not noticing what kind of dog you owned.

Or, for another example, as impossible as discovering that the two obvious imposters could not only replace your children but instantly alter existing photographs with such precision and accuracy so that there was only your memory to tell you otherwise...

Her breath began to come in short, panicky gasps.

"Annie, please—" Phil was trying to put his arms around her in a calming embrace. Annie shook her head and did her best to fend him off.

"What's wrong with you?" she cried, looking frantically from the photo to the floor and then to Phil, who kept coming towards her, trying to soothe her. "What's wrong with you? What's wrong with everyone?"

She moved around to the other side of the sofa, keeping her gaze locked on the now traitorous family portrait.

They shoot traitors, did you know that? Sean had said to his sister only yesterday; she remembered it very clearly, the way she remembered Sean and Tess and Czonka, Czonka the mutt; not the poodle but the mutt.

"They shoot traitors, did you know that? Did you know that, they shoot traitors, did you know that? Did you—"

"Annie, please—" Phil was saying. Now he had her backed up and off-balance with one faded, threadbare arm of the sofa behind her, still trying to gather her into his arms, still trying to soothe her. Still endlessly patient with her, still Mr "Steady-As-A-Rock"—

"Oh, God, Phil!" She seized him by his upper arms and held on, trying to look at every part of him all at once without taking her eyes off his face for longer than a fraction of a second. "I just thought of something!"

"Annie, please calm down," he begged her. "Please, you've got to—"

"No, listen! Oh, God, Phil, what if it happens to you?" she said clutching him even tighter for a moment and then running her hands over his shoulders up to his head, taking hold of his face. "What if you vanish next? What if—"

"I'm not going anywhere," he said calmly, pulling her close. "You know I'm not."

"But how do I know? How can I be sure?" She wrapped her arms around him as tightly as she could, refusing to look away from him at all now, trying to capture his gaze with her own. Nothing could possibly happen as long as they kept on looking into each other's eyes. "I don't want to lose you!"

He stroked her hair. "You're not going to."

She hung onto him fiercely, and then, instead of looking into each other's eyes, they were kissing.

But that was all right, Annie thought. That was even better than looking into each other's eyes. Physical contact was even safer than watching him every moment. She knew the way he felt, his smell, his lips as completely as she knew her own name, as she knew her children's names.

If she had been blindfolded and put in a totally dark room five hundred feet underground on a cloudy day and had to identify her husband out of a dozen other men only by kissing, she could have picked him out immediately.

There was only one Phil Macintosh, only one Mr "Steady-As-A-Rock", and although she believed him when he said he wasn't going anywhere, she was going to hang onto him with all her strength, just to make sure...

She sighed as the kiss came to an end and pulled her head back slightly to smile at him. If any husband deserved to know how much he was appreciated, it was hers.

She started to do just that, to tell him how much she loved him for being so patient, so indulgent, for letting her be silly without feeling like a complete fool, and saw that, as usual, he was already smiling at her.

And, also as usual, it was a very warm and loving smile. But it was the wrong smile, on the wrong face.

Annie could feel the physical sensation of the blood draining out of her face. She broke out of the embrace and backed away, touching her lips with one hand.

"No," she whispered, unaware that she was actually speaking aloud. "No, no, no!"

Somewhere deep inside herself, the temperature had plummeted to absolute zero and then somehow fallen past that, into inconceivable depths from which there would never be any return.

"Annie?" said the man she had been kissing. "What's wrong?"

The wrong smile, the wrong voice, the wrong face, the wrong man asking the wrong question, with no right answer.

"No," she moaned. "No, no, no, no..."

"What's wrong?" the stranger said. Taking another step toward her and looking hurt when she backed farther away. "Annie? What's wrong?"

Impossible. Like everything else. Impossible.

"Annie?" said the strange man.

How could he know her name when she had never seen him before? It was impossible.

"What's wrong, Annie?" he said again, and again and again, like a recording on a loop. "Annie? What's wrong? Annie?"

SEVEN

That man wasn't Phil. There was no way he was Phil.

But whoever he really was, at least he had the sense to leave her alone, Annie thought, as she paced around the cartons stacked in the bedroom, hugging the heart-shaped pink satin throw pillow Philip had given her last Christmas.

Philip had given it to her, the real Philip. Her Philip. Mr "Steady-As-A-Rock".

The real Philip Macintosh, whom she would know if she kissed him blindfolded in total darkness. Not every woman's idea of jaw-droppingly handsome or movie-star sexy but the first time she had ever laid eyes on him, she had thought he was easily the most attractive man she had ever met, and in the intervening years, she had had no reason to change her mind.

She knew every line and angle of his face, by touch and by sight, every contour of his body. She knew the texture of his exposed skin, on his face and throat, his hands and arms, and how it varied from the softer, paler areas that only she ever saw uncovered. She could have drawn the exact shape of his hairline more easily than she could have sketched a rough approximation of the United States.

She knew when and where his first gray hairs had come in (ten years ago, an even sprinkling all over his head), and how it had mixed with the natural gold tones giving him a full head of somewhat glittery highlights that most people had to fork over extortionate amounts of money for in beauty salons.

She also knew that except for the area over his forehead where most men's hairlines typically receded, he had lost very little of his hair, the rest of it being virtually as thick as it had been when she had first met him ages and ages ago.

The real Philip Macintosh, the one that she knew had a small scar on his right ring finger from where he had cut himself on a can of tuna fish and had to go to the emergency room for exactly one stitch, as well as a puckery patch of skin on his left knee from the time he had taken a spill on a bike ride during their honeymoon.

There was only one spot on his body where he was ticklish, and it was located on his right side in the area between the bottom of his rib cage and his hipbone, and it only ever took her one try to find it.

The only real Philip Macintosh had a small red birthmark on the little toe of his right foot. His bellybutton was an "innie" and there were three very curly hairs just below it.

His favorite fruits were strawberries and blueberries.

The only time he ever snored was in the winter when the air in the bedroom was a little too warm and dry.

Her Philip Macintosh liked light bulb jokes, caramel corn, Marx Brothers movies, and peanut butter and jelly sandwiches. The thought of never seeing him again or hearing his voice or feeling his touch made her want to curl up in a ball and cry herself unconscious. At the same time, she could not bring herself to believe that she really wouldn't see him again. That was too much of an impossibility to exist in the same world as anything even remotely normal.

Annie paused at one of the two large sash windows in the bedroom and stared down at the grassy area between her house and the one next door. Nothing strange down there, nothing wrong; just grass, where one yard left off and the other began. One unremarkable, mundane, normal feature of this unremarkable, mundane, normal neighborhood, where people lived their unremarkable, mundane, normal lives.

They were people just like her, just like Phil, with children just like Sean and Tess. And with pets like Czonka. Well, perhaps not all the dogs and cats and other pets in the neighborhood were pedigree breeds like her Czonka, but they were all someone's favorite pet. Perhaps their ideal pet.

Then it came to her, all at once in a flash that went on for what seemed like forever. She could remember the rest of the dream. At least, she could remember the rest of the story that her Great-Aunt Lauren had been telling in the dream. When she fell on the stairs, something must have jolted loose inside her head—figuratively at least—and now her memory of the dream was clear again.

Back in the dream, Annie and her friend Trish had managed to persuade Great-Aunt Lauren to resume her story while they sat in the cool of the kitchen around the old, dark wood table. They had been eating toasted muffins and honey. Lauren had been drinking Earl Grey tea, and the two eight year-olds had been drinking more lemonade.

"So," resumed the old lady, old and yet still so sprightly. "Susie woke up the next morning, Saturday, with a vague memory of a strange and mysterious dream. But the memory faded before she had a chance to wake up and then... it was gone. Just a feeling that something important had been forgotten.

"Susie spent the morning doing her chores, helping out her mother around the house. For you see, this may have been a magical land, but the dishes still needed to be washed, clothes had to be laundered, and furniture still needed dusting. For once, though, Susie was not worried about the chores, because they helped to make the time go more quickly. Her mother had agreed she could go again to see the magical cat Callie in the afternoon, and learn the solution to her elder sister's pet problem.

"When the time came around at about three in the afternoon to set off to see Callie the magic cat, Susie knew that she needed to go to a different place. When she left her house, she followed the river that ran through their settlement upstream for a while, until she came to a place where there was a large and deep pool, the stream spreading out between high cliffs.

"At the top of one of the cliffs, at the end of a path that could only be negotiated by mountain goats, skilled walkers, or by determined eight year-olds, was the place where the cat liked to watch over the deep pool and think deep thoughts. Susie knew that there was something amazing about deep thoughts, even when they were the deep thoughts of a normal human creature. Those of a cat endowed with special powers were likely to be even more amazing.

"Callie was sitting waiting for her, alert and almost eager, when Susie came into sight of the cat, emerging from the end of the narrow path and onto the flat top of the cliff. The cat was sitting under a gnarled and wind-bent tree that had some-how managed to establish itself in the thin soil at the cliff edge.

"Susie greeted the cat and gave her a new pre-sent, a small cloth pouch filled with aromatic herbs which were a special favorite of Callie. The cat thanked her and then waited for Susie to speak. Eventually, after some minutes of silence, Susie could contain her curiosity no longer. She asked Callie straight out what the solution to the problem of the ideal pet for her sister's dream home could be.

"'I think you already know the answer yourself,' said the cat. 'Look inside yourself look deep inside.

The answer has already come to you. You need only to focus and to remember clearly.'

"As the cat said this, she was looking intensely into Susie's eyes, drawing her into a deep and quiet place, as deep and quiet and mysterious as the pool they were sitting above. Susie felt herself drifting into that place, and then it came to her, like a light being lit in her head. It was the dream that she herself had had the night before, the one she had been unable to remember. The dream she had known contained some special secret.

"Now that dream came back to her, piece by piece and scene by scene. It concerned the old toy-maker, a man so old and worn by time and experience that no one knew his true name, so just called him Toy-maker. Some said that he had magical powers, but the general opinion was that he was a person who had lived for so long, seen so much, and made so many beautiful and clever toys, that he had a profound understanding of life.

"Susie knew the toy-maker, though not well, and had not seen him for more than a year. Not that he would have changed—he was already so perfect in his role that no change, no improvement was necessary.

"The old man greeted her warmly and invited her into his workshop, where all manner of wondrous toys were on display, some in the first stages of construction, others half made, and a few that were complete and ready for their new owners.

"The toy-maker directed Susie to one of these finished toys. It was a doll's house made of wood and glass, perfectly to scale and true in every detail. The style of the house was not familiar to the young girl, and she supposed that toy-maker had modeled it on something he had seen during his travels in the more modern parts of the land.

"The old man told Susie: 'You seek a solution to a problem, the ideal pet for your sister Karen and her dream home. Here is a doll's house that is someone's dream home. I do not know yet what lucky girl this one is destined for. One day that special person will walk through my door, just as you did today, and she will know it for her own. But for now, you can play with it. See how it has many different styles of furniture and decoration that you can change, mix and match to your own preference. See how it has everything to make a perfect home. This is your chance to play, to experiment, and to find the perfect pet for the ideal home of your sister Karen.'

"When Susie looked closely at the doll's house, and opened up the whole of the front, hinged on the left, so that she could see every room, she saw how right the toy-maker was. The detail in the house was meticulous. Fine woods had been used for the floors, which glowed with a rich, deep color, and for the furniture, which was lighter and brighter.

"As well as having all the furniture, the decorations and the ornaments that would be needed to make the doll's house into the model of someone's perfect home, Susie saw that there were also people. They were small scale models, and she could select from people of different heights and ages.

"They had tiny wigs, so she could change their hair color or style to suit her. Of course, because this was all about pets, there were cats and dogs, parrots and canaries, little fish tanks that glowed with the myriad colors of tropical fish. In fact, there seemed to be every kind of pet imaginable.

"Susie quickly selected her ideal family, the mother and father, the two children, boy and girl. But it took her a little longer to solve the central problem for which she had visited the Toy-maker—the perfect pet.

"Susie experimented, putting different animals in different rooms, seeing how they looked with the people and décor of the perfect home, and eventually settled on a small dog. It was elegant, with white fur, and there was an air of class and superiority about it. Somehow Susie knew that this would be perfect for her sister Karen.

"The pet animal that Susie selected and carefully placed in the kitchen of the doll's house, completing her collection for a perfect home, was a white poodle. The problem was solved, Susie thanked the toy-maker and went on her way.

"All this came back to her, a memory that had somehow been lost, as she stared fixedly into the deep and dark eyes of the magical cat, Callie. Gradually she felt herself pulling back from such close communion with the cat, and emerging into a full awareness of her surroundings.

"'You see,' said the cat. 'The answer was there all along. You only had to reach inside yourself to find it. You know your sister so well that you and only you could do this for her. You have determined that her perfect pet, the one which her true love the merchant must place in their new home, is a white poodle.'

"Susie thanked the cat for helping her to gain this insight, bid Callie farewell and then went on her way home, to share her secret with her sister, Karen. She had managed to find the answer through play and experiment by trying out different combinations of pets and people. The toy-maker's new doll's house had been the focus for her thoughts, a place where she could play out her ideas, a special place to solve problems. Even if it all existed only in a dream, the result, the solution to the problem was as real as it would have been if Susie had made an actual visit to the toy-maker.

"So you see, girls," Great-aunt Lauren had concluded, looking over at the young Annie Macintosh and her friend, "when we search for perfection, often the answer lies within our own minds, within our own hearts, at the center of our most secret desires. Remember that in the future."

Which was where the dream ended—or at least, where Annie's memory of it ended. It had come back to her by some mechanism she barely understood, to do with her fall and her period of unconsciousness. It was no surprise that the ideal pet in the story had been a white poodle, for here she, Annie Macintosh, no longer an eight year-old girl but grown, married and with her own children, had a white poodle as *her* pet in her dream home.

Annie shook herself and came back to the reality of her new home, focussing her eyes on the window in front of her. As she did so, she wondered if any of this made it easier to accept that her pet dog, the family pet dog, the dream pet in the dream home, was so different from the one she thought she remembered from before, from her old life.

She wondered if anything else about the changes that had been going on around her would be any easier to accept. Her eyes looked out of the window as she thought, and she realized she had no idea how long she had been standing here staring at the yard. Was it just a couple of seconds, or could it have been hours? She had no idea. What she was certain of was that outside the window, the yard was as basic as it had ever been. Just grass. She blinked her eyes a couple of times, just to be sure.

She looked and looked, and it was just grass. Grass and nothing else. She could lean out of the window and look towards the front yard and see the big old maple that was there. The developers of the house and its companions had left as many mature trees in place as possible. But there had not been that many to begin with. The natural vegetation of the area had been a light deciduous woodland, Annie had been told. Very few trees had grown to any significant size, just because the local farmer who owned the land had cut down most of them for lumber. Fortunately, however, a few had been left and the maple in Annie's front yard was one of them.

However, Annie would only see that if she opened the window, put out her head and looked into the front yard. Right now, with the windows closed, she could see just the grass at the side of the house. She knew that if she were to go and look at the back yard, there would just be grass there too. The development company had ensured that a hardy grass had been planted, so perhaps it would survive the ravages of teenage families and pets better than the grass in Annie's previous yard had done.

Not that she had to worry any more about the ravages of either teenagers or her pet dog. Czonka had turned into the kind of pedigree dog that would turn up its nose at the mere idea of going out in the yard, let alone dirtying its paws by tearing up the grass.

Her teenaged children were no longer the unruly, ill-tempered and downright difficult ones whom Annie remembered. They too were now unlikely to go out and tear up the yard, or make a mess. They were the kind of children she had once dreamed about.

Of course, with all that grass and just one maple tree in the front yard, her garden was a long way from any kind of horticultural ideal, and even further from that wonderful garden of her childhood, the garden of her Great-Aunt Lauren.

Just as Annie had been the only one of the family to take an interest in how the inside of the dream house would look, she'd been the only one to take an interest in how the outside was going to be. But although she thought about it, all she had found in her head were confused memories of her Great-Aunt Lauren's garden.

Annie thought again about the dream, so oddly incomplete until a few moments ago, that she'd had the night before. She thought about the story her great-aunt had been telling to Annie and her friend Trish, all those years ago when she was eight years-old. Annie now knew what the ideal pet in the story told by her great-aunt had been.

She supposed this was sign that she should accept the new version of Czonka. Perhaps there was something inevitable about such a fine pedigree poodle being ideal for the fine and beautiful home that Annie now found herself in. Not to mention, of course, her family, who had also been perfected.

Annie had her dream home and now she had a dream family too. Which put her into a kind of waking nightmare, in which her memories conflicted with what was all around her. At least, thought Annie, I don't have to worry about all that grass out there, the grass in the back, the grass at the side, the grass at the front (along with the lone maple). No-one seems to be interested in the front yard or the back yard or the sides or anything outside the house. Even Annie had trouble summoning up much enthusiasm about it. How ashamed Great-Aunt Lauren would have been of Annie.

Even now, Annie's great-aunt, who had "passed over," as people liked to say now, some fifteen years ago, was probably sitting in gardeners' heaven looking down at all of Annie's grass, and tut-tutting the way she used to when Annie fell short of Lauren's expectations.

Truth to tell, Annie had failed to live up to the qualities set her by her great-aunt, not least in the area of gardening. No borders, no flowering plants, no color in the garden except green and green and more green, the strong and resilient and, in its own way, oh-so-perfect grass.

She could turn away from the window and then look out at it again five minutes from now and it would be the same grass, the same color, the same size and shape, in the same neighborhood with the same people living the same lives. Because that was how the concept of normal worked.

Leaning her head against the glass, she listened to the white noise of the unremarkable, mundane, normal neighborhood: the passing of an occasional car outside on the street, a mild wind stirring the leaves of the big maple in the front yard, a man's voice calling out an affectionate but firm warning to Lizzie that she had only five more minutes to play and then it would be time to come and wash up and that was final.

In spite of everything, Annie had to smile faintly to herself, wondering in an absent way if the peripatetic Lizzie, whoever she was, took the five minute warning any more seriously than Sean or Tess ever had. Probably not; no child ever did, and there wasn't anything more normal than that.

So perhaps that was the answer. If she kept looking at normal things, hearing normal things, made sure that she was surrounded by the very essence of normal in every shape and form available, then somehow all this strangeness would melt away, reverse itself as suddenly as it had come about, when she might not be expecting it.

Five minutes from now, or just after lunch-time, or when the late news came on at eleven, or when she woke up tomorrow morning, she would leave the bedroom and go downstairs, and the first thing she saw would be Czonka. Her Czonka. Original-recipe Czonka the mutt.

Then she would go into the kitchen and find that Sean and Tess were waiting to show her that they were also recognizable again, and finally, finally, finally Philip would appear, Philip Mr "Steady-As-A-Rock" Macintosh, and not some strange man who insisted on answering to Phil's name and somehow knew hers.

Or maybe she should get out of here right now and go back to the old house in the old neighborhood? Oh, yeah, now there was one hell of an idea—no, it was a veritable inspired-by-the-gods stroke of genius, that's what that was.

All she had to do was climb out the window, shimmy down the drainpipe—if there was a drainpipe—and take off running. Very, very easy, nothing to it. She could do that. After all, she had done a little track in high school and she and Yasmine still went to the gym regularly.

Of the two of them, Yasmine was actually the jogger while she preferred power walking with light weights. But that didn't mean she was physically incapable of running if she felt she needed to. On the other hand, she had become so proficient at power walking—so powerful, in fact—that she could probably power walk faster than a lot of people could run. Outrun them without literally running. Okay, it wasn't exactly normal but at least it wasn't completely impossible, either.

But that was neither here nor there. Say she did actually run away—or power walk away, to be perfectly accurate—and she went back to their old rented house in the old neighborhood. What in the world did she think she could possibly accomplish with that?

After all, what was she going to do, break into her old house? And what for? To move back in by herself? She didn't have the keys any more because she had insisted on having Phil make a stop at the Friends and Neighbors Rental Agency so she could drop them off in person.

"You do realize, don't you, that even if you do return the keys in person we still don't have a hope in hell that they'll give us our deposit back?" Phil had said wryly.

"I absolutely do not care about that," she had replied airily. "I simply want to have the pleasure of knowing without a doubt that once I hand over those keys, we will never, ever, ever have anything to do with F&N again."

Phil had looked at her with his eyes twinkling. "I had no idea you were so big on the closure thing."

"Closure, my butt," Annie had laughed. "I just want to be able to say I know the exact moment at which I shut all house rental agencies in the world, and F&N in particular, completely out of my life for good."

Phil had laughed with her. "Then you had better make sure you remember to look at your watch before you come back out again."

She had done just that very thing, even going so far to pose for a second in the open door before getting back into the car. Phil had applauded her and they had had a good laugh about it. The whole thing had been terrific fun and that had been the end of that.

Now, she could not remember for the life of her, what the time had been. As if the rest of the day had just blotted it out.

The moving finger, having writ, moves on, and only then do you discover that it won't color inside the lines and it's scribbled all over your nice neat life. Annie shifted uneasily, wondering what strange, shadowy zone of her mind that little gem of a thought had come bubbling up from.

She hugged the pillow a little more tightly and pressed her face against it. Stupid things; she was thinking stupid things. Her head was filled with nothing but stupid things today, like warped versions of old proverbs or sayings, and jackass notions about running away, made even more jackass by the place where she was thinking about running away to.

But all right then, she told herself, if you want to be a jackass, be a jackass. Go back to that ratty old rental house. You don't have to have a key to get in.

True enough. All it ever took was a little patience and one of the windowpanes in the back door would just pop right out, allowing entry to any family member who had gotten locked out—accidentally or, in the case of both Tess and Sean, on purpose. Getting the pane back in was a hell of a lot harder than popping it out, of course (the pane was a pain, as Sean always put it) which was why everyone would always leave that little job for her.

She had tried to break them of that habit with dire warnings about how someday a burglar might be casing the neighborhood and see the empty space in the back door before she was able to put the glass back in. None of them listened, of course.

Surprisingly, they hadn't been burgled.

Annie was the only one who had been surprised, of course. The last thing she had expected was to come home from the grocery store one fine day and find that they had not been robbed. She had kept waiting for it to happen. She had tried to brace herself against the inevitable shock of having her home violated, as well as the aftermath—a screaming, hysterical Tess, a belligerent Sean, and Phil trying to get everybody calmed down while the dog romped merrily through the wreckage of whatever the burglars had decided to leave behind. Assuming they hadn't stolen Czonka, too.

But the burglary had never come. Nothing had ever happened. As far as she knew, no one had ever even tried to break in. When she had finally expressed her surprise about this, Tess had all but laughed in her face.

"Come on, Mom," she'd said in that whiny tone. "Go outside, take a good look through our windows and then tell me you really think any self-respecting burglar is really going to break in here."

Annie could remember thinking that if that was supposed to be the advantage of having only possessions which had seen better days, she would gladly have sacrificed it in favor of a burglar alarm, and damn the extra expense.

With her luck, if she really did go back and break into the old house, she would be arrested for burglary. And after they locked her up, none of the self-respecting burglars would talk to her.

She shook her head. Her head that was filled with stupid things. The stupidest of all being that she would even entertain the idea of going back to the old house. Talk about the last thing anyone ever expected; that would make a burglary next to last, she thought.

She had been dying to get out of that old house and when they had actually closed the sale on this one, she had felt absolutely no wistful nostalgia about that place, even though the four of them had lived there longer than they had anywhere else. It did not occupy a place in her heart as the old family homestead and she had always known for a certainty that when they did finally move up to something better, she wasn't going to miss it.

And she didn't. Her head may have been full of stupid things but really, there was stupid, and then there was a very special kind of stupid. She would have had to be that very special kind of stupid to miss the ancient plumbing that banged and rattled and always had at least one pipe that would burst at the most inconvenient moment possible after the weather got cold, or the perpetually leaky roof, the uneven floors, the sad excuse for weatherproofing, the lack of closet space, the world's ugliest wallpaper...

She sighed. No, she wasn't feeling homesick for any of that. She didn't want to go *backwards*. It was more like the other way around.

Now she blew out a disgusted breath. What was that about her head being filled with stupid things? She didn't want to go backwards, it was the other way around? What in God's name was that supposed to mean?

Yes, she thought suddenly. It was like the old stuff, things from the old life were pulling at her in some way. As if everything that she had left behind still had some kind of hold on her whether she liked it or not. Some force was trying to drag her back to where she had been before, she could feel it...

Uh-huh. Sure she could. She squeezed her eyes shut and pinched the bridge of her nose. The only thing she could feel was her own neurotic hang-ups pulling at her again. First it had been worrying about the moving men thinking her furniture was too shabby for such a nice house. Now she had graduated to thinking that she was too shabby for such a nice house—and nice life. That was her whole stupid problem, that and nothing else, and she already walked herself through that yesterday. It was supposed to be all settled.

EIGHT

All right, then, it was settled. The moving men didn't care one way or the other about her furniture, and it didn't matter one way or another who might think it was too shabby for the new house, even if she thought so, it didn't matter. And as for her thinking that she *herself* was too shabby to live like this; well, that was too neurotic even to be worthy of therapy. Even Tess would have told her how ridiculous that idea was. And so would Philip.

Oh, yes, definitely. There, now. Everything was settled and explained.

So how did that account for the fact that she didn't recognize her dog or the people who claimed to be her children and her husband?

Abruptly, there was a knock on the door and she almost jumped out of her skin.

No, she couldn't, she wasn't ready yet, Annie thought as she darted a quick glance out the window, telling herself that she wasn't checking to make sure the grass really hadn't changed. It was too soon for her to come out of the bedroom, she had not had enough normal yet.

There was a second knock and she jumped again.

"Philip or whoever you are, go away!" she shouted, reaching for the lock on the window.

She had no awareness of how her fingers were poised to flick the lever back, of how she had already decided to risk jumping out if any of them decided they had to come in after her.

"Annie, it's me," said a familiar voice. "It's Yasmine."

She froze with one hand still on the window and stared at the door. Yasmine was here? Yasmine had come to help her? Again?

Was that normal?

"Annie?"

Was it really Yasmine?

She ran across the room, unlocked the door, and opened it a crack.

"Yasmine?" she asked breathlessly, "Is it really you?"

The face peering back at her was absolutely and unmistakably her best friend's. Annie's breath came out in a relieved rush. Thank God! Yasmine's familiar, flawless, normal face. Normal.

"At least you haven't changed," she said. "Thank God!"

She opened the door a little wider, took a quick look up and down the hall to make sure no one else was lurking nearby, then pulled Yasmine into the bedroom with her.

"Did you see him?" she asked, slamming the door and locking it again behind them. "Did you see Philip?"

Yasmine flicked a nervous glance at the lock on the door. "Philip called me. He asked me to come over and speak to you."

Annie took hold of her friend's upper arm and gave it a little shake. "But did you see him?"

Although she didn't protest or try to pull away, Yasmine took a moment to give the hand clutching her arm a significant look.

"Well, of course I saw him," she said quietly. "He's downstairs."

Annie let go of her immediately but without apology. "And?"

"And..." Yasmine raised her perfectly shaped eyebrows. "He's very concerned about you."

Annie blinked at her and took a step back. "But you didn't notice anything different about him?"

Her friend's lovely face took on a slightly pained expression. No, Annie begged silently, feeling herself sag.

"Annie, I know that—for some reason—this is hard for you to believe," Yasmine said, taking her arm and guiding her over to sit down on the bed. "But you have to accept this; Philip is still Philip. Just like Czonka is still Czonka, and the kids are still the kids. None of them has changed. None of them."

Annie pulled away from her and held her head in both hands as if it might come apart at any moment.

"I'm not going crazy," she said. "I'm not."

"No one said you are," Yasmine replied, leaning closer to her and putting an arm around her shoulders. "I'm sure there's a perfectly rational explanation."

The words clanged as they echoed in Annie's mind. I'm sure there's a perfectly rational explanation. The keyword, of course, being rational. Rational as in from the realm of the mundane and the ordinary. Existing in the world called normal.

Rational also meaning not irrational; which was not necessarily crazy. She wasn't going crazy, but she didn't have to go crazy to be irrational, which was to say, irrational as in unreasonable.

Unreasonable standards and comparisons: what did that word "perfect" really mean anyway?

Unreasonable demands for things that were impossible to attain: she was going to wake up some morning and find out she had turned into one of those people who was never satisfied with anything.

Unreasonable expectations; just because we have a new house doesn't mean we're going to turn into a new family.

Oh, no? said a small voice somewhere in her mind. Guess again.

Annie put a hand to her mouth, horrified, and looked at Yasmine.

"You're right," she whispered. "There is a perfectly rational explanation." She took a breath. "I changed them."

Yasmine opened her mouth to answer and then stopped.

"Now you lost me," she said after a bit, frowning in bewilderment.

Annie put a hand to her head, as if that would somehow help her draw out the right words.

"I remember telling Philip," she said slowly, "that I wished we had the perfect family to go with all of this…"

Just because we have a new house doesn't mean we're going to turn into a new family, she rembered Phil saying.

Sometimes I wish we would, she had replied.

But that wasn't true.

She had been lying to her husband when she'd said that. She'd known what she was saying was a lie the moment it had come out of her mouth. She didn't wish for that sometimes.

She wished for it all the time.

"And…?" Yasmine prompted, moving so that she could look into Annie's eyes.

"Well, don't you see?" Annie hesitated. She wanted to hear the words in her mind before saying anything to Yasmine but for some reason they wouldn't come to her that way. It was as if they wouldn't exist even as thoughts unless she admitted them out loud. "My wish—the perfect family to go with all of this." She leaned closer and lowered her voice to a whisper. "It's come true."

Yasmine's lovely face lit up with a broad smile. Not as if she were trying to placate her, Annie saw as she drew back, but as if this were the most delightfully amusing thing she had heard lately.

"This isn't funny," Annie said, almost snapping at her. "Yasmine—"

"I'm sorry," she said her friend, still smiling as she shook her head and tried to look apologetic. "It's just that…" she hesitated. "Annie, do you trust me?"

"Well…" Annie drew back a little more, eyeing her warily now. "I want to."

"Then come downstairs with me."

"Why?" Annie pulled her hands away from Yasmine's.

Yasmine refused to acknowledge her openly suspicious expression.

"Because," she said, reclaiming Annie's right hand and pressing it between both of her own, "I want to show you something."

Annie tried to pull her hand away again and Yasmine tightened her hold.

"Look at me, Annie," she said, her tone acquiring a very slight edge. "Right now. Look at me." She waited until Annie obeyed. "I'm still Yasmine, right? I haven't changed."

But that's because you don't have to—you're already perfect, Annie told her silently. You always have been and you probably always will be.

Yasmine gave her hand a small, prompting squeeze and tilted her head to one side. Annie gave in and nodded.

"Good!" Yasmine said, smiling broadly again and stood up, pulling her to her feet as well. "Then come downstairs."

She meant to say no, resist, dig in her heels if she had to. She had no intention of leaving the room, at Yasmine's request or anyone else's. Exactly how long she was going to keep herself locked in and everyone else locked out was something she hadn't given much consideration to; she had thought only as far as refusing to come out until further notice.

But for some reason, she was letting Yasmine open the door and usher her into the hall, and instead of bolting right back inside and slamming the door in her friend's face, she was just going along with her, as if nothing out of the ordinary had happened and everything was really quite all right. Perfectly normal.

She told herself that when she and Yasmine reached the top of the stairs, she was going to call a halt right then and there.

She would turn to Yasmine, look her straight into her eyes and say, sorry, but I changed my mind. This is as far as I go. Something very odd is going on around here and until I get at least a hint of an explanation, I am not budging another inch... And I do not care how perfectly rational that explanation might be, I want a second opinion and I am not moving until I get one.

Then she followed Yasmine docilely down the stairs without a word or the slightest bit of hesitation.

It was like being in a dream, except that her mind felt unclouded, clear and alert and she had no sense of being controlled by some force that had sapped her will or taken her over in some way.

She knew that she had intended to stop at the head of the staircase and stay there, refusing to walk down.

But when the moment came, she went right on going after all, as if that had been exactly what she had meant to do all along. While Yasmine gave her a benign everything's-going-to-be-all-right smile to let her know how well she was doing with all this.

Ah, yes, how well I'm doing, Annie thought, suppressing the urge to laugh hysterically; now if only I knew *what* I was doing...

Then she reached the bottom of the stairs and all thought ceased as she stared at the scene in front of her in the living room.

Some time later, it crossed Annie Macintosh's mind as she was standing there motionless and silent, dimly aware that her hand was still sandwiched gently between both of Yasmine's, that this might be a dream after all.

It could have been that, in reality, she was still falling down the stairs and what she saw right now was just part of her life which was still currently in the process of passing before her eyes.

Except in true Annie Macintosh fashion, she not only saw her own life passing before her eyes, she also saw the life she wished she could have had. That was the only reason she could think of—or, as someone she knew had once phrased it, the only perfectly rational explanation—for the way the living room looked to her now.

Of course, it was hard enough trying to get her mind around the idea that all of the various boxes that had been stacked up all over the place were gone. Was she really supposed to believe that Phil and the kids would have simply gone ahead and taken care of the unpacking, put every single item away, and then broken down all the cartons and cleaned up all the crumpled paper and any other moving detritus?

That was about as likely as her coming downstairs with Yasmine to find that all the old, shabby furnishings had been replaced by the exquisitely tasteful and excruciatingly expensive items of décor that she seemed to be looking at in the room right now.

The broken down, threadbare sofa was gone as if it had never been at all, even though she could remember the feeling of the lumpy worn-out cushions under her when she had regained consciousness on it earlier in the day. Instead, there were now two sofas facing each other in the room, two matching sofas upholstered in rich, tastefully understated brocade; and light-colored brocade at that. As if none of the people in this house ever spilled food and drink with a routine, liberal hand. As if the family dog was a fancy, purebred poodle who hardly ever got dirty rather than a mutt who had never met a mud puddle he didn't want to wear.

There were half a dozen matching throw pillows on each of the sofas, artfully arranged, clean and in good condition. Obviously, they had never been used by battling siblings who were trying to bash each other's brains out.

The coffee table standing between the sofas had been converted to what Annie thought was an antique toboggan. She wasn't familiar with toboggans, antique or otherwise. She wasn't familiar with antiques of any sort for that matter. There was enough new stuff that she couldn't afford, there was no need to add on decades of old stuff to it.

But she could remember seeing this particular piece somewhere a long time ago. Probably just as a picture in an expensive catalog, which was where she saw most of the things she wanted. She had thought it was actually a very clever thing to do with an old toboggan; she liked the way the curving lines of the runners served as a framing accent and drew the eye along the length of the object so that when you looked at it, you somehow saw it both as the toboggan it had been and the table that it had been converted into.

She had thought it was a little like looking at an optical illusion, like the picture of the cup that became two people's profiles, or the old lady who became a young woman sitting at her vanity table. Only this was something far more artistic; cleverer, even wittier.

She also remembered that it had been incredibly expensive—like most things that caught her eye—and figured that it was just as well she couldn't afford it. She could just see herself coming home from the store some fine winter day to discover that Sean had decided to see if it could still serve its original purpose, either outdoors in the snow or right there in the living room. Or, God help her, both. So at least being unable to afford expensive antiques meant she had not had boyish pranks to worry about.

She still didn't—the boy who now claimed he was Sean would never have done such a thing. It probably wouldn't have occurred to him even as something to joke about.

Nor did she have to worry about the runners scratching her lovely living room floor; not with that nice, thick Oriental rug to protect the wood. It was a beautiful design, one that complemented the brocade upholstery rather than fighting with it. Everything went together so well that the leather easy chair to the left of the fireplace seemed to be sitting in placid approval of the arrangement in front of it.

She recognized the end tables from the same catalog she had seen the sofas in; she had lingered an especially long time over that page, admiring the rich old-gold sheen of the wood and the subtle tint of the glass tops. She remembered how she had studied the inset that showed how all the glass had beveled edges. The only furniture she had ever seen with beveled-edge glass were crème-de-la-crème antiques; also only in catalogs, of course.

The lamps standing on the end tables were the same ones she had seen in the photos, although according to the captions, they were just for the purpose of illustration: Lamps courtesy of Waterford Crystal; not offered. Nice of them to say so, she had said to herself wryly, as it saved her the minor embarrassment of having to decline with the made-up excuse that they already had far too much Waterford in the downstairs parlor.

But even now that would still be a white lie, she thought distantly as she finally gave in and let herself wander into the room for a closer look at everything. The lamps didn't constitute too much Waterford at all; they were exactly the right amount.

She could also see now that her theory about Waterford fixtures in general had been correct: they were classic enough to suit just about any décor, no matter how eclectic. Even if there was a state-of-the-art stereo system not ten feet away, the glossy, high-tech façade looking so intimidating, ultra-modern and complex and even more expensive than when Phil had showed it to her in the store with an expression of longing that she had no trouble relating to. Of course, she hadn't been able to look at the stereo for very long at the time since the price tag had made her eyes cross.

Her eyes certainly weren't crossing now, however. Her gaze traveled past the sound system to the framed print of the New York skyline from 1930. She knew for a fact that it was a limited edition print she had seen advertised somewhere, not something that she would have been able to buy in the plebeian form of a poster just because she had liked the image. She knew because she had tried.

Eventually, she realized that she had been turning around and around in a slow circle for some time in the middle of this perfect living room, letting herself admire it without questioning anything about what she saw, even though she knew that it was actually all wrong. It had to be, no matter how much she wished otherwise.

Yasmine appeared in front of her then with a happy, expectant smile. Waiting for her to say that, oh, yeah, she remembered now and everything was all right after all.

Annie shook her head. "This is not my furniture."

Yasmine looked at her skeptically with half-closed eyes.

Annie shook her head again, more emphatically this time. "Yasmine, it's not. It can't be. Our couch was ten years-old," she said. "This stereo—" she motioned toward the high-tech but tasteful unit. "Philip wanted this stereo but it cost ten thousand dollars." She turned to Yasmine, frowning slightly. "Ten thousand dollars," she repeated, wondering if her friend's lack of reaction was simply a matter of her not having heard the figure correctly the first time.

But apparently Yasmine felt that ten thousand dollars was too paltry a figure to bother raising her eyebrows over even slightly. "Okay, then," she said, sounding just a little bit tired now. "Let's just pretend that everything you've been telling me is true. This isn't your furniture."

She made an all-encompassing gesture at everything around them and then pointed specifically at the portrait hanging over the mantle.

"And this isn't your family," she added. "Let's pretend that somehow everything's changed. Okay?"

Annie was so baffled that she forgot to be frightened by the way the strange faces in the family portrait. "And?" she said after a bit.

"Oh, Annie!" Yasmine gave her a little shake. "Don't you get it? Don't you see? Any way you look at it, you got what you wanted."

Annie's frown deepened along with her bewilderment. "I... what?"

"Honey—" Grinning, Yasmine leaned toward her and lowered her voice conspiratorially. "You've traded up."

Upgrade.

Annie felt as if her memory had thrown the word at her like a brick. And hey, let's not forget that upgrade was your word for it, and no one else's. *Le mot juste*, remember?

Oh, yes, she remembered, all right. Upgrade. She couldn't deny that was exactly what she had wanted.

And who wouldn't want an upgrade? said a little voice in her mind tauntingly. No home or family is perfect without one. Right? Right?

Right?

NINE

If she no longer understood anything else in the world, Annie thought, she was utterly and completely clear on the concept of deafening silence.

The one presently hanging over the dining room with a virtually tangible force, as she sat at the table eating supper with three people who kept claiming to be her family, was so absolutely thunderous that she wouldn't have thought sounds as minor as the clink of silverware on china plates could be audible. And yet they were.

Chalk up one more impossibility among the plethora of the last twenty-four hours, then.

Annie glanced quickly at the three strangers sitting around the table and poured herself some more wine. If she could really call them strangers.

She was starting to think that she was wrong about how many strangers were in this house; perhaps there weren't three, but only one.

If she were going to be honest about it, they looked like they belonged here more than she did. They had the look of people who were used to living a quality life, people who went to the trouble of taking a shower and getting dressed up for dinner.

Compared to them, she might have been some homeless person they had invited in for the charity of a hot meal, in her ratty jeans and a stained T-shirt under a worn-out, plaid work-shirt.

There, she was doing it again. Thinking she wasn't good enough to live in a house like this...

No, that wasn't it and she knew it. That wasn't the problem. She could have been wearing an original Dior evening gown and a diamond-encrusted tiara and she would still have felt... what? That she was out of place?

Or that they were out of place?

She sneaked a glance at all three of them. Uh-huh. Maybe she should invite those proverbial or theoretical neighbors in after all and have them vote on who didn't seem to belong, Annie thought, looking down at the work-shirt. She had spilled some wine on it; not that that was the only stain. It was one of Phil's old ones that he didn't wear any more.

Her Phil, that was. Her Philip Macintosh, the one she remembered, with the unruly, thick hair that was becoming a little more silver every day and the worry lines that had gotten significantly deeper as the kids got older and the warm, compassionate smile that had always meant the world to her.

Her Phil, not the man sitting down at the opposite end of the table who claimed to be Philip Macintosh. He would never have owned a shirt like this, not even brand new. Anyone could tell just by looking at him that it wasn't his personal style, although he would have looked good in it anyway.

He would probably look good in just about anything he put on. He obviously spent more than a few hours in the gym and it was paying off for him. She couldn't see even the faintest beginnings of worry lines on his smooth, handsome face. And even though his hair didn't look quite as thick as her Phil's, it was carefully styled and still completely dark.

Abruptly, she realized that in spite of everything, she felt a stirring of attraction to him. To this man, to this stranger? She was horrified at herself and yet she couldn't help it.

She tried to compensate by keeping her eyes averted but without much success. Her gaze kept returning to the bone china dishes, the not just flatware but real silver—and the crystal goblets at each place. None of it, not a single piece, was chipped, cracked, worn, or even slightly damaged in any way. And it all matched.

The concept of matching tableware had been one more entry on Annie Macintosh's list of impossible dreams, like having a fireplace, but lo and behold and voilà... like the fireplace... and everything else... and *everyone* else... Inevitably, she would find herself once again staring at the man at the other end of the table, unable to look away again without enormous effort.

Naturally, the dining room table had been included in the general upgrade. What had once been a battered pine thrift shop cast-off was now a venerable Heywood-Wakefield elder statesman from the middle of the last century. Or elder states-table; which would make the dishes elder states-china and the silverware elder states-silverware. Elder states-knives and elder states-forks. And don't forget those elder states-spoons. Annie poured a little more wine into her elder states-glass, biting her lip against the hysterical laughter that wanted to come bubbling out at any moment.

No one looked directly at her as she gulped most of it down in one go but she knew they had been watching her all through dinner, and they were all well aware of how many times she had drained her glass. Or rather, her elder states-crystal goblet; it was genuine lead crystal, intricately cut, impossibly expensive.

There was that word again: impossibly. From the English word *impossible*, meaning could not be, but here it was anyway. Here it was, and here she was with it, and them. She finished the rest of her wine and clutched the now-empty glass in one hand as if it were a lifeline.

The wine bottle was within easy reach and there was still some left. Like everything else, it was awfully good, better than it should have been. One more upgrade among all the other upgrades; from cheap Beaujolais to elder states-wine.

"So how's the new school?" the man claiming to be Philip said suddenly. His tone of hearty good cheer was obviously forced but also obviously well-intentioned. He gave each of the attractive teenagers who claimed to be her children a thousand-watt smile. "The campus sure looks nice."

The girl looked up at him and hesitated, darting a quick glance in Annie's direction without quite looking at her.

"Well, I love the tennis courts," she said, and then sat up a little straighter, apparently bolstered by the sound of her own voice in normal conversation (there was that word again: normal). Her tentative smile blossomed into a real one. "They've got stadium seating and everything. One of the girls I talked to told me her dad played at Wimbledon a few times and he says the school's courts are practically just as good." She took a sip of Coke from her goblet. "Can you believe that? Man, I can hardly wait till they finish re-stringing my racket."

Still smiling, she looked at the boy. We all have to pitch in here. Your turn now—name something you really like about our upgrade.

"I met my new swim coach today," said the boy promptly. "You know he won a bronze medal at the '88 Olympics? I'm going to ask him about maybe setting up some extra training sessions."

Philip looked suitably impressed, pausing to make sure that she had not had so much elder states-wine that she couldn't take note of his reaction.

"Sounds like you two are really going to love it here," he said cheerfully.

Then all three of them turned their perfect faces to look at her expectantly.

We all have to pitch in here. Your turn now—name one thing you really like about this family's upgrade. Just one. Doesn't have to be your favorite or anything major, just something good. And, oh, yeah, don't start acting weird again, okay?

Suddenly overwhelmed with self-consciousness, Annie looked down at her plate. Her elder states-plate, delicately rimmed with gold.

She could remember looking at these plates years ago in the store where she had signed up with the bridal registry. One place setting had cost more than a month's rent on her first apartment, while a service for twelve complete with salad dishes and soup bowls cost more than her first car.

She had barely touched her food except to push it around with her fork. Her elder states-fork; the pattern was Aegean Weave and she had once joked about starting a high-interest savings account so that someday, she could buy a butter knife.

She raised her head and found to her horror that they were still looking at her, still waiting.

Immediately, she grabbed the bottle and poured the last of the wine into her glass, hating the way her hand was visibly trembling and hating the way they wouldn't pretend they couldn't see that.

And still they expected her to come up with her personal take on "Why It's So Great To Go On Living."

Defiantly, Annie picked up her wine glass with both hands, held it perfectly steady for a long moment, and then raised it to her lips. She had intended to finish it all in one gulp—if they were going to watch her like a goddamned TV show, then she would give them something to watch—but she barely managed a sip before she had to put the glass down again.

There was another long moment of thunderous silence with all eyes on her and her staring back like a deer in the headlights, unable to look away no matter how much she wanted to.

Abruptly, the boy turned to Philip and said, "So, how's work, Dad?"

Dad; no argument on that score. No matter what other claims they might make, it was obvious that, just as he and the girl were brother and sister, "Philip" was most definitely his father. It was also obvious that they had a good relationship; she didn't have to know them very well at all to see that.

"Well, remember that biotech company I made an offer on?" "Dad" was saying cheerfully. "We just closed the deal."

"Oh, cool!" said the blonde girl with a little too much enthusiasm.

"That's great!" the boy agreed in the same, slightly overdone tone and then turned to her with a too-bright smile. "Isn't that great, Mom?"

Annie blinked at him, trying to see something of the family she had always known in those three unfamiliar faces. But she couldn't.

There was nothing of the Sean she knew as her son in that handsome, blemish-free, candidate-for-a-boy-band face. There was nothing that she could recognize, not even the tiniest vestige of anything in his appearance or his attitude, his posture or his tone of voice that was even remotely like the Sean with the gang gestures and the skateboard and the endless taunts about his sister's weight. Who would no more have asked his father about work than he would have wanted to know what she thought. About anything.

Tess, the real Tess, could never be that demure blonde girl with her sweet disposition and her cheerful attitude. Circumstances being what they were, she had not actually displayed much in the way of active cheerfulness over the course of the day, especially not at dinner tonight but somehow Annie knew that was her normal mode. If this girl ever ended up on a psychiatrist's couch, she thought, it wouldn't be because she had been emotionally scarred by four years of high school. Not this girl. This girl was breezing through her classes, captaining the tennis team, and dating the male version of herself.

And Phil...

All right, maybe she had often wished that the kids could have been more like the two who were sitting at the table right now. But even so, she would not really have traded them away for completely different people. Not really. It was actually more a case of her having higher hopes for them, hopes that they would discover their strengths and talents and fulfill their potential. Hopes that they would succeed. Hopes that no matter what happened in the future, they would be happy.

These were things that all parents hoped for. She hadn't wanted to change Tess and Sean themselves so much as she had wished for an improvement in their attitudes, their dispositions. But if there was one person she hadn't wanted to change in any way, it was Phil.

She had never wished for anyone younger, more handsome, richer, or more successful; she had never wished he could change and become more

like someone else who was more successful. When
it came to Phil Macintosh, there was no upgrade.

Was there?

She realized that they were all watching her with
those wary expressions again.

Sean tried a friendly smile, which faded slightly
as he glanced at his father. He had asked her a
question, Annie recalled suddenly. They had been
having a conversation and it had been her turn to
say something.

But about what? Something about "Philip" and
his work. He had something... a company. Some
kind of company? He had bought—a company?

Suddenly she felt as if the knowledge were on the
edge of her awareness, that if she thought about it
for one more second, maybe even half a second, it
would somehow come to her. Like something she
had forgotten without realizing that she had ever
known it in the first place.

But she never had known it. How could anyone
remember something they had never known to
begin with? Things didn't happen that way. She
wasn't going to allow things to happen that way—

Before she was even aware that she was speaking aloud, she heard her own voice say, "Oh, yes.
It's great."

Judging from the way the boy's smile brightened
again, the utter astonishment she felt at herself
wasn't apparent on her face.

Because she was smiling back at him, she realized.

Her astonishment went up another notch and
then several more with the further realization that

she wanted to smile at him. And why wouldn't she want to smile at a boy like this? If she looked past everything else, the possible and the impossible, all the stuff that didn't make sense and all the stuff that did, what she would see was the ideal that she and every other parent in the world secretly wished for, whether any of them would admit it or not, even just to themselves.

"So, Mom," said the ideal Sean conversationally. "Is your head feeling better?"

Annie felt a sudden, powerful urge to answer him as if everything really were all right, to just let go of everything she knew to be normal—or thought she knew. Then everything would be all right again immediately. For the three of them, anyway. They would relax, stop looking at her with those faces, those uh-oh-what's-wrong-with-Mom faces, and finish their dinner with in the comfortable certainty that their life, their family life, would be going on as normal.

And after a while, it would be the same for her. All she had to do was go along with them. It wouldn't be hard. They wanted her and they were doing everything they could to let her know it. They wanted her and they needed her—the *real* Annie Macintosh. They weren't asking her who she was; they weren't insisting they didn't recognize her; they weren't claiming she wasn't who she said she was. They weren't the ones who were making everything difficult.

It would be so easy if she let it. She could just slip into this life with this son, this daughter, this husband, and that Czonka. Try them out like a new pair of shoes, see how she liked them. She had a feeling that she would find she liked them quite a lot.

"Hey—" the ideal Sean put down his fork for a moment and turned to her again. "Remember that time I got beaned in Little League?"

Annie blinked at him. "You played Little League?" The question was out before she could think better of it and the fragile hope that everything might possibly be returning to normal among them shattered.

"I-I guess I forgot," she added faintly, watching them all sneaking dismayed glances at each other.

Then she wondered why she had said such a thing, made such a ridiculous excuse. There was nothing wrong with her memory. Sean had categorically refused to have anything to do with: "something so one hundred percent lame-ass," as he had so delicately put it.

That had been the Sean she knew, though, not this ideal one.

Annie drained her glass just for the sake of doing something, anything at all, but this only seemed to heighten their dismay. Hardly surprising.

What's wrong with Mom?

Oh, nothing that six weeks in Betty Ford couldn't cure.

Might as well make it worth the cost, then, she thought.

"I-I think I'll get some more wine," she blurted as she got up and fled to the kitchen, leaving both her glass and the bottle behind on the table.

TEN

She didn't realize that she had been holding her breath until she sagged against the island counter and felt it all come out in a forceful rush.

Leaning heavily on her elbows, she started to put her head down and then jumped back as if the countertop had suddenly turned red-hot.

It hadn't, of course. The rose-colored marble surface was pleasantly cool; also clean and polished to a high gloss. There was not a scratch anywhere. Easy to see that it was real marble, too. God, it must have cost a fortune to put in, Annie thought, pressing her knuckles against her mouth as she looked around the kitchen, more than all those state-of-the-art, ultra-modern appliances put together.

And that was saying something. The stove was a self-cleaning marvel with a computer memory, built into the cabinets at shoulder level. No more bending over to check on the roast or the casserole or the duck à l'orange! Plus, the oven door opened sideways, closet-style, to make it easier to put things in and take them out again. Very impressive.

So was the high-tech microwave, which looked like it could track satellites and cook dinner in eight seconds. It too was built into the cabinet space, which left vast plains, virtual acres, of countertop area free.

Chalk up yet one more unheard-of luxury in the life of Annie Macintosh. She remembered the kitchen here as being better than the one in the old house, but she didn't remember it being this good. Did she?

Well, did she? Had the countertops all been genuine marble when they had first moved in yesterday, or had they just been a very convincing facsimile? If they had changed, when had it happened? Had the transformation occurred before Sean or after Tess? Or during Phil?

Or could it be that they had not changed at all, that she had been so wrapped up in wishing for that dusty rose-colored marble that she had actually failed to notice it was there?

Annie sighed. Yasmine would probably come over later and tell her she designed the kitchen herself.

If I could have, I would have, Annie thought, letting one hand trail along a rosy marble countertop as she wandered slowly around the counter in the center of the room. The island counter had its own white enamel sink, presumably for washing vegetables. Had that always been there? Had it always been white? She was getting more and more confused now about what she remembered, what she thought she might remember, and what she didn't recognize at all.

She turned to look at the stainless steel double sink; there was a high-tech water filtration system built directly into the faucet, which seemed to have an even more complicated system for turning the water on and off. The back splash tiles were the same marble as the countertops.

She didn't have to open the lower cabinet in the corner to know that it was a three-tiered revolving unit but she did anyway. Behind the cabinet doors to the left of it were all her larger pots and pans and baking dishes, neatly grouped by purpose and stacked by size; she didn't have to look to be absolutely certain about that, too, Annie realized suddenly.

She knew exactly how the cabinets had been organized and she also knew that if she went ahead and opened them anyway, she would find not only that she was right but also that every bit of the old mismatched and battle-scarred junk had been replaced by all the top-of-the-line cookware she had always wanted.

Except that was ridiculous, of course. She started to reach for the nearest cabinet door and then paused.

Oh, go ahead and look, said a small voice in her mind. Open the cabinet doors and feast your eyes on all the stuff you've always wanted. What do you think it's there for? At last it's yours. Yours.

That idea about slipping into this life, trying it on like a new pair of shoes—that's what's ridiculous. And the way you're wandering around this kitchen like a lost soul, that is ridiculous, too. This is what you have always wanted; the perfect home. And now you're try-ing to find excuses to reject it. God only knows why. If you really, really don't want it after all, step aside. Unless you want to get trampled by the stampede of billions of women who would all be only too happy to take your place. Add that to all those other things you're just so absolutely certain are true, but be sure to put it at the top of the list.

Annie took a deep, steadying breath and let it out slowly. All right, she certainly couldn't argue with that one. Her gaze came to rest on the refrigerator, which was, like everything else in the kitchen, top of the line: frost-free, with a temperature monitor and alarm, a handy water and ice-cube dispenser in the door, and, for all she knew, a direct line of communication to the microwave so it could call ahead and let it know that leftover lasagna was on the way.

The fridge's high-gloss, dirt and scratch-resistant front was covered with magnets holding up an assortment of family photos, as well as recipes, notes, quotations, and, most prominently, a Mother's Day card.

At least she recognized the card. The kids had given it to her with the coffee mug. Smiling, she took it down and opened it.

"To the best mom in the world," she read aloud. "We love you more than you'll ever know. Tess and Sean."

Her eyes began welling up just as they had when she had first opened the card on Mother's Day.

"We love you more than you'll ever know."

She could remember thinking at the time how lucky she was; there were people who'd have given anything to get a card like this from their kids but never would, for one reason or another. Of course, she had barely had a chance to read the card all the way through once before Sean inevitably began teasing Tess until she stormed off in tears to lock herself in her room. But even after that bit of unpleasant business-as-usual, Annie had still been able to tell herself in all honesty that she felt lucky.

That had been the old Sean and Tess, though. The original Sean and Tess.

She put the card back up on the refrigerator and looked at the photos. Sean and four other boys in bathing suits lined up on the edge of an Olympic-sized swimming pool, all of them holding gold medals and laughing happily as they let themselves fall backwards into the water. Annie couldn't help smiling at the way the camera had frozen the boys leaning back at a comically impossible angle above the pool.

Here was a photo of Tess looking trim and strong in immaculate tennis whites, sitting on a bench in front of some courts somewhere. The tennis racquet she was holding had a big, pink gift bow in the center of the strings and an oversized tag shaped like a dog biscuit that read HAPPY B-DAY FROM CZONKA XO dangling from the handle. Czonka the poodle was sitting next to her on the bench, looking dignified and rather proud of himself with a bright green tennis ball in his mouth. Annie felt her smile getting wider, even as she was thinking, but that's not my dog.

And here was a shot of Phil slumped in what looked like a brand-new wheelbarrow, pretending he was taking a nap while Tess made believe she was trying to wheel the thing away with him in it. Sean was crouched in front of them, obviously trying to persuade Czonka to jump in on top of Phil.

That had been Father's Day, she thought and then wondered what had given her that idea. Then, afraid that the answer might come to her, she distracted herself by looking at another photo, this one of herself and Phil in front of a Christmas tree, with him holding some mistletoe over her head.

Wow. To look at us, anyone would think we were a happy family.

But of course they were a happy family. Just because they weren't happy all the time, every single minute of every single day, didn't mean they could not be a happy family.

Yes, but this makes us look like we spend a lot of time doing things. And like we always remember without fail to have the camera handy.

A photo of her and the kids giving Czonka a bath in a big basin outside—they were all drenched and covered with soap bubbles. And laughing about it, of course.

She closed her eyes and let her head fall forward to rest against the front of the refrigerator. There were lots of other photos. If she looked at all of them over and over for long enough, would she eventually talk herself into believing that these were things she remembered after all?

Even though she could still bring to mind the family in the portrait over the fireplace—the girl she knew was Tess, the boy she knew was Sean, and their father, the one and only Philip Macintosh with herself by his side—that picture just wasn't there any more. No matter how well she could see it in her memory, there was no trace of it anywhere else. In light of that, how could it make sense to do anything else except let herself just slide into this life? Or to let it slide into her, whichever.

She raised her head and opened her eyes, focusing on a shot of her spraying a very much younger Sean and Tess with a garden hose. This was her life. It was right here in front of her. This was her life, this was her family. They knew who she was, they recognized her. They loved her. All of them, they loved her.

She turned away from the refrigerator and spotted the poodle sitting over by the kitchen door. He was watching her with a frankly speculative tilt to his frizzy head.

Probably wondering if I'm going to find something else to freak out about, Annie thought, feeling a mild wave of regret.

The poodle's tail thumped tentatively on the floor a few times.

"And you love me, too," she said to the dog softly. "Right?"

The poodle cocked his head in the other direction. Does this have anything to do with our agreement where I adore you and you give me food?

Annie put a hand to her mouth, suppressing a nervous laugh. "You're a good dog," she told the poodle. "You're a very good dog."

The poodle shifted position slightly and gave her
the doggy equivalent of a smile, tail thumping on
the floor again, sounding more confidently now.
No doubt he recognized "good dog" as the words
that usually preceded a treat.

Annie knew right where the dog biscuits were
kept, too, just like she knew where everything else
was in this kitchen. Without her actually willing it,
she walked over to the correct cabinet, found the
dog biscuits and took one out of the box for him.

"Good dog," she said again and held the biscuit
out for him between thumb and forefinger. "Good
Czonka. Good boy."

Instead of charging her in a greedy, affectionate
rush like the original Czonka, the poodle got up
and walked over to her with a calm and dignified
self-possession. He licked her hand once, presumably by way of a doggy thank you, before delicately
taking the biscuit between his teeth. Then he just
stood with it in his mouth, looking at her and wagging his pom-pom tail.

I adore you, I adore you, I adore you. Mother,
may I? By the way, have I ever mentioned that I
adore you?

"Good dog," she repeated, her voice dropping to
a whisper this time.

I adore you, I adore you, I adore you, said the
poodle's dark, bright eyes. Now, who's your
doggy? Say my name, say my name. Czonka. Just
say it for me, just so I know you haven't forgotten.

Annie put a hand over her eyes for a moment,
then shook the thought away and went to the sink.
So she was reading the dog's mind now, was she?

If things had not been out in the wild blue yonder before, they sure were now. She poured herself a glass of water and drank it down slowly, holding onto the edge of the sink so tightly with her other hand that her knuckles were white.

She had to regain her equilibrium, Annie told herself for what had to be the gazillionth time. She had to figure out what was going on but she wouldn't be able to do that unless she could pull herself together first. For the last couple of days, she had been dancing along the thin edge of a freak-out—no, scratch that, it was more staggering wildly than dancing.

She certainly couldn't go on like this, with everyone wondering what was happening her. There was no way she could even begin to explain anything to them because she didn't have the faintest idea of what was going on herself or what to do about it. That was the problem. She had no idea what she was doing and she was doing it in a state of high panic.

So she had to steady herself; she had to. Then she could tackle the problem of what the hell was going on. Otherwise, she was just going to get more and more panicky and disoriented until she didn't know which end was up.

Oh, who was she try to kid—she had no idea which end was up right now.

Annie closed her eyes and moved the cold glass back and forth across her forehead while she took slow, deep breaths. Maybe Yasmine was right; maybe she was simply in the middle of a melt-down from the stress of buying the perfect house of her dreams. After all, she had to take into consideration that Yasmine had come over to talk to her about it instead of dodging the issue by running off to an appointment with a client. That had to be significant. Nor had Yasmine seemed particularly alarmed or disturbed by anything Annie had told her.

I've had clients forget their own names, what year it was, how many children they have.

If anyone else had tried to sell her something like that, she might not have believed it for a minute. But Yasmine was such a hard-headed, high-powered businesswoman. She was confident, independent, capable, and not given to flights of fancy. In fact, she was the only person Annie knew who categorically refused to read her horoscope in the comics section of the newspaper.

Yasmine's livelihood depended on her knowing what she was talking about, all the hard facts and figures. So if Yasmine told her that the stress of buying a house had driven people to forget their own names, then maybe the best thing she could do was head back upstairs and start sewing tags in her underwear right now.

Too bad Yasmine hadn't thought to mention any of this to her before, she thought suddenly.

"Of all the people I've ever known, you're the only one that I would ever describe as someone who has her shit together." That's what she had said.

Annie winced. The fact that that statement had slipped her mind only proved how disoriented she really was. Yasmine hadn't thought someone who had her shit together would start bouncing her reality checks. Apparently the hardheaded, high-powered businesswoman did not always know what she was talking about after all.

Oh, and whose fault was that?

Annie winced again. She poured herself another glass of water and then dumped it out, watching the water swirl around the shiny stainless steel and disappear down the drain. So it turned out that she, Annie, did not have her so-called shit as together as she would have had everyone believe—everyone in this case being her best friend and her family—and the only conclusion she was drawing from that was that Yasmine didn't know everything?

Earth paging Annie Macintosh, currently doing business as Cleopatra, Queen of Denial. Get your ass back to the real world and start getting your shit together again immediately.

Small wonder she was having trouble recognizing her own family, let alone her furniture. If she kept up this kind of thinking, she wasn't going to be able to recognize herself.

She ran cold water over her hands and pressed them to her face, then automatically reached into the top drawer on her right for a towel. It was soft and freshly laundered and smelled wonderful and as far as she knew, she didn't own any dishtowels this nice.

Slowly, she lowered it from her face and looked down at the immaculate navy-blue and white striped terry cloth draped over her palms. No tomato sauce stains, no scorch marks, no rips or holes or loose threads.

One more nice thing along with your customized kitchen and your matching dinner service and your gorgeous living room. Oh, and your beautiful, loving family. So all of this is a problem for you... why?

She folded the towel neatly and put it on the marble counter. Her beautiful, loving family. Phil and Sean and Tess. She summoned the images and they rose up again in her mind's eye in a perfect family portrait, just like the one hanging over the fireplace in the living room.

Exactly like it, she realized suddenly.

The faces in her mind were not the ones she kept insisting were actually theirs but the new ones. She tried to recall the originals but now they refused to come to her. No matter how hard she concentrated, the only faces she could see belonged to these people she didn't know.

The images simply didn't exist in her memory any more. She could remember that they had been there in the past but not the images themselves.

It felt as if something cold and hard were gathering in the pit of her stomach. How was that possible? How could she have forgotten so completely those faces that she had been able to recall only a few minutes before? And these were not just any faces but the faces of her family. She could not remember the faces of her family.

The new faces appeared in her memory again, this time with a growing sense of familiarity about them. As if she hadn't really forgotten so much as sort of misplaced the recollection in some way and then recovered it and put it back in the right context or the right associations or something. She wasn't sure she even understood her own line of thinking.

But then, she didn't seem to be making a whole lot of sense today. What on earth did she mean by telling herself that she couldn't remember the faces of her family when she could picture them in her brain as clearly as if they were standing right in front of her?

No. Wait. That was wrong. Her family was—

Stop it.

Annie shook her head, trying to clear it. "This is your family now," she said firmly, aware only in a distant way that she was speaking aloud. "They love you. They need you."

She paused for a long breath, pretending it didn't sound shuddery at all on the exhale. Because now she had steadied herself. She had to be steady. If she had managed to remain steady through the lean years and the tough times, then she certainly could not go to pieces because life was getting better. That didn't make any sense at all.

"You have to make this work," she told herself. "You have to. You, Annie Macintosh, and nobody else."

She wasn't quite so far gone that she had forgotten her own name, or at least not yet. She could pat herself on the back for being one up on some of Yasmine's other clients.

She straightened up and turned away from the sink. She would go back out to the dining room and enjoy the rest of the meal with her beautiful loving family.

After just one more deep breath, she thought, reaching out to lean one hand on the counter again as she closed her eyes.

It was just that the quiet was so comforting, she told herself after a while. She had been such a nervous wreck for so long that the quiet was hard to give up. All those years in rented apartments with paper-thin, definitely not soundproofed walls. Relatively quiet was as good as it ever got, and there had never been a whole lot of that. Just an endless supply of noise, noise, and more noise: other people's TVs and radios, other people's children laughing, yelling and whining, other people's babies crying, other people's arguments becoming louder as they became more heated. Other people's doors swinging open and slamming shut, other people's footsteps in the hall.

And outside, the constant traffic noise, revving motors, blaring horns and screeching brakes occasionally punctuated by the unmistakable sound of a collision, sometimes major, sometimes minor, always unpleasant. And sirens, a dozen times an hour sometimes.

Like most people, she had learned to block it out most of the time so that unless it got really bad, she would hardly even notice it. Strange, then, that she should notice its absence so vividly.

Or maybe not so strange after all, not really. Maybe what she was actually noticing was not having to expend the effort to block all that noise out. Now that she let herself pay attention, she could hear all the pleasant sounds of normal life going on around her—things like the wind in the trees, a car passing on the street outside, Lizzie's father calling her again.

Busy Lizzie; a ghost of a smile touched Annie's lips as she wondered how old the girl was.

Makes you wonder what else you might have been blocking out, doesn't it?

She laced her fingers together and rested her chin on them in an unconscious attitude of prayer. It was pretty hard to live a full and satisfying life when you literally had to block out a major portion of the world you were living in just to keep yourself sane. No wonder she was having so much trouble adjusting.

All right then, if she could admit that to herself, then she could stop hiding in the kitchen and go out to her family, her beautiful, loving family who needed her, and she would make it work. She would.

She gave herself a mental push and, with what she hoped was a pleasant smile on her face, marched out to sit down and finish dinner with her family.

There was no one sitting at the table.

Steady, now. Do not lose your grip again. Annie closed her eyes, counted to three, and then opened them again.

She was still standing alone in an empty room.

ELEVEN

Okay, don't lose your grip again yet. Obviously they were here. Or someone was, anyway.

On the other hand, Annie thought, looking with apprehension at the plates of half-finished food on the table, how good a sign was it when you had to search for something that would prove that both your family and the dinner you had just been eating with them really existed and were not in fact hallucinations?

She looked down at the chair she was leaning on. This was where she had been sitting. Mom always occupied the chair closest to the kitchen during meal times; that was the rule, or the tradition, or whatever in just about any average, unremarkable, normal suburban middle-class nuclear family home.

Like this one, the Macintosh residence, where the four of them did all those average, unremarkable, normal suburban middle-class nuclear family things. Things like eating dinner and chatting about their respective days. And then leaving the after-dinner clean up to Mom while they plopped themselves down in front of the TV in the living room.

She could not actually hear the TV but maybe that meant they were waiting for her to join them before they put it on. Because it could have been that while her old, original children, the ones she remembered (or thought she remembered) would have stuck her with all the clearing away and washing up, her new ideal children were actually going to do the dishes for her later.

She made herself let go of the chair and moved around the table to the entrance to the living room. Maybe she would find them all sitting on the sofa—correction, sofas; there were two sofas now, as gorgeous and ideal as her children—waiting for her to come in, so they could tell her to sit down and relax, they would handle the cleaning up tonight.

The sight of the empty room was no less startling for the fact that she hadn't really expected to find anyone there. What if they had run away, she thought suddenly. What if her continuing crazy behavior had scared her entire family so badly that they had felt they needed to leave the house altogether, literally escape because they thought she might be dangerous? Even though she wasn't trying to be crazy.

Nobody tries to be crazy. Either you are crazy or you aren't.

She pushed the thought away and massaged her forehead with one hand. The quiet in the house that had been so soothing barely a minute ago now seemed to press in on her from all sides, as if it were part of some force that wanted to isolate her and then swallow her up.

Now that was a pretty crazy idea for someone not trying to be crazy. Even if such a force existed, why would it do that to you, what would be the reason?

The answer was in her mind before she could suppress it: to change me.

Annie put her face in her hands. My name is Annie Macintosh, she said to herself. As long as I still know my own name, it means I'm not a total loss. How many times would she have to tell herself that before she believed it, she wondered and moved slowly to the foyer.

She heard another car drive past the house followed by the man outside hollering for Lizzie to come in and wash her hands again. Annie lifted her head, frowning as she listened.

God, what was it with that guy and this Pavlovian thing he seemed to have with traffic noise and his daughter? It seemed like every time a car went by on the street, he took it as his cue to yell for Lizzie to come in and to wash her hands. Annie was also beginning to think that Lizzie just might be one of those kids best described as a pain in the ass.

Or maybe she was only hearing what she expected to hear now that she was paying attention to that specifically. Lots of cars, whole fleets for all she knew, must have driven past without anyone calling out for Lizzie or anyone else. Next she would start thinking that she could hear the sounds of neighbors who had lived upstairs in some apartment complex from however many years ago. And while she was thinking of it, how many years had it been since she had lived in a place where she had had upstairs neighbors anyway? She couldn't seem to remember that, either.

Don't, Annie told herself as she ran a hand through her hair and looked around the living room. Don't you dare start that. Do not start looking for stray threads you can pull that will cause you to unravel. You have to stay focused on the here and now. Wasn't that what all the self-help gurus were always telling people they were supposed to do, stay focused on "the here and now?" Annie had to bite her lower lip to stifle the nervous laughter that had started to build up inside her. "The here and now." What the hell did that mean anyway? What if "here" turned out to be some place you didn't recognize? And as for "now", wasn't it always "now" no matter where you were?

She looked around the living room again.

Well, the good news is, nothing in here has changed now, she thought. Or at least, none of it had changed since the last time everything had changed, anyway.

Nervous laughter threatened again, more strongly now and Annie had a strong feeling that if she gave in and let herself start laughing, she might never be able to stop. Automatically, she started to look at the family portrait over the mantel and then thought better of it.

No, she thought, averting her gaze downward and turning away. There was absolutely no reason for her to keep checking on that damned picture unless she really was determined to drive herself crazy. She had developed some kind of secret, weird obsession with it that she hadn't even been aware of until yesterday, when the stress of moving to a new house had fried her brains and crumbled her cookies. She had to stop telling herself crazy things.

She didn't try telling herself anything at all except that she should have a look around and find out where her family had gone. After she found Phil and Tess and Sean, everything else would either fall into place or become someone else's worry.

Her gaze fell on the staircase. Had they all gone upstairs?

Maybe Sean had suddenly reverted to his old ways, she thought almost hopefully. Maybe he had gotten bored with his new, nice persona and decided to reduce his sister to a weeping, hysterical bundle of raw nerves who had locked herself in her room. If that was the case, then Philip would have gone up after Tess and was now trying to persuade her either to come out of her room or to let him in so he could try to calm her down.

As soon as she started toward the staircase, she heard the murmur of voices just above her. There, she'd been right, Philip and Sean and Tess had simply gone upstairs. No sobs or shouting, but she decided that was all right; it wasn't really so bad not to have a hysterical teenaged girl to deal with. If that was a permanent change, she welcomed it.

She opened her mouth to call up to them about missing dessert or something equally innocuous and suddenly felt an overwhelming urge to keep quiet instead. Very, very quiet. She moved on tip-toe to the side of the stairs and flattened herself against the wall, straining to hear the conversation taking place only a few feet over her head.

"Dad, what are we going to do about this? She's just not getting any better," Sean was saying tensely.

"No, she sure isn't," Tess added. "I thought she was going to be all right. I thought she was pulling herself together, but then she said that thing about forgetting that Sean played Little League. If anything, she's getting worse." The girl sounded as if she were on the verge of tears, albeit the non-hysterical kind.

A heavy sigh; that was Philip. "I know, kids. I know."

"So what're we going to do?" Tess asked.

"Well, we have to help her, of course," replied Sean. "Only... Well, how? What are we going to do, Dad?"

There was no sarcasm, no impatience in his voice, only compassion. Her son was showing sensitivity and concern. That was something good, Annie thought; so why was it scaring her?

"We're going to do whatever it takes to make her better," she heard Philip promise them. "That's all we can do. I've already made some calls."

Annie covered her mouth with one hand. "Some calls?" What did he mean by that? And who had he made "some calls" to?

"Dad, will she have to... Well, you know... Go away somewhere?" Tess asked unhappily.

"Just for a while," Phil said gently. "But you two don't have to worry. You know that I'll always be here for you."

Annie was horrified to realize that he was speaking in the same soothing tone he had always used to tell her everything was all right.

No, not him, not this man. He had never made her feel better, he was some stranger, just some guy she had never seen before. The man who had taken her in his arms and reassured her, that had been the other Phil, the original. The one whose face she could no longer bring to mind but who she could remember all the same.

He had vanished in the middle of a kiss and changed into this new, improved Phil, or he had been replaced by him, to go with the new, improved Sean and the new, improved Tess and the new, improved Czonka.

The problem was, she wasn't the new, improved Annie, she was the same old one. She didn't go with them, she was the odd one out. So they had no choice. The only thing they could do was send her away.

Unless she did something about it first.

She turned around blindly, thinking that the first thing she had to do was get out of their vicinity and bumped her hip on an antique half-circle occasional table with a cut-glass vase of flowers on it. She managed to catch the vase before it fell and smashed to bits on the floor but the skinny table legs scraped on the hardwood floor, making a squeaking noise that seemed as loud as a fire alarm.

The murmuring she had been listening to upstairs abruptly went silent.

"Honey?" asked Phil after a long moment, raising his voice.

Annie froze with her hands on the vase, not daring even to breathe. Maybe if she held perfectly still, they would think it was just Czonka.

"Honey?" Phil said again. "Annie, honey, is that you?"

Now she could hear their footsteps starting to come down the stairs and she bolted for the kitchen. The cordless phone was lying on the island counter. Annie grabbed it up but her shaking hands fumbled the sleek receiver and she juggled it like a hot potato for what seemed like an eternity before she finally managed to grasp it right side up.

Fortunately, she did much better at dialing. Her fingers danced quickly on the keypad, tapping out Yasmine's number with the ease of long habit.

There was only one ring. Then she heard Yasmine's voice.

"This is Yasmine Haleem. Please leave your name, number and a brief message. Have a great day!"

Annie forced herself not to panic at the sound of the answering machine, remembering that Yasmine had told her she almost always screened her calls in the evening. Many of her more nervous Real Estate clients could often forget what time regular business hours began and ended, she had said.

Which Annie figured could not be terribly surprising if these were the same people who also tended to forget their own names or how many children they had. She waited for what seemed like another eternity before the answering machine finally beeped.

"Oh God, Yasmine, if you're there, pick up! Please!" she half-whispered into the receiver.

Nothing.

"Please, Yasmine. I need your help!" Annie begged.

Still nothing, not even mild static.

"I mean it, Yasmine. I don't know what to do!" she sobbed. "They're going to send me away! Yasmine, please pick up the phone, please—"

"Annie?" came Phil's voice from the living room. "Where are you, honey?"

She froze.

"Mom?" Sean's voice, a little bit closer.

"Oh God, Yasmine, they're coming. I have to get out of here—" Annie dropped the receiver. She flung open the kitchen door and received a fresh shock as she found herself confronting not the still-unfamiliar back yard, vague and indistinct in the late evening shadows but a darkness far too absolute to call night.

She teetered on the balls of her feet for a fraction of a second while a multitude of things whirled through her mind: the sound of her family, or whoever those people were, coming to get her so they could send her away, the living room furnishings that couldn't possibly belong to her, the expensive china on the dining room table still waiting to be cleared, the poodle that was not Czonka—no, he wasn't Czonka, he wasn't and he never had been—a cut-glass vase on an antique table she had never seen before, Yasmine and her perfectly rational explanation...

But most of all herself, standing in this house, this kitchen, trying to tell herself that these three strange people really were her family when she knew better.

How could she think something like that? What in God's name would make her think she should just go along with whatever everyone said, what in God's name would make her think she could do such a thing?

In the distance, that voice again, the man she had heard before, calling a familiar name. How many hours had that man been calling Lizzie for supper? Or had it actually been days? Or did it just seem that way because she used to hear him calling for Lizzie in the old neighborhood, too?

No, now that was ridiculous, too. She had been hearing that man call for Lizzie only since they had moved here, not back in the old neighborhood. Wasn't that right?

Or worse, maybe there really wasn't any Lizzie and what she was hearing was just some lunatic that happened to live in the neighborhood and oh, God, maybe she would end up the same way, calling for Sean and Tess and Phil over and over, all day long and into the too-black night.

Unless they sent her away...

Hurling herself out of the door and into that utterly unbroken blackness felt like jumping off a cliff.

She expected to stumble over something immediately and raised her arms to shield her face. But for some strange reason, she couldn't feel anything at all, not even her feet touching the ground. That had to be because she was already falling, Annie thought, and felt her body automatically stiffen, anticipating the impact. But that was exactly the wrong thing to do, wasn't it? She had to relax her muscles or she would hurt herself worse.

Relax, right. That was a good one. Falling in the dark? Well, that was no big deal, just chill out and hope for a happy landing. Her nerves were screaming as her muscles tightened even more and the impact didn't come and didn't come and didn't come and what kind of darkness was this, had she actually thrown herself over a cliff after all?

Her forearms hit something solid, and the sensation was completely wrong. Instead of grass or dirt and rocks, it was something smooth and hard, like a wall or a thick wooden board or—

The front door banged loudly against the wall behind Annie as she burst into the foyer. Blinking against the sudden light, she staggered all the way to the foot of the stairs and caught herself on the polished wood railing. For some unmeasured time, she hung there telling herself that at any moment her mind and her vision were going to clear and she would see where she really was.

Then she heard the voices coming from the kitchen, Sean saying he had just heard someone come in the front door and Tess agreeing. Obviously her mind still needed to clear if she was hearing things as well as seeing them, but as soon as it did, she wouldn't be so disoriented and it wouldn't seem like she had run out the back door and then almost immediately burst through the front door...

Phil called her name and everything snapped into focus. She backed away from the staircase, looking around wildly. It had happened that way. She had run out the back door and ended up bursting through the front door. It wasn't impossible.

Annie remembered something she'd once read, a science article about the structure of space. The article had speculated that the surface of space was like a Moebius strip, a continuous surface that went on for ever. However, if you could go through the strip, to the other side, you would be somewhere else on the surface, far, far away.

It was as if the house, her dream home, existed, but that when she went out one door, at the back, she punched through the Moebius strip and came in the other door, at the front.

No, thought Annie. It was somehow simpler than that. It was as if she could see the garden, the front yard, the back yard, the yards at the side of the house, but not actually experience them. She remembered how no-one was really interested in the garden or how it should look. Yasmine certainly had shown no interest in talking about the garden, ready as she was to talk for hours about the house.

But then, where did Phil go when he went to work? Where did the children go when they left the house to go to school? Annie didn't know. She cared, but she didn't know.

No-one else, Yasmine included, sensible, sane, rational Yasmine, seemed to care very much about what happened outside the house.

Annie cared, but she couldn't connect with the outside. Unless, of course, that too had changed since the last change...

Without thinking, she turned and ran back out the front door again. This time, however, the blackness she threw herself into was gone in an eye blink and she found herself skidding to a stop in the middle of the kitchen.

"Annie?" called a man's voice anxiously.

At least she thought he said Annie. She might have heard it wrong, however. Maybe it hadn't been Annie. Maybe it had actually been Lizzie. Suddenly she wasn't really sure any more. The two names sounded nothing alike in the slightest but that didn't seem to matter. Maybe it was because she had heard two different people call the two names at exactly the same time.

"Annie?" Lizzie?

She fell back against the marble counter, her breath coming in rapid, terrified gasps as the strange man who claimed to be Phil appeared in the doorway with the two strange teenagers behind him.

"What are you doing?" he asked her.

She shook her head, trying to catch her breath. The man watched her with a stricken expression and then took a step toward her. "Annie—"

"No!" she shouted at him, terrified. "You leave me alone!"

But she could see he was never going to do any such thing. None of them was ever going to let her be. They all really believed that they were her family and there was something wrong with her; they weren't going to leave her alone, they were never going to leave her alone, ever. They were going to do whatever they had to do to help her, whatever it took.

She looked at the open kitchen door and the impenetrable blackness beyond. There was nowhere else to go. The man took another step toward her and she rushed into the darkness beyond the door.

Immediately, she was running across the foyer all the way into the living room before she finally managed to stop herself against the back of the couch. The undeniable reality of the upholstery under her hands was too much for her and she broke down in sobs.

"Please, please help me," she wailed, with no idea who or what she might be appealing to. "Please... Please..." Smearing the back of her hand across one side of her face and then the other, she looked around the living room for some sign, some indication of what might be happening to her, some hint of how much longer it would last and when it might possibly stop, if it ever could stop—

Then, with no warning, she found herself standing in front of the fireplace, looking up at the portrait hanging over the mantle.

"No," she whispered, putting both hands over her mouth.

The perfect faces smiled down on her, implacable. Yes.

"No, no—"

Yes. Yes. Yes.

The purebred poodle, and the ideal Sean. The lovely, blonde girl who was now Tess. Handsome Phil, more handsome than ever. And in their midst, Annie Macintosh.

Only now it was the right Annie Macintosh, that was. Not her, not the one that didn't belong, that didn't know them and had no place among them but the matching Annie Macintosh, the one that went with this house, and with the rest of them. Not that woman, but the perfect Annie Macintosh.

And the perfect Annie Macintosh was not a hysterical housewife in an old T-shirt and worn out jeans who was too busy freaking out all the time even to run a comb through her stringy blonde hair or put on any make-up.

The Annie Macintosh who lived in this lovely home was a well-groomed beauty with a neat, short cap of shiny dark hair, fine bone structure, perfect skin, and a bearing that managed to be both regal and relaxed.

The Annie Macintosh who belonged in this family had the calm, self-possessed look of a woman who would never even come close to freaking out because she was secure in the knowledge that everything about her life was absolutely, positively perfect.

Perfect.

Perfect.

Perfect.

TWELVE

If he was going to put a stop to this business once and for all, Phil Macintosh thought as he went to close the front door, he was going to have to take some very definitive action.

He already knew exactly what that action would be. It was something that he had turned to before and it had worked like a charm. No doubt it would be equally successful in putting an immediate and permanent end to this peculiar outbreak of absent-mindedness that everyone in the house had seemed to come down with all of a sudden.

He would lay it down as law while they were all still at the table: from now on, whenever anyone forgot to the close the front door, it was going to cost them real money. The charge would be one dollar the first time, two dollars for a second offense, and ten dollars for every time thereafter. No exceptions; zero tolerance.

Of course, what could possibly make a person forget to close their own front door in the first place was beyond his understanding, Phil thought as he secured the dead bolt and put on the chain lock. But for some mysterious reason, every so often all the members of the Macintosh household would develop the affliction and, try as he would, he simply could not discern any particular cause for this sudden front-door-related amnesia.

And if that wasn't strange enough, it also seemed to be contagious. As soon as one of them started forgetting, they all did it, himself included. Very weird, indeed; one of those little family quirks, he supposed. Fortunately, a system of fines would cure all of them.

He was about to go back to the dinner table so he could make this announcement and finish his dinner when a flash of color in the living room caught his eye. Automatically, an enormous, happy smile spread over his face.

"Oh, there you are, Annie," he said, going over to his wife and slipping his arms around her from behind.

She was staring at that family portrait again. God, but she loved to look at that thing. He thought that she had to have memorized every line and color in it by now.

He could feel a certain amount of tension in her body as he hugged her, which he found rather surprising. She had been working extra hard over the last couple of days to get all of their belongings out of boxes and packing crates and settled in the house. But that was typical of Annie. She didn't like to waste a minute, everything had to be perfect. This time, however, she had been working so hard he had started to worry a little that she might be overdoing it.

Annie had quite literally pooh-poohed his concerns. She was the only person he had ever met in his life who actually said, "pooh, pooh" when dismissing something she considered to be a minor issue. And she had certainly seemed more relaxed today, even going so far as to lay on that superb five-course dinner for their first official meal together in the new house. Of course, no one would ever know just by looking at her that she had gone to so much trouble.

As always, she took her usual seat at the table—the one nearest the kitchen—with all the casual grace of someone who had a staff of twenty to prepare all the meals for her while she took a nap.

But as soon as he touched her, he knew she still needed to unwind a little more. This move must have stressed her out even more than she had herself had anticipated.

"Are you okay, Annie?" he asked, concerned.

She turned around in the circle of his arms and smiled up at him. She really was a classic beauty, he thought, the kind usually described as ageless. How had he ever gotten so lucky?

"I was just looking at our picture," she said, slipping her arms around his neck, "and thinking how lucky I am. I have a wonderful family, this beautiful new home—" she made a gesture that took in their immediate surroundings and paused to look over her shoulder at the family portrait again. "It's perfect."

"Just like you are," Phil said, meaning it. He stroked her short, dark hair—how he loved the way she wore her hair—and then lifted her chin so he could kiss her.

Somewhere outside, a man's voice called, "Lizzie! Dinner!"

"I mean now, Lizzie!" her father said, his good-natured tone starting to show a little strain.

"I'll be right there!" Lizzie called back from where she was sitting at the computer. "I just have to finish one last thing with my computer game!"

Sometimes it could really be hard to tear herself away, even when she knew Dad had made macaroni and cheese for dinner, which was her favorite. At times like this, for instance, when everything turned out so romantic. Lizzie beamed at the two figures with their arms around each other on the screen. They really were perfect together, she thought.

She switched to another angle so she could look at the whole living room, including both the brother and the sister in the background giggling while they watched their parents kiss. Abruptly the screen froze and for a moment, she was afraid that it had crashed on her and she would have to start all over again.

Then she saw the words at the bottom of the screen.

UPGRADE COMPLETE

What a relief! Happy now, Lizzie shut off the monitor, ejected the CD-ROM and put it back in its case. She started to put it back in the box and then decided to leave it out, setting it on top of the handbook.

She could hardly wait to get back up to her room after dinner and resume the game. It seemed like she had been waiting forever for the new release to come out. Of course, it always seemed like she had to wait forever each time they announced there was going to be an upgrade.

She had been moving her little family through the same settings for so long that she had honestly begun to think that even they had to be getting tired of everything.

What would the software company have thought if she had sent them an email to tell them that the Macintoshes from the computer game were demanding improved living conditions, better back-stories, and even complete makeovers for everyone in the family or they were going to crash? BSOD would stand for Boredom Screen Of Death.

Well, she didn't have to put up with all that old stuff any more. The Macintosh family were in the new house, and all of them had gotten the personal improvements they deserved. She couldn't help thinking of them in that way—she had been playing with them for so long and she knew the program so well. But things had only just begun for all of them.

As soon as she could be excused from the table, she was going to come back up here and read the handbook from cover to cover, to make sure she didn't miss any of the new features. If Model Home 2.0 was anything like the earlier releases, it would take her at least two weeks before she found even half of the Easter eggs.

She wondered if there might even be some way to play with the garden, to make that perfect and romantic too. Her Grandma Lauren had a beautiful old-fashioned garden. Perhaps it would be nice if her little family could go out in the garden? Perhaps it would be nice too if they had a grandmother, or a great-aunt maybe, who could come over and tell this little girl stories.

It would only work, of course, if the little girl were a lot younger, say around Lizzie's own age. She had always been entranced by stories, especially those old fairy stories that her grandmother had given her. Magical cats, toys that came alive, faraway countries where everything could be perfect and there was endless time for play: those had been the things she loved when she was younger. Just like the old doll's house, now resting in a corner of her room under a dust sheet. She had loved to move the furniture around, move the little model people around, and to make up stories about them.

How much better it all was now with the computer program—especially since it had been upgraded. She wondered whether her own movement, from fairy stories in books via the games with the doll's house to her computer and its upgraded program, was itself a kind of upgrading of herself.

Well, time enough to think of that after she had eaten. She put the program's box on the desk next to the CPU and then hurried down to dinner before her Mom and Dad got too impatient.

Is that really all there is to it?

Is it really the case that the things we want are actually out of our hands, as are our reasons for wanting them? Not to mention what it's going to mean for us if—no, make that when—we get them?

We all want to believe that, as good people, as responsible people, we know exactly what we're doing at all times. We need to believe it. Just as we need to believe that we are motivated by only the best of intentions—and that those intentions are strictly our own.

· But as virtual reality becomes less virtual and more real, how can we be certain that we ourselves are not just simulations after all? Can we really tell ourselves that we know beyond the shadow of a doubt that we're not images of light and shadow on some high-res monitor located somewhere far beyond the border of the things that are familiar to us, in that highly unfamiliar region of ever-shifting shadows called The Twilight Zone?

SENSUOUS CINDY

Based on the Teleplay
by James Crocker

It is one of those long-accepted truths that all human beings have both a real life and a fantasy life. In fact, it would seem that the happiest and most well-adjusted among us are those people who allow themselves to enjoy richly detailed and emotionally satisfying fantasy lives on a regular basis.

These fantasies inhabit a very special sort of realm, one that actually lies halfway between dreams and reality. It is a place where we can indulge freely in speculation as to the possible outcomes of certain choices we might be faced with. Or we might simply want to escape the rules and demands that we are obligated to cope with during the course of any given day, or week, or month, or year... or even lifetime.

While escaping reality is often seen as an activity that is somewhat less than worthwhile, it is also a long-accepted truth that we all need to escape sometimes. When we can escape for a little while from the ordinary world that we have to live in, we can often return to it with a fresh outlook and renewed energy to do the things we have to do, to handle our responsibilities. Those intangible things we call fantasies are meant to provide each of us with a personal time off, a break.

This includes fantasies of the sexual variety as well.

Every one of us has sexual fantasies. It's only a matter of human nature. The things that we cannot, do not, and/or will not do in real life, sexual or otherwise, are subject to no restrictions of any sort in the imagination. Our sexual fantasies are harmless of course, as harmless as any other kind of fantasy we might engage in. Aren't they?

But all fantasies, whatever they may be and whatever form they might take, can still have consequences—just like anything else in our lives. Then we quickly find out that the consequences are very real, when fantasy and reality change places, when time off turns into time too freely spent, and the break extends well past its usual limit to be acted out in The Twilight Zone.

ONE

Another night, another totally disheartening failure in bed.

Still, Ben kept trying to do it. He tried for hours.

He tried to do it in just about every position he could manage, with no success whatsoever.

Then he tried them all again, every single one of them, just in case he had been doing something wrong the first time through.

After that, he got desperate and tried to do it with his eyes closed.

Then he got really desperate and tried to do it blindfolded—literally.

The blindfold had been his fiancée's suggestion. Samantha had told him doing it that way always worked for her when all else failed. She had also claimed that it had the added advantage of being both cheaper and safer than resorting to prescription medicine, no matter how reliable everyone else claimed it was.

At distressing moments like this, Sam would sometimes take the opportunity to remind him of where she stood on the issue of medication, with only the extremely rare exception, virtually all pills could be at the very most only a quick fix for symptoms.

But none of them was really helping you, Sam had said, because what you actually had to do was address the more serious issues that caused the symptoms in the first place and there wasn't a pill in the world that had been designed to do anything so constructive.

What was even worse, though, was that simply treating your symptoms, no matter how unfortunate, by tossing pills down your throat tended to encourage you to go on ignoring those serious issues. You would take more pills instead of facing your problems head on and dealing with them in a constructive, proactive way.

Besides, you always seemed to run out of pills just when you needed them most. Then you would have to hop out of bed in the middle of the night—and it was always the middle of the night, wasn't it? Throw on your clothes and drive all over town looking for a twenty-four hour pharmacy.

That was not the sort of thing that she called a miracle cure or even a quick fix, Sam had said. The only thing she called that was a major pain in the ass.

Privately, Ben had been extremely doubtful despite Sam's impressive track record. Which was to say, she had certainly been right about a lot of other things—maybe even most things. Without a doubt, she was one very smart lady, which was one of the reasons Ben loved her so much to begin with.

But while doing it blindfolded may have had a one hundred per cent success rate for her, it did nothing for him. It certainly didn't help his concentration. Instead of shutting out any and all distractions, it became a distraction itself. Trying to do anything with his eyes covered made him feel too insecure and vulnerable.

It just was not going to work for him and that was that.

Exasperated, he tore off the sleep mask, glanced at the clock on the nightstand and then rolled onto his back to stare up at the ceiling in the dark bedroom, wishing he had ignored Sam's advice for once and stopped at a drugstore to pick up some sleeping pills.

Hell will be like this, he thought bleakly. Night after night after night without sleep. This had to be where the expression "No rest for the wicked" had come from.

He rolled over onto his left side and gave his pillow a couple of half-hearted slaps. But was he, Benjamin Baker, twenty-eight and recently promoted to senior photo editor for *Brash* magazine, really and truly that wicked?

His gaze wandered to the clock: 3:27am. That made it one whole minute later than the last time he had looked.

Yes, apparently he really was that wicked. Maybe even worse.

Ben sighed heavily as he pulled the covers all the way up to his neck and almost immediately kicked them off. Finally, he did the one thing he had been trying to avoid even more than looking at the time again. He rolled over onto his right side so that he was facing Samantha.

She was lying with her back to him, still as deeply asleep as she had been all night, almost since her head had hit the pillow beside him. Whatever chance he might have had of even just dozing lightly was unequivocally wiped out by the sight of the gently rolling landscape of her body under the covers.

Then, perhaps in response to a fleeting but pleasant dream, she sighed softly without waking, which made Ben decide that the whole business of sleep itself was overrated and a blatant misuse of free time. Whenever you were lucky enough to have a few hours to yourself, it was far better to spend them in the kind of activities that were a hell of a lot more gratifying than a periodic burst of rapid eye movements.

He raised himself up on one elbow and looked down at his fiancée's sleeping profile. His soon-to-be-wife, Samantha Ross. God, she was beautiful and it seemed to him as if she got even more beautiful every time he looked at her. Her luxurious dark hair, her perfect, porcelain skin, her features— exotic dark eyes set in a heart-shaped face with exquisite bone structure. She had that elusive and much-prized quality he had always called class, the kind of elegance associated with aristocracy. And at the same time, Sam had the most sensuous and sexiest lips he had ever seen, or fantasized about, or kissed, or fantasized about kissing.

And when he considered her from the neck down...

Great idea, Ben decided as a pleasurable haze filled his mind; he would consider her from the neck down right now, with enthusiasm and in great detail, and for a very long period of time. He slipped an arm around her waist and began to nuzzle her neck. Samantha stirred, smiling as she made a soft, happy sound.

Ben slid his hand down her side to her hip and moved on from there as she rolled over to face him. Her half-open eyes glinted up at him in the dark.

"Ben?" she asked in a sleepy, sexy whisper.

"Mmmm," he said into her neck.

"Ben?" A little louder now, and not quite as sleepy-sounding as before.

He said "Mmmm," again and went on nuzzling her neck while he caressed her.

"Ben," she sighed. "What do you think you're doing?"

"Shhh. This is a dream," he told her as he lifted his head and began to kiss her face. "It's just a beautiful dream..."

She caught his hand beneath the covers. "It doesn't feel like a dream."

"Ah, but it is." Freeing his hand, Ben put one leg over both of hers and rolled her over on her side to face him. "I'm not really doing this," he added, pulling her nightgown down from her shoulder so he could kiss the bare skin. "Or this... Or even this. And I'm certainly not doing this. I'm not doing anything at all, not a thing."

Did this nightgown have some kind of fastenings, or was it one that she just slipped over her head? He tried his hardest to remember.

"I'm sound asleep, just like you," he went on. "The two of us, we're really both sound asleep and nobody is doing anything."

He hoped this was one of the gowns that just had some kind of fastenings, buttons or ties; then he could just undo everything and—

Samantha pushed him away firmly.

"Benjamin Baker, you are not sound asleep and neither am I," she said, obviously wide awake as she sat up and pulled her nightgown back into place. "And this is not a dream."

"Then let's just pretend it is," Ben said pleadingly and tried to pull her down close to him again.

"Ben. In case you've forgotten, we agreed." She pushed his arm aside and turned away from him to lie down with her back to him again. "No more sex until we get married."

So much for that scheme. He should have known she wouldn't fall for it, he thought as he stared unhappily at the contours of her body under the covers. After all, she definitely hadn't fallen for it last night, or the night before that, or the night before that, or any other night when he had tried it.

What made him think that tonight would actually turn out any differently in spite of this unbroken string of failures was beyond all understanding, especially his own. The triumph of optimism over common sense, perhaps? Or maybe just naked desperation; no pun intended, but obvious and appropriate all the same. The only thing he knew was that he had to try something and he was not quite ready to concede defeat yet.

"Um, just give me a little memory-jogger here, Sam. When did we agree to that again?" he asked with a plaintive note in his voice that was sincere and unforced.

Samantha rolled over to face him. As surprised as he might have been, he wasn't too astonished to make the most of the opportunity by kissing her passionately. She surprised him further by kissing him back with equal enthusiasm, just long enough to rouse his hopes to the same level as his passion before she gently pushed him away again.

"This is going to make the wedding night special," she insisted. "It'll be like everything's new again, like we're starting over."

"In that case, why are we procrastinating? Why don't we start over right now?" Ben reached out for her again. "My name's Ben. And your name is?"

"Ben."

"Your name is Ben, too?" he babbled, hoping she wouldn't notice where his hand was. "What a coincidence!"

She removed his hand as he began caressing her. "We are not going to do this," she informed him with no-nonsense finality. "Didn't you give Father Brendan your word?"

He made a pained face.

"Well? Didn't you?" she prodded.

"Truthfully?" He gave her a deeply apologetic look from under his brows. "I had my fingers crossed."

"Fingers crossed. Oh, that's a good one." Samantha's sigh was long and weary. "I sometimes wonder how committed you are to all this."

"To all what?" asked Ben, honestly mystified and a little bit alarmed.

"To us getting married." There was an edge of impatience in her voice now.

"Hey, I'm committed, I'm committed," he said quickly. "I proposed, didn't I?"

Immediately, she softened. "Yes, you did. And very sweetly too," she said, smiling at him happily.

"Well, there you have it." He lifted her hand to his lips and then started kissing his way up her arm. "So maybe you could throw me a bone," he said, between kisses. "Once in a while? Now and then? Here and there? Or how about just this once? Hmm?"

As he passed her elbow, he looked up to see how she was reacting. When he saw the expression on her face, he let go of her arm and drew back.

"Okay, okay," he said and sighed mournfully. "No sex for six months."

Still staring at him with the same expression, she didn't answer.

"This is a test. Right?" he added. "Right?"

She remained silent.

Time to admit defeat, he told himself with enormous reluctance. "Don't worry, Sam. I'll pass," he promised her. "I really will. And with flying colors. You'll see." He lay down again on his back and stared up at the ceiling, wondering if he was going to be the only man in recorded history to die of enforced celibacy. "That is, if I don't explode first," he added.

"You are not going to explode," Samantha promised him in a soothing voice. She looked down at him fondly for a long moment and then cuddled up close to him so she could lay her head on his chest.

He responded immediately by making a noise like a bomb whistling through the air and then blowing up as it hit the ground. It was remarkably authentic considering he had not even attempted to make that kind of sound effect since back in the days when he and his best friend had waged daily military campaigns with an invisible army of thousands in the park at the end of their street. Back when his age had been in single digits. Perhaps it was his knowing firsthand how it felt to be on the brink of detonation that made up for his lack of practice.

After some unmeasured period of time, he realized that Samantha had gone peacefully back to sleep while he was lying there staring at the ceiling like a plank of wood with eyes.

No, no—he didn't have that quite right. He *was* a plank of wood with eyes. And he might as well get used to this new incarnation because there wasn't a damned thing he could do about it.

The silly boy, he had probably had the sleep-mask on for all of five minutes, Samantha thought as she settled in comfortably with her head on Ben's chest. Possibly not even that long but five minutes at the very most, even though she had told him more than once that you had to give it a lot longer than that. Of course, that was an improvement over the last time he had tried using the sleep-mask. He had only managed to keep it on for a grand total of a minute and a half before he had started complaining that it wasn't working.

She had had to explain to him—for what seemed like the ten billionth time—that sensory deprivation didn't work instantly, any more than any other highly rational solution to a problem, no matter what it might happen to be, whether it was getting a good night's sleep or ending world hunger.

But then, she couldn't even get the silly boy to stop calling it a blindfold, for heaven's sake. All those things that he, being a man, would associate with being blindfolded were no doubt only making the problem even worse than it already was.

Men—was there a single one among them who wasn't both his own worst enemy and favorite plaything?

Such big babies.

Of course, that was also part of what made them so adorable. They didn't call it "boyish charm" for nothing, after all. But good God, they could be so high maintenance. In every respect.

She had gone over the rationale behind the six months of pre-wedding abstinence to Ben more than once, but judging from his behavior, it had yet to take. And that certainly wasn't because the man was stupid. Every time she went through it and broke it down for him, he seemed to understand what she was saying.

Nor was he insensitive. Quite the opposite, in fact, which had been somewhat of a surprise, as her initial impression had been that he was a bit lacking in that area. Or, she had suspected, it might be more than just a bit, after all he was the senior photo editor at a men's magazine. Dirty pictures, hel-lo! But after she had gotten to know him better, she found out she had been quite wrong about him in that department.

One of the other things she liked so much about him besides his sensitivity, however, was the fact that he didn't simply lust after women, he genuinely liked them. And he liked them a lot.

Of course, any man who didn't have some special affection for women would have had severe problems in Ben's line of work. But with Ben, it went much further than a mere fondness for images of the unclothed female form.

Ben not only liked women, he also liked everything about women. He liked the whole idea of women, took pleasure in their company, and as far as she could tell, literally couldn't live without them. He appreciated women and respected them, which as far as Samantha was concerned made him perceptive, intelligent and sensible as well as sensitive.

A man who loves women will always love you, as her daddy had once advised her so many years ago.

So perhaps it really was much too unfair of her to make him go without for such a long period of time. Depriving a man like Ben who loved women so much, it was hardly surprising that he couldn't sleep. It was a wonder that the poor baby could do anything at all. God, he had to be going through pure hell.

Poor baby. Poor, poor baby!

A ghost of a smile played on Samantha's lips as she fell asleep again.

He would get over it. Eventually.

TWO

As was so often the case, the first person Ben saw the next morning as he got off the elevator on the twenty-fifth floor where the *Brash* offices were located was one of the ten most gorgeous women in the world, at least as the Top Ten List stood as of nine-thirty am.

Actually, he almost collided with her as he was heading for the receptionist's desk, only barely managing to stop himself in time. Just his rotten luck, he thought as he stuttered something that was trying to be both "Excuse me" and "Hi, there, I'm Ben, please let me be your devoted slave forever at the same time."

It would not have been a particularly forceful collision, just a minor bump that would have affected her nowhere nearly as much as it did him. Of course, he always considered it a pleasure to bump into a beautiful woman, whether it was literally or just figuratively. He didn't mind being bowled over.

But even as he was wishing the lovely lady with the long, shiny brown hair and green eyes and generous mouth had knocked him flat on his back and then fallen down on top of him as well, he was reminding himself that he was no longer available for that kind of happy accident and the only thing he should have been thinking about right now was his upcoming wedding to Samantha.

Wow, that was quite a mouthful, he thought. And so was the pretty lady gracefully sidling past him and out of the door. As luck would have it, she was followed by yet another of this morning's ten most beautiful women in the world. This particular knock out was a little bit taller, with perfect deep brown skin and exotic, almond-shaped eyes. Everything else about her was very nicely shaped, too.

Collision was not quite such a near thing with her, which Ben could not help feeling disappointed about. Not that he was supposed to be wishing that beautiful young women would knock him off his feet, he reminded himself again. Now that he and Samantha had agreed they were committed to each other, he had no business being in a reclining position in the presence of any other woman.

On the other hand, maybe if he were lying on the floor he might finally get some sleep. Lying on the floor alone, that was. Like that old saying by whomever goes, no rest for the wicked, Ben told himself as he made his way toward the receptionist's desk.

Naturally, a third member of this morning's ten most beautiful women in the world was sitting in the waiting area with her long legs crossed, leafing idly through a back issue of the magazine. As Ben strode past, she looked up and gave him a smile even brighter and friendlier than that of the first two women.

Ben knew she was a model who had come in for an interview which she hoped would lead to a pictorial feature. This was something that would have been obvious to Ben even if he hadn't seen the portfolio case propped up against the side of her chair. All the beautiful women who came in to be interviewed made a point of giving everyone who walked through the reception area bright, friendly smiles, just on the off chance that they might turn out to be someone important.

This was not something that made Ben think any less of them. He just happened to be one of the few who truly understood how tough they had it in the modeling business since he made his living by being one of the people responsible for making it so tough on them. While he would not have traded jobs with anyone else in the world (or almost anyone), he was sensitive enough to feel some regret at having to be one of the people who made the lives of beautiful women more difficult.

But he also knew better than to take any of those bright, friendly smiles personally. Not that they looked especially artificial or insincere. After all, these women were professional smilers. They all knew what they were doing, each and every one of them. In Ben's case, those smiles would be completely genuine and heartfelt when the ladies found out he was the guy responsible for the decision as to which photos would go into an issue of the magazine and which would be returned with a neutral apology and sincere best wishes for future success.

It was just that at his age and level of experience, he was no longer so easily dazzled. Well, it was that and Samantha. All right, it was mostly Samantha, "mostly" in this particular instance being a synonym for "virtually all." If he were going to be perfectly honest, which he might as well be.

Samantha was not a model, had no aspirations in that area, and in truth, had never entertained any, in spite of the fact that she was without a doubt, the most beautiful woman Ben had ever met in his life. And that was not merely the judgment of a man who was so smitten with a woman that the only way he could see her was through the goggles of love. Most of the people Ben had introduced her to had assumed that Sam was a model and that the two of them must have met during an interview at *Brash*.

He got a real kick out of seeing everyone's reaction when he explained that the gorgeous Samantha was actually a high-level computer scientist with the Fantadyne Corporation and, according to highly-respected and expert sources such as Cnet.com, MSNBC, and a certain Mr B*ll G*t*s, one of the country's leading programmers in dynamic three-dimensional virtual reality. To be dating and then to be engaged to this remarkable woman whose extraordinary beauty was exceeded only by her genius-level intellect had changed Ben's life more dramatically than just about anything else that had happened to him since the onset of puberty.

For one thing, he had a whole new perspective on relationships, or rather, what he had once thought of as relationships. Compared to what he had with Samantha, all of his previous attachments had been about as deep and meaningful as cocktail-party chatter. Life in general seemed to have opened up as well, becoming more interesting, more vivid, more stimulating; heavy on the stimulating. Being with Samantha made him feel more actively alive.

But if the real, completely unadorned, stripped-naked truth were to be told, Sam was also an enormous boost to his ego on every level and in every way. Going out with a stunning model on his arm wasn't exactly mission impossible, or even mission terribly difficult for him or for most of the guys who worked at *Brash*. Of course, they all would have bitten out their tongues before they would have admitted such a thing but they all knew it, each and every one of them.

Another thing they all knew at *Brash* but felt compelled to leave unmentioned was the fact that most people would assume that their fortuitous choice of career was pretty much the only reason gorgeous women would even give them the time of day. Ben himself had always preferred to think that while maybe that was a fair description of the way things worked for a few of the guys, it was not at all true in his case. He liked to believe that he had enough going for him in the way of sex appeal and personality that beautiful women would find him attractive for reasons that were completely unrelated to the progress of their developing careers.

At the same time, he was intelligent enough to know that all the other guys at *Brash* were thinking exactly the same thing, and that this was yet another hot topic that was never going to come up even hypothetically in conversation around the figurative water cooler.

But then Samantha had walked into his life and changed everything just by being who and what she was—so much more than an incredibly beautiful face. Not to mention her body (oh God, that body). You could see how extraordinary she was just by looking at her, Ben thought, but not just by her physical beauty. It was the way she carried herself and the manner with which she regarded the world around her, the cool reserve that never deserted her yet at the same time never made her seem cold and remote.

It had only taken a few minutes of conversation with her for Ben to understand that she was something very special, and unless he had something on the ball, he would never be able to hold her attention for longer than a few minutes, if that. He had discovered that to have a woman like Samantha involved with him in a serious way was a heady experience. When she had agreed to marry him, he had been happier than he had ever been in his life.

He had also been floored and deep down, he still was. Once in a while, an odd chill would touch the edge of his mind and suggest that none of what he had with this extraordinary woman was real. But then he would find himself lying in bed next to Samantha, tossing and turning, unable to sleep and trying to think of ways to persuade her to change her mind about the period of pre-wedding celibacy she had gotten him to agree to. That was when he knew without a doubt that everything in his life was all very real. He could not have made something like this up if he'd tried.

Now that he and Samantha were together, he had found that he was less inclined to eye hot young models in quite the way he had before. Not as if they were hot young models who made him hot in the way that they made the readership of *Brash* hot. But thanks to recent developments, he seemed to be making a return to his old habits.

The enforced celibacy Samantha had instituted between them was definitely taking its toll on his perspective as well as his behavior. All it took was a few standard hotties smiling at him and boom!—he was a total basket case. All right, maybe not a total basket case. But from the way he was staring at this woman and her long legs right now, any casual observer might have gotten the impression that he felt it was his duty to make her believe that he was a total basket case.

"Hi," he said a little desperately, hoping his smile looked more professional than dazzled. He finally managed to wrench his gaze from her only to find himself nose to nose (or more precisely, front to front) with a blonde surfer-girl type near the reception desk. She also gave him a bright, happy-to-see-you smile that began to interfere with his ability to walk and remember his own name.

"Hi," he told her as he backed away, almost stumbling as the nearly irresistible urge to stop and get better acquainted with her fought with the equally powerful impulse to run like a greyhound and lock himself in his office. If only his office had had a lock.

Smiling back at her helplessly, he finally managed to get himself turned around and then nearly bumped into three more beautiful models who were about to check in with the receptionist.

"Excuse me," he pleaded, suddenly finding himself surrounded. He had to hold onto the edge of the receptionist's desk as if it were the only thing keeping him afloat in the middle of a turbulent ocean.

The receptionist was a forty-ish knockout named Ruby Pandiscio who had been on the job for about six months. She was highly skilled at directing traffic and dealing with the quirky staff, and when it came to handling the gorgeous models who descended on them every working day, she was nothing short of a diplomatic genius; and that included the more highly-strung ladies who might put on a good show of being relaxed but were given away by their white knuckles.

Ruby seemed to be paying little attention to him and she said nothing to him directly, but Ben could tell that she found his current predicament highly amusing.

"Hey, there," he said, nodding at a petite brunette with bright blue eyes. She had a cute little chin that seemed to be begging him to take it between his thumb and forefinger so he could tilt her face up and kiss her.

No. He wasn't supposed to think of things like that, he told his brain.

His brain replied with the information that it, not he, was in charge of the thinking while everything else was his responsibility, thank you, and that was just the natural order of things.

Just his luck to have a brain with a mind of its own, Ben thought as the woman made a small move toward him, offering her hand and starting to say something. He couldn't help drawing away with a slight flinch, bumping into a pleasantly firm presence behind him.

"Hi, there!" he blurted, jumping back as if she had burned him—which she had, in a way—and knocked against a second woman. Or rather, he knocked against a part of her that he wished he hadn't been able to identify, didn't dare look at, and now couldn't stop thinking about.

From the way she brushed her shoulder-length, pale blonde hair back from her shoulders, he knew she wasn't going to take offense at this minor accident.

"Ho, there!" he added with a nervous laugh as a third woman smiled a warm greeting at him. This one was the worst of all. He had to force himself to stare fixedly at the spot between her eyebrows because it was the only way to keep himself from staring fixedly at the long, sexy bare midriff on display between her tiny bandeau top and her low-rise jeans. He did not dare allow himself to look at all that supple, naked and excruciatingly nearby flesh; otherwise he might not be able to stop himself from slipping his arms around it. Her, rather.

Even worse, the lady with the great abs did not seem as if she would have been terribly inclined to put a stop to this, judging from the way she was eyeing him. He already knew that he could expect no help from his brain, either. Damn, but it was getting harder all the time. Life as a whole, and certain other things in particular.

Ben snatched both hands behind his back and used the weight of his body to trap them against the desk. He could hear Ruby Pandiscio behind him chuckling deep in her throat.

"I, uh," he floundered. "I—uh, yes, I work here. I do, in fact, work here."

Of course, all the models wanted to shake his hand now, which was bad, very bad. If they touched him, he wouldn't have a chance. He would simply explode, melt down and die, leaving behind nothing more than a stain on the carpet to be steamed out by the janitorial staff after business hours.

He looked up at the skylight as if that might actually cause some kind of helpful sign or wonder to suddenly appear out of nowhere. Something like a rope ladder dangling from a helicopter, for instance.

Nothing appeared, not even a bird.

"I'm, ah, senior photo editor here at the, uh, the whaddayacallit—the magazine," he babbled at the women with only a vague idea of what actually might be coming out of his mouth.

His despair close to total now, he turned a pleading gaze to Ruby Pandiscio on her throne behind the desk although he didn't have the faintest idea of what she could possibly have done to help him out short of hitting the fire alarm.

For her part, Ruby pretended that she had forgotten he was even there at all as she murmured, "*Brash* magazine, how may I direct your call?" into the microphone of her headset.

As Ben stared at the models who were now standing side by side in front of him, he felt as if he were looking at an insurmountable wall of beauty. He was practically like the poor bastard in that famous story by Edgar Allan Poe: "The Cask of Amontillado." Only in this case, he was being walled up alive with beautiful women instead of bricks.

Beautiful women and their navels, he added to himself. There was the one with the bare midriff, of course, but while the other two were a bit more covered, their cute little innies were also on display for the world in general to see and for him in particular to admire.

"If you have any photos you'd like me to look at," Ben told the models and their belly buttons as he held onto the desk and tried as hard as he could to look casual while he backed slowly away from them, "I'd be very happy—very, very happy—to, ah... look... at, uh, you know... anything you've got."

The women were all even more delighted with him for this wonderful offer and hefted their port-folios by way of letting him know that this was definitely his day to be very, very happy because they just happened to have photos they wanted him to look at.

Fortunately for Ben, they had to step back to do so which opened up a space just large enough for him to dart through. He sprinted all the way to his office without looking back.

At its heart, *Brash* was, first and foremost, a men's magazine in the original, classic sense of that term, ie, it published photos of gorgeous, mostly nude women and advertisements from companies who also wanted a great deal of exposure and were will-ing to pay a fortune for the privilege.

Each issue of the magazine was carefully designed and laid out so that these two crucial and indispensable elements could be presented as beautifully as possible. Once those two things were taken care of, any space left unoccupied was filled in with whatever amount of text was necessary to give each ad a reasonable area of exclusive display. Competitors tended to object when they found themselves too close together.

Besides being a man with a fondness for photos of beautiful women, the founder of the magazine, now sadly deceased, had also been well-informed and well-read with a lively and curious intellect. As a result, the text filling the areas between the photos and the advertisements was, more often than not, worth reading.

Part of this was due to the fact that high advertising revenues allowed *Brash* to pay writers as much as it paid models. Not that it actually did pay anything of the sort. It actually paid writers only a fraction of what it paid beautiful, naked women to pose for photos. But it could have.

Even so, that fraction was still substantially greater than the rates offered by most other markets and each year, there was a token cost-of-living increase that in reality fell laughably short of the actual cost of living. Of course, the writers themselves were unaware of any of these discrepancies. Accustomed as they were to settling for much smaller amounts of money, it never entered their minds to question anything. The only thing any of them wondered about was how to sell to *Brash* more often.

This was why the department responsible for the smallest amount of the magazine's content was just as busy as any other area of *Brash*, and more often than not even busier.

Ben could not think of any time when he had run into anyone from editorial who wasn't literally running somewhere wild-eyed with panic—usually down to the production department to insert a correction and usually about ten seconds before it would be too late. It was Ben's opinion that the crew in editorial really had to work much too hard for a living, and he wasn't alone. This sentiment was shared by everyone else at *Brash*, including the editorial department.

Thus, whenever he felt the inclination to complain about his job, Ben would think of all those poor bastards in editorial, chained to their desks in a rat's-maze arrangement of cubicles reading through reams of text without so much as a single photograph to break things up. All they did day in and day out, week after week, month after month, was try to dig their way out from under an ever-growing mountain of text. That was it. That was all they ever did because it was all their job description said they could do.

Except maybe they took a break now and then so they could pray that medical science would find a cure for eyestrain in their lifetime.

Of course, it wasn't like Ben didn't suffer from a little eyestrain himself now and then, especially after a particularly long day of looking at pictures. But what pictures! Definitely worth getting eyestrain over!

Plus, he had the pleasure of working in especially nice surroundings. *Brash*'s late and sincerely lamented founder had paid top dollar to keep the best industrial designers in the country on retainer. Part of the reason was simply to provide an aesthetically-pleasing working environment for the employees. With the exception of the poor bastards down in editorial, of course. All they ever did was read, an activity for which they hardly needed an environment at all, let alone an aesthetically-pleasing one.

However, *Brash*'s founder had also felt it was just as important to impress the hell out of any and all visitors to the premises, whether they were bike couriers, account executives or beautiful women. But especially beautiful women, since they tended to get a lot more naked a lot more quickly when they were impressed with the surroundings.

What this meant was that every five to seven years, the staff could expect to suffer through a somewhat extended period of inconvenience due to substantial redecoration and/or re-arrangement (except, as previously mentioned, for the editorial department). The latest round had concluded about four months ago but for Ben the novelty had yet to wear off. Everything still looked and felt brand new to him, his office included.

As classy and appealing as the new décor was, it really had taken some getting used to, and Ben still wasn't terribly sure when he was going to feel completely acclimatized. Having an office with translucent glass walls and a mostly transparent door made him feel a little on the exposed side. Although it wasn't a total loss of privacy, as it turned out. Since the walls were only translucent, you couldn't actually see through them. So it was really not as if he had to spend eight or more hours a day at work in a fish bowl or on display in a store window.

But from outside in the hallways you could see shapes and movement, so it was usually possible to tell at a glance whether people were actually in their offices or not. This feature was extremely inconvenient for those times when you might want to slip out early without letting anyone else know. On the other hand, it did give you some advance warning if someone was waiting in your office for you, knowledge that was often useful or at least wouldn't do you any harm.

Ben was surprised to see that there was someone sitting behind the desk in his office this morning. But then he remembered that Garrett Wilson had mentioned he would be coming by early to do some kind of quick, after-care diagnostic on the computer for him. Just as a personal favor, from an alpha computer geek to his poor, technologically-challenged friend, as Garrett himself put it.

Sure enough, it was Garrett, who looked up briefly from whatever complicated thing he was doing on the keyboard as Ben came in.

"Have you seen the women out there?" Ben asked him, feeling only too glad of the company, especially since it was the sympathetic male variety. He paused for a moment to peer back down the hallway through the glass door, hoping that none of the women had followed him while at the same time wishing that every single one of them had. "Well? Have you?"

Garrett took a bite of a powdered doughnut without saying anything. Ben could not remember ever seeing him at work on a computer without a powdered doughnut close to hand. Powdered doughnuts seemed to be as much a part of his equipment as any of the other tools he used. And, in Garrett's case, they were about as fattening. As far as Ben could tell, the only way he ever gained weight was when he let his unruly black hair get a bit too long and wild. Like it was now.

The longish hair usually meant Garrett was on one of his periodic woman-hunts. The ladies, he had explained to Ben once, really liked long curly hair on certain guys, alpha geeks in particular. So Ben was pretty sure that Garrett had seen the women out in the reception area; they would have been impossible to miss. But Garrett had probably seen them in much the same way he had seen the women on numerous framed covers of *Brash* back issues decorating the walls in Ben's office, women who were wearing quite a lot less than the models in reception and looking unabashedly pleased about it, ie, without a whole lot of interest.

That was the thing about Garrett. For all that he claimed to be on the lookout for a nice lady to hook up with, preferably someone hot, what put him at a distinct disadvantage was the fact that his idea of hot was a naked motherboard. Or at least it had seemed that way to Ben in the dozen years they had been friends.

It wasn't a perspective that Ben could ever have subscribed to or even understood, but he was happy enough that Garrett did, if for no other reason than because Garrett had known Samantha longer than he had. In fact, Garrett had introduced them to each other.

At the time, Ben had understood immediately that Garrett and Samantha had known each other for quite a long time and were fairly close friends. His first thought was to wonder exactly how close they were. It was a great relief to find out that the only passion they shared had to do with computers and Garrett was nowhere near as close to this beautiful woman as he was hoping to get.

THREE

Later on, after his hopes had been realized, it occurred to him that if his friend Garrett had been even a little less fascinated with hardware than he was with females, it might have been a lot more difficult for him to get Samantha's attention. It would also have been a lot more problematical. Competing with a close friend for a woman was the sort of thing that was always extremely hazardous to a friendship. Having known Garrett for as long as he had, Ben wouldn't have enjoyed taking that risk.

Not that something so unfortunate would necessarily have stopped him, of course. He simply wouldn't have enjoyed it.

But to his way of thinking, when a woman like Samantha came into your life, giving her up was not an option. He would have given up almost anything else before he could have brought himself even to consider giving up Samantha. He would have given up his car or even sworn off driving altogether in favor of public transportation if she had insisted on it. Thank God he hadn't had to agree to anything of the sort, but he could see himself doing it for Sam's sake. He would have given up eating meat, if she had wanted him to. He would have given up beer and/or any other form of alcohol.

Hell, he would have given up air.

He was now beginning to suspect that it would have been easier to give up any of those things than the sacrifice he was currently making at her request.

Strangely enough, of everything he might have imagined she would ask him to forego, at least temporarily, sex was the last thing that would have occurred to him. Sam had gone out of her way to let him know that she had absolutely no complaints about that part of their relationship—making use of unambiguous terms like the best—as well as "no, really, I'm not kidding, positively the best ever and the only man I'll ever want for the rest of my life."

Given that sort of feedback, the one request he had never expected to hear her make, in bed or out of it, was celibacy.

"Have you seen them?" Ben asked again. "There are nines out there. There are nine-point-nines. There are whole tens. No, forget tens. I think I even saw a twelve."

"Uh-huh." Garrett finished the last bite of the doughnut and flicked a small cloud of powdered sugar from his fingers into the air. It fell like a fine snow onto Ben's desktop. "You and Samantha still not having sex, eh, big boy?"

Ben glanced down at himself and winced. "Is it that obvious?"

"I feel your pain, chief," Garrett said, his voice flat and unemotional as he turned his attention back to the computer screen. He typed something rapidly on the keyboard and then nodded, looking pleased. "Meanwhile, back here at the ranch, that was one nasty virus that attacked you," he added, real feeling returning to his voice. "Good thing you did as I told you to for once and backed up your hard drive. Otherwise you really would have been screwed, and way beyond anything I could have done to help you. Ninety-nine per cent of all computer disasters would actually be non-events if people would just take five lousy minutes to back up the hard drive."

Ben closed his eyes for a moment, thinking he should probably tell Garrett not to use words like screwed and hard drive right now.

It took him a few moments of carefully focused concentration before he was finally able to walk again, albeit still with some slight discomfort. He managed to make his way over to the desk where Garrett, oblivious to his difficulties, was busily fishing through his tech bag. Ben was about to ask him what he was looking for when he pulled out a jewel case with an unlabeled DVD in it, which he held up briefly for Ben to see before popping the disc out and slipping it into the computer.

"So, what's that. Some more of your famous post-virus computer after-care?" Ben said before he could think better of it. Most of the time, he made it a strict policy never to ask Garrett about anything that had to do with the function, maintenance or repair of any computer, his own in particular, if he could possibly avoid it. This was because Garrett would be only too glad to tell him, in detail and at great length, and, of course, Ben would have absolutely no idea of what he was talking about.

Once in a great while, however, Garrett would feel the strange need to take it upon himself to make an actual attempt at explaining something to him even though he had not asked. The only reason Ben could think of for Garrett doing such a thing was his relationship with Samantha—which was to say, somehow, Garrett had gotten the extremely mistaken impression that something of Samantha's techie nature had finally rubbed off on him.

Ben always did his forceful and unambiguous best to discourage Garrett from expounding on anything even vaguely concerned with computers by sticking his fingers in his ears and singing loudly. As far as he was concerned, any and all issues, facts, procedures, useful tidbits, amusing anecdotes, apocryphal stories and outright jokes related to computers were a matter of need-to-know.

Or, in his case, did not need to know—which was to say, since Garrett and Samantha knew about computers, it meant that Ben most definitely did not.

At the moment, his friend was pushing a very complicated-looking high-tech piece of equipment at him with more than the usual amount of insistence. Ben took the thing from him with a reluctant frown and looked it over. It was actually a fancy set of goggles, the kind that appeared to be used with the more expensive (and therefore, as far as Ben was concerned, more incomprehensible) variety of computer game.

"What's this?" he asked his friend a bit suspiciously.

"What's what? Oh, you mean this?" Garrett motioned at the hardware and grinned at him. "This is only the best sex you're not having. And it's absolutely, one hundred per cent guilt free." He gave Garrett's hand a small push upward, prodding him to put them on. Even more wary now, Ben took a closer look at them instead.

They were very complicated. All right, these were the full-immersion variety that Garrett was always trying to convince him were so great. Except Ben had never seen any goggles that were quite this fancy or sophisticated. The part meant to go over your eyes was small, sleek, compact; it looked more like something that had come out of the type of research and development laboratory that Sam worked in rather than the latest high-tech toys. Ben handled them gingerly, as if the sensors he could see in the straps might somehow cause them to come alive on their own and try to clamp onto him.

"A virtual sex program?" he said as Garrett reached over and pulled a slender cord out from the framework. "This is a joke, right? I mean, you really are kidding. Aren't you?"

Garrett gave him a smug, knowing look through half-closed eyes.

"Oh, come on." Ben wrinkled his nose in disgust. "Give me a break here, will you? In case you have somehow failed to notice, Garrett old buddy, I'm not sixteen years-old any more. I don't need something like this. I love my fiancée."

"And you make a very cute couple," Garrett agreed, plugging the cord into Ben's computer. "Believe me, all your friends think so, hers and yours both. But trust me, this has nothing to do with Samantha. Sensuous Cindy is the greatest program Fantadyne's ever cooked up."

Ben looked from the goggles to Garrett with a frown. "Fantadyne?" he said, puzzled. "*The* Fantadyne? The one that makes the game simulations? The one that Samantha works for?"

"Give that man a cigar," said Garrett and wiggled his eyebrows, adding, "But I'll bet you anything you care to name that she didn't work on this sucker."

Ben's frown went from puzzled back to suspicious. "So how did you happen to get a hold of it?" he wanted to know.

"Aw, that was easy," Garrett said with exaggerated carelessness. "Easy, peasy, lemon-squeezy, in the words of the prophet. It was none other than Mr Robert Newton himself who financed the entire project."

Ben's suspicious frown vanished as his jaw dropped. "Our Robert Newton, you mean? *Brash*'s dear departed publisher?"

"Give that man another cigar. Frankly, though, I haven't got the faintest idea what you could possibly do with a cigar if you had one," Garrett added with a smirk. "Samantha probably doesn't let you smoke, either. And even if she did, you still wouldn't have a single thing to smoke about in the first place."

He chuckled, hugely pleased with his own wit and then went on quickly as Ben started to say something in protest. "Yes, indeed, that was *Brash* magazine's good old Newton. Man spent millions to finance a crash project to produce what he was hoping would be the perfect sex program. Then the minute it gets good enough to put into beta testing, the poor guy dies of a heart attack." Garrett chuckled again. "But you know what they say—every cloud has a silver lining. Even a dear, departed publishing cloud like Newton. Besides, you've got to admit that it was probably the way he wanted to go."

"Uh-huh," Ben said with a grimace of displeasure. "As fascinating as all of this may be—not to mention lurid, tasteless, and unsavory—I'm afraid I've also got to admit that I'm not real sure it's a whole lot in the way of a truly attractive or compelling recommendation." He looked down at the goggles in his hand again. "And pardon me for mentioning it, but you still haven't answered my question," he added. "How did you get your alpha geek paws on it?"

"No problemo, not for an alpha geek, chief." Garrett shrugged, looking modest. "Or at least, not this alpha geek. I've got a friend on the inside who sneaked me a copy of the beta."

"Okay, I was just curious," Ben told him. "But something else I'm a lot more curious about here. Have you tried this thing?"

"Oh, please." Now Garrett drew himself up with an air of mock dignity and mimed straightening a tie that Ben had never known him to wear. "I live by a code, sir, and in this case I am not referring to binary. I would never kiss and tell. Not this alpha geek."

"Uh-huh," Ben said again, his suspicious expression returning. It was his experience that one-upmanship was in fact the real code that just about every geek, alpha or otherwise, lived by. Any time one of them got lucky in any way, the news was usually all over the Internet in a matter of minutes, and that went double for Garrett.

If a virtual sex program like this had become in any way available to the alpha geek elite—the most alpha of the alphas—then Garrett certainly would not have been the only geek who had gotten access to it. Even if Garrett had for some reason really overcome his natural inclination and managed not to broadcast his good fortune far and wide, it was hard to imagine that any of the other geeks would actually have decided to keep quiet about it as well.

"Oh, come on now, chief," Garrett was saying as he began packing up his equipment. "Just how long have you got left on your sentence now? Six more months of solitary celibate confinement until your wedding night? And still not a chance in hell of parole?"

Yeah, it had definitely been a mistake for him to have confided in Garrett about the little agreement that Samantha had managed to talk him into, Ben thought unhappily. Even as he had been telling Garrett all about it, he had been wondering somewhere in the back of his mind if he might somehow come to regret letting his friend in on that particular bit of information about his private life after all.

But instead of following his better judgment, he had decided that of all the people he was close to, Garrett would have been the last person to give him a hard time about it. Besides the fact that Garrett was his oldest friend and had always shown himself to be trustworthy in the past, there was also the fact that the guy really was an alpha geek and most alpha geeks were acquainted with all kinds of celibacy. Particularly the kind that didn't involve a woman speaking directly to them, even to say no. Or to say anything else. Or even, for that matter, to be in close enough proximity to ignore them in the first place.

Well, chalk up another lesson he'd had to learn the hard way: when it came to matters of sex, no one would show you any mercy. But Ben supposed it could have been worse. His friend might actually have had a girlfriend himself.

Garrett picked up his tech bag and turned to him with an expectant look. Ben only made a pained face at him. "Hey, this is all your decision and no one else's, chief," Garrett said with a shrug. "I'm certainly not going to tell you what to do." His gaze fell on a small scatter of photos on Ben's desk and he helped himself to one of them, tucking it into one of the many pockets on the geek vest he always wore. "Or what not to do, as the case may be."

How about that, Ben thought, staring after his friend as he headed for the door. Apparently Garrett did find a woman now and then whom he thought was more interesting than a naked motherboard to look at after all. Those famous wonders that would never cease had struck yet again.

He knew that what he ought to do was tell Garrett to get his alpha geek ass back over to the computer and get this program, whatever it was, off his hard drive right now. But it seemed that celibacy had had an adverse affect on his reflexes; Garrett was out of the room before Ben could even make a sound.

Oh well. It would have to wait till Garrett's next service call. Which, given the computer's track record of malfunction and downtime, would be fairly soon. But seeing as how the cranky thing happened to be running just fine right now, however, the wiser course of action would probably be for him just to get busy with whatever he had to do and try to accomplish as much as possible before his computer decided it had to start working on its next nervous breakdown.

After all, it wasn't like he could afford to sacrifice any more time to computer maintenance, especially if it wasn't something that absolutely had to be done. If he got any further behind, he was going to end up looking as frantic and bloodshot as one of those poor bastards down in editorial.

And besides, if he did call Garrett back now, he would have been forced to utter the words hard drive aloud himself, which he was pretty sure he couldn't do without losing it completely.

Feeling slightly at a loss, Ben turned back to his computer and saw that the screen was now lit up with the words "Sensuous Cindy" spelled out in orchids, irises, and various other kinds of exotic flowers with highly suggestive shapes.

"Control, alt, delete," he murmured, setting the goggles down next to the keyboard.

The escape sequence was one of the very few bits of computer-related knowledge that he'd gone out of his way not to forget. Although just as soon as someone came up with a single panic button he could press that would perform the same function, he was going to forget that as well, along with all the rest of the computer stuff he didn't remember any more.

As he positioned his fingers on the keyboard and prepared to shut down the program, another line appeared under the flowery title.

Put the goggles on to begin.

Ben hesitated, lifting his fingers from the keys. When it came to instructions, these were pretty generic, and they hadn't presented themselves in the same flowery letters, just a basic typeface. But for some reason, the words felt like a personal message aimed specifically at him.

Hey, you there, Ben Baker, what do you say? How about you put those goggles on right now so we can get our freak on?

Now, as dumb ideas went, that was pretty damned dumb. Actually, it was more than pretty damned dumb. It was major-league damned dumb, dumb enough to be right up there with wearing an aluminum-lined baseball cap to keep satellites from reading your thoughts. Control-alt-delete was the only idea that made any sense at all right now.

But then again, on the other hand…

Ben thought it over. Garrett was probably the only person in a thousand-mile radius who could have undone the considerable amount of damage to his computer from the latest virus. Well, he was the only person Ben trusted to get the job done right, at least. So any program Garrett put on his computer had to be worth taking the time to check out. Even if it was some silly piece of soft-core called Sensuous Cindy.

He grabbed the goggles and put them on quickly before he could think better of it.

FOUR

Computer gaming was one of those things that Ben had never been able to work up much in the way of enthusiasm for.

Even back in the days of his extreme youth, he had not been able to get terribly interested in an activity that would require him to spend long periods of time thumbing a control pad in front of a TV or a computer screen, no matter how good the graphics were. The control pads were kind of flimsy anyway and never worked quite the way you wanted them to even before they got so worn out the buttons gave out altogether.

Then there were the games themselves: they were expensive even when they were on sale at fifty per cent off. And to add insult to injury, at least to Ben's way of thinking, the games in question were most definitely not worth their exorbitant price tag since the graphics were never really all that great. In fact, they weren't even what he would have called good.

People always seemed to be raving about computer game graphics, how they were getting better

all the time but he had never found them to be
even remotely as praiseworthy as everybody else in
the world seemed to think. When it came to the
animation, the old Looney Tunes from the 1930s
were far and away superior to the stiff, blocky
action you got with a computer game—if you could
really even call that stuff "action" in the first place;
Ben certainly couldn't. And that was the crap that
everybody kept trying to tell him was such a
twenty-first century state-of-the-art big deal? Not
hardly.

Ben considered Bugs Bunny a hundred times
more believable than that girl—what was her
name? He could never remember—the one with
the braid and the short-shorts and the big knockers
who went around swinging on ropes and getting
chased by badly-drawn Dobermans.

Hell, Bugs Bunny in a dress, even.

But what he really found most bewildering of all
was the fact that the computer-game chick was
seriously supposed to be hot—which was to say, it
wasn't a joke or a put-on. He had just never been
able to see anything remotely hot or even mildly
warm about her himself. Who on earth could look
at such an obvious cartoon and get aroused? Was
it really just the big cartoon knockers? And if that
was the case, then how incredibly sad was that?

Well, all right, he was willing to grant that big
cartoon knockers would do the job for some guy
shut up in a room who was resigned to the fact that
he was so incurably geeky, he had simply given up
all hope of ever seeing an actual woman's breasts
up close and personal in the real world.

Except even someone that tragic would know he could buy an issue of *Brash*, if he had so much as half a brain cell. So the question remained: what the hell was it with these guys?

It could have been something really simple—like incredibly bad eyesight brought on by long hours sitting in front of a monitor thumbing loose buttons on a piece of crappy plastic. Or maybe it went beyond that. Maybe it was actually some kind of serious brainwashing. Hell, a lot of cults didn't bother to use anything nearly as sophisticated as even a simple videogame and they could have you selling flowers in the airport twenty-four hours after you'd bought one yourself.

Whatever it was, Ben had long ago decided he was not going to have any part of it. To that end, he made sure he ate a lot of carrots for good eyesight, never, ever bought flowers in airports no matter how cheap they were, and paid absolutely no attention to the constant and ever-increasing hype about how computer graphics were getting better and more lifelike all the time.

After all, if there had been any actual truth to that last claim, he thought, then computer-game chicks would have taken over the world already and there would not have been any real, live gorgeous women waiting out in the reception area. And if eliminating the need for the presence of real, live gorgeous women was really the sort of advanced development that all the tech-heads considered progressive or desirable, then as far as Ben was concerned, they could keep it.

At least, that was how he had felt before putting on the goggles.

But if what he was looking at right now constituted the current standard of quality for computer graphics, he thought as he gazed in stunned astonishment at his surroundings, then it wasn't going to be very long at all before every chair in the reception area would be empty for good.

Some years back, one of Ben's old girlfriends had taken him to an Imax theatre and expected him to be impressed. He had been, but not to the degree that she had hoped.

It had simply been a movie blown up to several times the normal size—pretty neat, but not exactly a groundbreaking revolution in cinema. Compared to this, however...

Well, there was no comparison and that was because there simply couldn't be one. It was impossible to compare this to anything except reality itself and at the moment, Ben was not prepared to say for certain that reality would actually have come off as the winner.

The more rational, down-to-earth part of his brain was reminding him that he was in his office at *Brash*, and about to start another workday—a very long workday—of poring over photographs of absolutely gorgeous women. A very, very long workday. Then he would hop in the car and head home to spend the evening with an even more gorgeous woman, the most gorgeous woman he had ever met—a very, very long evening—which would then be followed by a very, very long and mostly sleepless night.

But everything that his rational mind told him was completely overruled by his senses. His senses were telling him in no uncertain terms that he was standing in the middle of a fancy bedroom suite. It was an extremely high-class fancy bedroom suite, the type of accommodation you found at one of those extremely fancy island resorts where the going rate per night was slightly more than the annual budget for a third-world country because it would put you right on your own private beach.

Whenever you felt the urge for a little sun and sea, all you had to do was step out of the door—or in this case, the diaphanous white curtains billowing slightly in a soft, cool breeze—with your sunglasses and your waterproof sunblock.

Neither sunglasses nor waterproof sunblock would be necessary right now, however, as it was night-time.

The sound of the ocean came to him faintly in the candle-lit room. And there sure were a lot of candles. He saw candles on shelves, candles in baskets hanging from the ceiling, candles in wall sconces, candles in freestanding candelabras that were taller than he was. Someone had certainly gone to a lot of trouble for romantic lighting. And someone had gone to even more trouble to make it all look positively realistic, indistinguishable from real life. He wouldn't have believed it if he had not been seeing it for himself.

If Garrett had tried to describe this to him, he would not have believed it for a moment. Hell, he wouldn't have believed it even if Samantha herself had told him about it.

He went over to the nearest freestanding cande-labra for a closer look at one of the candles. Damn, this was really good, he thought, studying it first from one side and then the other. If this was state-of-the-art, then things had really changed a lot. He could remember Samantha talking to him about how hard it was to simulate things like flames or running water and have them look even halfway real. Obviously, they had worked the bugs out. Even when he squinted at the candle flame side-ways, he couldn't see any telltale pixel blocks that would indicate a small breakdown in the resolu-tion. That was really one hell of an accomplishment.

But as amazing as that might be, Ben thought, would it stand up to a real test? He dabbed at the flame with a fingertip.

He burned himself.

The sensation was instant, unmistakable, and more than a little painful, and it startled him so much that he forgot all about checking to see if the fancy graphics had faltered or not. Since when had it become possible to hurt yourself with a com-puter simulation, Ben wondered as he sucked on his wounded finger? Just when had computer graphics become so realistic that the power of sug-gestion could actually achieve such a high level of effect? He would never have believed anything like that could happen, not for a moment.

And even if someone else had claimed it not only could but already had, he would never have believed such a thing could work on him. He wouldn't have tried to claim he wasn't suggestible at all—everybody was, to a certain extent. But to this degree? No way.

All he needed now was an explanation for the blister he could feel coming up on his fingertip.

He then heard a soft rustling noise behind him and turned to see that a gentle wind coming in from the water was making the candles flicker and stirring the diaphanous white curtains.

The curtains suddenly blew open wide enough to reveal what must have been the private beach. A full moon riding high in the dark sky was turning the water silver as the waves rushed up gently on the shore. The curtains billowed some more and fluttered as the wind became a little more forceful. The candles flickered again and began to dance so that the soft light shifted and the shadows in the room rearranged themselves, and all at once, Ben could feel that he was no longer standing there all by himself. Something new—no, someone new—had been added.

But then it seemed to him as though the beautiful young blonde woman standing in front of the softly billowing curtains had actually been there all along. He had simply not been able to see her until the wind from the beach had blown in to make the candles flicker and dance, which in turn had caused the light in the room to change so that the shadows fell differently.

If so, he thought that was one very neat trick even for a computer-generated virtual reality. In any case, it was obvious that this room belonged to her, although judging from the way she was smiling at him, he felt it was safe to assume that she did not regard his unannounced arrival there as an unwelcome intrusion.

That feeling was most definitely mutual, Ben thought, taking in the sight of her. So this was the famous Sensuous Cindy. Apparently. She certainly had not been over-sold. He stared openly at her silky chin-length blonde hair, her large exotic eyes, flawless skin and full lips that demanded to be kissed, her firm, well-shaped and perfectly proportioned body, lithe but not too skinny, It was like encountering someone who comprised all of the best features of the world's most attractive women in the best possible way.

The ten most beautiful women in the world he had seen only a few minutes ago had just experienced a very substantial demotion, he decided, feeling utterly dazzled in a way that he hadn't felt since he had been very young. Sensuous Cindy now occupied all Top Ten spots all by herself. And maybe even the next ten after that.

Unless he was hallucinating, of course. He had to consider the possibility whether he liked it or not. Maybe he really had been hypnotized or brainwashed so that he was now in some weird sort of a waking dream, a state produced by the power of suggestion mixed with a healthy amount of wishful thinking. The only thing was, would a hallucination or a delusion be wearing the red negligee set that happened to be his current favorite item in a certain very well-known catalog? Right down the smallest detail of lace on the bra?

Ben squeezed his eyes shut briefly and opened them again.

The blonde woman was still there and she still looked perfectly real, not to mention perfectly beautiful. Not a hair or a pixel out of place.

Now that he had been confronted by Sensuous Cindy, Ben thought, nothing was ever going to be the same, particularly in his case. He had no other choice, he was going to take back every critical word he had ever spoken about computer graphics. This image—this woman—was most definitely not some sad excuse for a fantasy where a pair of big boobs were supposed to make up for the obvious cartoon quality. Or, rather, the obvious and total lack of any quality.

The Sensuous Cindy program was to all appearances an honest-to-God, living, breathing woman. There was no room for any doubt about that. There couldn't be. The way she looked, the way she moved—every detail was there. He could even see for himself that she was breathing; he could actually see her chest rising and falling as she came toward him.

Of course, he could also see a lot more than that as she walked over to him in her teddy set, including the most interesting fact that she was a natural blonde. Not that he would really have minded if she had been an unnatural blonde, Ben thought dazedly. He had absolutely no problem at all with unnatural blondes, or, for that matter, unnatural redheads, unnatural brunettes, or even, under the right circumstances, the unnaturally and deliberately hairless. Some people might be biased for or against certain features. But not him, not Benjamin Baker. He was not burdened by prejudices of any sort, not in the slightest, no way. And he never would be.

Why, he would never have been able to do his job properly if he'd had that sort of hang-up. The one quality a photo editor for *Brash* needed above all others was the capacity to recognize and appreciate all kinds of beauty.

After all, beauty was always beauty in all its myriad and wondrous varieties, whether it was the dark, exotic and mysterious kind of beautiful woman or Sensuous Cindy's kind—the blonde, curvy, outgoing kind of beautiful woman who was obviously well-adjusted enough to be comfortable with the fact that every heterosexual male with a pulse was going to stare at her until he was distracted by, say, being hit in the face with a sledgehammer.

Or until she got so close that it was simply impossible to see all of her at once. As was the case right now, Ben realized.

Smiling up into his face with undisguised delight, Cindy slipped her slender arms gracefully around his neck, which necessitated his finally removing his wounded finger from his mouth to accommodate her. As stunned as he might have been, he was not so far gone that he had completely forgotten how to behave. It was only good manners to stop sucking your finger when a beautiful woman embraced you. Now if only he could think of some suave thing to say by way of conversation, or even just to let her know he was not actually brain damaged.

But apparently Sensuous Cindy did not have any immediate worries about any possible damage to his brain. Thanks to her out going personality, she was far more concerned with putting him at ease.

"Hi, Ben," she said in a low, sexy voice. "I've been waiting for you."

After a greeting like that, there was no other polite choice for him to make except to kiss her. Any other course of action just would not have been right.

FIVE

Kissing was one of a very few select things that, in Ben's personal opinion, could not be in any way overrated. It was also probably one of the main reasons he had never taken to videogames or similar kinds of things.

He had always liked kissing far too much to spend any more of his free time than he absolutely had to, engaged in activities that were not in some way, related to kissing. Within reason, of course, and if he could possibly help it.

The turning point in Ben's life had come for him in junior high school. He had been in the eighth grade when he had discovered the hitherto unknown (to him) joys of kissing with Faye, a slightly older, more experienced woman of fourteen. Faye had also been a kissing enthusiast, and it so happened that she was one of those girls who had been blessed with lips that were naturally like pillows.

Consequently, Faye's adolescent pout was world-class, easily the stuff of legends—not to mention fantasies—and much sought-after by a large and diverse group of young men ranging from the experienced and discerning ninth-grade make-out artists to the eager and mostly untouched novices just starting junior high.

Ben had always felt thankful that he had had the good fortune to get his first kiss from those extraordinary lips and not from someone like the girl who sat behind him in history class. That particular girl had a crush on him and she had made no secret of it. She was also one of those early bloomers who already wore a bra.

While these were considerations that fell squarely in the plus column of Ben's pubescent check list for what made pretty girls even more attractive, the single, solitary entry in the minus column negated them completely; which was to say, her very unfortunate orthodonture work.

The girl wore braces of the heavy, barbed-wire variety. That alone would have been bad enough, but to make matters worse, her lips were pale, thin little things that did not look like they would be able to offer much in the way of protection from the hardware behind them. And as for slipping her a little tongue—well, the obvious dangers made that idea positively (not to mention excruciatingly) unthinkable.

As the years went by and Ben had grown a little older, he eventually became acquainted with the many other delightful activities that two people could progress to from kissing if they let nature take its course. Once that had happened, he never looked back. After gaining the understanding of what kissing usually led to, he became an even more devoted and enthusiastic kisser, which, in turn, made the women he kissed even more enthusiastic about kissing him.

Most of them told him he was the best kisser they had ever locked lips with and, times being what they were, he was pretty sure he could believe them. For his part, however, Ben had never felt even the slightest inclination to single out any one of them as being the best, even just privately to himself. As far as he was concerned, all of the women he kissed started out excellent and only got better with practice. If there had to be a best, then it was whomever he might have happened to be kissing at the moment.

But as soon as this woman had pressed her lips to his, however, all of that had changed. He felt as if he were now being kissed by the woman who had invented kissing and then, not content to rest her lips on her laurels, she had re-invented it in the new, improved version. There was a distinct possibility, in fact, that this could have been the fabled yet legendary One True Kiss, and the only way he could ever hope to achieve that level of excellence was to practice with this woman for the rest of his life or until the end of days, whichever came last…

Something about the tailend of that thought woke him from whatever semi-hypnotized, semi-enchanted state he was in and gave him just enough strength of will to pull his head back and break free. Sensuous Cindy made nothing in the way of a protest; she only continued to smile up at him with those lovely and incredibly talented lips. Ben felt a wave of dizziness pass through him.

Forgot to breathe, he thought. That's what happened to me, I actually forgot to breathe. Anyone would think I was thirteen years-old again and this is my first time. One kiss—just one—and all of a sudden, a lifetime of experience gets wiped out and I'm reduced to an amateur.

Raising her eyebrows very slightly, Cindy ran the tip of her tongue over her lips and Ben knew she was about to start round two, which he was not certain that he would be able to survive unless he could have a brief time out at least. Any more kissing like that without a break would cause his brain to melt and run out his ears. He had to do something to put her off, at least for a few seconds.

"You…" he said faintly, then had to pause and take a deep breath before he could go on. "You, uh, you taste… uh… great."

"Well, thank you," she purred. "So do you."

She took her arms from around his neck so she could run her hands affectionately over his shoulders and down his arms. Immediately, Ben seized the opportunity to move several steps away from her on the pretense that he was utterly fascinated by the room and he just had to take a look around at everything in it.

"Hey, you know, this is really something," he babbled. "Never seen anything like it myself, not ever. And by that, I mean never, not even once. How is this happening? I mean, how does it work?"

"Well, if you're really that interested, I suppose I could draw you a diagram," Sensuous Cindy said, gliding toward him in a graceful billowing cloud of transparent red negligee. "But it would kinda ruin the mystery. Dontcha think?"

Ben tried to back away from her without actually looking as if he were backing away and tripped over a large throw pillow on the floor. The sensation of losing his balance was realistic enough to make him think he really was falling before he managed to catch himself against a curtained window.

His clumsiness did nothing to discourage Cindy from being sensuous. She kept coming at him in an unbearably sexy slink, keeping her dark-eyed gaze fixed on his face and beaming her sexy, full-lipped smile, which he now thought was beginning to take on an aspect that was more than slightly hungry.

"So, Ben, darling, tell me. Now that I've finally got you alone, what did you have in mind?" she asked him. One hand was now toying with the top fastening of her teddy. "Something naughty? Or something nice?"

The words naughty and nice had never been so imbued with erotic connotations until now. Ben knew he would never be able to think of Santa Claus in the same way again. Or, to be completely honest about it, he would never be able to think of Santa Claus at all, period. Never again for as long as he lived. The association had already become just too bizarre. Not to mention disturbing.

"I, uh—" Ben flattened against the window as Cindy came closer. Some impulse made him pull the curtains around in front of himself as if they could actually offer some protection from her. "I don't, I—"

Cindy paused to smile at him in amusement. She put her hands on the small of her back and took a deep breath. She did it in a very casual way that did not seem at all calculated, and yet was very much a classic pin-up pose. Ben found that the effect was extremely impressive.

Oh, God, he was doomed, he thought and looked down at the material he was clutching so desperately to himself. "Wow, just look at these—uh, these curtains, will you?" he said, rubbing his thumbs on the cloth. "Amazing. Just really amazing! You know, they feel just like silk. How about that, huh?"

Sensuous Cindy stepped closer to him and, without taking her eyes off his, pulled the curtains gently out of his grasp, tossing them aside.

"Did you come here to play with the curtains?" she asked, moving in even closer to him now so she could slide those long, graceful arms around his waist and press her impossibly perfect body against his. "Or did you come here to play with me?"

Well, he certainly could not deny that this was a reasonable question, Ben thought, feeling another wave of dizziness. God, but he needed some breathing space. He needed a time out. If only he could have one, even just for a few moments—

But he could, he realized, suddenly feeling foolish.

He put both hands up to his temples as if he were about to remove a pair of glasses. To his vast and unutterable relief, he could feel his fingers touching the goggles just as vividly as he could feel

Sensuous Cindy touching him. Or, well, almost as vividly, anyway. He gave a quick tug upwards—

—and immediately he found himself sitting behind his desk in his office at *Brash*. Alone.

The suddenness of the change made him jump, which felt a little like he had dropped into his chair from a small height. Damn, this simulation stuff was. It was…

Oh, the hell with it. He had no idea what it was, except that there sure was a lot more to it these days than he had ever suspected. Slightly breathless, he swiveled around to lean his elbows on the desktop, still holding the goggles in both hands. He turned them over and peered at the inside, wondering if Sensuous Cindy was still running or whether his abrupt departure had paused the program like a freeze frame in a movie. There was no image on the lenses, or at least none that he could see from any of several angles he tried.

When it came right down to it, these were just goggles after all, he thought. They were very fancy, high-end, and high-resolution, and most likely far better than anything available even to the hard-core aficionados with deeper than average pockets. But in the end, they were just goggles. Yet when he put them on, somehow he didn't just see an especially vivid movie, he could hear and feel, as well.

He could also smell and taste, he reminded himself, licking his lips while he remembered how Sensuous Cindy had licked hers. And his.

But… with just goggles? Just goggles and nothing else? How the hell could anyone have managed that?

Sure, the power of suggestion could be a much stronger thing than most people realized. There was the placebo effect, for one thing. But even the placebo effect didn't work on everybody the same way. Nor was it really all that reliable. Not everybody who took a placebo felt any effects.

He had always doubted that he himself would. No, not doubted. He was absolutely sure that a placebo would not have affected him in any way. He had never been able to bring himself to believe for a moment that he would have felt anything from a sugar pill just because someone in a white coat claiming to be a doctor had told him he was supposed to.

But still, even if it turned out that he were really a lot more suggestible than he had ever imagined he would be, the situation with the Sensuous Cindy program seemed to be patently impossible. No matter what his eyes saw, he could not bring himself to believe that it would be so convincing to his mind that it could take over all his other senses. As if his whole body were in some weird kind of sensory conspiracy against his brain.

No. No way. That kind of thing just did not happen, not to him and probably not to anyone else. A good pair of simulation goggles—even goggles this good—could not confer something like instant mind control. That was a degree of brainwashing far beyond merely persuading someone to sell flowers at the airport. If something on that level was even possible in the first place, it would have taken a hell of a lot more than a sophisticated computer program and the latest and greatest in hardware.

And he could prove it, Ben thought suddenly. He could prove it and he would. He knew exactly how to do it.

Regardless of what he saw when he was wearing the goggles, he told himself, he knew that he was sitting at his desk in his office. He knew for a fact that he was alone and no one was talking to him or touching him. Nobody here but us chicken, singular. Therefore, having acknowledged those irrefutable facts outright to himself, he simply had to keep them in mind when he put the goggles back on. As a result, he would be able to talk his brain into only seeing the graphics, that and nothing more. Once the illusion had been identified, then there would be no hearing, no feeling, no smelling and no tasting.

He would see Sensuous Cindy moving as if she were embracing him but no matter what she did, he would not feel anything other than what he was feeling right now. Because he knew that in reality—the reality that counted—he was sitting at his desk. Elbows on the desktop. Feet flat on the floor. He knew all this because he had confirmed it, in person. Of course, that would mean that the whole experience with Cindy had to be substantially diminished and that was too bad in some ways.

Well, okay, it would be too bad in a lot of ways. But that was not what was actually important here, he thought. The important thing to consider was the matter of consent. If you were going to get that disoriented, you should only do it voluntarily, not because you didn't actually know what you were getting into.

"Okay," he murmured and raised the goggles to put them on again. "Welcome to my office, Cindy. You don't mind if I call you Cindy, do you? Can I offer you some coffee? Or would you prefer something else in the way of refreshment?"

He fitted the goggles over his eyes and discovered immediately that it was most definitely something else that Sensuous Cindy wanted.

He found himself flat on his back on the bed, looking up at her while she undid each of the buttons on his shirt one by one with her very deft fingers. Trying to sit up, he opened his mouth to protest, or thought he opened his mouth, but no sound came out. Cindy's extraordinarily kissable lips stretched in a delightfully sexy smile.

"I have an idea, Ben, darling. Why don't you just lay back and relax," she suggested in a low sexy purring growl as she pushed him back down on the satin sheets, "and let me drive?" She knelt on the bed next to him and, as she undid each button, bent down to kiss the small area of newly-exposed skin.

Ben was helpless to do anything except watch, while noting in a distant, almost absentminded way, that his traitor senses had not hesitated to resume their delivery of false information to his poor, besieged brain. But at least he could console himself with the knowledge that it was false information of a very high quality.

The bed, for example; those satin sheets covered a mattress of the kind his chiropractor was always telling him he should be sleeping on, unless he wanted to use his retirement income to pay her mortgage off early and put all her kids through Harvard. Having been to a party at his chiropractor's rather lavish home, Ben was pretty sure that, given what she charged, she had paid her mortgage off long before his first appointment. It so happened that he had also met her kids at the same party and he was absolutely certain that none of them stood the slightest chance of getting into Harvard.

But if, on the other hand, he had actually known what it felt like to lie on a mattress like this, he would have bought one for every room in the house. After which, he probably would have stopped leaving the house altogether. Which would have been a shame, since he'd have been missing so much—God, so very much. Of something or other. Of whatever he had just been thinking about.

Cindy was still kissing her way down his chest. There was something about the way she did it, something about the way she touched him, that made it seem both innocently spontaneous and premeditatedly wicked all at once. Ben thought he had never experienced anything so unbearably erotic. At least it would be until whatever it was that Cindy decided to do next.

Finished with his buttons, Cindy smoothed her hands over his chest by way of moving to put herself nose to nose with him. Or rather, eye to eye.

She had incredibly beautiful eyes, of course. They were unique, otherworldly, a sort of hazel-sea-green with shiny gold specks here and there. Eyes that Ben knew he could get lost in. Literally.

Some fleeting thought involving his own eyes, or maybe eyesight went through his mind. He didn't really want to bother pursuing it, but it seemed to nag at him. Something to do with eyeglasses. No, not eyeglasses, exactly. Goggles, perhaps.

Goggles? What goggles?

He raised his hand to stroke her cheek and felt it brush against something near his temple. Oh, right... Those goggles.

Ben pulled back from her with a pained expression. "Cindy," he said, "I—uh, listen. I don't know if I can go through with this."

She gave him a dreamy smile; he caught her hand as it began to make its way downward from his chest.

"Please," he said. "It feels too real."

"Well. Gee, Ben." Her sexy smile turned mischievous, which on her was even sexier. "I am just a computer program."

"Yeah," he said with a weak, nervous laugh. "Some program."

She moved closer to him for another kiss.

"I'm engaged to be married!" he added in a desperate yelp.

Those lovely, otherworldly eyes widened. "You are? That's so sweet," she told him, fondness and approval warming her voice as she slid herself even closer. Then she was half on top of him and he could feel the full length of her body pressing against his as clearly as he had ever felt anything in his life. "But Ben, darling, you're not married *yet*," she said, her voice slightly playful. "Are you?"

"Uh, no," he admitted, staring into those amazing eyes. "No, I am not."

No, I am not married and no, I am not getting out of this.

"Well, then—" She pressed her lips against his and gave him another head-spinner of a kiss that left him breathless. "Why don't you just consider this good practice."

He was only human, Ben thought, as she overpowered him with a follow-up kiss. He was only human and she was not, which meant he did not stand a chance against this onslaught of sensuality. No, indeed, he had no choice in the matter, no choice and no chance. He was just going to have to practice. A man had to do what a man had to do, and as those certain things that were what a man had to do went, this was really not so bad. This was really not so bad at all. In fact, it was even quite—

Abruptly two strong hands shoved him away and he found himself floundering on the bed under Cindy's now stern but still beautiful gaze.

"Hey, mister," she said sharply. "Don't you know there's a speed limit in this town?"

Everything stopped. Including, Ben was fairly certain, his heart.

Oh God, how stupid was he? He should have known, he thought, defeated. He should have known that it would turn out to be nothing more than a big practical joke—Garrett's idea of pre-wedding humor. After Ben had been foolish enough to tell him all about the little "agreement" Samantha had talked him into, Garrett just hadn't been able to resist having a little fun by playing on that.

Sure, that was it. Good old Garrett had decided that he would arrange for his pal Ben to get all revved up and ready to rock, and as soon as he was in high gear, *blam!* Road closed, nowhere to go after all. When he got hold of that bastard...

And then his arms were full of Sensuous Cindy again and he could feel her breath as she licked and nibbled his neck.

"Just kidding," she murmured.

Ben felt his heart start up again as if nothing had out of the ordinary had happened. Okay, he thought, so humor wasn't her forte.

The bedroom around them disappeared and became beautiful blue sky. Nice effect, Ben thought and decided that in spite of everything, this was really not the time for him to mention to her that she had damn near given him a fatal heart attack. It was also probably not the best moment to give her an ultimatum to the effect that if she ever did such a thing to him again, it would put a very serious strain on their friendship.

Aw, what the hell, it would just be a waste of his energy if he let her little attempt at being funny remain an issue between them. After all, some people just could not tell a joke. It wasn't her fault if she was one of them. She couldn't help it, it just wasn't in her nature. Well, sort of nature. Which only underscored the point, what could anyone reasonably expect a computer program to know about humorous timing?

And besides, he thought as he resumed practicing, she was so good at so many other things.

SIX

SIX

Ben felt as if he were drifting on a cloud.

Or maybe that was what he had been dreaming just now. Or maybe he was half-dreaming and half-remembering in a sort of a half-doze after an encounter that had been both dreamy and the stuff of dreams. Or, what the hell, maybe he was still dreaming, in which case he had no reason to be in any hurry about waking up. After the last several weeks he'd had, it wasn't like he couldn't have used a little more sleep to begin with.

Then he shifted position slightly and he knew that he had to be awake after all. But if the unreal dreamy feeling had faded away, the sensation of lying in the most comfortable bed in the world with his arm around a woman who was as naked as she was gorgeous was still very much with him. He tried opening his eyes just a tiny little bit, in an attempt to peek at his surroundings without waking himself up completely. The bedroom seemed to have vanished for good in favor of the limitless horizon.

Ben dared to open his eyes a little wider. Nothing but blue sky everywhere. Yeah, it sure seemed to be limitless, all right.

It was like being in a hot air balloon, only without the balloon or anything else attached to it. This method was definitely quieter and much more restful, though. It was probably safer, too. He opened his eyes all the way now so he could look around at the heavenly blue sky, dotted here and there with fluffy white clouds.

Beside him, Cindy made one of those little purring noises that he had come to recognize as an indication of her deep contentment. She certainly looked deeply contented, Ben thought, gazing down at her she was practically glowing. And she wasn't the only one, as he found out after sneaking a quick look at himself under the covers.

Still got it, he thought happily. Samantha may have benched him for the time being but that did not mean he was completely out of practice. He still had what it took to make a woman glow, and to hell with modesty. He was only being honest about his own abilities. Although if he were actually going to be completely honest about the whole thing, Cindy herself had done a splendid job of providing him with more than an adequate amount of inspiration.

Well, it wasn't like there was anything wrong with that, he thought, feeling even happier. After all, this was her bed. If he had been inspired to make her feel like she was floating on a cloud in an endless blue sky and literally glowing with deep contentment, that could only be a good thing.

Despite this happy train of thought, however, he could feel his own contentment begin to damp down now. Craning his neck, he peered over the side of the bed but there was nothing else to see other than a few small puffy white clouds in the pleasant blue sky around them. He was very lucky that he had no tendencies toward agoraphobia and he could enjoy such nice imagery, Ben mused idly. It was all very lovely, and so very sweet, really, when you thought about it.

But what should he have been really thinking about right now? And what should he have been thinking about before?

Never mind "what." Try "who," suggested his conscience.

Samantha's face appeared in his inner eye. She looked beautiful, of course, all tender and loving. And trusting, of course.

Ben sighed. If he was going to torture himself, he might as well do it in his office.

He looked down at Cindy's tousled blonde head, wondering if he could slide his arm out from under her without managing to disturb her too much. Too late. She had already sensed the change in his body that meant he was waking up and now she, too, was becoming more alert.

She stretched her perfect body luxuriously. Then, with a sigh, she slid one arm all the way across his chest to give him a firm squeeze that felt oddly possessive, something he found not only surprising but a bit unsettling as well.

"I don't know about you, Ben, darling, but I could stay like this forever," Cindy told him dreamily.

As she spoke, she wrapped one leg around both of his and gave him another squeeze, making a happy sound that was somewhere between a sigh and a purr.

"With most guys, it's just that same old routine— wham, bam, thank you ma'am," she added.

"Yeah, well." Ben laughed nervously. "You know what guys are like."

He was certain now that it would definitely be too rude if he just started struggling to work his arm out from under her. No matter what he tried, he was just not going to be able to get his arm back unless she let him up and it seemed like a pretty safe assumption that she was not going to be inclined to move any time real soon. Damn, she had not looked anywhere near as heavy as she felt right now.

The memory of an old joke suddenly popped into his mind, something about finding yourself in bed with a woman so ugly that you would gladly chew through your own arm to escape rather than face the terrible prospect of actually waking her up.

Therefore what he was looking at now had to be the flipside of coyote ugly, he thought. Coyote Lovely—when you wake up and find that the woman lying next to you is so beautiful that you would gladly let her chew through your arm if she happened to want breakfast in bed.

Maybe he should just try asking her nicely if she would mind shifting around a little, maybe just her head or something.

"Mm-hmm," Cindy said, snuggling closer and somehow managing to trap his arm even more securely. "But you're not like most guys. You're so different. You're sweet. Considerate." She gave one of those sexy, purring laughs. "So very considerate."

All right, he could see that it was going to be a lot harder to bring up the subject of her getting off his arm as politely than he had originally thought (or hoped) it would be. He looked down at her and sighed, feeling a mixture of various regrets.

"Oh, but don't get me wrong," she opened her eyes and looked up at him without raising her head. "You were a real tiger when it counted."

In spite of everything, Ben smiled. Still got it. "Well, I have to say that you were pretty terrific yourself," he told her.

"Oh, Ben, darling, you are so sweet!" She squeezed him tightly enough to cut off his breathing for a moment before she snuggled even closer. Her body was half wrapped around him now and he still could not move his arm. "You know, I could really get used to this."

A small alarm bell went off in Ben's mind; he suppressed it immediately, feeling stupid. Because it was stupid, incredibly stupid, even though it was just an old reflex, the last vestige of an old conditioned response left over from an old life he didn't live any more.

Back in his younger and less responsible days, hearing a woman say I could really get used to this (or some variation thereof) usually indicated that she had actually already gotten used to it, and she was, in fact, far more used to it than he was comfortable with.

It inevitably signaled that in the very near future, she was going to want to have a discussion about that little thing called commitment, ie, she would vote yes on commitment, how about him? Unfortunately, it would not actually be a genuinely open discussion as to where he might stand on the matter because by that time, she had also already voted yes on commitment. Any reluctance on his part to do likewise would be indicative of a very sad and serious flaw in his character, or possibly even an especially severe variety of incurable personality disorder.

The seemingly obvious solution to the problem, of course, was simple; tone down the sexual performance to something that would not inspire such a reaction. There was a rather unfortunate drawback to that particular solution, however: the kind of sexual performance that a woman did not have any desire to get used to would definitely not get a guy any encores or even make for much in the way of a congenial kiss-off.

In fact, anyone who performed that badly in bed would be lucky not to get his ass kicked out of it early. Even worse, two hours later, he would most likely discover that the word had gotten out far and wide, and the entire world had been informed of what a lousy lay he was, which made getting past it and moving on somewhat difficult.

But then he had met Samantha and everything had changed. Right away, he had known she was someone special in a way that went far beyond matters of a sexual nature. This was the kind of woman who would never be impressed by a man simply because he found her attractive. He was going to have to demonstrate a lot more than merely that he was interested in her if he wanted her to even notice he was alive, let alone have dinner with him, or just a glass of wine, or even just think about it. And without laughing her head off, either.

As for the matter of commitment, there had really been nothing to discuss except, to Ben's enormous relief, the exact date for the wedding. The only thing that had scared him about commitment in this case was that Samantha might not want it. He had already voted yes and did not know how he could possibly undo it if Samantha had not felt the same way.

Now, looking back on all those years he had spent artfully dodging the thing that he now wanted more than anything, Ben could not help feeling that at last he understood more about human behavior than he ever had before, especially when it came to his own. His skittishness about commitment, he told himself, had come out of his subconscious knowledge that he was actually afraid that he would not be able to find the woman he was looking for, a woman with some very specific qualities, someone who would be so much more than just a pretty face and a dynamite body. And maybe most of all, a woman who wasn't going to settle for a guy just because he was willing to make a commitment.

He looked down at Cindy, who made another contented purring noise as she snuggled closer. Of course, there was no reason why a person's high standards would have to stand in the way of a rich and satisfying fantasy life.

If only the fantasy did not have to be so heavy that it had made him lose all feeling in his arm, everything might have been just about perfect.

This was probably not going to be the most graceful exit he had ever made, Ben thought as he reached up to his temple with his free hand.

Or, who knew, maybe it actually would be?

The transition, or lack of it, from Cindy's boudoir floating in the clouds to the earthbound reality of his office was more than jarring. It was actually sort of alarming and, at the same time, more than just vaguely depressing. After cloud nine in seventh heaven—literally—his real-life office was quite a let-down, drab and lifeless by comparison, something that was, in its way, even more depressing. Now that he was thinking about it, it was actually the most depressing thing he had contemplated lately since celibacy.

The idea that regular doses of virtual reality might have the unwanted effect of turning him into the kind of sad bastard who found real life less stimulating and exciting than computer simulations had about as much appeal for him as giving up the good life for a career in the fast-growing industry of trash removal. No, working in professional trash removal was actually slightly more attractive. Maybe the fact that being a garbage man would come with a paycheck (and a fairly sizable one at that, according to what he had heard) gave that option just enough of an edge.

Troubled, Ben dropped the goggles on his desk and sat back in his chair, staring at them with a deepening frown. How he had spent the last couple of hours was not really the simple matter it would have seemed to be just on the surface. He actually had a great deal to think over.

There was no denying that, in the area of stress relief, Sensuous Cindy was absolutely world class. Being with her was like going away for a long weekend with the perfect lover and having every single one of your needs seen to in exactly the right way. Only there was no her to be with, just it, and it was a computer program.

Of course, it was a very sophisticated computer program, not to mention the fact that it was incredibly realistic as well. But there was no way that any of those considerations could transform "it" into "her." Sensuous Cindy was still a computer program, not a living person.

That was the whole point of using the program, of course—to be able to forget, temporarily, that Sensuous Cindy was not a living person. Unfortunately, that was also the whole problem. Once you forgot Cindy was not a genuine woman, it did not leave much in the way of incentive to remember what she—what it, he corrected himself sharply, not she, it—really was.

Well, all right, the notion that you could be with the perfect lover had absolutely no basis in reality in the first place. Anyone with half a brain would know that such a thing could not exist as anything other than a fantasy. Of course, that in itself was hardly any sort of argument to refrain from indulging yourself by suspending your disbelief, at least for a little while.

But then, the encouragement to do so was a direct product of the physical sensations. Your senses were telling you in no uncertain terms that this was not a fantasy at all, this was really happening to you. Even if you could not, or would not, believe in anything else, you had no choice but to believe the evidence from your five senses. After all, seeing was believing, as the old saying went. But it was even more than just a matter of seeing. If you were also hearing, smelling, feeling, and tasting all at the same time, you had gone way, way past simply a state of believing. That would put you in the territory commonly known as being certain beyond the shadow of a doubt.

And the problem with that was, it just did not seem like anything to be afraid of. It didn't even seem like something to be a little bit nervous about.

Even when he analyzed the experience in terms of the raw, unadorned truth, when he considered what had actually taken place and how it had happened, Ben was strongly tempted just to go ahead and overlook anything that suggested he should feel even just mildly uneasy about it. Then he suddenly remembered touching the candle flame and looked at his finger.

The blister he had felt coming up on the skin was still there.

Okay, that was creepy, he thought and snatched his hand behind his back, thinking he would feel a lot better if he did not actually look directly at it.

But to his dismay, that did not help even just the slightest bit. Even with his finger out of sight, he somehow could not resist the urge to run his thumb over the injured spot.

It still hurt, but half a minute went by before he was able to make himself take another look at his finger.

Maybe it was not really a blister, he thought with faint hope. Or if it was, it wasn't necessarily from a burn. And even if it was from a burn, it could have been something that had happened this morning at home. He could have accidentally touched the hot plate on the coffeepot and just been too distracted to notice.

As far-fetched as that might have sounded, it was not really impossible—far from it. Anyone who had gone without sex for as long as he had already would be plenty distracted. Another week of this celibate regime and he probably wouldn't notice if someone burned off his arm with a blowtorch.

Well, however he looked at it, he had just had one very rare, very major experience of the kind most people dreamed about even if they didn't believe it was possible. But at the same time, however he looked at it, he was looking at it.

Which was to say, not she, he corrected himself quickly, but it. Sensuous Cindy was a thing, an inanimate object, a sequence of computer instructions which was now and always would be "it." And, like all inanimate objects deserving of the pronoun it, Cindy would never argue with him, never get on his nerves, never do things wrong, never fail to please him.

Cindy was a nice idea. No, try again, he told himself stubbornly. It was a nice idea.

The memory of that happy, satisfied, all's-right-with-the-world after-glow he had felt in Sensuous Cindy's heavenly bed came back to him. As if some other part of his mind, an area which was much less concerned with more elevated notions like virtue and honesty and loyalty were deliberately reminding him that the existence of the Sensuous Cindy program meant that the deep contentment of gratification was just one of those nice things that was now available to him whenever he wanted it.

But if all those days of youthful, carefree, unfettered sex—supposedly carefree, anyway, definitely unfettered—had taught him anything, it was that all the things he really wanted out of life were actually unattainable for those people who insisted that everything in their lives had to be convenient, stress-free, and easily replaced.

Remembering how he had felt with Cindy was a lot like remembering being drunk. Whereas recalling how he felt with Samantha—not to mention how he felt about Samantha—was a reminder of why he was glad to be alive.

There was simply no comparison.

Ben sighed. In many ways, he had to plead guilty to the charge of being a typical guy after all.

To be absolutely honest with himself, he knew very well that even if he and Samantha had been going at it three times a day, it would not have prevented him from having the standard male response to the models in the reception area.

Beautiful sexy women were still beautiful sexy women, no matter what. And thank God things like that never changed, he thought, cheerfully.

But he also liked to think he was also a grown-up. He had known from the beginning that a woman like Samantha would never have been interested in him if he hadn't been. It was also his belief (or hope, at least) that he had had grown up even more since they had been together, and being a grown-up meant knowing the difference between things that could really make you happy and things that could only make you feel good.

Unbidden, an image of Cindy making him feel good appeared in his mind. Okay, he still had a serious yen for all the stuff that made him feel good. What the hell, he was only human. And a guy.

But it was not as if he had asked for any of this. He had not deliberately gone out in search of something like Sensuous Cindy, he had not been making a conscious attempt to take at least some of the sexual edge off. Sensuous Cindy had been Garrett's own bright idea. Garrett had just gone ahead put it on his computer without bothering to check with him first and see if it was okay.

And all that notwithstanding, he couldn't really blame Garrett. He knew the guy hadn't meant any harm by what he had done. Hell, Garrett was his best friend, he was a good guy with a good heart. This was just his alpha computer geek idea of a stag party. Just all in good fun, really.

Well, it certainly had been good. Real, real good, as well as being the most fun he had had lately.

After all, who said being a grown-up meant you couldn't have fun? And now that he thought of it, part of being a grown-up was understanding that nobody was a grown-up all the time.

But it was not until he hit on the idea of bringing Samantha flowers that his conscience finally shut up and let him get some work done.

SEVEN

Letting himself into the house, Ben was very surprised to find that Samantha still had not come home yet.

His conscience promptly kicked back into high gear and then went into overdrive, letting loose with a fresh onslaught of twenty-four carat guilt. Poor Samantha—the one thing that was always first and foremost in her mind was their future together and how she could make him happy. Every day his beautiful fiancée would go into work and knock herself out with the long hours she spent slaving away at her demanding, high-tech job—a job he himself could not have done in a million years.

And what was he doing? Well, anyone could just see for themselves—here he was, home at the usual time even after he had spent part of the day goofing off by having hot compu-sex with a hot compu-bimbo. That in itself would have been bad enough, his conscience reminded him, except that he had promised his hard-working fiancée that he would refrain from all sexual activity until...

Shut the hell up, he told his mind firmly and buried his nose in the bouquet of roses he was carrying, trying to fill his head with something other than conscious thought, at least for a short time. He kept sniffing the roses aggressively as he crossed to the dining room table. By the time he started going through the mail the cleaning lady had left in a neat pile, he had lost the capacity to smell them at all.

Nothing special in the mail, he saw as he scanned the envelopes quickly. Just the usual come-ons from credit card companies, a bill or two, and oh, Christ, an invitation for Samantha to subscribe to a new magazine called, God help them, *All Things Bride and Beautiful.*

Ben gave a short, humorless laugh. And they'd criticized *Brash* as being too, well, *brash.* Personally, he would take either *Brash* or *brash* over bad puns any day. Or maybe he just didn't think the world needed yet another how-to-have-a-monster-wedding magazine. Simply leafing through the ones that Sam had left lying around the house had been incredibly off-putting, to say the least.

The sight of all those wedding dresses and designer tuxedos and hair-dos and articles with titles like "Trimming Their Guest List Without Tears" and "Camouflaging Your Broken Leg—Easier Than You'd Think!" and "Chiffon vs. Tulle—The Debate Rages On" had made his eyes glaze over, which to be fair was only to be expected since he was, after all, a guy.

But what really got to him more than anything else were the honeymoon ads in the back. They were stacked up in columns like oversized classified ads with cheesy cut-out photographs, most in black and white although more and more of them seemed to be switching to color, showing happy couples in heart-shaped bathtubs, toasting each other with champagne amid mounds of strategically-placed bubbles, with a video camera on a tripod set up off to one side, so that every precious, golden moment could be recorded and preserved. Those little horrors made him want to run screaming into the street.

He had wondered why they didn't seem to affect Sam in the same way. Mostly because he had trouble reconciling the idea that any of these bridal magazines could actually have any credibility at all with his brilliant fiancée. When he had finally worked up enough courage to ask her where she stood on the matter of cheesy honeymoon ads, she had only given a careless shrug and told him that she hadn't noticed them. What a relief that had been.

Of course, she had felt compelled to tease him unmercifully for weeks after that, sending away for honeymoon brochures with larger pictures of people in heart-shaped bathtubs, which she would then sneak into his laptop case or his pockets or even leave on his pillow.

That Sam, he thought, smiling. You just did not mess with her unless you were prepared to take a really hefty dose of payback.

Just then, he heard her car pulling up in front of the house and some impulse told him to duck out of sight and wait till she was checking out the mail

on the dining table to surprise her with the flowers.
Oh, she'll be a lot more than just surprised, said
his conscience nastily. Once she gets over the
shock, she'll be suspicious, too.

Nope, no undue optimism around here today,
Ben thought, not a trace. He was in absolutely no
danger of breaking out in a rash of yellow happy
faces.

He hurried silently into the living room as he
heard Sam's key in the lock and positioned himself
carefully in the entryway to the hall, making sure
he didn't crackle the paper that the florist had
wrapped around the roses. He heard the front door
close and then Sam's footsteps as she crossed the
hallway and headed for the dining room to have a
look at the mail he had just been skimming.

Tiptoeing up the hall, being extra careful to avoid
the two creaky floorboards he knew for sure about,
he paused at the doorway to the dining room to
peek around the corner. Sam had just put her laptop computer case down on the table. Now she
was standing with her back to him while she shuf-
fled through the envelopes he had scanned earlier.

He saw her pause to take a second look at one
and then gave a small chuckle. *All Things Bride
and Beautiful*, probably. God, but he hoped she
didn't think it was amusing enough to subscribe
to. He wasn't sure his sanity could survive having
something called *All Things Bride and Beautiful*
showing up in the mail once a month. Not even if
he knew it was just a joke, just Sam's way of teasing him. After all, what if it backfired and she
actually started reading the thing?

He would be doomed. Hell, they both might be.

Better distract her now, he thought, because in another moment it might be too late. Hiding the roses behind his back, he managed to scurry up next to her just as she started to turn around.

"Oh!" Her dark curls bounced as she jumped back from him, much more startled than he had expected or intended. "It's you!"

Smiling at her, he produced the bouquet, slipping it directly under her nose so she could get the full benefit of the fragrance immediately.

Her eyes widened with delight as she started to smell them. Then she seemed to hesitate. "What's the occasion?" she asked him, a faint wariness in her voice.

"No occasion," Ben said expansively. "Does there have to be an occasion?" He made an exaggerated, formal bow. "Very well, then, if that is indeed the case, you are the occasion. You gorgeous woman, you."

Samantha took another step back and folded her arms in front of herself. "We are not—I repeat, *not*—having sex, Benjamin."

"And that's just fine with me," he added smoothly, as if he were finishing her sentence for her.

Now she frowned at him with suspicion. "And reverse psychology is not going to work, either," she warned him.

"Aw, what are you talking about, Sam?" Ben said, laughing a little as he shrugged. "It's only six months. Six tiny little months. That's just—" he snapped his fingers. "A drop in the bucket. Besides, you were right," he added, wiggling his eyebrows at her. "It really is going to make for one hell of a wedding night."

He moved swiftly over to her before she could retreat again and kissed her on the cheek. "I love you, Samantha," he told her quietly, almost solemnly. "I really do."

She gave him a searching look that went on for so long, he started to feel a mild pang of worry. "Do you?" she asked him finally.

"Do I? Well, hey," he said and put the bouquet under her nose again. "These flowers weren't cheap, you know."

"Come on, Ben," she said, rolling her eyes, "you've got to be serious for a minute—"

"But I am being serious, Sam," he told her, taking her gently in his arms before she could move away again. "About loving you, I mean. Not the flowers. Not that I would ever buy you some cheapo cut-rate bouquet, of course," he added quickly.

She hesitated and then put her arms around his neck. "Well, in that case, I have a confession to make. There's something you ought to know," she said, smiling up at him in a dreamy way.

He laughed a little. "Go ahead, tell me everything. Give it to me straight—I can take it."

"You, Benjamin Baker, are the only man I will ever love."

Ben felt his heart do a funny little dance. He was damned lucky to be the man who heard that from her and he knew it. He was bending his head to kiss her when the phone rang.

Samantha moved to answer it and he tightened his hold on her slightly, looking pained, making sure that she knew he did not want to let her go. Her smile widened mischievously as she broke away from him and went over to the sideboard to pick up the cordless handset from the recharging stand.

"Hello?" she asked, watching him with that mischievous expression while he made exaggerated sad faces at her. "Yes, he's here." She chuckled and handed the telephone to him. "Why, it's for you. Imagine that."

He made even sadder faces at her as she took the roses into the kitchen to look for a vase to put them in. She only stuck her tongue out at him playfully.

"Yeah, hello?" he asked in a pointedly unenthusiastic tone of voice as he put the phone up to his ear.

"Hello, Ben, darling," said a warm female voice.

Ben frowned. The woman on the other end sounded familiar but he could not quite place her. "Who is this?" he asked, baffled, and then had a sudden, awful thought. Oh, God. On top of everything else Garrett had done today, he had not gone and signed him up for some kind of a subscription to a phone sex service as well, had he?

"It's me, lover," the woman went on in her sexy purr, laughing a little. "It's Cindy."

"Cindy?" Ben lowered his voice. "Cindy who?"

The woman laughed again in a musical way that tickled him in places he didn't want to be tickled right now. "Sensuous Cindy, you silly man!" she said. "I had such a great time with you today, darling. Now I just can't stop thinking about you—"

Ben groaned. Yeah, this had to be more of Garrett's doing, obviously. He had to admit that signing him up for some customized phone sex was a lot more creative than he would have given the guy credit for. But Jesus, creative or not didn't matter. Garrett had gone way too far over the line this time. Ben was going to have to have a very serious talk with him and make it as clear as he possibly could to his well-meaning friend that he shouldn't do him any more favors. Beg him not to; even offer to pay him not to, if that was what he had to do to convince him.

"Okay, very funny. Now who is this really?" he asked impatiently. "If Garrett put—"

"I just told you who this is," the woman said, her sexy voice becoming even sexier. "Aren't you listening? I said, it's me. It's Cindy."

"Cindy?" He did not want to believe it; moreover, he told himself, he should not have been able to believe it even for a split second. On the other hand, he had not wanted to believe that merely putting on a pair of goggles could deliver an experience that could become far, far more than something solely visual.

But all right then. If seeing something was believing, and additionally hearing it, tasting it, feeling it, and smelling it was knowing for sure, beyond the shadow of a doubt, then what in God's name did it mean if you were talking on the phone to it?

"Cindy-from-this-morning-Cindy?" he asked uneasily. "That Cindy?"

Her pleasurable moan confirmed it. "Darling, just hearing the sound of your sexy voice again gives me... ooohh... butterflies..."

"What butterflies?" Ben said, trying to convince himself not to freak out. "You're a computer program! Computer programs don't have butterflies, they have bugs. You have bugs! Your system needs a defrag!"

He turned around just in time to see Samantha coming back into the living room carrying the flowers in the vase she had found for them. She smiled brightly at him with mild curiosity as she set the vase in the center of the dining table.

"Who is it?" she asked, cheerful and unsuspecting.

"Nobody!" he said, a little too loud.

She stared at him in surprise.

"I mean, it's someone from work but it's nobody you know—" He cleared his throat and spoke into the receiver again in his best official at-work voice. "This, uh... you know, this is something that can wait until the morning. Regular business hours. We will discuss it in full detail then. All right?"

"All right... But," Cindy's laugh was throaty and highly suggestive; the sound went all the way through him to his core and back out again, making him feel like he was a bug. A butterfly, to be specific. Impaled, trapped, and with no possibility of escape. "Will you promise to come see me? First thing? The very first?"

"Sure, sure," Ben said hurriedly. "Absolutely. You can count on it. On me."

"I can't wait." Her dreamy sigh was more torture. "Oh, Ben, darling, I just can't wait for you to hold me in your arms again. It was so—"

Ben hit the disconnect button. It was all he could do to keep himself from rushing out onto the front steps of the house and hurling the telephone handset as hard and as far as he possibly could.

"Everything all right?" Samantha asked innocently, still giving him that bright smile. She certainly wouldn't have been smiling at him so brightly if she had had any idea what that phone call had really been about, Ben thought, slightly nauseated now. Sam wouldn't have been smiling at him at all. She would have picked up that vase of roses he had brought her and—

Immediately Ben stamped down hard on the thought and forced himself to smile back at her. "Yeah, great. Really, everything's great!" he told her. "Really. Oh, something came up—nothing really, just—well, something—you know how things can get at the magazine, it's crazy there, something's always coming up. But it's really nothing. Everything's under control. Really."

Well, that was mostly true. Everything was under control; everything except him. Ben turned away from her in a way that he hoped looked like any other perfectly natural, casual, and aimless sort of movement, and not one little bit like a guy who didn't want his fiancée to get the idea that he was panicking because another woman had just called him on the phone to request a few more rip-roaring hours of hot, nasty sex.

Even if it was actually a computer program rather than another woman.

He looked down at the cordless receiver in his hands and went over to put it back in its stand.

Samantha was saying something about dinner. Would she be suspicious if he told her that he had suddenly lost his appetite?

I've had such a long day with an awful lot of hard work. You know what some days are like, don't you? Yeah. So, if it's all the same to you, Sam, honey, sweetheart, darling, I think I'm just going to watch a little junk-food television and then turn in early.

Then he could lie awake for most of the night and wonder how in the world a computer program could call him at home of its own volition.

At the very least, that would be a change from lying awake most of the night wondering how he could survive six months of enforced celibacy.

It would not be an improvement, of course. Nowhere near an improvement. Just something different; a change in routine.

EIGHT

He had come in so early this morning that there was no one sitting in the reception area except Ruby Pandiscio, who was enthroned behind her desk with her headset on, as usual. She looked up as the elevator doors opened and eyed Ben with what seemed to be arch amusement.

Sorry, Mr Baker, but the first of the hotties isn't due in for another half an hour. The only hottie around here for you to feast your eyes on right now is me.

In which case, he was in no danger of starving to death, even if she was old enough to be—well, not his mother. Not quite. Although he had the definite impression that she regarded him as young enough to be her son, in spirit if not in fact. This perspective of hers wasn't limited to him—Ruby seemed to regard all the *Brash* staffers the same way.

From time to time, it occurred to Ben to wonder why Ruby had chosen to locate her lofty perch of maturity and experience behind a receptionist's desk at a men's magazine. In particular, a men's magazine like *Brash*, that once in a while decided it did not have to bother publishing any of the incisive articles that its target readership could pretend they were far more interested in than the photo spreads. Especially if it meant reducing the number of pages occupied by a photo spread. Fewer pages meant fewer pictures of ladies—this was never a good thing.

The idea of actually asking Ruby Pandiscio such a question, however, was something Ben found far too intimidating. For one thing, he wasn't sure how to go about putting it into words; for another, he was afraid that the answer would turn out to be something so reasonable and obvious that by the mere act of asking he had exposed himself as callow, shallow, and intellectually deficient.

Or she might just haul off and slap his face. Judging from the subtle but well-defined muscles in her arms (on display in warm weather), there was a good chance that she would take his head off if she did, which he was pretty certain was not the kind of on-the-job injury covered by his HMO or workmen's comp.

Ruby's smile seemed to soften a little as she put a small stack of phone messages on the desk for him along with some interoffice envelopes. Apparently she wasn't going to behead him today.

Ben's answering smile was a bit tense at first; then for some reason he felt himself relaxing. His smile widened as he stood there sorting through the While-You-Were-Out slips of paper under the woman's benevolent gaze.

What would she say if he asked her why she worked there?

That was assuming for the moment that she did not come back at him with a response like: Since when is that any of your business, punk? Or I'd tell you but then I'd have to kill you, of course.

For all he knew, she might even tell him something completely mundane. For instance, she might answer that this was the best she could do as a single mother with a limited education or as a divorcee re-entering the work-force after her husband had run off with someone who looked like a model for *Brash*. Or she might tell him simply that she was on parole.

Okay, that last one was maybe not terribly mundane in a setting like this, he thought, frowning at one of the phone messages. The call back box was checked and then circled, with a note in Ruby's precise, ultra-legible hand saying: Asked me to tell you, "Don't forget!" Ms S C (only gave initials).

On the other hand, having a receptionist who was on parole was a lot more mundane than some things he could think of. Or rather, didn't want to think of. He put the message down on the stack he had already looked at and went on to the rest.

When he finished, he folded them all into a sloppy wad and tucked them into his pocket, then decided to have a quick peek at what treasures had arrived in the interoffice mail.

"Mm-hmm," he said to himself, peering busily into an oversized manila envelope stuffed with four-by-five color transparencies for his perusal. He made a business of pretending to count them while also pretending that he wasn't finding ways to delay going into his office. At the same time, he also had to pretend that he was completely unaware that Ruby knew exactly what he was up to and was watching him as if she thought he might be on parole, but from the loony bin.

After a bit he dared to look up and give her a friendly smile. "There are some days that you just gotta ease into, instead of diving in head first," he said, by way of pretending he wasn't making a really lame excuse in a really lame way.

Ruby raised one perfectly-shaped eyebrow at him but just as she seemed about to make a comment, the phone rang. "Good morning, *Brash* magazine," she said, turning away from Ben slightly. "How may I direct your call?"

She put a finger to her headset in a way that reminded Ben too much of a similar action, one involving a very high-tech headset that included a pair of full-immersion goggles.

He ran down the hall to his office.

It was an enormous relief to find that all was quiet on the glass-walled front, or more precisely, in the office behind it. Apparently, whoever had been calling so early had not asked to speak to him. He could be glad about that, Ben thought, closing the door. Then he just leaned against it for a few seconds, staring at his work area.

It did not look like a place where odd or unusual things could happen. In spite of the fancy design, it was still nothing more than a mundane, boring old office setup—desk, computer, phone, all the standard office stuff, along with the light-box on the wall behind. Nothing unusual was going on.

Nothing unusual was happening now and nothing unusual ever had or ever would happen here, he told himself. This was nothing more than the office where he spent a major portion of every day poring over hundreds of photos and transparencies of unusually beautiful women, which was nothing unusual for his line of work. In fact, he had a whole bunch of new transparencies of unusually beautiful women to look at again today. Anyone would have thought that the world's supply of unusually beautiful women would have run dry ages ago but somehow, it never did.

Unlike fossil fuels, rainforests, and white rhinos, unusually beautiful women only became more plentiful as time went by, at least if what he saw in the course of a typical workday was any indication. Day in, day out, week in, week out, it was the same old same-old and it just kept on coming. So, Ben told himself, the sooner he got down to some real work, the better.

He paused to turn on the light-box mounted on the wall behind his chair before he sat down. Oh, yeah, he'd really better get to work, he told himself as he poured the transparencies of unusually beautiful women out of the interoffice envelope onto his desktop in a messy heap. There had to be a hundred and fifty images there, which he was supposed to get through before lunch.

Excuse me, did somebody actually say lunch? Not today, not by a long shot; he was going to have to work through lunch, because there would be another one hundred and fifty slides for him to look at this afternoon. At least that many, probably more. This was the world's fastest self-replenishing resource, after all. Now if he could only figure out where had he hidden his magnifier...

As luck would have it, he found it in the first drawer he opened. Right next to the goggles. Ben stared down at them, feeling put-upon and more than a little doomed.

After a bit, he took both the magnifier and the goggles out and placed them side by side on the desktop in front of him. What the hell. He could just put on the damned goggles, go visit Cindy—correction: run the program—and get it over with. It would not take more than a few minutes, and it would be just for the sake of getting it out of the way. Once he was finished with that, he would be able to take care of everything else he had to do today and he wouldn't have to give it another thought.

Of course, it would be kind of hard to do anything at all when he was slumped behind his desk in a drooling, semi-conscious, post-orgasmic haze.

But never mind that. After he pulled himself together enough to drag himself out of the building and find his car, what then? Another bouquet of just-because-I-love-you roses for Samantha? Another evening to get through grinning like an ape and hoping Sam bought the whole if-you're-happy-I'm-happy-everything's-swell act? Another sleepless night feeling guilty about his iffy celibacy?

And that would be followed by what—another day of this new brand of same old same-old? How many more days like that could he take? He would lose his mind; he would go completely loon-a-rooney, and all because of... what?

A computer program.

Congratulate yourself! You, Benjamin Baker, are a bona fide idiot.

Ben blew out a breath and picked the goggles up in one hand. Okay, that was a little melodramatic. Or a little over-melodramatic. Or more than a little. Like maybe grand-Wagnerian-opera ridiculous. But that was just all the more reason to shelve Sensuous Cindy permanently, forget about her—correction: it. Forget about it. Later, he would give Garrett a call, tell him that he wanted him to come back in and get it cleaned out of his computer as soon as possible. It was bullshit and it was interfering with his life. It was even getting in the way of him being able to do his job. Nobody in their right mind would let an inanimate object have that kind of power over them. Not even if they got all freaked out because it called them on the phone.

And hell, it wasn't like a computer dialing a telephone was really anything to get freaked out about anyway. It wasn't even anything particularly unusual, thanks to that wonderful, twenty-first century development called telemarketing, computers made phone calls all the time. If he were to ask Garrett, his friend could probably name twenty different kinds of glitches just off the top of his head that could cause a computer to auto-dial numbers by mistake. And that was a completely logical explanation for what had happened last night, he told himself firmly as he put the goggles back in the drawer.

"Had to be a glitch of some sort," he said aloud— hearing the words aloud made them feel more real—and shut the drawer with a little more force than was actually necessary. "That's all it was. Just some glitch. Had to be. Had to."

Okay, now that he had that settled, it was time to get busy. Ignoring the small sting from the blister on his fingertip—it was practically all healed up already anyway, no big deal there—he put half a dozen transparencies up on the light box and began to examine the first of them with the magnifier.

Yes, indeed, I love my job, he thought happily.

"Hey, lover," said a familiar sexy voice behind him. "Whatchya doin'?"

Ben let out an involuntary yelp of surprise. The magnifier he was holding went flying out of his hand and off into parts unknown as he jumped back and turned around. Then he gave another yelp when he saw the display that was now on his desktop computer screen.

"Aren't you forgetting something, darling?" Sensuous Cindy said, staring out at him from where she was lounging on her bed. Today's negligee was different and as he might have expected, even sexier. "Did you or did you not make a little promise to me last night, lover? Hmm?"

Ben squinted at the screen in disbelief. She—it—seemed to be looking right at him, as if she could see him as easily as he could see her. Some bit of half-remembered techno-babble he'd heard from Garrett once about high-definition touch-screen technology flitted through Ben's mind.

He decided to try a little experiment. Keeping his back flat against the wall, he leaned slowly and carefully to the right, returned to center, and then leaned as far to the left as he could. Damn, he thought. It really did look as if her eyes—its eyes, damn it, its eyes—were tracking his every move but even what little he knew about computers told him that was just absolutely impossible.

Wasn't it?

"I'm confused," he said shakily, just for the sake of saying anything at all. "Is this, uh, you know, like, part of the program?"

"I'm not sure I know what you mean, Ben, darling." Sensuous Cindy leaned forward which, in her current state of partial dress, was a very interesting move. "All I know is," she said, licking her lips, "I've never felt like this before."

She slid herself toward him on the bed as if she were really getting physically closer. The silky, chin-length blonde hair fell forward and she shook it back without taking her eyes off him. Even just on his little computer screen, those eyes were remarkable, deep and powerful. He felt as if her gaze were boring into him.

"I-I, uh, I have no idea what you... uh, you could be... uh, talking. What you're talking about," he said with some difficulty. He knew that he wasn't actually having any physical trouble breathing but for some reason he still felt as if he couldn't get enough air.

"What I'm talking about is chemistry, you silly boy," she said, laughing a little. "You know what chemistry is. That mysterious attraction between two people who belong together."

She reached the foot of the bed and sat up, throwing off the diaphanous robe so he could get a better look at what she was barely wearing. Her lacy bra and thong were another set Ben that had seen in a sexy-underwear catalog, and quite recently, in fact. It also just happened to be another one of his favorites, as worn by his favorite lingerie model. Who, now that he was thinking of it, did nowhere near as much for the outfit as Sensuous Cindy did. But Sensuous Cindy could not possibly have known that.

Could she?

"You know what I mean, like pheromones," she added with a sexy sigh. "And all that other good stuff. Mmm." She hugged herself. "So good."

"Pheromones?" It came out of him as more of a groan than a word. "No, that's not right, don't be ridiculous. Humans have pheromones. You have to be human like me to have pheromones."

She raised her eyebrows and sat up even straighter, crossing her legs and using her arms to cover herself primly. "Well, Ben, darling, I was certainly human enough for you yesterday," she told him with a sexy little pout.

It was the pout that was the last straw for Ben. Ever since he had discovered the beauteous and bountiful mouth of Faye in junior high, he had been powerless in the face of a really good pout.

The still, small voice of his conscience promptly reminded him that his very own Samantha had the all-time best pout of anyone he had ever known, Faye included. It was promptly drowned out by the blare from his more instinctive nature pointing out the rather obvious fact that Samantha didn't happen to be there while Cindy was.

The only thing Ben knew for sure at the moment was that if he could do nothing else, he had to make her—it—whatever this was—stop looking at him like that.

"Look, I, uh, I—" Ben swallowed, tried again. "I'll—hey, how about I come visit you after I finish work?"

"Hmm. After work? Well. I don't know about that..." Cindy pretended to think it over for a second or two before leaning back on her hands and uncrossing her legs. "And afterwards, you will stay for awhile and hold me? Keep me company so I won't have to be so lonesome?" she asked, making a sad, slightly swelled little face at him.

"You got it." Ben nodded frantically. "Holding, touching, whatever you want. Just tell me and I'm there. Absolutely."

"Well..."

"I promise," he added. "Lots of holding. Mass quantities of holding."

"Well, when you put it that way..." She pretended to think it over some more while Ben kept repeating silently to himself, "it," not "her." "It," not "her." "It," not "her." "It," not "her." Then her lips widened in a slow, sexy smile. "All right. See you later—" she winked. "Lover."

The computer screen went blank.

Ben's breath came out in a noisy, relieved rush. Then, as if the only thing that had really been holding him up was that gaze of hers, his legs just gave and he sat down on the floor hard.

He had known when he had come in this morning that he had a long day ahead of him. That had turned out to be the good news, Ben thought unhappily as he pulled himself up off the floor and into his chair. The bad news was that for the first time he could ever remember, no matter how long his workday might run, it actually wasn't going to go slowly enough or last long enough.

Slumped in his chair at the tail end of the day, Ben regarded the photo layout on his computer screen through watering, half-closed eyes.

He found it amazing that he was still able to see the screen, or anything else, for that matter. He would have sworn that no human eyes could actually withstand the degree of eyestrain he was suffering with right now and remain intact. Rather than, say, melting into some inert substance akin to egg whites and running down his cheeks like viscous and rather disgusting tears.

There really was no damned justice, he thought wearily. Otherwise, he wouldn't have had to go through hell to design pictorial page layouts for photos that were heaven to look at. Worse, it seemed like the more heavenly the photos were to look at, the harder it was to design a layout that did justice to them. But that only figured. Because, as he had pointed out to himself bare seconds ago, there was no justice in the first place.

Bare seconds. He gazed lovingly at the computer screen, taking a moment for each photo, singly and then as a group. Tough as it was, he had done the job. "That's why they pay me the big bucks," he informed the ladies on the monitor. "Because in the end, I always do the job."

The ladies gazed back at him with what might have been admiration and approval mixed in with their various expressions of simmering animal lust.

"Yes, indeed, it certainly is a dirty job, but—" he sat up and did a final save on the file. "Only if you do it right."

He took a last look at the layout before closing the file and emailing it to the production department.

"All this and the big bucks, too." He chuckled. "Maybe it's a good thing for me there's no justice after all. Sometimes, anyway."

He rubbed the back of his neck and rolled his shoulders before he let himself fall back into a slump in his chair again. God, he was exhausted. Maybe in a minute or two he would give some serious consideration to moving a muscle. It would be just one muscle to start with, nothing too ambitious, he decided. If that worked out and it didn't kill him, he would go ahead and move another, and then another, until eventually he had enough of them going to get him up on his feet. Then he could work on a plan of movement that would eventually allow him to get home...

His cell phone rang and he groaned loudly. Answering it meant having to move a muscle right now, before he'd gotten any rest after the last time he'd moved. Damn. No justice, that was what it was. No justice anywhere at all. He slipped the tiny phone out of his shirt pocket and thumbed a button.

"Ben here," he sighed.

It was Samantha and in spite of his fatigue, he smiled at the sound of her voice. If only he could just teleport home somehow—email, or fax, even—and just melt into a little pool on the couch or the bed and spend the evening doing nothing more than listen to the woman he loved talk to him. Even if she just wanted to tell him he was late, which was what she was saying right now.

"I know," he said apologetically. "I had to work late. There was this photo layout I had to finish and it was such a bitch. Unlike a certain other person I could name—"

"Oh?" she said, amused.

"Who is the very opposite of that word, in every way. But as soon as we hang up, I'm so outta here that it's unbelievable."

"Well, I'll believe it when I see it," Samantha promised, laughing a little. "I guess I'll just have to find something to keep me busy till you get here."

She had such a sweet laugh, Ben thought. That was the good news. The better news was, he was going to get to hear it every day for the rest of his life.

"I love you," she added.

"Love you, too," Ben said, utterly content. "See you soon. Bye."

He hung up and dropped the cell back into his pocket.

Okay, he thought, and now to try that thing where he tried moving a muscle, even if he wasn't as completely rested as he had intended. Going

home to Samantha was something definitely worth
tiring himself out for.

Just as he sat up, he saw the magnifier sitting on
the desk next to his keyboard.

Maybe if he remembered to put it back where
he'd found it, he told himself, he might not have to
devote so much time to searching for it. He would
be able to find it again in no time.

He opened the drawer and then stopped dead.

Of course, there were also a number of disadvantages to having a policy of remembering to put
everything back where you found it, he thought,
staring at the goggles, the chief one being that you
really could always find it again in no time.
Whether you wanted to or not.

For some reason, the sight of the goggles made
him think of some kind of small but ferocious animal, dozing while it lay in wait for its next
unwitting meal to present itself. Ben hesitated.

Maybe if he wasn't just so damned tired, he
would have been able to appreciate the special
pleasures involved with being the main course on
Sensuous Cindy's menu. Or not. Maybe if he
wasn't just so damned married to Samantha
already, in spirit if not in actual, legal fact. Maybe
that, or maybe if he was nine or ten years younger
and still in his raw youth, he would have been able
to muster the necessary enthusiasm for an imaginary playmate. Especially if she happened to be a
lot less imaginary than she was imaginative.

Or maybe if he was ten or twenty years-older,
approaching his middle age full of disappointments
and unrealized dreams and ambitions. Then he

probably wouldn't hesitate to give himself over to the fantasy of Sensuous Cindy for an hour or two of badly-needed escape.

But kid stuff just didn't interest him any more. And as for finding himself ten or twenty years down the road bemoaning the disappointment of unrealized dreams and ambitions—well, he wasn't there yet, and he didn't have to end up that way if he really didn't want to. On the other hand, if that was what he did want, then all he had to do was waste the time he had right now on dumb shit that didn't do anyone any real good.

Like, say, having sex with a computer program, instead of appreciating what he had.

His real life was, in fact, what millions of people could only fantasize about and Ben knew it. He lived well, with no money or health problems; he had a career rather than just a job, and he was making steady progress in it. Plus, he liked his job. Considering that his work involved his getting paid to look at numerous photographs of gorgeous, scantily-clad women, what was not to like?

But just to make all of it perfect, Samantha loved him. She loved him and she was going to be his wife. There wasn't a fantasy that anyone could come up with that that could even begin to approach the experience of real life with Samantha Ross. Sorry, Cindy, Ben thought at the goggles. It was nice while it lasted, but that's true of all fantasies.

He slid the drawer closed with a sense of satisfied finality. It felt like case closed, the end, that's that. Done. Finished.

Because it was, of course. And the fact that he closed the drawer very gently meant nothing. It was just that he kept his magnifier in there, too, and he didn't want it to slam against the goggles and break.

It wasn't like there was some kind of small but ferocious animal sleeping in there that he didn't want to disturb. There was nothing alive in the drawer. Just his magnifier, which he didn't want to break.

Oh, and some goggles that he didn't need any more.

Just as he was locking the door to his office, he imagined he could hear Cindy calling his name, wanting to know what was keeping him and how much longer she was going to have to wait. Hearing things, now, there was one more very strong argument for breaking the virtual reality habit before it actually got to be a literal habit, Ben thought as he marched to the elevator bank.

His determination pleased him so much that he could feel his fatigue began to lift a little, along with his spirits which refused even to acknowledge the small twinge of pain when he hit the down button a little too hard with his injured fingertip.

The Sensuous Cindy program was just too vivid, too thoroughly overdone. That power-of-suggestion thing was a double-edged sword: nice for the virtual reality business since it meant the only thing they had to provide besides the program was a pair of goggles, but very troublesome and highly annoying for people who might find themselves hearing a program's voice like it was a tune stuck in their heads.

Yeah, he could definitely see where that could happen all too easily, and it was just the sort of thing that geeky geniuses like Garrett would over-look because they were too busy writing their geeky genius programs.

There was a hushed *ding!* and the doors opened on an empty elevator. He stepped in and pushed the button for the lobby. As the doors closed, he suddenly became aware of how quiet everything was. He was probably the last person to leave the building tonight. Again.

He had had an awful lot of long days lately where he didn't get home until well after eight, some-times nine. That may have been okay in the past when he had been a single guy but it wasn't the sort of thing that would make for a happy marriage or a good family life.

It was time for him to start thinking about how he could avoid having to work so many late hours. He had to start planning his time better, maybe map out his tasks for each day; or better yet, orga-nize everything by the week. He could get himself some kind of chart. That would be very efficient. And now that he was thinking of it, wasn't there some software made specifically for scheduling all those things you had to do in the course of a day? Garrett could probably tell him which one of them was—

There was a shrill mechanical screeching sound and the elevator's smooth, rapid, almost silent descent came to a sudden noisy and very bumpy halt. Ben lost his balance, falling first against the wall on his left and then rebounding to hit the wall behind him. He was trying to steady himself when the elevator dropped another couple of feet before it jerked to a stop again.

Then just to make sure he was getting the idea that he might be in more than a little bit of trouble, the lights flickered—with the requisite unpleasant buzzing noise of imminent doom, of course—and Ben felt his mouth go dry.

Dizzy with panic, he had to look around several times before he managed to focus on the panel of buttons. Even then, he was unable to focus well enough to make out which button would activate the alarm. What the hell, he figured, and pounded on all of them, splaying his hands as widely as he could in order to hit as many buttons as possible. One of them had to be an alarm. The blister on his fingertip twinged more intensely; he tried to ignore it even though it suddenly seemed to be getting worse again.

No bells went off, no buzzer sounded. He couldn't hear anything except the sound of his too-rapid breathing and the faint click of the buttons themselves. Maybe it was actually a silent alarm, he thought with sudden desperate hope. The builders had put in a silent one on purpose, so it wouldn't deafen the poor people who might be unlucky enough to get trapped between floors. No point in adding injury to insult, after all. Sure, that was exactly what it was. It had to be. After all, it was bad enough to be trapped until help could arrive.

Trapped with no idea of what had happened or how to get out.

Trapped with nothing you could do except hope that when help finally did show up, it would get there before whatever was holding the car in place gave out and it started falling, out of control, going faster and faster and faster—

"Hey, there, mister," said a voice from a small speaker just above the top row of numbered buttons.

Ben jumped back startled, while thoughts pinwheeled crazily through his mind. He'd been right about the silent alarm thing and boy was he glad he wasn't stuck in here being deafened as well as scared. Why the hell didn't they put video cameras and TV screens in every elevator in the world while they were at it? And of course, he couldn't possibly be the last person to leave the building. Obviously, there must be a security service, rent-a-cops on patrol just for this kind of emergency; the building's insurance company probably made that mandatory as part of the coverage.

At the same time he was thinking all of this, however, he knew he was wrong. He knew he was wrong because the voice was wrong.

It was not a voice that belonged to some rent-a-cop hired by the building management to take care of the odd elevator emergency. Not even a female rent-a-cop. No female rent-a-cop on earth would have a voice like that.

This female voice was one he knew very well because he had heard it before. In fact, if the truth were to be known, he had heard it too much and he had made the decision not to hear it again. But here it was again anyway, because it wasn't done talking to him. Ben yanked at his collar, trying to loosen it.

Suddenly a tiny little video screen lit up behind the large dark plastic panel where all the buttons and the speaker were located. As tiny as the screen was, it was also very high definition.

Not that Ben would have had trouble recognizing the face gazing out at him from the display anyway. The face went so perfectly with the voice.

"Aren't you forgetting something?" Cindy asked archly.

She did not look happy.

NINE

"Cindy, please—I'm asking you nicely now," Ben said, hoping that he actually sounded a lot nicer than he felt. "Please start the elevator. Please?"

"Nothing doing, lover," she said. "Not until we get a few things straightened out. First we talk. Then we'll see about the elevator."

She looked down at him coolly from the tiny screen, her eyes tracking him as he paced from one side of the elevator to the other, back and forth, over and over again. His brain kept telling him to knock it off, calm down and get a grip while his gut insisted that constant movement was the only way he could keep the walls of the elevator from closing in on him completely and mashing him flat.

"Boy, Ben, when you sweat, you really sweat," Cindy added. "Did you know that?" She sounded sincerely fascinated, which made the whole situation even more surreal and nightmarish for him.

"Listen to me, Cindy," he panted. "I have a thing about being trapped in small spaces, I really do. I am not kidding about this, it's a very serious thing.

Right now I'm approaching meltdown here and it ain't gonna be pretty."

She was still watching him with fascination.

"I told you, I'm not kidding, Cindy," he said, trying to quell his rising panic. "I'm really not. This isn't a joke."

"Well, how do you think I feel?" she said defensively. "I can't eat, I can't sleep—"

She had not really just said that, had she? Ben clutched his head with both hands. "You never eat! You never sleep!" he wailed. "Am I the only one who knows this?"

But apparently she didn't listen, either. "I keep dreaming about you—"

Ben let out a wordless howl of frustration. "But you just said you can't sleep!" He clutched his head even more tightly. "Oh, Jesus, did I just say that?" he muttered. "I can't believe I said that. I can't believe I'm arguing with a computer."

Cindy still wasn't listening. "Ben, darling, please," she said, "I'm not asking for much. All I want is for us to be together—"

"Oh, for crying out loud," said Ben. "We can't be together!"

"We can't?" Cindy was staring out at him from the tiny screen with a mixture of hurt and astonishment puckering her pretty forehead, as if this ghastly idea had come from somewhere so far out in left field that she could never have imagined such a bizarre thing. "But Ben," she murmured, her voice threatening tears. "Why not?"

He stared back at her in disbelief. God, she really wanted to know; she was expecting a straight answer out of him, she really was. "We can't be together," he said, speaking slowly and clearly, "because I am engaged. We can't be together because. I. Am. Getting. Married."

She blinked and then broke into a sunny smile of honest delight. "Oh, really?" she asked, thrilled to the point of actually clapping her hands a little. "So when's the big day?"

He saw with some amazement that she really didn't remember what he had told her earlier. Maybe all that high-definition realism meant sacrificing a lot of capacity in the memory-bank area.

"In six months," he said.

"Well, congratulations, darling!" she said warmly and blew him a kiss.

"Thank you," he answered politely and tried to smile just as warmly. "Now, if you—"

"But, darling," she went on, not listening again, "I don't see what that has to do with us."

Ben heard the buttons popping off his shirt as he tore the front open from top to bottom. He ignored them. "That's okay," he said, as breathless now as if he had run a twenty-five mile marathon, or maybe paced it in panicky five-stride installments back and forth in a small, enclosed space. "Maybe after I have my panic attack, I can explain it to you. In detail." His breath was starting to come in whoops now. "If I live."

"Oh, come on, Ben," Cindy said and gave a small, sexy, purring laugh.

But the only reaction that sound stirred in Ben at the present moment was a new surge of panic. It took every bit of self-control he had not to start screaming for help.

"I know you like me," she was saying. "Don't try to tell me otherwise. I know you too well—"

"Yes, okay, I do like you," he said, mopping his sweaty face with the front of his shirt. "You got me there, I admit it. I like you. I like you. Like. But I love Samantha."

Just speaking her name gave him a moment of hopeful solace, very brief but very intense. And there was an extremely good reason for that, he realized. If there could be a single absolute truth in his life, then his love for Samantha was it.

His love for Samantha was more solid, more substantial, and more real than anything and everything else he knew of; that included more widely known facts such as who was on the cover of the current issue of *Brash*, what the capital of Venezuela was, and the existence of gravity, even in direct connection to stalled elevators, including the one he was currently trapped in.

"I love Samantha," he said again, just to hear it.

Cindy gave another of her sexy, purring laughs. "I'm okay with that," she assured him.

"You may be all right with it, Cindy, but I'm not." Ben stopped pacing and looked up at that impossibly beautiful face, feeling the same degree of guilty regret he would have had if Sensuous Cindy had been a real woman. "It was sex, Cindy. It was good, but it was just sex. That's all. Nothing more." He took a deep, uncomfortable breath. "I'm sorry. I really am."

Her blonde head tilted to one side as she regarded him through half-closed eyes for some unmeasured period of time. At last she seemed to have heard him, Ben thought. He had finally managed to get through to her. Now they were getting somewhere; they could settle this whole thing and that would be the end of that.

"Are you trying to tell me," she said after a bit, speaking slowly with a tearful edge in her voice, "that I was just—just a fling? A—a booty call? A roll in the hay?"

Ben winced. "I really don't want to hurt you," he told her, "but yes. That's exactly what you were. As wonderful as you are—and you are wonderful, really—for me you were just a fling. A booty call. A roll in the hay."

The expression on her face went from hurt to stony.

Ben had the distinct sensation of his heart sinking as he became aware that having this discussion with her while he was still trapped in the elevator might not have been one of his more brilliant ideas.

Abruptly, Cindy stood up and folded her arms, regarding him with a stern frown. "I am so disappointed in you," she said coldly and turned her back on him.

"Cindy—" he started and then cut off as the screen went black.

Ben stood motionless in the middle of the elevator, nursing the faint hope that in spite of her disappointment, she would decide to give him a break anyway and in the next few seconds, he would hear the sound of the electric motor coming to life up again so the elevator could continue its descent.

The next few seconds ticked by in silence. These were followed by several more, also soundless.

Oh, good God, he thought, feeling something akin to a tidal wave of intense panic sweep through him, this really had been a bad idea. No, not just bad—incredibly stupid was what it was. Nobody but nobody dumped a woman at a time like this, whether she was real or not.

"Cindy," he called pleadingly, "please don't leave me here like this. Please. I told you, I don't do small spaces. I'm in a bad way here. The walls—they're starting to close in…"

Desperate, he pounced on the control panel again and pounded the buttons with both fists, yelling for help. The blister on his finger was stinging badly now, as if the burn had happened only moments before. He kept pounding on the control panel anyway and yelled even louder.

There was no answer, no sound at all except for the ambient hum coming from the lights, a hum that was somehow becoming more intense without actually getting very much louder. Which was what happened when the walls were closing in, he thought and realized with horror that he was sucking on his burned finger again. He snatched his hand away and jammed it into his trouser pocket.

"Okay, okay!" he wailed at the speaker. "I'm sorry, Cindy, I made a mistake! I made a big mistake! Please, Cindy…"

The screen lit up again but she was still standing with her back to him.

"You're absolutely one hundred per cent right. I should have come to see you, Cindy," he babbled, unable to help himself. "I really should have. You were right and I was wrong. I know that I should have come to see you, I know better than to behave like that—"

She tossed her hair and looked over her shoulder at him, pouting but obviously listening.

"I'll do anything you want, really, I will!" he promised, his voice rising half an octave along with his level of hysteria. "Anything, anything at all no matter what it is, if you'll just forgive me. Please, please, forgive me, Cindy, I wasn't thinking straight. I must have been crazy, over-work or something. I didn't know what I was saying!"

It seemed like forever before Cindy finally turned slowly all the way around to face him. Her gorgeous pout was now a sexy invitation. "Ben, darling, don't you understand? I just want to be with you," she pretend-scolded, shaking her finger at him playfully. "Is that really such a bad thing? Really?"

He shook his head solemnly. "No, Cindy," he said with as much sincerity as he could force. "Of course it isn't a bad thing. It's actually a very good thing."

The elevator motor came to life just as suddenly as it had died and the car finally began to move again. Limp with relief, Ben let his head fall forward to rest against the control panel. The elevator was going up instead of down but the direction no

longer mattered to him. He didn't care which way
the elevator went, up down, or sideways, just as
long as it ended up someplace where the doors
would open so he could get out.

But of course she would bring him back to the floor
where the *Brash* offices were, Ben thought as he
stepped off the elevator. Under the circumstances,
maybe he should consider putting in for overtime.

There was still no one sitting in the chairs or
behind the desk in the silent, dimly-lit reception
area, of course—Ruby Pandiscio had left hours ago
and wouldn't be back until tomorrow morning.
Which Ben thought was a real shame, as he had an
odd certainty that if anyone would have known
what to do, it was Ruby, although he could not for
the life of him have explained what made him
think such a thing.

He glanced back at the elevator. It was just sitting
there with its doors open and he had a sudden
powerful urge to jump back on it and try for the
lobby again. Except that would have been the sec-
ond-stupidest thing he had done in the last
twenty-four hours—or the third, if he counted his
running the Sensuous Cindy program in the first
place. Which he probably should, he told himself
gloomily.

The elevator doors slid closed then, almost as if
in acknowledgement of his thoughts. He heard the
smooth whir of the motor as it began a rapid
descent. Right—I guess I passed that test, Ben
thought, grumpily. I may be stupid but I'm not
totally stupid.

Maybe that meant he was actually getting smarter, he thought as he forced himself to start walking back through the reception area. Just as he got to the hallway, he saw his office light up brightly behind its translucent glass wall while all the other offices remained dark.

That Cindy—not just sensuous but also considerate. Not to mention careful not to waste electricity

"Ben? Darling?" Her voice came from the PA system speakers in the ceiling. "I'm waiting..."

He stopped, thinking that he could try a run for it in the stairwell. He'd have to go down twenty-five flights, sure, but that would be a piece of cake compared to trying to go up that many.

"Where are you?" Cindy asked, a faint but definite edge of impatience in her voice now.

"I-I'll be right there!" he called up at the ceiling. "I just gotta—uh—I just have to use the men's room!"

He went back to the reception area and then just stood, wondering exactly how safe it actually would be to use the men's room. Something told him not to take any more dumb chances. The PA system extended to the bathrooms as well, but even if it hadn't, she had already proved she could just call him on his—

Abruptly, he fumbled his cell phone out of his pocket and hit speed dial.

"You just better be home," he muttered as he listened to the ringing on the other end. "You just better be."

* * *

"Ben...   Beeeeeeeeennnnnnnnnnnn...   oh,
Beeeeeeeeeeennnnn!   Where
arrrrrrrrrrrrrrrrrrrrrrrrrrrrrrrrrrrre
yoooooooooooooouuuuuuuuuuuuuuuuuu..."

Ben didn't answer her. He had no idea how long
he had been sitting in the reception area bent over
with his elbows on his knees and his forehead resting on the knuckles of his interlaced fingers,
listening silently to Cindy calling him. He only
knew that it was too long. But then, even a second
was much too long a period of time to have to listen to that deceptively sweet voice singing his
name over and over like a twenty-first century,
high-tech siren.

He was way beyond the point of it driving him
crazy now. He had already gone crazy, with fear,
with exhaustion, with anger, with frustration. He
had gone all the way past the limits of sanity and
then come all the way back again. Now all he
could do was sit and wait for whatever came
next, feeling neither hope nor fear. Regardless of
what happened, good or bad, it was completely
out of his hands, at least for the moment.

"Be-en." The siren voice turned sulky and impatient. "This isn't funny any more."

It wasn't? That was news to him, he thought
darkly. The only thing was, he had no memory of
any point at which there had been anything he
would have called particularly funny, or even mildly
amusing about this situation. Damn—how could he
have missed something like that? Maybe there was a
glitch in his sense of humor. Maybe he was one of
those poor souls who was lost without a laugh-track.

"I know you're out there," she said ominously.

Ben winced. Yes, she most certainly did; no bluffing on that one, none whatsoever. In terms of her skill in precision locating, she was not quite up to the demanding standards of the Global Positioning Satellite system, but Ben was sure that all she needed was little more time and she would get the hang of that, too.

Without warning, there was an earsplitting bang that seemed to shake the entire reception area. Terrified, Ben jumped out of the chair and then scrambled to regain his balance, looking around wildly.

"Are... you... trying to... kill me?" huffed a tortured male voice.

He turned to see Garrett just barely holding himself up in the open doorway to the stairwell, clutching his chest as he fought to breathe. Ben ran to him and managed to get his shoulder under his arm before he could fall on his face.

"Tell me... again," Garrett gasped as Ben helped him over to a nearby chair, "why... couldn't I... take..." he plumped down on the seat still clutching his chest with one hand and gestured limply toward the bank of elevators with the other. "One... of those..." He paused and almost slid out of the chair as he breathed in with a bronchial whooping noise that Ben found almost as frightening as his own situation. "An... elevator."

Ben leaned close to his ear and spoke in a low voice. "It isn't safe. Nowhere's safe."

Garrett made a pained face and shook his head.

"God," he wheezed. "Twenty... five... stories... straight... up. You think... that's... safe?"

"Oh, Beeeeeeennnnnnnnnnn," sang the siren voice.

Garrett's head snapped up and he looked around. "What... who..." he swallowed with some difficulty and took another big, labored breath. Who... the hell's... that?"

"Who's what?" Ben asked, feigning an innocent, puzzled tone as he put his shoulder under Garrett's arm so he could help him walk to his office. "Oh, you mean, that?" He glanced up at the ceiling briefly and then looked at Garrett again, his expression hardening along with his voice. "That is why you couldn't take the elevator."

"How much longer?" Ben asked for what might have been the zillionth time, hovering over Garrett who was sitting at his desk and typing in rapid-fire bursts.

Garrett didn't take his eyes off the computer screen. "Don't rush me," he said, also for the zillionth time. He was still panting and wheezing to the point where Ben was starting to wonder if he wasn't putting it on a little, or even more than a little. Oh, sure, the guy was hardly any kind of athlete but it wasn't like he smoked a hundred cigarettes a day and weighed three hundred pounds, either.

Whatever impatience or irritation Ben might have been feeling, however, would have to stay under wraps until after Garrett took care of this little situation. But the moment Garrett told him he was finished, he was going to give the guy a thorough rundown of what was bothering him, starting with the way he had just gone ahead and installed the Sensuous Cindy program on his computer in the first place.

"Man, you know, I really can't believe I'm doing this," Garrett added sadly. "I mean, it's a crime is what it is. It's a real crime."

"A crime? Oh, you want to talk crime here?" Ben asked him, forgetting why he had been keeping things friendly. "How about attempted kidnapping? How's that for a crime?"

Garrett paused to look over his shoulder at him with exasperation. "Come on, Ben, the elevator got stuck. It happens. Accept it."

"I'm telling you, she wasn't going to let me out!" he said as his friend turned back to the computer.

"Listen, man, you really need to stop talking about her like she's real," Garrett told him, forgetting to pant. "You're weirding me out. Big time."

"Hey, have I got some news for you, Garrett old buddy. Big time," Ben replied, openly snapping at him now and not caring. "You know she's not real, and I know she's not real. But Cindy? She's not on the same page with you and me. She sees things a little differently."

Garrett sighed with undisguised irritation. "She's nothing but a series of ones and zeroes," he said wearily, as if he were sick and tired of having to remind non-geeks about binary code. Then he sighed again, sounding more wistful this time. "Ones and zeroes, and they're all wrapped in the cutest, hottest little body—"

"Stop that," Ben snapped at him. "Now you're weirding me out, big time. Plus I feel guilty enough as it is." He paused as his gaze fell on the framed photo of himself with Sam that he kept on his desktop. "But not as guilty as I would feel if Sam ever found out," he added, turning the photo face down.

"Sam?" Garrett gave him a look and then forgot all about wheezing in favor of laughing heartily. "In case it's slipped your mind, Sam just happens to be one hell of a primo software developer herself. She would probably think Cindy was pretty damned cool."

"Oh, for God's sake, don't you get it?" said Ben, raising his voice with exasperation. "Samantha and I made a vow: no sex until our wedding. That means not with each other, not with other people, and not with any sex-happy computer program!"

Garrett shook his head and went on typing rapidly. "Your loss. Your great big fat gigunda mother of a loss." He continued to type for several seconds longer and then sat back, holding one finger over the keyboard. "All right, Ben, this is it. I push this key and whoosh! Cindy vanishes out of your life forever." Garrett looked at him with raised eyebrows. "I say that's a real shame. What do you say, chief?"

In spite of everything that had happened to him, even his getting trapped in the elevator, Ben hesitated. On some level, Cindy had become—well, not a person, exactly, but more than the inanimate object he kept insisting to himself that she was. Now that he had come right down to the moment of truth, he suddenly felt himself in the grip of an odd, vaguely superstitious apprehension.

Then the phone rang.

"I say, terminate her," Ben said promptly as the blister on his finger throbbed. "Now."

Garrett hesitated, looking from him to the phone and back again, the expression on his face plainly stating that if Ben really thought it was Sensuous Cindy who was calling, he had completely lost his mind.

Ben glared back at him. Garrett shrugged and dropped his finger down on a key like a bomb. The computer screen went black; then two words appeared, all the letters capitalized: PROGRAM DELETED.

As soon as the words appeared, the phone cut off in mid-ring. Garrett blinked at it, startled now, and then turned to Ben again.

"Told you," Ben said absently. He wasn't looking at the phone but at his fingertip.

The blister was gone.

TEN

He couldn't remember when home had been so much of a refuge as it was tonight, Ben thought as he let himself in.

The relief he felt at being able to close the door—literally—on the day he had just had was intense enough to make him a bit lightheaded. For a few moments, all he could do was stand there with the paper sack in his arms and stare unseeingly down at the wine he had stopped to buy on the way home.

He had splurged on a couple of bottles of full-bodied reds, the sort Sam was so partial to. It hadn't been some minor, lightweight splurge, either, but something more akin to what women referred to as retail therapy. Even the guy behind the counter at the liquor store had been impressed, asking Ben if he was celebrating because he had won the lottery while he rang up the sale.

"Oh, you could put it that way," Ben had replied, wondering what the guy's reaction would have been if he had told him the truth.

Actually, I'm celebrating my narrow escape from the clutches of a computer program in the form of a hot babe that keeps trying to sex me to death.

Oh, sure, any guy could relate to that; there were probably even support groups. Hi, my name is Ben and I'm a Cindy-holic. Ben shook the thought away and called out, "Hi, I'm home!"

"In here!" came Sam's voice from the small room she had set up as her home office.

Ben stopped to set the wine and his laptop case on the dining room table and then went in to find her frowning at the computer on her tidy, uncluttered desk. The whole room was equally neat. How she managed to keep everything that way was completely beyond his understanding. Who needed virtual reality when there was Samantha Ross, woman of mystery, wielder of unknown and possibly unearthly power?

He swept her gorgeous dark curls to one side and bent down to kiss the back of her neck. Sam made a small noise of approval that turned into a sigh of pleasure as he began to knead her shoulder muscles in the slow, gentle but firm way that she liked.

"Mmm," she said happily. "That is so nice." She leaned back and looked up at him, raising her eyebrows at the sight of his face. "Tough day?"

"Shows, does it?" He sighed. "I won't bore you with the details." Especially since you would definitely not find any of it all that terribly boring, he added silently.

"Poor baby," she sympathized. "I know just how you feel, believe me. I'm having trouble with my hard drive. It was working fine yesterday. Now all of a sudden I can't access any of my files. Stupid thing."

The array of icons and boxes with error messages in them made little if any sense to Ben but he had a strong urge to make himself useful, or at least try.

"Want me to check it out for you?" he asked her.

Samantha gave a surprised laugh as she twisted around to look up at him. "Remind me, will you—who's the computer expert around here again?"

"Hey, a fresh set of eyes—" Ben kissed the top of her head. "Like the proverbial yet legendary chicken soup for the computer expert—couldn't hurt, might help."

He moved her shoulders gently, turning her so that she could see the store logo on the bag just visible on the dining room table from where she was sitting.

Obviously pleased, she stood up and gave him a kiss. "Have at it," she told him. "I'll get us some wine."

He sat down at the computer, enjoying her exclamation of delight when she saw exactly what he had brought home—not just something good but something great. That was what he wanted, Ben thought as she took the wine into the kitchen to open it.

More than great sex, more than winning the lottery, more than the adulation of millions, what he wanted was to be the man whose purpose in life was to make Samantha Ross happy. He wanted every part of their life together to be better than she might have expected. A woman like Samantha deserved nothing less.

He moved the mouse around the screen idly and then clicked on a random icon. Instantly, the display changed and he found himself looking at something he did understand but which made absolutely no sense at all.

"'Terminate her'?" Sensuous Cindy said, gazing hard at him from under her brows. "Did I actually hear you say, 'Terminate her'?"

The world tilted sideways as Ben's mouth went dry.

"No," he said, shakily, "no, you can't be here, you can't. We got rid of you—"

"Oh, that," Cindy said, waving one graceful hand dismissively. "You mean you tried to get rid of me, but I was hiding in the computer in the office next door." She made a *tsk*-ing noise. "Ben, really, who do you think you're dealing with?"

He could hear Sam coming out of the kitchen just then saying something about needing a certain man with muscles to get the cork out of the wine bottle. Almost blind with panic, he did the only thing he could think of and kicked the plug out of the wall-socket. The screen went dark as the whole computer shut down.

"Having any luck with that?" Samantha was twisting the corkscrew into the wine bottle as she came over to him.

"N-nah," he said, hoping he didn't sound as shaky as he felt. "The whole dammed thing froze up on me. Why don't we forget about it for now? We can, uh, you know, pop some popcorn, watch a movie?"

She looked from him to the expensive wine she was holding and back again. "Wine and popcorn?" she asked, sounding slightly skeptical.

"Sure," he said expansively. "You stick a bag of the good stuff in the microwave and I'll see what's on."

Sam laughed as he made little shooing motions at her. "Wine and popcorn," she said again. "Honestly, sometimes you can be so cute."

She headed back to the kitchen while Ben all but ran for the entertainment center.

Thank God for satellite TV, his mind babbled, and for each and every one of those five hundred and some-odd channels broadcasting junk from the very early morning to the wee hours of the night. For when you absolutely, positively wanted to do anything but think, and keep someone else from thinking, too.

He picked up the remote and thumbed the On button.

"Why are you trying to hurt me, Ben?" demanded the larger-than-life-size Cindy face on the TV screen. She seemed to be very close to tears now.. "What's the matter with you? I love you, can't you understand that? I love you—"

Ben reached around the back of the TV, grabbed a fistful of wires and yanked as hard as he could. Everything went off.

Right away, the phone started to ring.

"I'll get it!" Ben yelled, charging across the room like a linebacker to pounce on the cordless handset.

"Maybe it's time Samantha and I had a little talk," Cindy said by way of hello. She didn't sound even a little bit like someone on the verge of tears any more.

"No, don't!" Ben said frantically. "I'll come back to the office, right now I'll—"

"Oh, don't do anything on my account," she told him with a definite edge underlying her otherwise airy tone. "I mean, really, after all—"

"No, no, no, it's on my account! I want to come see you!" he said desperately, lowering his voice to a half-whisper. "I really do, Cindy, I want to. We can, you know, we can, uh, we'll, we'll talk."

Her purring, sexy laugh. It had begun to sound a whole lot like doom to him now, and it was laughing at him, not with him.

"And once we're done talking…?" she said.

Wincing, Ben lowered his voice even more. "I'm a tiger. Remember? Grrrrrrrr." Hearing what he was actually saying made him wince again.

"You are just so cute!" She all but squealed with delight. "And will you stay the night? Please? For me?"

"Stay the night," Ben echoed bleakly before he could think better of it. "Oh, uh, yeah, yeah, yeah, sure. I'll stay the night, anything you want. Anything."

"Okay," she said with a contented, sexy sigh. "But hurry—"

"I'm already out the door," he said, started to replace the receiver and then put the phone back to his ear to add, "Baby," before he hung up and bolted for the front door.

"Ben?"

He whirled to find Samantha looking utterly baffled as she stood in the middle of the living room carrying a tray with two wine glasses and a big bowl of popcorn on it.

"What's going on?" she asked.

"The office called! There's a fire I have to put out!" he babbled at her, yanking the door open. He caught himself and ran over to give her a quick kiss on the cheek first. "Gotta go, be back as soon as I can—"

Oh, God, please let her buy that, he prayed as he sprinted for his car.

"Ben, darling!" Cindy raised up on the bed where she had been stretched out waiting for him. "What took you so long?"

Ben looked around the fancy bedroom. "Well, what can I say?" Good question: what could he say? He spread his arms helplessly, looking around while he tried to think of something.

He was back in the resort bedroom on the beach again. If he could ever really get out of this mess once and for all, he would take Samantha away to a resort in the Caribbean that would make this place look like a boudoir in a trailer park.

No, when he got out of it, he corrected himself as Cindy slithered across the bed toward him; when. This was a computer program and it would come to an end.

"Uh, traffic was horrendous," he said weakly. "Man, it just gets worse by the day. By the hour, for crying out loud. I was going to stop for flowers but it was so bad—"

Cindy reached over and tapped his hand with her perfect index finger. Instantly, he felt a familiar throb of pain from his finger; at the same moment, he found himself holding a bouquet of what he knew must have been rare and exotic blossoms, all of them in fantastic colors. He offered it to her without missing a beat, as if he had been holding it all along

"Hope you like them," he said conversationally.

She accepted the flowers and buried her face in them with a dreamy sigh. "They smell beautiful."

She raised her head and smiled up at him for a long moment. Then she tossed the bouquet over her shoulder and pounced on him, wrapping both arms around him and jamming her mouth against his.

Apparently, she wanted to start hot and go on from there; fine with him. He felt her surprised delight and increased enthusiasm as he went from cooperation to full participation

Even if he were to do this every day, Ben thought, he would never get over how utterly real it felt.

It was so complete and so perfect in detail that even just remembering it was like remembering something that had actually happened in the real world. Illusion didn't really seem to be the right word for it, didn't begin to describe it.

This felt a lot like it was some gray area between real life and illusion, where Cindy was more real than he wanted, but less real than she wanted. He turned the idea over in his mind for a few moments; the more he thought about it, the creepier it got. And that was even before the twinge in his finger reminded him that the burn had come back.

On the surface of it, this was no doubt some kind of major cutting-edge breakthrough in computer programming, the kind of thing that might result in a Nobel Prize for the lucky bastard who developed it.

It would be lucrative, too—like a license to print money. There were probably billions of people, and only a very tiny percentage of them genuine computer geeks, who would have given anything, done anything, paid anything for even just a small taste of what Garrett had bestowed on him for free, just as a well-meaning favor for an old friend.

But well-meaning didn't necessarily make it good and that was a problem that had been around as long as humanity itself. Every time people came up with something that was supposed to do some kind of good, it always ended up creeping up behind them and biting them on the ass.

Creeping. Because it was creepy.

Unbidden, the memory of Samantha showing him one of her favorite books popped into his mind, a big art book full of reproductions of newspaper advertising from a hundred years ago.

One of the ads had been for that miracle drug of 1898: heroin, developed by the Bayer Company in Germany for the treatment of morphine addiction. It had worked, too. It had done quite a lot more as well, but the fact remained that it had done exactly what it had been designed to do.

Well, there was one other good thing—well, vaguely good, sort of—to be said for heroin: it couldn't literally phone you up at home to demand sex, Ben thought as Cindy became even more enthusiastic. If this went on much longer, he would have genuine bruises on his lips.

He felt something change then. Cindy felt it at the same moment, or possibly a fraction of a second before. She gave a little jump and then pulled back from him, looking puzzled.

"Ben?" she asked, her voice uncertain.

Her lips flickered slightly. Only her lips and only briefly, but it was obvious that she could feel something happening and it was a rather strange sensation. She touched a fingertip lightly to the corner of her mouth.

"Ben?" she asked again.

Abruptly, mixed groups of ones and zeroes were rapidly streaming by on her lips, as if the lipstick she was wearing had suddenly become animated. Now she rubbed her index finger on her lower lip and then took a close look at her fingertip.

There was a bright pinpoint of light on it. It flickered and then began to spread out, covering her hand with more streaming groups of ones and zeroes. The streams traveled up her arm to her shoulder where it merged with the ones and zeroes spreading down from her neck.

Damn—Garrett had been absolutely right about that, Ben thought as he backed away from the bed. It really was all just binary codes and, weirdly enough. On Cindy, it actually looked sexy.

It figured—only Sensuous Cindy could make ASCII erotic, he thought.

"What did you do to me?" Cindy asked him, looking down at her arms and her torso with fascination.

At least it didn't seem to be hurting her or causing her any sort of distress, Ben thought guiltily. He would never have been able to forgive himself if this had meant she would have to suffer the computer program equivalent of pain.

"I'm afraid it's a virus," he told her a little sadly. "I stopped by Garrett's on my way over here. He wrote it for me and I gave it to you."

"But why?" she asked, watching as the binary codes flowed down her legs.

"I'm sorry, Cindy," he said, meaning it. "But I had to. Being with you made me realize how much I really do love Sam."

She was so covered with binary codes now that they had completely obscured all of her human features except for the outline of her body. She was nothing left of her but a Cindy-shaped silhouette with ones and zeroes running through it.

"Oh, Ben," she said adoringly and he wasn't sure which surprised him more—the fact that she was still able to speak or that she was still all lovey-dovey.

The binary codes were spreading out from her to the rest of the room, which was disappearing much more quickly than she had.

"That is soooooo romantic! You are such a sweeeeeet..." Her voice died away.

There was nothing to see now except ones and zeroes but Ben took a last long, hard look. Then he removed the goggles and, with a ceremonial flourish, tossed them into his waste basket.

Two points, he thought, satisfied.

ELEVEN

God, what an ordeal that had been.

Putting his feet up on his desk, he slumped down in his chair. This time, however, it was really over. He had told Garrett there couldn't be any more surprise comebacks and Garrett had promised him that there wouldn't be, that nothing could survive the virus he was making up for Ben to give to Cindy.

Even better, it hadn't required any special knowledge on Ben's part, no complicated programming for him to learn or codes to remember. He'd simply had to put a floppy disk in the drive before he plugged in the goggles and then make direct, active contact with Cindy. After that, he was home free. Or he would be, as soon as he got up the energy to move.

His gaze fell on the goggles in the waste basket. Even after everything he had been through, he could still see how, from Garrett's perspective, it was a shame, really. Kind of a waste—

The phone rang and he nearly went through the ceiling.

"No," he said firmly, looking from the telephone to the goggles in the waste basket and back again.

No. Garrett had promised him, he'd even given him a somewhat simplified explanation of how the virus worked so he would understand why he didn't have to worry about Cindy coming back any more.

"No—"

Oh, for crying out loud, he thought, suddenly feeling like an idiot. Was he was really going to jump out of his skin every single time the phone rang for the rest of his life? He picked up the receiver and forced himself not to hesitate before he said, "Hello?"

"So what happened?" asked Garrett, his voice sad and resigned. "Is it over?"

Told you. Ben closed his eyes for a moment as relief spread through him with an intensity that made him feel even more wrung out. "Yeah, it's over," he told Garrett, unable to keep from sounding a little bit regretful about it. "It's over and done with and I can't thank you enough. I really mean that."

"Don't mention it." Garrett gave a laugh completely devoid of any merriment. "And I really mean that. Don't mention it ever, to anyone. Otherwise they'll think we're both crazy."

"But Garrett," Ben said, "you are crazy. All you computer geeks are crazy. And I probably am, too."

"Yeah, fine, whatever," said Garrett. "You can do whatever you want, but I don't want anyone thinking that I might actually be the kind of crazy that would erase something like Sensuous Cindy permanently."

"Jeez, will you take it easy?" Ben said, starting to get annoyed with him again in spite of everything. "You're making it sound like you erased every copy of the program everywhere in the world. You only took her—it—off my computer, okay? She's still out there. You might try to keep that in mind if it makes you happy."

The idea gave him a small chill and he realized that he was going to have to try not to keep that in mind if he wanted to be happy himself.

"Hey, why don't you just ask that friend of yours at Fantadyne for another copy of the beta?" he went on quickly.

"I ought to make you ask for me," Garrett said a bit sulkily.

"Hey, if you want, I'll even see about getting you a note from a doctor," Ben told him, laughing a little. "How about that?"

"Good idea," said Garrett sourly. "You going to see a doctor, I mean. But not for my benefit."

Ben laughed. "I'll talk to you tomorrow."

He shut the phone off and, still laughing, started to put it back in his pocket when it rang again.

No, he thought and then made himself answer it before he could change his mind.

"Oh, yeah, I almost forgot," Garrett's voice said, still a bit sour. "Take those goggles out of the waste basket, will ya? You can't just throw them around like that, they cost a fortune!"

"Gotcha," Ben said, laughing again as he hung up. "Just as soon as I can move a muscle," he added to the air.

Abruptly, the phone in his hand rang for a third time.

Please, no, he thought, staring at it, knowing somehow that this time it would not be Garrett on the other end. His thumb hovered over the keypad and he almost hit the off button. Then he realized that there was no sensation of a blister or even a slight burn on his finger.

"Hello?" he said, putting the phone to his ear.

"Ben?" asked a familiar female voice. "Are you okay?"

Samantha. For crying out loud, it was Samantha. Thank God. He slumped down in his chair again, resisting the urge to kiss the handset he was holding to his ear.

Then he couldn't help feeling like a complete and utter fool. Of course it was Samantha on the phone, and even if it had not been Samantha this time, it would have been Garrett again after all, giving him one more call just so he could rag his ass even more about Sensuous Cindy. As it was, he could probably count on the fact that he was never going to hear the end of it from Garrett anyway.

"Yeah," he said, sighing with relief. "Yeah, I'm okay, Sam. I'm just fine."

"Glad to hear it," she told him. "Did you get your fire put out?"

He glanced at the contents of the waste basket again. "Looks that way," he said.

"Good. Listen, darling, I know it's awfully late, but could you stop by the store on the way home?"

"Sure," he said happily. "No problem. What do you want me to get?"

"I e-mailed you a list of what we need," she said. "Oh, and the computer's working fine again, by the way." She chuckled. "Maybe it was the way you looked at it with your fresh pair of eyes."

"Great," he told her. "See you soon."

"No need to hurry," she told him.

"No problem," he said again, glad that he could finally say that in all honesty. "Sam?" he added suddenly.

"What?" she asked.

"I love you."

"Me, too," she said breezily. "Bye now." Then there was a click and all he heard was the hum of the dial tone.

Apparently the enormity of what he was feeling right now just could not in any way come through to her over the telephone, Ben thought as he hung up. Which was one more good reason to stick to real life for all those things that really mattered. He opened the email program on his computer so he could download Sam's shopping list.

Damn, but he couldn't wait to get home.

I love you.

Sam could feel herself smiling more than a little wryly as she pressed the disconnect button on the phone. Some people—in particular, some men—could say that so easily. Like it was just one more thing to throw into a conversation: Hi, how are you? Gesundheit! Think it'll rain tomorrow? I love you.

But she supposed she shouldn't have even thought of finding any fault with something like that, Samantha told herself as she put the cordless handset back in the recharging base. There were an awful lot of women in the world stuck with guys who were just the opposite—you could not have gotten them to say I love you if you put a knife to their throats and pointed a double-barreled shotgun at their balls.

Well, maybe if you held both the knife and the shotgun to their balls.

Men! Men, God help us all, men, she thought and laughed silently to herself. Can't live with 'em, can't shoot 'em, as her mother had always said, speaking the absolute truth at least where Sam's father had been concerned.

Sam knew that it was her father's example that had made her a bit skittish about having a serious relationship with any man, no matter how nice he seemed or how much she liked him. Not that she had any hard feelings toward her father—not really. For all his faults as a husband, Frankie Ross had still been her daddy and just judging from the way her friends talked, he had been a better daddy than most.

He had always been Frankie Ross, never Frank or Frannie or Francis. He was in sales, he said whenever anyone asked him what he did for a living. Sam could remember him selling advertising for a local radio station for a while. Then he had been a regional representative for some kind of fancy designer soap that was, he had told her and her mother in a very serious, almost solemn voice, especially good for those ladies whose complexions needed extra help.

That hadn't lasted very long, though, and Sam had wondered if it had been his tendency to be rather generous with free samples that had been a problem, or whether it was that he kept giving the samples to ladies whose complexions did not seem to need any extra help.

Then he was back with the radio station for a while—a long while; she remembered going to at least five annual employee picnics in a row. Then he was with a gourmet food distributor and he kept bringing home cases of cans of turtle soup and bouillabaisse.

Then another stint at the radio station. Eventually she was old enough to understand about downsizing and being laid off. But somehow, he always managed to get another job before very long. Your daddy is one heck of an ace salesman, he would tell her. He can sell anything to anyone. He can sell ice cubes to Eskimos.

You can say that again, her mother had added.

Frankie Ross had looked up at his wife with that twinkle in his eye—it was still a real twinkle then—and said, "Another satisfied customer."

Really, Mommy? Sam had turned to her in all innocence. What did you buy from Daddy? But for some reason, neither her mother nor her father would answer that question.

Good time Frankie Ross, always up for a few laughs, always ready to have some fun. You could tell just by looking at his big, friendly smile that he was one of those easy-going, good-natured guys who could be counted on to be the life of the party. A real likeable guy, a hell of a swell, that Frankie. The more perceptive among the crowd of those likeminded party animals that seemed always to surround Frankie Ross no matter where he went would sometimes whisper to each other—strictly behind good old Frankie's back, of course—that the never-ending party was probably nowhere near as much fun for anyone who was part of the Ross household.

Guy's wife has to be a saint, you know what I mean? And don't they have a kid as well? Yeah, a little girl—Frankie's pride and joy, he's always showing her picture around, cute little thing, cute as a button. But the most serious eyes you ever saw on a kid, like she already knows what's what. Guess any kid with Frankie as a father would be kinda wise beyond her years, you know what I mean?

Sam had known what they meant; she had overheard that conversation and variations of it often enough when Frankie brought his friends home in the middle of the night. As perceptive as some of them might have been, that did not make any of them less inclined to party on anyway.

Inevitably during the course of the night, she would be discovered crouching on the stairs by one of these enlightened souls on the way to use the bathroom. Whoever it was would always alert Frankie so he could put her back to bed and tuck her in.

Frankie never scolded her for getting out of bed and spying on the party, probably because he realized he was the one who had woken her up in the first place and he had enough sense to feel at least a little bit guilty about it. He would just take her back to her room, slurring his words only very slightly as he told her she needed her beauty sleep. The feel of stubble on his cheeks—he was a two-shaves-a-day-man, her mother used to say—and the smell of beer were still vivid in her memory.

Guy's wife has to be a saint, you know what I mean?

Oh, yes, indeed, from a remarkably early age, Samantha had understood and accepted it as a given: her mother was indeed a saint. In Sam's eyes, her mother was a saint just by virtue of her beauty alone. Much later, when she looked through the family photo albums, she could see that her assessment of her mother's beauty had not been solely a matter of filial love and adoration—Maggie Ross had been a classic beauty well into her later years, even after her dark hair had gone completely white.

What the family photos documented was not her beauty fading but her weariness increasing. Each year, her smile appeared to be a little more strained and the look in her eyes a little bit sadder as the resignation in her expression became more marked. Sam had not failed to notice any of this while it was happening; the photos simply provided confirmation of her youthful impressions.

And yet, she had always thought of her parents' marriage as a happy one. They had never stopped loving each other in that special way of two people

who were still in love. In fact, she had been surprised and somewhat disturbed when she learned
that not all of her friends' parents had the same
intensity of emotion—those who were even still
together. And this in spite of the fact that none of
the other mothers seemed to find the men they
were married to as tiring to live with as Frankie
Ross was for her mother.

Sam only found herself becoming more bewildered as the years went by and she grew up. The
party around good old, good-time Frankie Ross still
seemed to be in full swing but her father's laughter had begun to acquire a hard, effortful sound
and more and more often the twinkle in his eyes
was a little too twinkly, the look in them not so
much happy as it was manic.

Somewhere along the line, her father's insistence
that life was something to celebrate had taken on a
very definite quality of desperation. Slowly she
came to realize that the only reason her father was
working so hard to keep the party going was
because he was afraid of what would happen if he
stopped.

Guess any kid with Frankie as a father would be
kinda wise beyond her years, you know what I
mean?

When she had gone to her mother with this startling insight, however, Maggie Ross had shut her
down right away, refusing in no uncertain terms to
listen to her. Sam's initial surprise at her mother's
reaction had been immediately replaced by a realization so instantaneous and fully-formed as to be
a genuine satori: her mother didn't want to know

because she already knew, and had known for some time. Long before Sam had first perceived any outward signs of her father's secret anguish, Maggie Ross had known all about it. Moreover, she had known even before Frankie himself had begun to suspect, before he had even started to build up his denial about it.

And still she had stayed with him, cleaning him up and putting him to bed after everyone else had taken off, clearing away the bottles and the pizza boxes and restoring their home, particularly the living room and the kitchen, from the ruins left behind before she went off to work at the Maxi-Mart.

She had stayed even after some of the parties turned into two-day benders. She had stayed after Frankie Ross could not tell her the names of the people who had passed out in the living room because he could not even remember bringing them home. She had stayed after the police had come to investigate a noise complaint and ended up arresting everyone in the house except her and Sam.

She had not even blinked when Frankie had brought home the stripper who had claimed her abusive boyfriend had thrown her out with nothing but a black eye, a thong, and a pair of three-inch spike heels. The stripper had spent one night on the couch and left wearing Maggie Ross's Go Lions! sweatshirt and a pair of her old jeans with enough money for a one-way bus ticket home to Salt Lake City in the back pocket.

She had left and Maggie Ross had stayed, setting out a glass of water with three aspirin on the

nightstand next to Frankie's side of the bed so it
would be the first thing he saw when he woke up
before she went off to work at the Maxi-Mart.

Maggie Ross had kept the books for the local
branch of Maxi-Mart, which happened to be the
largest one in the region. A classic beauty with a
good head for numbers and business in general,
she had managed, by virtue of competence and
attrition, to get to the head bookkeeper position in
a shorter-than-usual amount of time and then par-
lay that into a higher level managerial spot in
Accounts. This had required a great deal of computer training, which Maxi-Mart had provided on
the job, including a laptop, of course, so that she
could study at home.

Sam had used computers at school since kinder-
garten but the fascination that had led to her
pursuing a career in Information Technology had
been kindled in her during the evenings when she
had sat on Maggie Ross's lap at the dining room
table, watching as her mother plumbed the mys-
teries of exotic things like programmable databases
and spreadsheets. Then afterwards, Maggie would
let her explore the rest of the programs on the computer as well as the operating system itself.

Between the curriculum at school and her
mother's indulgence, Sam's interest grew naturally
and easily into a talent and then a passion. Her
father talked to some people who talked to some
other people and somehow managed to get her
admitted to advanced courses of study after school
and on the weekends and during the summer. By
the time she graduated from high school, she had

been accepted into an honors program at the Mass-achusetts Institute of Technology.

Frankie Ross had asked her if she wanted a grad-uation party and had actually been surprised when she had said no. Then he had gone ahead and thrown one anyway. It was the only time she had ever been angry with him. She had expected her mother to be angry with him as well but she wasn't, which had made Sam angry with her, too.

"I don't get it," she had raged at Maggie. "What's the matter with you? I thought you at least would care about my feelings."

"Getting mad at your father for throwing a party," Maggie Ross had informed her more than a little wryly, "is like getting mad at the weather."

It was then that Sam had suddenly had a per-fectly clear if wordless understanding of why her mother had stayed with her father all those years, and not just why but how as well. But even more than that, she now knew the state of Maggie Ross's existence. The image was there in her mind: her mother standing outside in the rain, alone.

Her mother was lonely. But she had stayed with Frankie Ross because without him her life would only have been lonelier. Sam had decided then and there that no matter what else happened, whether she shared her life under the same roof with a part-ner or just a room-mate or whether she lived alone, she would not end up lonely.

Men! Men, God help us all, men. Can't live with 'em, can't shoot 'em.

So her mother had said, standing all alone in the figurative rain and dedicating her life to not getting mad at it. But that was how Maggie Ross had chosen to make the best of her lot. This was the twenty-first century and things had changed. Boy, had they changed.

Sam went back to the desk in her office and picked up the goggles she had left next to the keyboard. The advantages of being a computer expert, she thought, handling them gently, almost lovingly; if the rest of the world only knew the perks to being a so-called computer geek. She couldn't help feeling glad that was still the world's best-kept secret.

Sam glanced at her watch. Now that she had given him an errand to run for her, Ben wouldn't be home for at least another hour, which would give her enough time. Maybe not as much time as she would have preferred, but it would be adequate.

She slipped on the goggles and the office around her vanished.

It was replaced by a perfect recreation of the bedroom in her favorite beach-house. The design was one that Fantadyne had licensed at her suggestion—her very strong suggestion, she remembered, smiling to herself. The consistently high ratings that all the beta testers gave it had borne her out and as a result she had become management's golden girl and The Next Big Thing at Fantadyne, something that came with even more perks.

"Sorry I'm late," she called out, sprawling on the bed luxuriously and undoing the buttons on her blouse. "I've been dealing with my fiancé. He's been acting a little strange lately." She shrugged

out of the blouse and rolled over with a small sigh
of pleasure. "If I didn't know better, I'd think he
was cheating on me. You know?"

The diaphanous white curtains billowed as a
breeze blew in from the beach.

"Men," said someone, speaking in a sexy purring
growl. "You just can't trust them."

Smiling with happy excitement, Sam held out her
arms. Sensuous Cindy flowed into them, pressing
that perfect body along the full length of her own.

God, it was so real, so real, and yet so much better than reality. Six more uninterrupted months of
private happiness—it was like contemplating six
months in heaven.

"Well, you can't, you know," Cindy added,
stroking Sam's cheek.

Sam laughed, feeling delicious. "Yeah, I do
know," she said and then let Cindy shut her up
with a kiss.

The question under consideration is: what will happen once we are all able to act out our sexual fantasies? What kind of a world will that be?

If it turns out to be the sort of world where things like betrayal and infidelity only take place in our fantasies and never create any problems in real life, then who could possibly be hurt by such a development? That can't possibly be harmful to anyone, can it?

Because it's what we really do, in the real world that counts. Those are the only things that truly make any difference. Whatever we fantasize about doesn't matter. It can't matter if it didn't really happen... right?

It is not yet possible to create a personal fantasy world that not only feels just as real as the world we all have to live in, but that more than a few of us may decide is ultimately preferable to it as well. Not yet, but perhaps someday, and that someday may well come much sooner than we think.

But until then, this is something that will itself remain just another fantasy... except, of course, in The Twilight Zone.

ABOUT THE AUTHOR

Pat Cadigan lives in the gritty, urban North London borough of Haringey where the traffic never lets up and the trees grow out of the sidewalk. A recovering American, she has been a professional writer for twenty-five years, having penned the novels *Mindplayers, Synners,* and *Dervish is Digital,* but to name a few. Acclaimed by the Guardian as "The Queen of Cyberbunk", Pat's Hugo and Nebula Award-nominated short stories have appeared in *Omni* and *Asimov's Science Fiction Magazine,* as well as numerous anthologies. Fellow housemates include hubby and main squeeze Chris Fowler, son Rob Fenner, and Miss Kitty Calgary, Queen of the Cats.

Also from Black Flame
Twilight Zone #1

MEMPHIS · THE POOL GUY

by Jay Russell

The free clinic near the intersection of Pico and Sepulveda was packed to the rafters as usual. As ever, there was a preponderance of withered old people and young mothers with screaming babies sitting around, but also a surprisingly broad array of Angelinos from across the age, race and cultural strata. Ritchie saw African-American gang-bangers in their colors and a tidy Korean family reading from their Bible. There was a leather-clad biker with a patch over one eye, and an Aryan surfer dude who looked like he'd just walked in off the beach at Point Dume.

Every chair and bench in the place was taken and there were old Latino ladies sitting on the floor waiting their turn to be seen by one of the medical staff. Many of them would be examined initially by a nurse, but Ritchie never put up with that kind of treatment. He had been coming to the clinic for years, and he always made a fuss when they tried to foist him off with a mere nurse. Just because he couldn't afford health insurance, it didn't mean that he shouldn't be seen by a doctor when he needed to be. At least, that was always Ritchie's position and he made it very clear to all concerned. Because the truth of the world was that if you made a big enough stink—complained loudly enough, behaved stubbornly enough, gave people enough grief—they always gave in because it was easier for them in the end. The staff at reception knew Ritchie well enough by now that they didn't even try to send him to the nurse first. But he still had to wait his turn, and wait and wait, before he could see the doctor.

"Rosoff," Ritchie had demanded when he checked in at the reception desk. "I want to see Doctor Rosoff. And don't try to stick me with nobody else."

The receptionist nodded wearily, knowing better than to get into an argument with him. She remembered the fuss Ritchie had made the last time he was in. She gestured at the waiting area, indicating that he should take a seat. Ritchie saw that there was a tiny sliver of space on a bench between an eighteen year-old Latina juggling three kids and a middle-aged African-American man with his arm in a sling. He wedged his way between them—he wasn't about to sit on the floor—garnering a pair of dirty looks and a pained grunt from the man with the sling, but no more significant protest. The Latina woman's oldest child, who looked about four, tried hard to engage Ritchie in a game of peek-a-boo, but he was too self-absorbed in his problems to play along. That earned him another sneer from the little girl's harried mother.

Fuck it, Ritchie thought.

Truth be told, Ritchie didn't much care for children. But then he didn't much care for any of the types he had to share bench space with. Ritchie had long lists of people and things he didn't like. Not that anyone was asking.

As Ritchie sat there on that hard wooden bench, among the coughing, sneezing, broken-boned detritus of the uninsured, he couldn't help but rub at the mysterious scar on his chest through the thin material of his white T-shirt. The scar had started to fade almost as soon he noticed it, but it was still there. The moistness, the *freshness* of it had dissipated, but the exposed folds of skin had consequently started to go hard and crusty and it itched liked a son-of-a-bitch. He tried his best not to scratch, but like a missing filling or toothache that your tongue can't help but find and irritate, he couldn't resist the urge to scratch the bizarre wound. And every time he scratched at the scar, or found himself fingering it under his shirt, the whole awful episode of the dream came back to him with a remarkably vivid sense of reality.

He could see those beady black eyes of the dark-haired man boring into him, his glare burrowing into Ritchie's soul much as the bullet had dug its way into his heart. He could taste all over again the terror that he'd swallowed down as the gunman squeezed the trigger and discharged his deadly load of lead into Ritchie's heart.

He could feel, almost as if it was happening again then and there, the eruption of pain in his chest as the bullet carried out its fatal work.

Ritchie found himself shivering slightly in that warm clinic waiting room, and the sweat started to pour out of him afresh.

Must be that I've got some kind of bug, he thought. Maybe some weird new kind of flu from China or something, and the mark on my chest is just some crazy symptom that the doctor will know.

After all, it couldn't really be a gunshot scar, now could it?

Could it?

If nothing else, Ritchie's shakes and sweat encouraged his neighbors to increase their distance from him. The mom and kids got up altogether and moved away. Ritchie took advantage of it to spread out a little on the bench. A few hardy invalids tried to use Ritchie's own ploy on him and made an effort to squeeze in next to him, but none succeeded. The hard look on Ritchie's face and his wretched-looking condition were enough to scare them away.

After what seemed like an eternity, Ritchie's name was finally called over the crackly loudspeaker and he was directed to an examination room. Once inside, he was told to remove his shirt and wait for the doctor. He started to do so as the attendant left the room then decided that he would prefer to leave his shirt on for the moment. Much as he couldn't resist scratching at the itchy wound, Ritchie realized that he didn't want to sit there and have to look at it the whole time. He would wait until Dr Rosoff arrived and take his shirt off only when he really had to.

Another long wait ensued in the examination room. Ritchie sat on the exam table for a while, but his impatience grew. He got up and paced around the perimeter of the room, reading the dull charts and posters on the walls about measles vaccines and sexually transmitted diseases and the amazing advantages of breast feeding. That one made Ritchie snigger as he read it twice: he was all in favor of breast feeding whenever possible. Heh heh.

Ritchie was re-reading the detailed instructions over the sink on the proper way for medical professionals to wash their hands, when the exam room door flew open and Rosoff came in. She didn't look up, but continued to read a chart in her hand as she walked. She was carrying a whole stack of them under her arm. Her stethoscope was draped around her neck like a boa and she wore black denim jeans and a plain, pale yellow blouse under her stained white lab coat.

Rosoff wasn't an unattractive woman, though with her dark brown hair pulled back tightly in a bun she looked more than a little severe. Probably on purpose, Ritchie guessed, to keep the patients at a distance. He tried to imagine how she might look after hours and he suspected that with her hair down, a little make-up on and a blouse with two buttons undone, Rosoff wouldn't look half-bad. She could certainly breast feed Ritchie from that ample chest of hers any old day. Ritchie reckoned that Rosoff was about his age, thirty-seven, which for some reason always made him a little bit angry. He knew it was foolish and irrational, but the fact that a contemporary of his could be so much better off than he was—so much smarter, richer, capable, professional—just plain cheesed him off. Deep down he knew that the feeling was all about him and had nothing to do with the doctor herself, but it still bristled at something inside of him.

Even so, Ritchie had come to sort-of like Dr Rosoff. The first time she'd come through the door to examine him he had demanded to see a different doctor because he didn't like the idea of being examined by a woman. But that complaint had fallen on deaf ears. He was told, in no uncertain terms, that he could see the doctor assigned to him or he could walk out the door. Ritchie had been so sick with the flu that day that he couldn't say no and so Dr Rosoff it was. As it turned out, he decided that women doctors were okay; after all, they were a little easier to talk to than men about some things. That was why, today, he'd been so insistent that he could only be examined by Dr Rosoff.

"Ritchie," Dr Rosoff said, still reading the chart. "Long time no see. Always a good thing in a patient."

"Heya, Doc," Ritchie replied.

Doctor Rosoff offered him the briefest of smiles then flipped through the pages on the chart. She tossed the rest of her paperwork down on a stool and gestured for Ritchie to take a seat on the examination table. Surprised by his own high level of anxiety he climbed aboard, dangling his legs over the edge.

"So, how have you been, Ritchie? I knew it had been a while and I see from your records that you never showed up for your last appointment."

"I've been okay, Doc. I mean until today. I... I didn't think I needed that other appointment. At the time, you know?" Ritchie nervously licked his lips and drummed his fingers on the hard padding of the table.

"Uh-huh," Rosoff said. "So what happened today then? What brings you here?"

Ritchie realized that he didn't know where even to begin. The entire experience was so crazy, so weird. How could he explain what had happened in his dream, how terrifying it was, to this stern looking doctor standing in front of him with a million other patients—old ladies and kids, for Chrissake—demanding her more immediate attention?

"Ritchie?" Rosoff said, a hint of annoyance in her tone.

"It's..."

"I haven't got all day, Ritchie. You know what it's like here."

Ritchie nodded in reply, then shook his head and finally, in exasperation, lifted up his T-shirt.

"Here," he said. He pointed a finger at the scar above his heart.

Doctor Rosoff leaned in to take a closer look. She gently prodded the skin around the scar, then turned and pulled a pair of rubber surgical gloves out of a box hanging on the wall. She carefully slipped them on and walked back over to Ritchie who was still sitting there holding his shirt up.

"Why don't you take that shirt right off?" the doctor said.

Ritchie slipped the T-shirt off over his head.

Doctor Rosoff ran a gloved finger along the inside edge of the scar. It wasn't itching so badly now, but it still felt slightly raw as she poked at the loose flaps of skin. In Ritchie's mind's eye he saw the dark-haired man with the beady eyes standing in front of him. As Rosoff pressed a little bit harder against the center of the scar, Ritchie could have sworn he felt the bullet once more penetrating his chest. He flinched and let out a little grunt.

"Is that very sore?" the doctor asked.

"It's a little sensitive, yeah," Ritchie told her. "It's crazy, huh?"

Doctor Rosoff stepped back and looked Ritchie in the eye.

"How did you get the scar, Ritchie?" she asked.

"That's what I mean," Ritchie said. "It's totally crazy."

"I'm afraid I don't understand."

"I just woke up this morning and it was there."

Rosoff did a double-take.

"I'm sorry?" she said.

"It was worse this morning, though. First thing, I mean. It was kind of... weepy I guess you'd call it. And it was a lot redder too. Kind of wet, you know? Like it was fresher or something."

"What happened to you in the night, Ritchie?" the doctor asked.

"Nothing! Well, I mean nothing really. I had this dream, see?"

Doctor Rosoff picked her papers up off the stool and tossed them onto the counter by the sink. She dragged the wheeled stool over and sat down on it, taking a good measure of her patient.

"You had a dream," she said.

"It's crazy, I know. I can hardly believe it myself."

"I'm just not following you here, Ritchie. You're going to have to make a little bit more sense."

Ritchie shook his head. "That's just it, don't you see? It doesn't make no sense at all. I mean it was just a dream, right? And they don't always make sense, I know that. But I dreamed that someone shot me, you know? Right here." He pointed to the scar on his chest. "And in the dream it was so real, it was just like it was really happening. It hurt like a sonofa... It really hurt. And I could feel myself dying, you know? I could feel that my heart stopped beating. And I started to scream and my roommate, Leonard, he... Well, it don't matter about Leonard. But he had to come and wake me up out of it I was screaming so loud, and when I woke up in my bed, I had this."

Ritchie ran his finger along the scar again.

Doctor Rosoff slid the stool back and slipped the gloves off her hands with a pop. "Look, Ritchie, if you don't want to tell me where you got this injury that's up to you, but—"

"I just did tell you!" Ritchie shouted. The doctor eased her stool back another foot. "I dreamed that someone shot me, right? A man with dark hair and nasty, tiny black eyes. He had a big gun and he pointed it at my chest and he pulled the trigger and when I woke up..."

"You had this," Rosoff said.

She sounded doubtful. Who could blame her? Ritchie knew how loco it sounded.

"I knew it," Ritchie exclaimed. He slapped his hand against the table with considerable force. The tissue paper sanitary sheet tore and fluttered to the floor. Doctor Rosoff watched it fall then flicked her eyes back to Ritchie. He was staring down at the floor and said: "I knew you wouldn't believe me."

Ritchie started fiddling with the scar again. It was itching like crazy now, starting to feel sore again.

"Calm down, Ritchie," Doctor Rosoff said. She pulled her stool back closer to Ritchie and rested a calming hand on his knee. "Do you remember the last time you were here? Before the appointment that you skipped?"

Ritchie nodded his head. He felt a nervousness in his stomach, though, suddenly as distressing as the itching of the scar on his chest. He started to sweat again, too.

"Do you remember what we talked about then?" Rosoff asked him.

"That was when I hurt my hand."

"Yes," the doctor said. "You put your hand through a plate glass window, remember? You cut yourself quite badly."

Ritchie involuntarily shuddered. He was feeling very cold now without his shirt, but he made no move to put it back on. He wrapped his arms around his chest, covering up the scar there but displaying for the doctor the vestiges of the scars on the back of his right hand and wrist.

"And you were experiencing a number of other difficulties at the time as well. Insomnia, loss of appetite, you reported some depression..."

"It was at the Eumenide place," Ritchie said, staring off into nothing. "They had that pool house out in back. I was reaching back with the skimmer and I busted right through the window of the little house. Mrs Eumenide was inside changing at the time. She said I gave her a real scare. Cut my hand up bad, but she didn't even notice that. I finished the job off, though, and then I came over here."

"Ritchie?" Doctor Rosoff said. He gave a little shake of the head and came back to the present moment. "You complained of feeling depressed. I just looked over my notes from that appointment and you told me you were in some despair at the time."

"I remember that," Ritchie said. "Just some rough times. It's been a tough couple of years. You know, the economy and all. Even rich people been cutting back."

"I understand that. At the time, we talked about the possibility of you going to see a therapist. A psychiatrist maybe. You were supposed to come back for an evaluation appointment with our counselor here. But that was the appointment that you never showed up for. That was six months ago."

Ritchie was shaking his head. "I don't need a shrink. What would be the point, anyway? I know exactly what a shrink would say to me."

"And what would that be?" Doctor Rosoff asked.

Ritchie snorted in reply.

"Ritchie?"

"I'll tell you what he'd say. He'd say: 'Ritchie, you are a thirty-seven year-old pool guy with no home, no wife, no kids and no life worth mentioning. You live in a ratty little apartment with a dickhead of a roommate you can't stand because you can't even afford your own goddamn apartment. You are depressed, my friend, and you have got every right to be depressed. Because you, Ritchie Almares, are a big time loser.' That's exactly what he would say."

"That is definitely not how it works, Ritchie. Therapy is not like that at all. It can be an extremely useful tool to—"

"Not be a loser?" Ritchie asked.

"Do you think you maybe have some self-esteem issues, Ritchie?" Doctor Rosoff asked.

"I got plenty of self-esteem," Ritchie told her. "For a loser."

A silence ensued between them. Ritchie began idly playing with the scar on his chest again. It was suddenly itching like mad.

"Are you telling me the truth, Ritchie?" the doctor asked.

"What? About being a loser? You bet your ass. You look in the dictionary under loser, you see my picture."

"No, Ritchie," Rosoff intoned. "I'm referring to the scar. Are you telling me the truth about that? How did you really get that injury? It looks at least two months old to me and if not for the location, I'd swear it was a bullet wound."

Ritchie leaned forward. "What do you mean there about the location? Why couldn't it be a bullet wound in that location?"

"Because no one could receive a bullet wound in that spot and live to tell about it. If that was a scar from a gunshot wound, the bullet would have blown your heart to little wet bits. And while I haven't actually listened to your chest today, since you're sitting here talking to me, I have to assume that your heart is still beating in there."

Ritchie reached up and covered over the scar with the palm of his hand. He rubbed it up and down then took his hand away. He looked down.

"Still there," he said softly. He looked back up at the doctor. "But I promise you that this scar was not there when I went to bed last night. I swear to you, Doctor Rosoff. It wasn't there last night. Not before I had that dream."

Doctor Rosoff shook her head, scratched it then threw her hands in the air. She leaned forward and took another look at the scar. Ritchie felt a burning sensation in his chest every time she touched him and had to work hard not to let the pain show. Rosoff sat back once again and let out a long breath.

"I have read of instances where extreme stress can cause certain... psychosomatic reactions."

"What does that mean?" Ritchie asked.

"Psychosomatic. From the mind. Rare occurrences such as... Oh, stigmata is an extreme example. I'm talking about physiological manifestations of psychological disturbances. Things in the mind made real. I've never seen such a thing in my entire career, though. And I thought I'd seen it all at this clinic."

Ritchie felt deflated. He scratched at the scar yet again and visibly shuddered. The doctor didn't miss it.

"So you're telling me that I am nuts," Ritchie said. "What do I need a psychiatrist for when I got you, Doc? Diagnosis complete. Rubber room this way."

Doctor Rosoff dropped her weary head into her hands. She pulled at her cheeks with her fingertips. Then she looked up at Ritchie and said, "Let's tackle this from another angle. You say you had a dream last night in which you were shot and when you woke up you had this scar."

"That's exactly what happened," Ritchie affirmed.

"Then let's see if we can't analyze this more carefully and systematically. Let's try and take it apart a little bit. The man in your dream, the one who you say shot you. How was it that you described him?"

Ritchie shuddered again. "Cold. He had really dark hair, black like the night, and wavy. And eyes just the same: black, I mean. They were the tiniest, death-like eyes you've ever seen. They weren't human eyes."

"Okay," Rosoff said. "This dark-haired man. Did you recognize him? Was it someone that you know or have met before?"

Ritchie thought about it. He had been so terrified by the dream, and its aftermath, that he realized he hadn't much thought about who the man was until now. His face had been so awful, but...

"You know," Ritchie said, closing his eyes, "I'm not sure. I don't think I know him, exactly, but now that I think about it, there was something familiar about him. Distorted like, but familiar."

"Dreams always distort the familiar, don't they?" Rosoff asked.

"I guess so. But I can't think for sure who he might be. It's like on the tip of my tongue now, you know, like the answer to a sports trivia question. I know it, but I don't." Ritchie opened his eyes and shook his head. "No, I can't figure it out. Anyway, who would want to kill me? I'm just a pool guy, you know? What have I ever done? Put too much chlorine in the water?"

Doctor Rosoff studied him, but couldn't provide any answer to his question. She glanced at her watch. Ritchie realized she'd been in with him for a very long time on this busy day.

"Ritchie," she finally said. "Would it be all right with you if I asked one of my colleagues to help out with this? Get some additional input on what might be going on here?"

Ritchie shrugged. "I don't mind. I need all the help I can get about now. Bring 'em on."

"I'll just be a minute then," Rosoff told him. "He's just down the hall and if he's not in with a patient, I'll have him come in. Just wait here."

Rosoff pushed the stool back into the corner and walked out of the examination room. Ritchie took advantage of the moment to slip his shirt back on. He still felt a chill, but having his chest covered left him feeling less exposed and vulnerable. He sat back down.

He waited.

Doctor Rosoff didn't return.

So he waited some more.

Ritchie started to grow impatient. He began pacing around the edges of the room again. He was about to take yet another lesson on hand washing techniques when he noticed his file still sitting on top of the counter where Doctor Rosoff had left it. He glanced at the door, then at the clock on the wall. Feeling only slightly guilty, he flipped open the file and started to read.

The doctor's handwriting was typically hard to make out and he had a difficult time negotiating his way through her tiny italic scrawl. The notes on the top page were from his previous appointment six months earlier. Some of it was the standard recording of his complaints and the various data which had been collected about his height, weight, urine, blood pressure and so on. But there was a section for the doctor's comments at the bottom of the page and though this was even harder to decipher, the notes made Ritchie's heart start to race. Ritchie began to read:

Patient is at extreme risk for clinical depression. Possible bi-polar? Family history! Definite risk to self, possibly to others? Severe anger management issues related to stress and yet origin to be ascertained. Recommended for...

The door to the exam room opened behind him and Ritchie quickly closed the file and tossed it back on the pile where he had found it. He'd only managed to take one step back in the direction of the exam table when Doctor Rosoff came through the door. She was speaking to someone Ritchie couldn't see behind her.

"Ah, sorry to be so long. The doctor was in with a patient and then I got called away to answer the phone. In any event, I want to introduce you to an associate of mine from the clinic. I've given him a brief rundown of the situation, Ritchie, and I believe that he can help you out with some of your problems. I think he knows exactly what it is you are going through."

She stuck her head back out the door and said: "Come on in, now, he's ready for you."

Ritchie took a step forward and started to raise his arm to shake hands with the new doctor.

He threw himself backwards, staggering against the examination table and sending it flying over with a loud, metallic clatter.

The dark-haired man with the tiny black eyes entered the room. He was wearing a white lab coat like Doctor Rosoff, but his face was as cold and hard as the last time Ritchie had seen him in the dream. The dark-haired man drew his thin lips back in that death's head mockery of a smile. Ritchie knew that it was time to die.

"That's him!" he screeched.

He scrambled back to his feet, looking for some place to run. He was trapped in the corner of the examination room.

"Doctor Rosoff!" Ritchie pleaded. "That's him! That's the guy who shot me!"

Rosoff leaned over and whispered something in the ear of the dark-haired man. The man nodded and his awful smile grew broader across his pale, white face. He reached inside one of the big pockets of his white coat.

He drew out a gun; a hand-cannon. The same gun he had used to shoot Ritchie with next to the Hunts' pool.

He aimed the broad black barrel at a point in the middle of Ritchie's stomach.

"Wake up," the dark-haired man said.

He fired the gun, which exploded with the noise of a howitzer.

The bullet ripped apart Ritchie's guts. As he fell, he saw a ragged strand of intestine spill out from the gaping wound in his belly. He could smell his own feces bursting out through the newly-blown hole in his middle.

Ritchie screamed.

It was, as the great prophet once said, déjà vu all over again.

The scream went on and on and on. And then, for good measure, it went on some more.

"Ritchie! Ritchie, dude, wake up. WAKE UP, DUDE!!"

Ritchie's eyes shot open. He can hear the screaming. It is so loud, so awful. Someone must be undergoing torture.

It's him. Ritchie is the one who is screaming. He realizes it.

He stops.

Where is he? What's happening? How did he get all wet?

Ritchie sat up in his bed. His roommate, Leonard, was standing in the doorway to the bedroom, a half-drunk bottle of Starbucks Frappuccino in his hand and a look of astonishment on his face. Leonard doesn't shock easily; most of the time he is too stoned to achieve a state as emotional as shock. He is usually too high to achieve a state of anything. Other than being stoned. Ritchie has never been able to figure out how Leonard managed to hold down a job. Of course, it was just as a script reader for one of the big film studios...

"Dude," Leonard said. "What be the haps, my man? Are you going to audition for *King Kong* or something? 'Cause that was, like, totally Fay Wray in execution."

"Shit, shit, shit," Ritchie croaked.

"I hear you, dude. But what was that shit?"

"A dream," Ritchie gasped. He looked cautiously around him. His room appeared to look exactly as it was supposed to. Everything was precisely in the lack of place it normally was. Leonard was stoned as he should be, even at—he glanced at the clock radio—eight-thirty in the morning. And all was right with the world.

But not with the inside of Ritchie Almares's sweat-soaked head.

"You had a dream, dude?" Leonard asked.

Ritchie threw off his thin cotton blanket. It, too, was so sweat-soaked he could practically have wrung it out and filled a glass. He could have sworn that there were pools of sweat in the creases of his dirty sheets. Probably little crabs swimming around inside them too.

He got up and looked out the window. The sun was shining, the birds were singing, the mustard-yellow smog was already crawling across the sky. Another archetypical Los Angeles day.

"I ain't never had a dream like that before," Ritchie said, suppressing a shudder. "It wasn't just a dream, man, it was one of those dream-within-a-dream things. Nightmare-within-a-nightmare, I guess you got to say. You think you've woken up from it only to find that it's still going on. Very scary."

"Awesome," Leonard said.

The dream was playing itself back now on the DVD inside of Ritchie's head. In widescreen and THX/DTS sound. There was probably a director's commentary available somewhere in there, too. And extras.

"First time around; right? I mean the first dream. I'm there cleaning the pool at that new client's house. That Hunt guy. You know, the guy who you said you knew?"

"Only by reputation, dude," Leonard said. "I mean it's a small town, you know?"

"Uh-huh," Ritchie said. "So I'm there working on the pool and I'm talking to the gardener, who's an asshole by the way. Kind of creepy."

"Ain't that always the way?" Leonard said nodding. He downed the rest of his Frappuccino in a swallow.

"Then I go to collect my money and this dude just shoots me. Out of nowhere. Just bang. Dark-haired son of a bitch with scary, black eyes."

"Was he, like, in a fight or something?" Leonard asked.

That derailed Ritchie's train of thought for a moment. Leonard had a shining talent for doing that to conversations.

"No, not that kind of black eye," Ritchie explained. "His eyes, the color of them, you know? His eyes were pitch black."

"Aww, that can't be good," Leonard told him.

Ritchie went on: "He just shoots me with this huge black gun, point blank. Straight through the heart. Blam!"

"Ouch, dude. That's gotta hurt."

"Oh, man, you have no idea. It really did hurt, too. I mean like I could really feel it happening, like I was dying. There was no sense of it just being a dream, you know? I screamed real loud and then I heard you calling my name, waking me up."

"Leonard, like, totally to the rescue," Leonard said, a great dopey smile spreading across his face.

"Uh-huh. So then I wake up, right? Only when I do, there's a big scar on my chest where the bullet went in. It's like still wet and fresh and gross."

Ritchie suddenly pulled down the collar of his T-shirt, tearing it slightly, in order to expose the area over his heart. He nervously glanced down.

No scar.

The skin is as smooth and whole as it has ever been. Nothing but his deep, dark suntan and the seeds of potential old age melanomas.

Ritchie breathed out a big sigh of relief and let go of his collar.

"Your head sure holds some freaky shit, dude," Leonard said.

Ritchie ignored him.

"There's more, though," he said. "That's not really the end of the dream, see? I only think it's the end. I think I'm all up and awake and just freaked out. And I've got this scar on my chest and it hurts so I go to the doctor. The free clinic on Sepulveda. I go to see Doctor Rosoff and she's examining me and all and she thinks I'm, like, nuts."

"Freaky shit, dude," Leonard repeated.

"And then suddenly the same guy shows up. The dark-haired guy with the gun."

"Let me guess!" Leonard yelled. He thought about it for a second, then said: "He shoots you again?"

Ritchie nodded. "This time in the belly. Oh, man does it ever hurt. I could see my guts spilling out. Could feel myself dying again."

"Gut shot is bad," Leonard said. "Remember *Reservoir Dogs*? Gut shot has got to be the worst."

"I don't know," Ritchie said. "I think the heart is worse. It sure was for me, anyway. I wouldn't recommend either, though."

"You're the man," Leonard admits.

"So then I was screaming again. Screaming from the pain and knowing that I was dying. Until you came along and woke me up out of it."

Leonard high-fived himself. "The dude is two-for-two," he said.

Ritchie just shook his head. He couldn't get over the experience he had just been through. Both of the dreams were so vivid, so real. No dream he had ever had in his life even came close to how these had affected him. Ritchie could swear that he could still feel the violation of the bullets in his flesh; could still hear the

deafening report of the explosions that killed
him—*twice*—still echoing in his ears.

"Anything like that ever happen to you, man?"
Ritchie asked his roommate.

Leonard shook his head. "No. I never remember too much about my dreams, dude. I sleep the
sleep of the just. And you know; Leonard strives
to maintain very solid walls between his fantasy
life and his real life."

Ritchie gave Leonard a look, but Leonard just
stared down and nodded his head at the wisdom
of his own lifestyle choice.

"Well, you're goddamned lucky then," Ritchie
said. "I wish I could forget what happened to me
this morning. Forget these awful dreams."

Ritchie stood there shaking his head, still feeling the horror of what he'd been through.
Leonard shifted uncomfortably in the doorway.

"Uhh, dude?"

"Huh?" Ritchie said.

"I hate to bring this issue up at this particular
juncture in time. Especially considering your,
like, total upsetness over the dream and all,
but—"

"What?" Ritchie demanded.

"You know that, like, the rent is about due
again—time, huh? ain't it, like, a thing?—and I
can't really cover your half this month."

"Oh, man! I told you I'd have the money this
week and I'll have it. You know I got this new
client and all. He's supposed to pay me today."

"It's cool, dude," Leonard said, holding up his
hands. "Leonard is a no-hassle zone. I'm just,

like, reminding you, okay? Leonard is just doing the things that Leonard has to do."

Ritchie shook his head as Leonard walked out of the room. He'd never entirely gotten used to Leonard's tendency to refer to himself in the third person. Ritchie flopped back down on the bed, staring up at the filthy ceiling.

I have got to do something about my life, he vowed for the millionth time that month. No wonder he suffered bad dreams living the way he did. Living with *who* he did. A change had to come and it had better come soon.

The dreams came back to him like a cheap pastrami burrito. Ritchie saw the face of the dark-haired man, heard the roar of the gun, felt the bullets in body...

Leonard poked his head back through the door.

"Dude?"

"What is it now, Leonard?"

"What time do you have to get to work today?"

"I told you, I'll have the money, man" Ritchie started.

"Nah, dude, that's not it. Leonard is most definitely cool. But, like, the cable guy is supposed to come this morning to install the upgrade, remember? You going to be here or should I tell the super to let him in?"

"What time is he supposed to come then?"

"Morning, dude, that's all they ever say. And they don't always mean it."

"Goddamn cable guys. Now that's the damn job to have. Who do you got to blow in this town to get one of those jobs, anyway?" He shook his head.

Then he said: "I don't have to go out until around noon to get to the Hunt place on time. I'll let the super know if the guy hasn't come by then."

"Righteous!" Leonard said. "Later for you. And those dreams."

Ritchie heard him go out the front door. Leonard always slammed it.

The bang brought the dreams to the front of his mind again.

Ritchie went into the kitchen and made himself a big mug of coffee. He and Leonard kept their food separate, but while Leonard's cupboard was always fully stocked, Ritchie's was invariably as empty as Old Mother Hubbard's. Good thing he didn't have a dog. He had to swipe some instant— and some milk—from Leonard's stocks to make his breakfast.

As Ritchie drank Leonard's coffee, he couldn't stop himself from playing the dreams back in his head yet again. He ran a hand over the unbroken skin over his chest for reassurance. He scratched his stomach.

Scratched it again.

He had a terrible itch down there. Ritchie got to his feet and pulled up his T-shirt. He looked down.

He tumbled backwards over the kitchen chair, sending the coffee cup flying. It smashed against the cupboard.

A raw-red wound the size of his fist was spread out across the middle of his belly.

It was in the precise spot where the dark-haired man in Doctor Rosoff's office shot him.

"No—o—o—o," he whimpered.

The doorbell rang.

In a daze, Ritchie got up. He was running his hand over the now very sore wound stretching across the center of his stomach. He was in disbelief. This could not possibly be happening to him. *Again.*

Ritchie staggered out of the kitchen and down the hall toward the front door. He felt like he was in hell. He had to be. What other explanation could there be?

The doorbell rang again.

"Leonard?" Ritchie called out weakly. The pain in his stomach began to intensify. It was as if the bullet was still twisting around inside him, grinding up his guts.

Ritchie collapsed to his knees. The doorbell rang again.

He dragged himself down the hall to the front door. He reached up for the doorknob, using it to pull himself off the floor. Ritchie was in a state of shock. He didn't know what he was doing, running on pure adrenaline now.

He opened the door.

The dark-haired man was standing there, his wavy hair mostly covered by a white baseball cap with the legend: Century Cable. He wore gray coveralls and carried a heavy metal toolbox. His thin lips drew back slowly in that now murderously familiar grin.

Ritchie was frozen with naked terror. Nothing came out of his mouth, though urine dribbled out of his penis.

The dark-haired man opened the toolbox and drew out his big, black gun. He pointed the barrel directly at Ritchie's balls. His skeletal grin grew broader.

"No. Please," Ritchie squeaked.

"Wake up," the gunman said.

He fired.

He screamed.

Read two more awesome stories with a sting in the tale in The Twilight Zone #1: Pool Guy / Memphis out now from Black Flame!